RICK PARTLOW
MAELSTROM STRAND

ALSO IN THE SERIES

WHOLESALE SLAUGHTER

TERMINUS CUT

REVELATION RUN

MAELSTROM STRAND

PROLOGUE

Rhianna Hale was a beautiful woman.

Colonel Ruth Laurent didn't usually give much thought to the comparative looks of other women, but it was worth noting, given her heritage. A beautiful woman from a rich, powerful family, yet she had forsaken the easy life running the lucrative Hale family gas mining operations for a career in the military. She still wore her uniform here, as risky as it was. Spartan Mobile Armored Corps flashed red and blue on the shoulder patch of her fatigue top, resplendent in the glow of the morning sun, a major's rank still fresh on her collar from a recent promotion.

Yet here she was, deep within the heart of the enemy.

"Being Lord Prime of the Starkad Supremacy has its privileges," Hale said, leaning on the balcony railing, staring out at the snow-capped peaks of the Jotunheim Mountains from the fourth floor of the mansion. "The view is majestic."

"Appropriately, I think," Lord Aaron Starkad replied, arms crossed in the unquenchable smugness that was a counterweight to his perfectly sculpted features and long, flowing blond hair. "My great-great..." He rolled his eyes. "...whatever grandfather, the first Lord Starkad shed the blood to establish the Supremacy, and his sons and daughters have devoted their lives to defending and expanding it. A nice little getaway in the mountains seems a fitting recompense."

Laurent successfully suppressed the involuntary snort at the idea of the thirty-room mansion and its hundreds of square kilometers of land being referred to as a "nice little getaway," and got down to business.

"The question, Major Hale," she interjected, "is what would *you* consider a fitting recompense for allying with our cause?"

"Colonel Laurent," Hale said, turning away from the towering wall of mountains that divided Stavanger's largest continent in two to face her, "I have spent most of my life trying to live down the deeds of my uncle." Her lip twisted into a sneer, marring the wonderful symmetry of her face. "Duncan Lambert the Traitor. The man who killed the Guardian of Sparta and lost the battle for the throne to his grandson, Jaimie Brannigan." The sneer softened into something just as bitter but less strident. "Sometimes I think the lost battle is what people hate him for more than the regicide. I attended the Military Academy when I could have avoided service, fought and clawed my way up through the ranks in the Mobile Armored Corps despite the prejudice my family faced. Why do you think I'd be interested in your offer?"

"You've maintained connections with the proscribed members of your family," Laurent pointed out. She stepped closer to the railing, motioning at the expanse of pale blue above them. "When they called, you came. You left your unit without permission and travelled all the way to Stavanger. You didn't take this sort of risk to tell us no thank you, that you're happy where you are. You're not satisfied being the good little girl, the devoted patriot."

Hale's eyes flashed with anger, a fire behind the soft hazel.

"There was a reason Uncle Duncan's treason came so close to succeeding, why he attracted so much support. That reason still exist today. The Brannigans have turned the Guardianship into a hereditary monarchy much like your own Supremacy." She nodded politely to Aaron. "All due respect to your institutions and traditions here, Lord Starkad, but that is *not* what Sparta was meant to be. The Council is supposed to choose the most qualified candidate, not simply validate whichever of the current Guardian's children or grandchildren he or she chose to replace them. They've put the glory of their family over the good of Sparta, and their self-serving policies of containment and defense have allowed Sparta's enemies to consolidate their gains and allowed the Jeuta to operate without fear of reprisal."

Her hands worked themselves into fists, then relaxed with a visible effort.

"I know I'm not the only one who feels this way. I've heard the rumblings in the general staff about dissatisfaction with the Guardian's lack of aggressive action against the pirates and bandits and Jeuta raiders. They remain silent out of fear, but if they thought there was a realistic chance of a regime change..."

"If our two Dominions were to ally," Aaron Starkad proposed, taking a step closer to Hale, "we would present a strong enough front against our rivals and enemies to make it possible to take real action against the Jeuta, to finally do what the Empire couldn't, and put those beasts down for good."

Hale was a tall woman, statuesque even, but Lord Starkad still towered above her. Sheer odylic force radiated from those piercing blue eyes. Hale's nostrils flared slightly, her pupils dilating. Laurent watched, fascinated, as if she were witnessing a nature documentary about the mating habits of bull elk.

"All you have to do," Starkad went on, voice smooth and seductive, "is rally those disaffected elements in the military, and perhaps a few among the Council families who feel they're being overruled by allies of the Brannigans. With our aid, with a few strategic realignments of forces to draw attention where we want them to be looking, it should be possible for you to finish what your uncle started and bring Sparta back to the dream of its founders."

There was a tinge of skepticism to Hale's smile.

"You make it seem so easy. Brannigan is no fool and he's surrounded himself with strength. General Anders, General Constantine..."

"Anders is a straightforward man," Laurent judged, remembering the files and reports she'd reviewed. "He'd be more likely to recognize a threat from without than one from within. But Constantine..."

"He's been Jaimie Brannigan's Chief of Intelligence for twenty years," Hale said with a tone of grudging respect. "We'll need to get him out of the way before we move."

Laurent couldn't quite keep the grin off her face. Hale had bought in.

"He'd be a valuable source of intelligence himself, if we can take him alive," she said, something akin to hunger twisting in her stomach, the feeling she'd used to get as an analyst from following a lead back to the nugget of truth at its source.

"I'm sure we can work something out," Lord Starkad said, taking Hale's hand in his. She looked up into his eyes, licking her lips perhaps unconsciously. "For now, I'd dearly love to show you my riding stables. Perhaps a nice horseback ride to show you the borders of my land?"

Laurent motioned to a line of dark clouds blowing in from the east.

"There's a storm coming," she warned them. "You'd best hurry."

1

Wholesale Slaughter, follow me!"

Logan Conner fell out of the sky with fifty tons of metal wrapped around him and a fusion rocket strapped to his back. He'd never done a high drop in the Sentinel before and his stomach told him exactly what it thought of the idea of dumping a twenty-meter-tall strike mech out of the bottom of a drop-ship two hundred meters above a surface too shrouded in fog to even see. The external lift pack rumbled in a murmur of raw power, braking his forward momentum with a six-gravity deceleration thrust and pressing him into the mech's padded "easy chair" with enough force that he nearly blacked out.

Wouldn't matter much if I did. Can't maneuver worth a damn with these things.

It was times like these he missed the lighter, more versatile Vindicator assault mech he'd piloted when he'd simply been a platoon leader in the Spartan Mobile Armored Corps instead of...

Well, instead of whatever the hell I am now.

Technically, he was a colonel, though he still commanded a company of mecha, but not in the Mobile Armored Corps. Most company commanders didn't also have their own starship and a Ranger Company at their disposal and certainly didn't get to make policy decisions that could change the course of Dominion politics. But then, most weren't also the son of the Guardian of Sparta and commander of the most intricate and far-reaching covert military operation in Spartan history.

"Colonel Slaughter, this is Bohardt, come in." The voice in the earphones of his helmet was keyed up, on edge, which wasn't unusual for a mech-jock running his first ballistic insertion. Logan checked his Identification Friend or Foe display and saw Bohardt's transponder below his, almost on the ground, with his mercenary mecha company arrayed in a diamond formation around him.

"This is Slaughter," he replied once the thrust pack had dialed back to a more reasonable gee-load, beginning the controlled descent. "Go ahead Captain Bohardt."

Jonathan Slaughter had been his cover for two years now, head of Wholesale Slaughter Private Military Contractors LLC. Once, when he'd first begun this mission, he'd nearly lost himself in the role, even *thinking* of himself as Jonathan rather than Logan, but the stakes had levelled off a bit since then...and the mission had evolved.

"Bohardt's Bastards are on the ground and ready to move," the older man reported. "It's your show, sir, you give the order."

Logan bit down on the mouthpiece of his helmet and tensed up as a flashing yellow light signaled landing was imminent. The Sentinel vibrated violently enough to blur his vision and he was pushed down into his seat again as the lift pack burned out its engines on one final, heavy-gee landing blast. Sucking in a breath through creaking ribs, he pushed a lever downward at the rear of his cockpit and felt the Sentinel stagger as the lift pack fell off its shoulders. Through the transparent aluminum of the cockpit canopy, he saw little more than he had on the way down. The fog was so thick, he could barely make out the hulking, shadowy masses of the mecha around him, their jump-jets still glowing yellow from the drop in the blackness of the moonless night.

"First platoon is down, Boss," Captain Valentine Kurtz reported, sounding cheerful about it. The IFF display showed his Golem and the other four assault mecha in his platoon lined up along Logan's right flank. "We're all good to go."

"Second platoon down, sir," Lt. Summer Prevatt chimed in from the other side. "No damage reported."

"Captain Bohardt," he finally replied to the mercenary commander, "lead the way. Your people have point."

It was a hard order for him to give. Bohardt's Bastards had a good reputation, but they hadn't proven a damn thing to him, and he was about to trust them with the lives of innocent people instead of counting on his own troops. It wasn't the choice he would have made a year ago, maybe not even a month ago.

David Bohardt seemed competent and his people moved out smartly for a group of guns-for-hire. Mercenaries in general were unreliable, deserters and rejects barely better than the bandits and pirates they were hired to fight, but once in a while you came across mavericks who just didn't fit in with the military in their Dominion. He was hoping Bohardt was one of those.

At least he's better equipped than most of them. No slapped-together Hopper scout mecha fabricated in backwoods shops or ancient wrecks salvaged from battlefield spare parts. Bohardt piloted a broad-shouldered Valiant assault mech, in good repair and freshly painted with all-season camouflage and the Bastard crest, while the rest of his company were in a mix of older but still serviceable Warlocks and Agamemnons. No strike mecha like his Sentinel, but mercenaries tended to stay with machines no heavier than assault models since they were the most versatile and easier to transport.

Bohardt led a standard company, five platoons of four mecha each, which was also decent for a mercenary unit. No dedicated Arbalest missile carriers, but a nice variety of payloads and certainly enough for the enemy they were after today. They kept to a textbook double-wedge formation, staying in perfect alignment despite the treacherous footing of the muddy plains and the nonexistent visibility. Thermal and infrared were fine for spotting enemy forces, but they weren't much good for making out a mud puddle from a ten-meter deep trench.

"Move out, Val," he told his second in command. "Stay close and keep an eye on them."

"You sound like a damn mother hen, Boss," Kurtz said, his low chuckle a burst of static in the headphones. "It's just a bunch of half-assed pirates. Even Momma Salvaggio's bunch could have taken them, and these guys are a damn sight better than they were."

"They pay me to be nervous." Logan wanted to snap at the man but controlled himself. Val had been with him since the beginning and if he thought Logan was being a nervous mother hen, he was probably right.

Kurtz led his platoon off behind the mercenaries in an echelon left formation, the hunchbacked Golems plodding along like toddlers splashing through rain puddles, then disappearing into the dense fog. He envied their agility. His Sentinel strode forward ponderously, circular footpads two meters across sinking a meter deep into the mud with each step, then yanking free with a series of shuddering jolts.

Prevatt's platoon trailed behind him in echelon right, stretched out in a straight line with the platoon leader's mech to the left end of the formation and farthest forward, the opposite of Kurtz's array. It was all glowing lights on a screen to him, a collage of thermal, infrared and sonic sensor readings mixed with the transponder readouts and converted to the best simulation the Sentinel's computer systems could provide on his Heads-Up Display. That was the reality for him, not the vague, nebulous darkness outside his canopy. He'd learned to work off the display, to convert it to an image of the world inside his head and move through it instinctively.

The objective was five kilometers due north, and the enemy had surely seen the drop-ships inbound, detected the mecha insertion. They'd be coming out to meet them, sending everything they had because running was no longer an option. Their next move would be to try to use the hostages as a shield and bargain for safe passage. He'd trust Lyta to handle that end of the battle. She and her Ranger platoon had parachuted in along with Bohardt's infantry force on the first pass before the mecha insertion. He wondered if she was just as hesitant about letting the mercenaries lead the way as he was.

Ah, the hell with it. I'm the boss and I need to see these guys in action.

"I'm moving up, Val," he transmitted. The other man didn't argue, even though he must have wanted to.

The Sentinel had long legs and a lot of power to play with despite its mass and the deep mud, and all it cost him to move past Kurtz's lighter assault mecha was pain. The strike mech concussed like a drumhead with every plunging step, shuddering violently each time it pulled free of the muck. The easy chair was padded and fitted with a pneumatic suspension but he still felt as if he were being shaken in the teeth of a gigantic beast.

Just one bad step, worry nagged at him, *and this thing will wind up face-down in the mud and I'll look like the galaxy's biggest idiot.*

But the ground grew firmer the closer they came to the pirate base and he quickly caught up with the Bastards' formation, passing between a pair of gangly Warlock assault mecha and coming even with Bohardt's Valiant before he slowed back down to their patrol speed.

"Coming to look over my shoulder, Colonel?" Bohardt asked him, his tone light, his clipped Clan Modi accent coming through a bit stronger than usual, the only sign he wasn't joking.

"Just wanted a front-row seat, Captain," he assured the man.

"You're in luck, then, because the show's about to start."

Logan didn't have to ask what he meant. The Sentinel's radar and lidar were flashing red icons across his threat display, a dozen of them coming overland and nearly as many flying in on jump-jets, on a trajectory to touch down only fifty meters ahead of them. It was a heavy company, numbers wise, a lot for a half-assed group of bandits, but mostly scout mecha.

If they had any brains, they'd just run off into the swamp and hide until we left. He shrugged. *Of course, that would mean being stranded on this barely-habitable rock, so maybe I'd fight to the death, too.*

This place didn't even have a name, just a number on a star map. The star it orbited was unstable and given to bursts of radiation every few millennia, but the Empire had terraformed this world anyway...or, half-terraformed it. Most of the world was too hot for humans to live without special equipment, and the areas near the poles were wet and miserable half the year. You had to be desperate to be here in the first place, which was why it made a good location for pirates to have a base of operations.

He used to wonder why pirates didn't just make their bases on lifeless worlds or asteroids or someplace no one would look... until he'd spent weeks and weeks on a starship without touching land. It did things to you, psychologically, made you a bit crazy after a while. Military crews could get away with it because of strict discipline and a lot of experience on how to handle troops cramped together in an enclosed ship for that long. Pirates, not so much.

It's not like they were the most mentally stable people to begin with.

"First platoon!" Bohardt was barking out his orders. "Meet 'em in the air! Second and Third, advance!"

The lead platoon in his formation blasted off on columns of superheated air, sucked in via turbines and run through their fusion reactors. The overhead fog glowed brilliant yellow and white with the plasma of their exhaust, four comets streaking upward. The next two broke from a plodding trot to a loping gallop, rushing forward to meet the pirate armor.

It was a ballsy strategy. Doctrine back home was to let the enemy touch down and then attack, but he could see the idea of not ceding initiative to them. Not reckless though, he'd still kept two platoons in reserve. Bohardt had struck him as level-headed when they'd first met in person, but it was nice to see the judgement confirmed when the real bullets flew.

"Everyone else," Bohardt went on, "launch missiles at the ones coming in overland. Soften 'em up!"

The remaining two platoons had closed up into a single wedge formation as the others had advanced, and from the arrowhead formation, fire arced into the sky trailing billowing white smoke as shoulder-mounted missile pods belched out a full spread from each of the eight machines. Logan's fingers had toggled his joystick trigger over to missiles by instinct, but he held off. This was Bohardt's fight unless and until he proved he couldn't handle it.

Fireballs erupted in a chain over a kilometer away, burning through the fog and replacing it with sprays of dirt and rock and mud heated to steam. The pirate mecha had been running Electronic Counter Measures and he couldn't tell for sure how many of the enemy had been hit; the radar was scattered by their ECM, the lidar was blocked by the smoke and steam and thermal was useless in the heat of the fireballs.

Above, it was even less clear. Jump-jet exhausts merged in an inferno of roiling heat, smoke, steam and lasers cutting super-heated streams of plasma across the sky. Something exploded fifty meters over their head, a sun rising in the deep night, sending tentacles of plasma arcing away from them, and flaming debris tumbled downward. Then another, and a larger, and then a whole Hopper scout mech burned into the mud and dirt only thirty meters ahead of their lines, crashing with enough force to shake the ground. A rain of fire followed it, more debris and more machines, some more or less intact, others missing arms, or legs, or wreathed in the flaring plasma of a breached reactor.

Finally, the enemy mecha touched down, their jets over-heating, but only six of them. Their numbers had been cut in half in seconds and one of the six could barely stand, its left leg still glowing orange from a laser strike. They were strung out between fifty and two hundred meters away, some turning to fight and others ready to run. Logan was worried for a moment that Bohardt's First platoon would land right in the line of fire of his reserve forces to blindly pursue them, but the man was already speaking before the thought had the chance to echo from one side of Logan's brain to the other.

"First, get behind us," Bohardt snapped smartly, all trace of his accent gone in bland professionalism. "Fourth and Fifth, take them down."

The reserve platoons didn't need to be told twice. Lasers, missiles and Electro Thermal Chemical cannon rounds converged on the skinny, bird-legged scout machines, more of a firing squad than a battle. A few ragged lines of tracer-fire answered back from the 20mm Vulcans the Hoppers mounted, but none came close to the mercenary mecha. In seconds, the pirate machines were down but for one Hopper sprinting away at top speed, back toward the base. A missile streaked out from the shoulder of a Warlock and took the pirate Hopper in the right hip, blowing its leg off in a shower of sparks.

The mercenary Second and Third platoons were closing on the pirates' heavier mecha, ancient and obsolete Reapers cobbled together from parts but still capable of carrying heavier laser weapons and cannon. Less than three hundred meters separated the ranks when firing began, almost point-blank range but still far in the thick fog. The images teased at his vision, shadows cast in the light of burning metal and scintillating laser discharges, not quite solid enough for his sensors to give him a complete picture.

Logan felt an itch he couldn't let himself scratch, the unnatural feeling of being a spectator in a battle. People were dying while he sat and watched, unable to even follow the fight much less take part in it. If this was what command meant, he was ready to call it overrated. He remembered back when General Anders had been a Colonel, his battalion commander, stuck behind the battle, barely able to fire a shot. No wonder the man had been so ill-tempered in the field.

He noticed in his threat display that First platoon had landed behind their lines and was forming an echelon left of the reserve force. *Well trained for mercs. Borhardt is as good as I heard.*

"Advance at the run," the mercenary Captain ordered. "Hold fire until I give the order."

"Val," Logan called back to his executive officer. "Keep up but maintain the interval between us. Keep an eye on our rear and watch for runners."

"Oh, I got it covered, Boss," Kurtz replied, his backwoods colony drawl pronounced. "You have fun, y'hear?"

Logan's Sentinel was a grown man jogging beside a twelve-year-old, towering over Bohardt's Valiant by nearly five meters, the smaller machine taking a step and a half for every one of his, and it felt maddeningly slow. It would be so easy to blow past him and the rest of his force and charge into the fight with his plasma cannons blazing.

"Be nice to have the command and control suite you got on that Sentinel," Bohardt commented, only ten meters away, close enough for him to feel the footsteps of the mercenary's Valiant vibrating the ground in antiphonal chorus to his own.

"I don't know," Logan responded, impressed by the man's calm demeanor. "I used to pilot a Vindicator and I doubt I ever would have left her if she hadn't been shot out from beneath me."

"Grass is always greener," Bohardt said, then chuckled softly. "Not that there's any fucking grass here."

They were close enough to see the battle now, close enough for stray lasers and ETC rounds to test Logan's resolve not to flinch. It was much harder when you weren't shooting back. The pirate Reapers put up a better fight than their scout mecha, but he could see them falling one at a time, overwhelmed by the superior numbers of Bohardt's Bastards. He found himself nodding, not simply for the victory, which had been nearly inevitable barring gross incompetence, but for the efficient and well-disciplined formation the mercenaries maintained under fire. No one broke off and did their own thing, they kept to their assigned target and poured fire in until it was down.

A Reaper stumbled on a molten, glowing knee joint, trying to limp away. An Agamemnon speared it through the torso with an Electro Thermal Chemical cannon round, the hypersonic tungsten projectile ionizing a stream of air behind it and flashing red plasma when it cored through the older mech's fusion reactor. The Reaper dropped, powerless and lifeless, the crash of metal resounding in the sudden silence.

As far as he could tell, the Bastards hadn't suffered a single casualty.

"That's the last of them," Bohardt said, satisfaction evident in his voice. "First platoon, dismount and check for survivors. Second, you stay and cover them. The rest of you follow me."

Logan saw the glow of the pirate base in the fog across the plain, and started to make out the details of the place, even at a kilometer and a half away on the flat plains of the swamp land. Despite what Bohardt had said about grass, there *was* some vegetation out here, tenacious brush and weeds deeply rooted beneath the water-turned dirt, trees twisted with the effort of standing their ground against the flood, but nothing tall enough to block the view from the canopy of his Sentinel.

Calling it a "base" was something of an exaggeration. It was a mech hangar thrown together from corrugated aluminum on a cement foundation laid in a day and dried by fusion air jets. Makeshift tents had popped up around it like mushrooms in a fairy ring, raised off the mud with cargo pallets, while a couple of hundred meters out, a cargo shuttle converted with welded-on armor and jury-rigged cannons to resemble a poor man's idea of a drop-ship squatted on heavy-duty landing gear already centimeters deep into the mud.

On thermal, his mech's sensors picked up human-sized forms moving between the hangar and the tents in a methodical search. Either Lyta Randell's Rangers or the Bastard infantry platoon scouring for any pirates still hiding out. He hoped that meant the dismounted part of the operation had been success-ful. He didn't need more images of slaughtered civilians haunting his dreams.

"Cap, this is Chandra." The call was to Bohardt, but Logan heard it in his helmet speakers, sharing the mercenary's commo net. "Chandra" was, he knew, Lt. Rani Chandra, Bohardt's infantry platoon leader. "Compound is secure. We have located seven crewmembers from the *Vikrant* and they confirm they are the only survivors."

"Shit," Logan hissed. The Clan Modi freighter *Vikrant* had carried a crew of twenty.

"Any prisoners, Chandra?" Bohardt asked her, voice subdued as if he, too, realized the implications of what she'd said.

"You want any?" The question was a challenge and Logan felt the corner of his mouth turn up. He didn't necessarily appreciate bloodthirsty attitudes in soldiers, but when it came to pirates...

"No, I got no use for 'em."

"Then we're fresh out," the woman reported. Muffled gunshots sounded, barely picked up by the infantry leader's throat mic. Single shots, repeated, three different places. "A couple of the civilians are pretty banged up. We're letting the Wholesale Slaughter medics handle them."

Logan switched to a private network, happy to listen in on Bohardt's people but not quite prepared to extend the courtesy in the other direction yet.

"Lyta," he called, "how'd they look?"

"They're not Rangers," Colonel Lyta Randell told him, sounding as if she'd just been running tactical training lanes back on Sparta instead of raiding a pirate compound. "But they'll do against bandit trash. I got the word from the boarding team in orbit," she added. "Katy relayed it down. They took the *Vikrant* back with no casualties. There were only handful of pirates up there and they were so clueless about the freighter's security systems, they didn't even know they were being boarded."

"Any more survivors up there?" He let hopefulness creep into his voice, even though he knew better.

"Negative. A few bodies though."

His teeth clenched and he had to work to relax his jaw before he spoke again.

"Roger that. Let me know when the medics say this group is ready for transport and we'll give them a ride back up to their ship."

"Colonel Slaughter, let me ask you something," Bohardt said. "Just between us."

He checked the communications display on his cockpit control board and saw Bohardt had opened up a private net between them, visual as well as audio. The man's slightly chubby cheeks seemed squeezed into his helmet, the beard an affectation to make him look less baby-faced.

"Sure."

"What's in this for you? For Wholesale Slaughter, I mean. You're letting us keep the reward from the owners of the *Vikrant*, you're paying our expenses. I know you've got the same arrangement with Salvaggio's Savages, the Cossacks, at least four or five other outfits. Where do you make your money out of all this? Mercenary, man, I mean it's right there in the word."

He considered telling Bohardt it was none of his business, but this man was an intelligent and effective leader and deserved a better answer.

"I'm building a network," Logan told him as honestly as he could, "off the books, extra-governmental, to start taking care of the problem of pirates and bandits who cruise the borders between Dominions to hit cargo ships, who prey on Periphery colonies not protected by any of the Dominion militaries. I'm going to use you and all the others to wipe them out and make it unprofitable for anyone else to move in once they're gone."

Bohardt nodded slowly, a canny understanding in his dark eyes that belied his looks.

"You mean you're working black ops for some government's military intelligence agency."

Logan smiled thinly.

"Do you care?"

"Not as long as the deposits clear."

Kathren Margolis sighed as she leaned into the galley table, sipping hot coffee from a mug instead of a squeeze bulb.

"Remind me to buy Terrin and Franny dinner when we get back to Argos," she told Logan across the table. He grinned between bites of a prepackaged sandwich, knowing exactly what she meant.

"You still going on about the artificial gravity?" he asked her.

"Dude!" Kammy protested from across the compartment where he was filling his plate from the food dispensers. "Your brother managed to do something even the old Imperial researchers couldn't do! He turned the field output from the stardrive into an artificial gravity generator with just a few plates under the deck! The man's a damned genius!"

"He'd win an Academic Prestige Award for it," Katy agreed, "if the whole thing weren't so incredibly top secret no one will ever hear about it." She shot a knowing smile at the ship's captain, Kamehameha-Nui Johansen, 130 kilograms of muscle stuffed into a grey Wholesale Slaughter uniform that she still thought looked out of place on the big man. "The only reason Kammy is so happy about it is he doesn't have to eat food paste out of a tube anymore."

"Amen, sister," Kammy agreed, holding the tray full of soy protein and spirulina dressed up by the food processors to look like chicken breast and potatoes under his nose and taking a deep whiff. "And I can *smell* it, which you can't do in free fall."

She understood his relief. As odd as it sounded, starship crews didn't spend that much time in microgravity. They accelerated constantly between jump-points and only experienced free fall once they'd arrived at their destination—and most of the time, that was a planet or moon where the crews could rotate down for shore time in the gravity well. It was different for Belters and other deep-space crews, but Kammy had spent most of his life crewing a starship.

Not one like this, of course. There *were* no other ships like the *Shakak*. It was, as far as they knew, the only operational stardrive in existence, and even now it couldn't use the Imperial tech engine for faster-than-light travel because they lacked the antimatter power plant to provide that level of energy. It still made a great sublight drive for getting around between jump-points and allowed them the equivalent of dozens of gravities of acceleration without the fatal gee-load they would have faced with a conventional drive. Which meant there was no way to use acceleration to simulate gravity, and the whole crew had been fairly miserable until Terrin Brannigan, Logan's brother, had developed a way to turn the gravimetic field generator that was the core of the stardrive into a means of artificial gravity for the ship.

Katy didn't pretend to know how it worked, but she was damned glad it did.

"Are we forgetting why we're here?" Francis Acosta said, seated across from her, arms folded. Of course, Francis Acosta wasn't his real name. He was Military Intelligence and he'd been pretending to be her co-pilot for over a year. His real name was Bray, but it felt weird calling him that and she still thought of him as Francis. He *looked* like a Francis, darkly earnest and with a stick up his ass. "This is supposed to be an After-Action Review for Bohardt's Bastards." He snorted a skeptical laugh. "Given that General Constantine is probably going to have a damn coronary about how much Military Intelligence funding we're dropping into this Wholesale Slaughter Initiative of yours,

I should probably have a complete report for him when we get back."

"They're squared away," Logan declared. "Their tactics and training are top notch, nearly as good as Spartan military standards." He glanced over at Lyta Randell but the older woman was staring down at her coffee cup as if the secrets to the universe were concealed in it. Colonel Lyta Randell's face was a road map of a life spent on the razor's edge, and something seemed to be dragging it down with more force than the artificial gravity field.

"Colonel Randell," Logan prompted, his tone formal, "would you care to share your impression of Captain Bohardt's unit?"

"They're fine," Lyta said, still seeming distracted. "Better than most of the shit we've had to sift through."

Katy frowned. Lyta hadn't been herself since Revelation, and she hadn't been able to drag out a reason why. *Maybe I should see if Kammy can talk to her. He's known her longer.*

"I'm just glad you've still managed to accomplish what you set out to do originally," Katy told Logan, resting her hand on his arm. "Even if we haven't been able to get any immediate military benefits from the Imperial technology we got off Terminus, you've still found a way to take the fight to the bandits and pirates."

"If anyone can make headway on that Imperial tech, it's Terrin," Logan said.

"No argument from me," Kammy said, toasting the declaration with a bottle of fruit juice. "At this point, I'll believe the kid can walk on water."

"We've been gone too long," Lyta said, shaking her head. She still stared through the bulkhead at something none of them could see. "I have a feeling we need to get back."

"I'm sure everything's fine at home," Katy said carefully, not wanting to sound patronizing.

"We'll find out in a few days," Kammy said cheerfully around a mouthful of faux-tatoes. "A few days! God, I love this ship."

2

Are you seeing what I'm seeing here, Doc?" Terrin Brannigan asked, a broad smile slowly spreading across his lean and normally dour face. He straightened from the readout, pointing at a sine wave displayed across the screen. "I think we can duplicate that."

Dr. Kovalev ran his fingers through his greying beard as he peered over Terrin's shoulder, a tic Terrin had first noticed when he'd worked for the man as a graduate assistant two years ago.

"Yes, I think you're right," the older man said, words trailing off upward as if they were a cloud wafting away from him. He paused, eyes unfocussed, and Terrin knew he was running the calculations in his head. The man was a mathematical genius, which was one reason he'd brought him into the research staff here. "If you can manage to procure a few hours with the ship you discovered..."

"The *Shakak*," Terrin reminded him. Technically, it was the *Shakak II*, since the first iteration had been a conventional cargo ship destroyed in a battle with a Starkad cruiser in orbit around Terminus.

"Yes, if you can get your father to authorize some experiments with her stardrive out away from any gravity wells, I think you could use the artificial gravity field you rigged up for her to duplicate this effect."

Kovalev's interest seemed purely academic, but Terrin was about to start hopping up and down with excitement. It must have been obvious because Franny noticed all the way across the lab and hurried over from her computer terminal.

"What is it, Terry?" she asked, eyes lighting up. "Did you finalize the sequence?"

"We sure did!" he enthused, laughing. He wanted to kiss her, but it would have been unprofessional here in the lab, surrounded by two dozen other scientists and technicians, all of them so absorbed by their own part of the project they barely spared his exclamation a glance. "I think we can do it. We can at least set up a test."

"Oh my God!" Franny gasped, motioning expansively, her smile nearly too large for her elfin features. She pounded him on the shoulder with her fist almost hard enough to hurt. "If you can generate enough of a gravity field, we'll be able to manufacture exotic matter! You could duplicate the stardrive!"

"Maybe," he cautioned, trying to sober up and be realistic, though it was difficult. A few heads had popped up at Franny's words and he didn't want anyone getting *too* excited. "We're just talking about small scale experiments right now. What we'd have to do is..."

"Save it for General Constantine," she said, holding up her wrist 'link to show him the time. "He's supposed to be here in a few minutes, remember?"

"Oh, shit!" he blurted. "I totally forgot about that!"

Kovalev laughed, nodding towards Franny's Spartan Navy uniform.

"You work for the military here, boy," he reminded. "Even

when you're the Guardian's son, you still have to justify your funding."

Terrin moaned under his breath, the air going out of him a little. He wanted to ask, "Why me?" but he already knew the answer. He *was* the son of the Guardian and he'd also spent more time researching this technology than anyone else, which was why he was in charge of the project.

"Get going," Franny gestured toward the door. "He's a general and he's your boss, you go meet him."

"Right, got it," he said, nodding. He looked down at his rumpled shirt and tried in vain to smooth it into something more presentable. "Do you want to come with me?" he asked her hopefully.

"I'm an NCO," she reminded him, smacking him on the arm lightly. She grinned. "A Chief Petty Officer now, but still an NCO until they get around to sending me to officer's training. They don't send NCOs to meet generals."

"You'll be fine," Kovalev assured him. He waved at the read-out. "If you need to impress him, bring him back here and I'll explain all this to him like I used to in class to my students."

"I want to impress him," Terrin told the old professor as he headed toward the exit, "not put him to sleep."

A chill wind blew through the door when Terrin opened it, threatening to push it back closed before he could slip out. The rush of air funneled downward from the gap in the snow-capped Bloodmark Mountains, looming over the lab facility like giants of legend, their cloud-shrouded peaks still wrapped in the talons of winter despite the spring flowers blooming in the fields of the isolated valley.

He paused just outside the doors, entranced as always by the jagged silhouette of the mountains and the incredible isolation of the place. There were no roads to this valley, by design. Construction equipment and supplies had been flown in on military drop-ships and the only way in or out was by a VTOL jet or a shuttle. Even ducted-fan helicopters couldn't generate enough lift to clear the tops of the mountains. Nobody happened across this place by accident.

Why doesn't the lab have more windows? he wondered. *Probably because everyone would just stare out them and not get any work done.*

The sun was behind him, the mountains basking in the late morning glow, which was how he spotted the jet. It sparkled against the majestic backdrop, a faceted diamond low in the sky. It was less than a kilometer away before he could pick out the whine of its engines from the background roar of the wind, and by then the lines of the plane were clear. It was small, a private passenger jet, gleaming white with the slanted grey design of the Spartan military running down its fuselage and across its wings. Just the sort of thing you'd expect the Guardian's Chief of Intelligence to have at their beck and call to visit a top-secret research lab.

The whine turned into a screaming roar as belly jets brought the angular little aircraft down onto the paved landing pad at the center of the cluster of buildings, touching down beside the VTOL jet they kept on hand for emergencies. The utility bird seemed bulbous and dumpy by comparison, but then, no one at the base was a general. Terrin waited until the turbines had cycled down to a tolerable volume before he jogged down the stairs from the lab and headed for the pad.

The grass was still wet from the morning dew, soaking through his comfortable, indoor shoes almost immediately. He winced, hating the feel of wet socks and knowing it would be hours until he had time to change them. Franny kept telling him he could get away with wearing a uniform since he was techni-cally sworn into the Spartan Navy Technological Research Division, and he thought he should have at least taken her up on the combat boots. He'd worn a set of Wholesale Slaughter fatigues on the mission to Terminus, but he felt like an imposter in a Navy uniform.

General Constantine didn't climb out of the jet's side door as much as unfolded, a praying mantis of a man, a head taller than Terrin. His tan uniform was spotless and perfect, as always, and the sharp edges of his face seemed to share the pressed creases of his jacket, as if the man himself were a weapon honed to a razor's edge. He regarded Terrin with dark eyes and a hint of a smile, approaching in a long-legged stride that ate up the meters between them in seconds.

"Good to see you again, Terrin," Nicolai Constantine said.

"You too, sir," he said, shaking the man's hand with a bit of tentativeness he hadn't experienced back when he'd been a student and Constantine just someone his father worked with instead of his immediate superior. "How was your flight?"

"I feel like I'm in that damn plane every day now," Constantine lamented, waving back at the VTOL aircraft. The whine of its turbines had died down to a low hum now, the blast from the belly jets a light breeze across the grass. "I don't think I've slept in my own bed in a week. I may as well be a Captain again and running field operations from a starship. At least then I'd get to go someplace new once in a while!"

He was walking as he complained, long, loping steps towards the main lab, and Terrin nearly had to jog to keep up.

"But tell me, lad, have you made any progress on all this technobabble I keep reading reports about?" Constantine went on. "I swear to whatever god is fashionable this year, between you and your wayward brother, you're going to bankrupt the whole damned Guardianship!"

"Actually, we have," Terrin said, trying not to gasp the words —he was out of breath already from trying to match Constantine's pace. They were already at the stairs and the general took them two at a time. "We just figured out...well, I *think* we've figured out a way we might be able to duplicate the stardrive."

Constantine stopped in his tracks halfway up the steps and faced Terrin with a look he could only describe as a starving wolf staring at a wounded deer.

"There's an awful lot of weasel-words in that statement, boy. What do you think you might have figured out?"

"Come in and I'll show you," Terrin urged him, pulling open the door to the lab.

"Officer on deck!" The bellow was so loud and echoing, it took Terrin a moment to realize it was Franny who'd yelled the warning. He blinked, not believing that much sound could come from the skinny, waifish woman. She was braced at attention, as were the other Spartan Navy technicians in the lab, while the civilian scientists seemed to hover uncertainly over their seats, unsure whether they should stand or not.

"At ease, at ease," Constantine waved at them, clucking with impatience. "I don't have time for that shit. Show me this think-might-maybe stuff before I yank your funding and send everyone home with no supper."

Terrin knew the man was kidding—if for no other reason than his father would have something to say on the matter—but he still hurried over to the monitor where the computer simulation had been running.

"It's right here." He waved Constantine over. "You see this gravimetic scale in the frequency of the gravitons coming off the..."

"Son," Constantine interrupted, raising a hand to stop him, "if I've done or said anything to make you think I've ever taken any hyperspatial physics classes, I apologize."

"Oh, uh...," Terrin stuttered until Dr. Kovalev stepped up and rescued him.

"General," he said, "you are aware of the principles upon

which the Alanson-McCleary stardrive is based? The idea that rather than moving the ship through spacetime, it contracts spacetime ahead of the ship and expands it behind?"

"I've heard the explanation," Constantine agreed. "That doesn't mean I understand *how* it does that."

"To generate the gravimetic fields necessary for the drive to work, you need exotic matter, material with negative energy density. The only places to get such material are inconvenient to reach."

"Inconvenient?" Constantine raised an eyebrow.

"The inside of a neutron star, for example," Kovalev explained, grinning now. Terrin remembered the look from when he'd really gotten started on a subject in his graduate classes. "They require massive gravity fields. But the young Mr. Brannigan here has recently come up with a way to achieve that without the necessity of tracking down a neutron star."

"I read about that!" Constantine exclaimed, snapping his fingers in realization. "You worked out a way to make artificial gravity on the *Shakak*!"

"And we can use the same method," Terrin said, nodding, "to generate the conditions to manufacture exotic matter. We just need some time with the *Shakak* at the secret proving grounds out away from any planets."

Constantine snorted a humorless laugh.

"Well, you'll need to talk to your brother about *that*, but I think he'd be willing to let you borrow her for a while, as long as this won't damage the ship..."

"It shouldn't," he assured the general. "I mean," he dithered, "there's always a slight *chance*..."

"Oh, sweet Lord," Constantine sighed, rubbing at his eyes. "You really need to learn how to sell a proposal. Look, just put everything in writing and send it to me. When Logan gets back, we'll run it by him together and set something up."

"This still won't go FTL," Terrin reminded him. "We know how to make antimatter, but it would just be unrealistically, impractically expensive."

"Even a couple more ships with that drive and the defense shield it provides could turn the tide in any future conflict," Constantine said, the grin on his face as if the starving wolf had gotten his deer.

He seemed about to say something else when his 'link chimed on his wrist and he checked the notification.

"Damn," he murmured. "Have to take this. Excuse me."

Terrin let out a breath as the general stepped away and Franny put a supportive hand on his shoulder, grinning triumphantly.

"I knew you could do it," she whispered.

If Constantine noticed the interplay, he didn't comment, just said something Terrin couldn't hear into the pickup of his 'link, then hit the button to disconnect it before coming back over to them.

"I'm afraid I have to take off," Constantine told them. "Something unscheduled popped up. Tell your cooks I apologize if they'd already fixed up a special lunch." His smile had a wry twist. "Be sure to enjoy it without me." He waved, heading for the exit.

Terrin started to head after him, feeling like he should walk him back to the plane, but Constantine stopped him with an upraised hand.

"Stay," he insisted. "I'll see myself out. And get some sensible shoes, boy, it's wet out there."

And then he was out the door, leaving Terrin between one step and the other, mouth open.

"That was easy," he said.

"Selling the idea was easy," Kovalev corrected him. "Now let's figure out how to actually do it."

Nicolai Constantine didn't like surprises. The greater part of his job for the last twenty years had been to avoid them. He wasn't sure if it had been a personality trait uniquely suiting him to the position or whether the position had shaped him into the man he was, but it carried over from professional to personal.

Which is likely why I haven't remarried.

"We're almost there, sir," his pilot called back from the cockpit with all the equanimity of a woman who loved flying and didn't give a damn about any inconvenience to his schedule this detour might be.

Would that my job were so uncomplicated.

The sun was bright over the Bloodmarks now and he guessed it was nearly noon, but didn't bother to check his 'link to confirm it. Wesley Martens was a friend and he had few enough of those. He could spare the man however long he needed.

A rich friend, he amended.

The mountain estate was proof of that. Wesley Martens had inherited it from a line of Martens going back to the days of the Empire, a proud lineage until recently. It was large enough to be considered a mansion, though he'd never heard the man refer to it as such. Wesley kept no servants despite the size of the place, depending on cleaning robots, automated kitchen machinery, and mostly on the fact he rarely brought anyone out here. The place had intrigued Contantine nearly as much as the man when he'd received the message.

A single gravel track stretched down from the hillside estate, winding for kilometers in switchbacks until it reached a main road. Constantine doubted anyone ever used the road, or had since the place had been built. Wesley didn't want people out here. It was his refuge, a retreat from the slings and arrows of outrageous fortune.

"Set down next to his flyer," Constantine told the pilot, gesturing to a flat area at the back of the sprawling, single-story structure.

The rear seemed less pretentious than the front, as if the Corinthian columns and statuary were for casual passers-by even where they wouldn't be any. In the back, the doors were smaller and more personal, the only decoration some well-tended rose bushes.

Some architectural comment on the duality of human nature? Or maybe his great-great-grandparents just ran out of money before the house was finished?

Wesley was already standing out there, waiting for him. He was dressed casually in the sort of clothes rich people wore when they wanted to look normal. They never quite pulled it off, in his experience. There was always an air of being too clean, too well-groomed for them to pass. Wesley covered his face with his hand to shield his eyes from the clouds of dust the jet kicked up as it landed. Constantine wondered if it made him a bad person for enjoying the feeling it gave him to see people come to meet him when he arrived, to see them guarding their eyes.

I should probably see an analyst about that, when I get the time. It was a joke with himself; he'd never have the time. He hadn't had time for a wife, a family, friends, hobbies...and he certainly had no time for therapy.

The jet's fuselage sank into the suspension of the landing gear, rising slowly a few centimeters before finally settling down. Normally, Constantine would have been out of his seat already, but he stayed motionless until the turbines began their mewling, petulant decline from a roar to a whine. He was almost reluctant to cut loose his safety restraints, knowing whatever his old friend wanted from him, it likely wouldn't be easy or pleasant. Easy, pleasant favors didn't require last-minute urgent requests to meet in private in the middle of nowhere.

"Nicolai!" Wesley bellowed with all the bombast Constantine remembered from twenty years ago. His arms were spread wide, giving him the look of a grizzly standing on its hind legs, challenging a rival, but Constantine knew it was all for show. The man was soft and the hug he gave was warm and welcoming. "You haven't changed a bit!"

"I must have looked like shit then, too," Constantine said. "You look old as the hills, my friend."

And he did. His hair had gone grey in great streaks down the side, leaving salt-and-pepper at the top, and deep grooves had worked their way into his long, horsey face, drawing his mouth downward despite his perpetual smile.

"Ah, I see you with my heart, then," Wesley said, waving it off. "Come on inside."

Constantine motioned to his pilot to get her attention.

"I may be a while, Lieutenant," he told her. "Feel free to get out and stretch your legs."

"Aye, sir," she acknowledged, pulling off her flight helmet to reveal jet-black hair bobbed short.

She might have seemed attractive to him once, though now all he saw was her skill at her job. He shrugged it off, just another melancholy musing of an old man, and followed his old friend into the house.

The interior of the place was unassuming, built for comfort rather than ostentatiousness, with couches sunken into niches in the marble floor, arrayed around a firepit burning warm on this chilly spring day. There was a bottle of wine and glasses ready, laid out on a low table beside the seats and Constantine accepted the drink gratefully, settling into the plush cushions before taking a long sip. The tinted, one-way windows stretching across the rear of the house painted an idyllic land-scape of the meadows behind and the mountains beyond and he wondered why the man didn't spend all of his time here.

"I assume there'll be lunch," Constantine said, eyeing Wesley balefully over the rim of his glass. "You pulled me away from the best a military crew ready for an inspection could provide."

"Of course," Wesley assured him, falling into his own seat with the grace of a side of beef falling off a carcass. He poured himself a glass of wine and raised a glass in toast. "Steaks are being prepared by the finest automated chef programs Spartan technology has to offer. Shouldn't be more than a few minutes."

"I know you love your toys," Constantine said, shaking his head, "but I prefer the human touch. The difference of a few seconds, a fraction of a dash of seasoning, it makes a meal unique." He speared the man with a glare, changing subjects abruptly in a tactic he'd learned from an old, experienced colonel many years ago. "What was so important for you to call me here at such short notice?"

"You are one of my oldest friends, Nicolai." He wasn't sure if the statement was supposed to answer his question or not, but he let Wesley continue through a pause to take another drink. "When you were new at school, your parents just emigrated from Mbeki, without a single soul to call your friend, with the older boys taunting you for your accent, I stood up for you. And when some of my acquaintances and extended family were so unwise as to back Duncan Lambert in his attempted coup, when others would have thrown me and my wife in prison merely for knowing the wrong people, you returned the favor and stood up for me."

"The point, Wesley," he urged, cocking his head to the side. He blinked his eyes. It was too comfortable in here and the warmth of the fire and the wine was reminding him how little sleep he'd managed the night before. *Going to nod off on this damned couch, stretched out like this.*

"The point is, I feel I owe you a debt, Nicolai." He sniffed the wine in his glass, eyes closing in appreciation of the bouquet. "I just wish there was some way I could have prevented all this."

Constantine blinked again, shaking his head. His head was fuzzy, much fuzzier than one glass of wine could...

The wine.

"Wesley, you fucking bastard." He'd meant the words to come out in a growl, but they were a whisper. He clawed for the handgun holstered beneath his jacket, but his fingers were numb, his arms strengthless.

Wesley Martens had stood up, though Constantine hadn't noticed it because the world was spinning around him now. The big bear of a man leaned over him, pulling aside his jacket and yanking the gun from beneath it. There were booted footfalls echoing around him, dark-armored figures swarming, rifles in their hands.

"Why?" he asked, barely able to get the words past his lips. Darkness was swimming around him, a predator impatient to swallow him up.

"Because sometimes," Wesley told him, a hint of sadness in those hound-dog eyes, "people are just what they seem to be, and all those relatives of mine who were so quick to deny my involvement in the conspiracy were keeping me in play for another day. But I have tried to do the best I can for you, Nicolai," he insisted, crouching down beside Constantine, peering into his fading eyes. "I have tried to make sure you will not be killed in the evil days which are coming." He shook his head. "Though I doubt you will see this as a favor."

The words slipped away from Constantine's grasp and the darkness finally claimed him.

3

Jaimie Brannigan leaned his elbows on the solid, polished oak of his grandfather's desk and stared at the troop disposition map as if he could make it go away.

"What the hell is Starkad doing, Donnel?" he asked the tall, imposing officer pacing on the other side of the holographic projection. "They have every single warship in their fleet sitting at their largest jump-point hubs. They're either worried about an invasion or they're getting ready to invade. Do we have any idea which?"

"I talked to General Constantine about it a couple days ago," Donnel Anders said, shaking his head. "He's heard chatter about the orders going out, but it's all rumors in the lower ranks, no solid intelligence."

Jaimie chuckled softly.

"You're a general too now, Donnel. You can call him Nicolai if you like, he won't mind."

Anders seemed mildly scandalized by the thought.

"I am too newly minted a General to be calling General Constantine anything but 'sir,' my lord," he protested. He shook the idea off with a visible shudder. "As for the Supremacy, if I was forced to guess, I'd say they could be finally making the big move we've all been expecting against Clan Modi to seize the Disputed Territories once and for all. But it could just as easily be a move to test our defenses and our response."

"So, how are we responding?" Jaimie asked him. "You're my Chief of Staff now that General Vardalos has retired. Earn your money, Donnel."

He was joking but he wondered for a moment if Anders understood. The man *was* new to the rank and the job and, while he more than deserved it, he still seemed a bit cowed by the altitude up here in the Palace.

"I've deployed Third and Fifth Fleet," Anders told him, adjusting the image in the very expensive and ostentatious holographic projector's tank until it showed the Spartan systems.

Like the desk and most of the décor in the Guardian's private office, the projector had been one of the eccentricities of Jaimie's grandfather, the last Guardian, who had been given to much more outlandish displays of wealth. For his part, Jaimie was a soldier, used to simple frugality, and the conspicuous consumption bothered him still.

Anders' forefinger traced a line through the floating image, showing the small groups of ships moving from one jump-point to another.

"They're heading to the jump-points where the Starkad flotilla would have to emerge if they came after our border systems. I've sent Second and Fourth to reinforce the defenses along our border with Clan Modi just in case it is a bid for the Disputed Systems. Don't want the fighting to spill over into our territory." He eyed Jaimie sidelong. "That's assuming we would stay out of the fight in the event of a Starkad incursion into Modi."

Jaimie sat back in his chair and whistled softly.

"Well, now, that would be a bold gamble, wouldn't it?" he

mused. "We don't have the forces to take on Starkad alone, but if Modi threw everything into a defense of the Disputed Systems..."

"It's a big 'if,' sir," Anders admitted. "I wonder if your son's pet project might bring us some intelligence about the mood in Clan Modi?"

"Don't let him hear you call it that," Jaimie warned the man. "He's as fond of the Wholesale Slaughter initiative as if he'd personally squatted down and gave birth to it." He smiled, pride filling his chest with a welcome warmth. "I have to say, I'm as proud as hell of him for it. He took a huge risk, both him and Terrin, but they not only brought back invaluable technological data, he also came up with a way to take care of the bandit problem without tying up our military forces." He ran a hand over his cheeks. He needed a shave, unless he wanted to go ahead and grow that beard again. "I think he's proven he's more than capable of taking over this job when I decide it's time to step down."

"It's been quite a while since Sparta has had a Guardian step down voluntarily," Anders mused, hands clasped behind him. "The ones who haven't died in combat have usually served until they dropped over from age or disease."

"Not me," Jamie insisted. "I will be quite happy to hand all this over to Logan and enjoy my retirement." He shrugged. "Not anytime soon, of course. Maybe just in time to spoil my grandchildren. Logan will talk Katy into getting married some-time before too long, even stubborn as she is. And even Terrin seems to have found himself a girlfriend, for which I offer many thanks to Lord Mithra." He hissed a relieved sigh. "Spenta Mainyu witness, I thought the boy had forgotten about women entirely, as obsessed with his work as he is."

"Hmmph," Anders grunted, smiling. "I wonder where he ever got that from, sir."

Jaimie scowled, though he couldn't put any true anger into it. "You're all cowering at the thought of taking Nicolai Constantine's name in vain, but you think nothing of giving a ration of shit to the Guardian. A lesser man might feel insulted."

"I'm not worried, my lord," Anders insisted, "because you could never be considered a lesser man."

"Nice save. At any rate, getting back to the point, the *Shakak* should be arriving in orbit within the hour, so you can ask him yourself."

The 'link on Anders' belt beeped for attention and the general glanced down in obvious consternation.

"I told them not to bother me during the damned meeting," he murmured, pulling the device up to check the message. His face paled and Jaimie came halfway to his feet at the shocked expression.

"What is it?" he asked, his first thought that there might be bad news about Logan, his second going to the Starkad fleet.

Anders didn't answer, just hit a control on Jaimie's desk and the holographic display changed from a star map to an image of the broad, multi-lane road between Argos and the military base at Laconia, just twenty-five kilometers away across the plains. A line of mecha marched down the middle of the road, one arrowhead formation after another, a hundred meters between platoons. They stretched for kilometers, as far back as the view of the road camera could reach. Above them, assault shuttles roared only two or three hundred meters up, screaming toward the city from the Navy base.

"What the hell is that?" Jaimie demanded, springing from his seat. "Are those from the Guardian's Own?" He knew the answer before he finished asking the question; his personal guard didn't *have* that many mecha.

"No," Anders said, sharp eyes zeroing in on the image. "Those are the Home Guard."

"Is there some exercise going on that General Delacorte didn't bother to tell me about?" Jaimie asked, anger beginning to crowd out the uncanny prickling down the back of his neck. His first thought had been an invasion, as impossible as it would have been for enemy troops to land without them knowing far in advance.

"If there is, he didn't tell me, either," Anders said. He didn't seem angry, just worried. He hit a control on his 'link and a flashing notification in the corner of the hologram showed he was syncing the device with the room's communications system.

He scrolled through his contacts and hit Georges Delacorte's name, touching the red toggle beside the call button to put it through over any other call the man was getting with Anders' priority override. A tilting hourglass flashed on the screen as the call was sent...and then nothing.

"Delacorte isn't answering," he said tightly.

"Try Nicolai." The words were steady, matter-of-fact, but Jaimie's stomach roiled with worry he hoped might be premature.

Anders sent the call to the Intelligence Chief, but the result was the same.

"Can't get through to him, sir."

Jaimie Brannigan sucked in a breath, trying to wrap his mind around what that could mean. At first and last, he was a soldier, so he didn't allow himself the luxury of emotional shock. Instead, he leaned over his desk and reached through the holographic projection above it to hit an emergency sequence on the physical keyboard there, one he'd never used except in drills. The one his grandfather hadn't had the time to use.

"Karras here," a woman's voice responded, as sharp and unyielding as the point of a sword.

"Colonel Karras." Jaimie Brannigan kept his tone calm and commanding. There was no use panicking at this point; and even if there was, he'd be damned if he was the first one to do it. "It seems like the whole contingent of Home Guard mobile armor is on the march from Laconia and General Delacorte doesn't seem to be answering his phone. I think it's probably time to take some precautions. Contact orbital defense and put them on notice. I want some assault shuttles on Combat Air Patrol for the palace."

"Roger that, sir," she said, as businesslike and professional as if he'd asked her to schedule an inspection of her troops. "Wait one."

"Wait one," he repeated, rolling his eyes at Anders. "Sure, no problem. Do me a favor, Donnel, go to the wall safe over behind the portrait of my wife..." He nodded toward the opposite wall of the office where a painting of Maggie from the year they were married hung as the centerpiece of a cluster of family portraits. "...and grab my sidearm and one for yourself, just in case."

Anders looked a bit lost but did as he was told, carefully tilting the painting aside and finding the silvery metal safe inset in the wall behind it, a half a meter on each side, with a blank ID panel at its center. He motioned toward it, shaking his head.

"Is there a code?" he asked.

"Just use your palmprint Donnell. I had it coded in when you took the position."

"Lord Guardian," Glory Karras came back on the line, and he thought he detected a hint of strain in her stoic façade. "I am unable to contact the orbital defenses. My technicians tell me there's extensive EM jamming across the whole city, but I had him try using laser line-of-sight with a relay satellite and there's still been no reply. I have taken the liberty of recalling all pilots and I will be putting the Guardian's Own into defensive positions around the palace." She paused. He could see her face in his imagination, sturdy and matronly like one of his tutors as a child. "You should evacuate immediately. We'll buy you what time we can."

And there it was. The vocalization of the thought he'd kept trying to deny, the realization of a nightmare from twenty years ago.

"Here." Anders pressed the cool metal and warm polymer of a gun into his hand, as if forcing him to confront the situation.

Jaimie didn't have to look at it. He'd practiced so often with the weapon it might as well have been an extension of his arm.

"It's a coup, Donnell," he said, watching the approaching mecha in the display. They seemed so real, so solid he could reach out and touch them marching across his desk, tip them over with a finger. "By God, it's a coup."

"It's more than that, sir," Anders told him, slapping a control he *did* know about, one Jaimie had shown him personally the first day he'd taken the job. An alarm began to sound and a heavy, BiPhase Carbide shield as thick as the hull of a starship slid into place across the front of the office. He turned back to Jaimie, features firmed up with resolve despite the nightmare sheen of unreality that had fallen over them. "The Starkad maneuvers were designed to draw our ships away...and they must have known the officers we trusted the most would be on the fleets we sent out to guard against invasion."

"This has been planned for months," Jaimie said, nodding with the realization. And with unwilling admiration. It wasn't like Aaron Starkad to be so forethoughtful.

Anders pulled a plush throw rug away from the floor just in front of the desk and yanked upward on a fold-out ring set in the heart of pine. A trapdoor rose, revealing a ladder heading into darkness.

"We have to reach your shuttle, sir," Anders told him, motioning for Jaimie to precede him down into the escape tunnel. "We can regroup off-planet, bring the fleets back with us."

"The hell with my shuttle, Donnell," Jaimie shot back. "Logan is walking right into this, and I can't think that's a coincidence. And Terrin is out at the research lab in the Bloodmarks."

"General Constantine was scheduled to visit him today," Anders said.

Jaimie began climbing down the ladder one-handed, his right filled with the welcome mass of the pistol.

"The hell with escaping," he told Anders. "We're going to save my sons."

"Damn it!" Lt. Lambeti snapped over the headphones of Logan Conner's helmet. "Hang on back there!"

The pilot's warning came a fraction of a second before the blast. The explosion rocked the drop-ship and Logan clenched his teeth, fingers going white on the control yokes of his Sentinel, wracked by a feeling of utter futility. A nightmare unfolded before his eyes, played out on the display screens of his mech's threat display, tied into the external cameras and sensors of the drop-ship.

Assault shuttles and dual-environment fighters swarmed through the afternoon sky like clouds of mosquitoes coming across the lake by their farmhouse in the summer, so many of them he thought he could have walked down from orbit on their backs. And yet fewer every second. Missile warheads filled the space between the aircraft with fiery globes of destruction and, where they struck home, debris rained down toward the surface of Sparta, only two kilometers below. Tracer rounds from shuttle-mounted Vulcans cross-hatched with the plasma flash of laser pulses and coil gun rounds ionizing the air in their wake, creating a pattern of light and death that it seemed nothing could penetrate.

Aircraft and aerospacecraft died and fell tumbling towards the city below. Fires already burned and pillars of smoke rose to merge with a black pall hovering over the heart of Argos, over the area he knew marked the spaceport...and the palace. He'd never seen destruction or war on this scale, not in a career with more combat time than almost any mech-jock in any conventional unit, never seen a whole planet ripping itself apart. And he'd certainly never expected the first place he'd experience all-out war to be Sparta. His home.

They'd arrived through the jump-gate only hours before and he'd suspected something was amiss almost immediately. They hadn't been hailed, hadn't been challenged, hadn't received so much as a friendly hello from orbital traffic control, and their messages to the home fleet ships in cislunar parking orbit had sailed out into the black unanswered. Lyta had been the first to get suspicious, and it had spread like a plague on a virgin field. They'd been running on the decoy fusion engine affixed to the rear of the ship for the sake of *maskirovka*, its fuel and boost capacity limited, mostly there just to provide a fusion signature so casual observers wouldn't wonder why a ship was moving at a tenth lightspeed without any noticeable means of propulsion. Once Logan had embraced the paranoia, he'd told Kammy to secure the decoy engine and burn for Sparta on the stardrive at maximum boost.

The command might as well have flipped a switch. The moment they'd surged forward at an effective acceleration of nearly fifty gravities, the four heavy cruisers had abandoned their LaGrangian point posts and headed out to meet them at maximum sustainable boost. Which was not nearly as fast as the *Shakak*, but also didn't have to be because they were heading right into the teeth of the fleet.

"Hey boss," Tara Gerard, the *Shakak's* tactical officer had reported, her tone unusually reserved, her characteristic bloodthirstiness seemingly reined in since they'd been dealing with Logan's homeworld. "I'm picking up what looks like a battle on the surface, just between your capital at Argos and the military base at Laconia." She'd squinted at the readouts for a moment and looked back at him again. "Some fighting going on in the air, too, but no orbital weapons used yet." She'd shrugged. "Don't know why."

"I think it's pretty obvious why," Lyta had said, her voice and expression as flat and final as a judge handing down a death sentence. "Whoever's behind this couldn't recruit anyone in a high enough position at the Orbital Defense Command to take over the defense grid, so they took it out, instead."

"Can you take on that many ships?" Logan had asked Kamehameha-Nui Johansen, pointing at the threat icons on the forward display screens.

"Mithra knows, boss," the big man had admitted. "One at a time, sure, but..." He'd eyed Logan with discomfort on his rounded, homely face. "Are we sure they're all bad guys? What if some of them are just being dragged along into this shit?"

"We're all being dragged into this shit, Kammy," Lyta had answered for him. "They're probably counting on us not wanting to fire on our own."

"We have to go help dad and Terrin," Logan had decided. He touched a button on his 'link to hook himself into the ship's public address system. "All shuttle pilots, all mech pilots, all Rangers, gear up and report to the drop-ships." He'd turned to Katy. "We're going in and you're going to watch our backs. Don't get killed."

She'd kissed him, brief but fierce and headed out of the bridge without a word. He hadn't hesitated. He knew what his father would say.

"Kammy, take us in. If anything gets in our way, warn it off, then shoot it down. Whoever's behind this is going to find out why staging a coup against a Brannigan is a bad fucking idea."

He hoped things were going well for the *Shakak*, because everything looked pretty horrible down in the soup.

"Katy!" he yelled her name, not caring about professionalism or radio discipline, not even sure if his signal could pierce the web of EM jamming. "How are we looking?"

"*You're* looking fine," she said, her voice low and steady, as if she were half-asleep. He knew what the tone meant. Combat pilots didn't yell or curse or sound uptight when the real bullets started flying. They shut down their emotions and ran on instinct, not letting their fear or anger interfere with the instincts of flying. "I personally have had better days," she went on, "but I'm not exactly the only target up here, so I think I'll be okay, barring Murphy's intervention."

He tried to access the feed from her bird and the second assault shuttle, but the interference from the ECM was too much. The air practically crackled with it. The world tilted crazily, throwing him against his restraints and the view from the drop-ship's external cams swung with it, showing sun and blue sky and mountains all rushing into one, stomach-churning kaleidoscope of colors. Something erupted into a gout of flaming debris only a few hundred meters away and their attitude gradually levelled out.

"Thanks, Commander," Lt. Lambeti radioed, relief strong in his voice.

"Get them safe to the ground, Tony," Katy replied.

"We have a transmission coming in," Lambeti said with all the subtle coolness of a puppy finding a bone. He was a young officer and still not quite up to the cool detachment of Kathren Margolis. "It's for you, Colonel Conner! It's from the Guardian!"

"I see it, Lieutenant."

He'd kept his voice calm, but inside Logan felt the weight of a planet slipping off his shoulders. His father was alive...they were in time. Logan tapped a control on the base of the mech's steering yoke and a still picture of his father popped up beside the audio-only message. There wasn't enough bandwidth available through the jamming to get an image.

"Logan, are you there?" Jaimie Brannigan asked, his bellicose voice strong enough to cut through the static and interference. "Do you read?"

"Read you five by five, sir," he replied. "We're on our way down right now. Coming in over Argos right now, heading for the palace."

"No!" his father exclaimed, surprising him. "Forget the palace. The Guardian's Own is still fighting there, but they're up against the entire Home Guard, or at least mech pilots enough to fill all the armor the Home Guard had. I think they brought in outsiders for this. Starkad is behind it, that's for damn sure. They have two squadrons of assault shuttles supporting them and it's a lost cause. We have to go get Terrin at the research facility in the Bloodmarks and get him and that data secured."

"Roger that, sir," he said. "We'll divert and meet you there."

"Be careful, son, but hurry your ass up. They have dropships and assault shuttles on the way and I don't want to have to fight them all by myself."

"We'll take care of it, Dad." He grinned, despite everything. "We're Wholesale Slaughter. That's what we do."

4

Terrin opened the safe with trembling hands and pulled out the lead-lined case, the scuffs and scratches on its surface as familiar as the touch of Franny's fingers.

"You still have it?" Jaimie Brannigan asked from behind him, a hint of disbelief in his voice along with what Terrin thought might be a touch of outrage at the security risk. "I'd have thought you'd erased the data crystals after you read them into the systems here."

"I was going to," he said, not bothering to shut the door to the safe—there was nothing else in there to secure. "I should have," he admitted. "But we went through so much to get this out of Terminus and keep it away from Starkad, I couldn't bring myself to get rid of it."

"It's just as well," Jaimie Brannigan allowed, wiping sweat from his brow with the back of his sleeve. It was cool in the office, but his father had been sweating since he rushed off the ramp of the drop-ship. "Saves us the time of copying everything."

"Sir," Dr. Kovalev said, clearing his throat. He'd followed them into the office along with Franny and it was a close competition as to which of them looked the most worried. "I have the technicians working on purging the databases here, but..."

"This isn't the only facility with the data," Terrin finished for him, closing his eyes for a moment and letting out a sigh at the realization. "We had to farm some of the work out to a few universities."

"It's scattered," Kovalev explained, hands working as if he were molding the explanation out of the air. "No one of them has all of it, but it's all there and it's only a matter of time before someone pieces it together."

"Plus, there's the Imperial weapons we shipped out from Terminus before Starkad got it," Franny pointed out. "They're at a couple of different weapons manufacturers' research and development labs off-planet."

"Nothing to be done about it now," Jaimie declared, though Terrin could see the concern in the man's face.

Well, there's a lot to be concerned about.

"Come on," he motioned to Terrin, "we need to get you and the data on the drop-ship and out of here before the enemy arrives."

"Who's behind this, Dad?" Terrin asked, knowing he was wasting time, but needing to know.

"Starkad at third and last," Jaimie told him, a door-slamming certainty in his tone. "As for who they set up to be their figure-head here..." He shook his head. "Unfortunately, it could be one of a dozen. My grandfather's old advisors told me I should have anyone even suspected of being involved with his assassination put to death twenty years ago, but I didn't do it because I knew Maggie wouldn't have approved."

Terrin tried to picture his mother, Maggie Conner, but the only image that came was of her with a rifle in her hands, heading off to face the traitors coming to try to kill her children.

"No, she wouldn't have," he agreed, voice breaking on the last word.

A muscle in Jaimie's cheek quivered, as close to his father would ever come to crying. He grabbed Terrin by the shoulder and pulled him into a hug, surprising him.

"Your mother would have been so proud of you, Terrin. *I'm* proud of you. You've accomplished more than anyone had a right to hope."

Terrin returned the hug, his throat clenching at the rare compliment from his father...and then he stiffened and pulled away, realizing what it could mean.

"We're getting out of this, Dad," he insisted.

"You will," Jaimie told him. "You and Francesca get on that drop-ship and head up to the *Shakak*." He turned to Kovalev. "Once you wipe the databases, get your people on the jet out there and take them as far as your fuel holds out, far away from the population centers. No military bases, no universities."

"Yes, sir," the professor said, nodding firmly. "I'll see to it."

"What about you?" Terrin asked his father.

"I'm going out to my mech and give you the chance to get away from here," Jaimie said. "It's a Guardian's duty to defend his people..."

"Lord Guardian!" The voice was small and tinny, coming over the external speaker of Jaimie Brannigan's 'link. His father hated using an earbud; he'd always said it made him seem like some madman talking to himself. But distant thought it was, Terrin recognized the voice as belonging to Donnell Anders. "Enemy forces incoming!"

Terrin swayed and nearly lost his balance as the explosion rocked the entire building, a rolling crack of thunder punctuated by the crash of furniture and equipment and screams from the main section of the lab outside the office.

"What the hell..." Terrin coughed the words out as he

caught himself against the desk, saw his father helping Franny to her feet. The opaque, smoke-dark polymer of the office walls were cracked and splintered, and the door had swung open, admitting a haze of pale smoke.

"The drop-ship, sir!" Anders said over the 'link. "They got the drop-ship! Mecha inbound!"

Jaimie Brannigan seemed preternaturally calm as he pulled the 'link off his belt and held it beside his mouth.

"Hold them, Donnell. I'm coming out." He eyed each of them, his gaze lingering on his son. "Logan's on his way. I'll do the best I can to buy you time till he gets here." He shoved the door open, checking outside in the corridor before he hesitated and threw a final command over his shoulder. "If there're any guns to be had, I suggest you arm yourselves. Don't let those data crystals be taken."

"I love you, Dad," Terrin tried to say, but his father was already gone.

Logan Conner charged down the ramp of the drop-ship and straight into hell.

He'd visited the research facility before, when Terrin had first arrived; and he'd been struck by the beauty of the place, the isolation of the little transverse valley sliced out of the mountains by the narrow stream running down from the glaciers. Now, the narrow valley seemed more like a smelting furnace, barely able to contain the flaring, sparking, molten madness within its borders.

The sight through his Sentinel's canopy was a kinetic light show impossible to separate into its coherent parts, so he ignored it and let the picture from the threat display filter through to his thoughts. Distinct packets of data moved in blue or red triangles, neatly separated into friend and foe, mecha, infantry, and aircraft.

That picture was clearer, but no less intimidating. Jaimie Brannigan and Donnell Anders had cobbled together a company from Mithra alone knew where, probably mech-jocks who'd happened to be in the palace during the attack. It was strike-mecha heavy with the Sentinels both his father and General Anders piloted, three bulbous, ugly Nomads and a pair of Scorpions at the heart, lighter assault mecha and a couple of Arbalests crowding close on the edges. They'd arrayed themselves in an offset line running from the furiously burning wreckage of what he assumed had been their drop-ship nearly all the way over to a three-meter drop off down into the creek bed. Not quite all the way though, there was a hundred-meter gap between the last of them, a broad-shouldered Valiant, and the terrain limiter.

Facing them from nearly two kilometers away down the length of the valley, partially obscured by scattered clumps of pines and aspens, was nearly a full battalion, still pouring out of half a dozen drop-ships, one or two still settling down on heavy landing gear. Fifty mecha, not yet deployed into formation but already spraying missiles and lasers across the distance between the two forces.

Poor fire discipline. Probably hard for traitors to train together and establish leadership authority.

"Fourth Platoon, fill the gap," he ordered, trusting Captain Gerald Paskowski to understand his intent. Paskowski's strike mecha would be ideal to seal up the hole in the line, heavily armed and armored and able to soak up a lot of damage without going down.

"Roger that, sir." Paskowski's tone was all business, as if this was just another operation and not the end of the world.

"Arbalest Platoon, standard launch diamond two hundred

meters behind the line and concentrate on the enemy's front ranks."

Captain Mandy Ford was still leading her fire support mecha off the second drop-ship, five blue icons he automatically translated into the hunched-over, top-heavy missile carriers, useless in a short-range fight against enemy armor but good as a stand-off weapon. She didn't respond, which was a breach of protocol but then, they were all pretty rattled, even if some were trying not to show it. He could see her moving into the formation he'd ordered, which was all he cared about.

"Val, you, Hernandez and Prevatt take your platoons around the left flank of the formation and stack up, get ready to jet over for a flanking attack on my command."

He'd been plodding along in his own mech as he spoke, walking just fast enough to avoid standing in one spot for too long, heading for the center of the line where twin Sentinels waited.

"Glad you could make it, son," Jaimie Brannigan's face appeared in the communications display, more haggard and drawn than Logan remembered, looking unnatural and wrong somehow squeezed into a helmet. "Terrin's inside, you need to..."

"Lyta's taking a platoon in there now, sir," he said. "Katy and her wingman are trying to keep the other side's assault shuttles out of the fight, but that means we won't have any air support. What we *do* have..." Logan grinned fiercely as wave after wave of missiles began streaking out from behind them, arcing over their lines. "...is artillery."

The Arbalests wouldn't have the luxury of a reload train out here, but they carried enough of a load to keep the barrage up for nearly a solid minute. A rolling chain of explosions tore divots in the valley floor, gouts of flame and dirt and, here and there, plasma from a ruptured fusion reactor rising into the air, chased upward by mushroom clouds. By the time their tubes shot dry, the entire far end of the valley was aflame, fire licking at centuries-old trees and spreading across the tall grass despite a few pockets of stubborn snow still cowering in the shadows, unwilling to melt away. White smoke billowed off the burning trees and grass and joined the darker haze from flaming metal, where enemy machines had fallen. Men died inside them, the unlucky who hadn't perished in the explosions that had crippled their mecha now consumed by the flames.

It was a bad way to go. Logan hoped when his time came, the end would be quick.

He couldn't see a damn thing through the smoke, not on optical, infrared or thermal, and Katy was far too busy above them to bother her for a report. He hoped against knowledge and experience that the missiles had taken the fight out of them, that they would head back to their drop-ships and be satisfied with the capital and the palace. He knew it was a fantasy before he saw the first of the black silhouettes striding through the white smoke, their march purposeful and vindictive, seeking vengeance for their fallen comrades. They might not be better trained or better led, but General Constantine liked to say that quantity had a quality all its own. And there were still a lot of them.

"For all my sins, I do penance, I repent." The words were murmured, barely audible, and it took Logan a moment to realize it was his father saying them. They were from the Baj, the Zoroastrian prayer of thanks and purification. It was said at meals and before trials.

"For all my bad thoughts, words, and deeds, that I have thought, said, and done in the world," he took up the next line, remembering nights together at the dinner table with his mother.

General Anders took up the chant, his voice strong and

faithful and perhaps fatalistic. "Or which occurred because of me or originated with me."

Valentine Kurtz spoke up next, surprising him. He knew the man was a follower of Mithra, but he'd never seemed very devout and didn't ever talk about it. "Of those sins of thoughts, words, and deeds, sins of the body, sins of the soul, material sins, spiritual sins."

They all spoke the next line together, along with many other voices, both his people and the pilots his father and General Anders had picked up. "I reject, I repent, I regret; with three words I repent."

"Fire at will!" he barked as the first rank of enemy mecha cleared the smoke, not even considering it was his father's command to give until the words had already taken flight. "Give 'em hell!"

5

Logan Conner emptied the tubes of his shoulder-mounted missile pod in a long volley, one load after another, risking burning out its launch tubes because he wouldn't have time to get it rearmed anyway. The enemy was firing off its own return volley, somewhere north of forty mecha launching their pod loads in billows of swirling smoke. He barely registered his Sentinel's automated anti-missile systems tracking incoming threats and neutralizing them with blasts of ECM jamming or shooting them out of their arcing trails with bursts of machine-gun fire.

A few mecha went down on each side from the exchange of missiles and Logan winced as blue icons from his unit's IFF transponder list began blinking yellow or solid red, but the time for long-distance attacks had passed. The enemy armor had closed to 300 meters and waiting for them to batter through their lines would be a losing strategy.

"At them!" he yelled. "Val, hit the jets! Take them from our left!"

Valentine Kurtz was his Executive Officer and he'd learned to trust the man in a fight over the last year, but Logan wished it were him soaring out over the battlefield fifty meters up, landing in the midst of the enemy. Instead, he and the rest of the center, fifteen massive, ponderous strike mecha, lumbered forward, slowly at first but picking up speed with each thundering step.

Lasers and plasma guns and ETC cannons fired on the run, ripping apart the very air between the two forces, melting metal until it flowed like blood, spearing through centimeters of armor. Logan couldn't imagine being an infantry trooper on the ground during a battle such as this. There was a reason mech-jocks called foot soldiers "crunchies," and it wasn't just interser-vice rivalry.

He was close enough now to see his targets with the naked eye instead of magnified targeting optics and thermal signatures, close enough to make out the bulbous, thick-legged Scorpion strike mech hammering its oval footpads into the soft, loamy ground with each step, firing twin blasts of plasma from its arm-mounted guns every few seconds. Logan toggled the trigger on his joystick to his own plasma gun and triggered a blast of his own, the coherent packet of ionized gas the temperature of the heart of a star flashing across the 300 meters between them in the blink of an eye.

There were times in a battle when you knew before you fired a round that it was right, it was true, it was going to hit. He knew it this time and wasn't surprised when the plasmoid took the Scorpion at the left hip and burned through the thinner armor over the joint in an echoing crack of violently sublimated metal. The joint gave way under the stress of the massive machine's unrelenting gallop and it collapsed, plowing into the dirt with its right shoulder, throwing up a spray of sod and grass and brush.

He had no chance to celebrate his victory. A tungsten ETC slug passed just under his Sentinel's left arm, smashing through the 20mm Vulcan mounted at that side and carrying it away in a shower of sparks. The Sentinel stumbled, but he kept it on its feet with the help of a personal sense of balance transmitted to the movements of the mech through the neural halo in his helmet. Red flashed in his damage display where the rotary cannon had been and yellow blinked from a handful of other hits he didn't remember taking. He couldn't let himself think of the enemy fire lashing out at him and the others, couldn't give in to the gut-punch feeling when he saw one of the people he'd come to view as his friends take damage to their machine and didn't know if they'd survived it. There wasn't even anything to command in this naked carnage; his troops were beyond maneuvers and tactics. This was an ancient battle in its way, the fire support gone, the air cover tangled up and useless. It was warrior against warrior, the mecha a latter-day equivalent of armored knights, each seeking out a foe to run down under the lance.

He'd settled on his next opponent, a slump-shouldered Nomad, when he saw his three assault platoons come down behind the main body of the enemy charge, falling upon them like leopards pouncing, slicing through their ranks with brutal efficiency. The traitors hadn't been well-formed even at the beginning, their attack rapid and almost desperate, an attempt to deal with a force they hadn't expected, and now any organization they'd had originally began to fall apart.

"Stay on them!" Jaimie Brannigan urged over the general communications net, his voice a rallying cry they all recognized from history class, echoing over the troops moving through the streets of Argos. "Don't give them time to breathe!"

Logan touched off a blast at the Nomad, accidentally hit an Agamemnon rushing in front of it in the melee. The left shoulder of the unlucky enemy mech glowed white with molten metal but it kept running, its left arm slumping against its torso with most of the servomotors and tensor fibers vaporized, only a few centimeters of BiPhase Carbide holding it in place. The Agamemnon didn't make it another twenty meters before it took another shot from one of Logan's assault mecha and stumbled to a permanent halt, its cockpit a smoking ruin.

He sensed the tipping point, a shifting of the balance of the battle. It was as if the field were tilted downward ahead of them and the enemy was tumbling backwards with the inertia, scrambling to get back to their drop-ships and perceived safety.

If they'd stayed together, they could have won.

Instead, the retreating mecha took shot after shot and couldn't return fire, couldn't cover each other's withdrawal. All he needed now was...

"Katy," he said, switching to her comm channel, "can you free up for a pass on the drop-ships?"

"I just dusted this asshole," she told him, voice as calm and satisfied as if she were relaxing with him on a sailboat down in the islands south of Golden Beach. "Give me ten seconds."

He felt a feral smile crossing his face, partly because this battle was nearly won but also because Kathren Margolis was a lioness in battle and he loved her. He aimed another burst of plasma at the same Nomad and hit it this time, burning halfway through the heat shield over its fusion reactor before it rammed straight into the trunk of a burning aspen tree and shattered it into splinters, spinning away from the collision off-balance.

A laser snapped out in a lightning strike of ionized air and took the massive machine in the right knee, not quite burning through but locking the joint up in mid-stride while it tried to regain its balance and sending it crashing into the heart of an oak two and a half meters across. The tree toppled over with a crack of splitting wood nearly as loud as the sonic boom of the laser and the Nomad went down with it and didn't move.

Logan was nearly through the trees, could just make out the landing zone where the drop-ships clustered together as if huddled for safety, wagons circled in some ancient legend against the predations of savages. Then Mithra reached down from the sky and showed them the divine punishment for traitors.

Or maybe Jesus did it, since it's Katy. No, Jesus was about love and forgiveness, so she said. This was more like the Old Testament God she talked about, the One who kept wiping out foreign nations so the Israelites could take over. Logan liked that version better.

The burst of laser-fire from her shuttle surely seemed like the wrath of an old God, splitting the sky with an eye-searing flash of actinic plasma that was only the after-effects of the weapon, not the destructive concentration of coherent light that did the actual damage. The nose of the closest drop-ship blew apart with a concussion of liberated energy, the metal frame and BiPhase Carbide armor turning to vapor in a single microsecond of the focused heat of a fusion reactor. The front landing gear collapsed and the huge lifting body lurched forward, prostrating itself to whatever ill-tempered God, Christian or Zoroastrian or otherwise, had struck it down.

Katy's assault shuttle screamed across the startling blue of the morning sky, a delta-winged angel of death in matte grey, and the 20mm Vulcan built into the portside wing belched out a stream of fire, almost anticlimactic after the terror of the laser but effective nonetheless. Tungsten slugs stitched a pattern of destruction into the side of another enemy lander, the penetrators blasting out the other side of the fuselage with sparks of burning metal.

The drop-ship pilots panicked, again showing the lack of discipline symptomatic of a force with experience but no unit cohesion. Two of the four undamaged landers tried to take off, their belly jets scorching the already-charred earth beneath them before their loading ramps had even begun closing.

Surviving enemy mecha rushed at them, those with jump-jets trying to fly into the closing doors ten meters off the ground. The first couple made it, but a third, a Valiant assault mech, slammed into the fuselage instead and bounced off, tumbling out of the air and smashing back to the ground with percussive finality. The drop-ship lurched from the impact, belly jets burning fiercely to right itself...until Katy sliced through the center of the bird with her shuttle's laser.

The massive lifting body split along the cut of the beam, the front section immediately losing thrust from the jets and crashing back into the clearing, smashing into one of the already damaged landers, crushing it beneath its weight and collapsing all seven sets of landing gear beneath the combined mass. The rear half of the bird pitched into a wild yaw, the belly jets out of control, tossing it in a descending spiral into the hillside several kilometers away. Plasma flared in a half-dome of star-bright fire and dirt and rock cascaded down in a landslide, the dust clouds billowing away from the convection heat of the ruptured fusion reactor.

It was victory. Logan knew the taste, knew the smell, felt it coursing through his veins like a drug.

We can still put down this damned coup attempt. We just need to hit them now, when they think they've won, hold them off until we can get the fleets back here...

"Shit! Incoming!" That wasn't Katy, it was her wingman, Lt. Duane, someone without the concerted cool that came naturally to her.

Still, there were moments when panic was the appropriate response.

"Break, Duane," Katy told the other assault shuttle pilot and Logan saw her go from a hover a hundred meters up to a reckless, ascending roll just ahead of a flight of three missiles seeming to come out of nowhere.

They curved to follow and she burned away at top acceleration, her sonic boom rolling over the plain. Logan felt a flash of worry for her, followed quickly by the internal question of where the missiles had come from.

All that was forgotten in an instant when he saw the wave of missiles following them, not air-to-air like the ones that had chased her out of her support position but heavy, slow, air-to-ground, launched by at least a dozen VTOL gunships buzzing through the air like lethal insects, lightly-armored and used only by the Home Guard. They were impossible to transport on spaceships, incredibly vulnerable to even shoulder-fired missiles, and mecha could swat them out of the air with the machine guns they carried to handle dismounts. But there were so many, and they were way too close, probably coming in low along the mountain passes to avoid radar.

"Scatter!" Logan commanded, knowing it was too late, that there was no way.

He tried anyway, spinning the Sentinel with grace learned through dozens of hours in the simulators and hundreds more in actual training, slamming the footpads into the dirt with enough force to make his teeth clack together, stomping into a run. He'd made it only ten or twenty meters before the first of the missiles hit.

The world shook beneath him, and he felt for one of the few times in his career like he was walking on stilts, barely under control, about to crash to the ground. Fire rose angry and vengeful, ready to consume, and consume it did, sweeping across the valley in the opposite direction of the missiles from the Arbalests in one of the little perverted ironies that could turn men to atheists. IFF transponders winked out, one after another, blinking red and then fading immediately to black, their signals lost forever and maybe the lives inside them as well.

Logan kept running because there was nothing else to do, no

defense against the death stalking them from above. His mech's anti-missile systems could take out one or two, but there were ninety, a hundred, launched one after another as fast as the gunships could cycle their pods. If they had more shuttles, more mecha, more of *anything*...

He saw their drop-ships in the lee of the research facility, their ramps yawning open, waiting for them to take shelter, to break and run. If they could get Terrin and the data on the landers, cram everyone left aboard and take off, maybe they could make it back to the ship.

The thought was still echoing inside his head when the missiles hit.

Logan had been around plenty of explosions both in training and in actual combat—it was a hazard of the profession and he'd reached the point where he'd lost his ability to flinch at them. Not this one. When the drop-ships blew, the concussion was fierce enough to knock his fifty-ton mech backwards, sending it sprawling onto its left side and jerking him against his restraints. A screech of static filled his headphones and his displays blanked out for several seconds before flickering back to life, mirroring the deadening haze over his thoughts and the flare of afterimages across his vision.

The numbness was a blessing, a defense against the reality he'd have to deal with when his vision and his thoughts and his readouts all returned. He wasn't sure how long it lasted, how long he let himself lay on the ground, stunned and helpless and drowning in sweat from the overpowering heat, but it was the incessant red and yellow flashing of the IFF transponders that finally kicked his brain into gear. The butcher's bill showed in lines of solid black, the only memorial the dead here would ever get.

But you're not dead, so haul your stupid, worthless ass back up, damn it!

For an instant, he thought the words were General Anders or Lyta Randell or any of a dozen instructors he'd had in armored combat tactics over his years in the Academy, yelling in his ear to continue the mission and not get bogged down in the casualties and the details. And they might have been, but now their lessons had crystallized into the little voice inside his head, the one he had to listen to when all the others faded.

The drop-ships were gone, replaced by a mass of flame where they'd been, a firestorm so violent and turbulent his mech's alarms were warning him of overheating simply from being this close. He forced himself to move, to roll the Sentinel onto its feet despite the plaintive beeps of the damage indicators and the moaning, grinding protests of actuators and servos strained nearly to their limit. If the Sentinel were a building, he thought, it would have been condemned.

He stood amidst the inferno and forced himself to check the IFF display. He'd tried to prepare himself for what he'd see, yet he still grunted as if he'd been slapped. The whole Arbalest platoon was gone, their mecha unpowered and disabled at the least, and at the worst...

"Logan!" It was his father, not in his head this time but in his earphones, and his voice was a relief, a small shifting of the load on his shoulders.

"I'm here," he croaked, his voice a dry rasp. He tried to take a sip from the nipple of the water hose hanging beside his head on the easy chair, but the water was hot and he spat it out.

"I'm here, Dad," he tried again, staggering through the fire, unable to see on either optical, thermal, or infrared through the heat and smoke. His sonic sensors and radar were offline and blinking red on the damage display. He switched to an open channel. "Wholesale Slaughter units, do you read? Is anyone there?"

He emerged from the smoke clouds, or perhaps the wind

shifted and took it the other direction. Things looked even worse without the camouflage of billowing darkness, scorched and cratered, with the remains of mecha scattered like body parts.

"Second Platoon here," Kurtz reported, coughing into his mic in a burst of static. "All of us, thank Mithra." And they were, miraculously. He saw their transponders blinking yellow or sometimes intermittent red with damage, but they were moving, all five of them.

"Third Platoon," Aliyah Hernandez sounded off, as clear and calm as ever. "I've lost Rennie and Pascal. KIA. Robbins' mech is toast but she managed to eject."

"Uh, this is Warrant Officer Southard, First Platoon." The voice was unfamiliar. Southard had been recruited recently and Logan hadn't had a chance to get to know him, except he was a senior Warrant and had been in the Armored Corps for nearly twenty years. "Lt. Prevatt is...she's gone. So are Coughlin and Scardino. Troyan's Golem can't walk and I told her to evac it."

"Fourth?" Logan asked when he hadn't heard anything from Paskowski or the others. "Where's Fourth?" The IFF transponders were dark. He could have sworn he'd seen a couple of red flashing indicators just seconds ago. "Did anyone see Fourth eject? What about Ford and the Arbalests?"

Desperation was slipping into his voice, a bad look for a leader and he fought to push his feelings back down and make his brain work logically.

"Logan," his father called again, his voice quiet and calm, accepting. "We have enemy forces incoming."

The Sentinel's radar was out, but he didn't need it. The drop-ships were huge and looming and coming down at the other end of the valley, not far from where the others had landed only minutes before. *Great God, has it only been minutes?*

"Katy?" he broadcast. He couldn't see her shuttle, couldn't pick her up without radar and lidar. There was no response, but she might not even hear him past the jamming and ECM.

He sucked in a breath and let it out slowly, calming himself. There were no drop-ships, there was no support to be had. There was nowhere to run.

"Wholesale Slaughter," he said with the reverence of his earlier prayer, "form up and prepare to attack."

"Terrin, damn it, what's taking you so long?" Lyta Randell snapped with uncharacteristic impatience, leaning back in through the ruined front door of the building. "Get out here and get your ass in the lander!"

She didn't like losing her temper, not because of the feelings it would hurt or the harm it would do to others' opinions of her, but because it was a loss of control. Lyta Randell couldn't afford to lose control, because people would die, and not the *right* people. But she felt like a reactive target in a box full of them and more than losing her temper, she did *not* like sitting in the middle of a battlefield full of giant machines capable of killing every one of her people without much effort.

The ground shook with their steps, with the reverberation of the missile warheads exploding downrange. Even this far away, the air itself seemed to crackle with the static electricity of discharging lasers and plasma guns, making the hair on the back of her neck stand on end. They were titans of old come to battle amidst the children of men. Many times, she'd fought in cities where the mecha stalked and not thought twice about it, but here there was no next street to escape to, no way to slip out. The burning hulk of Jaimie Brannigan's drop-ship seemed a testament to the fact that this valley was a death trap and there was only one way out.

"We're coming!" Terrin called from the other end of the central laboratory, jogging far too slowly as he pushed a haggard and frightened-looking older man ahead of him. "We had to find the pilot for the VTOL outside," he explained apologetically. "None of the scientists or techs know how to fly it." He paused in his pace to yell back at the others, who were huddled together in the back of the lab, away from the cracked front walls and blown-out doors. "Everyone!" he yelled, a commanding tone to his voice Lyta hadn't noticed before. "Get to the transport! You need to get out of here now!"

They hesitated, everyone waiting for someone else to be the first to move, but finally a Navy technician in a dress utility uniform ran toward the front door in a crouch. Lyta moved aside to let him through. The squad she'd brought down from the *Shakak* would guide him into the jet, which was the only reason she'd pulled them off the drop-ship in the first place.

"Go on, Mr. Gregson," Terrin urged the pilot. *Civilian pilot,* Lyta corrected herself, noting his casual clothes and longish salt-and-pepper hair. *Corporate hire maybe.* "Get the jet warmed up and get out of here."

The prospect of leaving seemed to embolden the old man and he was nearly sprinting by the time he hit the doorway, beating the rest of the rush from the lab crew. Except for one. Dr. Kovalev, Terrin's old hyperdimensional and astrophysics professor and doctoral advisor, was still hunched over a computer terminal with Francesca Hayden next to him, working furiously on two separate input screens.

"Doc, Franny, let's go," Terrin said, waving at the door.

Kovalev didn't look up but made a shooing gesture at Franny.

"You go. I'll finish."

"We're still running a deep scrub on all the databases," Franny explained to Lyta when the Ranger commander shot her a questioning look. "We erased the data, but the patterns are still there, just unprotected. We have to go through and over-write the matrix or the..." She hesitated, fumbling for the right words. "...whoever is out there, whoever's behind this will be able to reconstruct it with the right software. I need to stay and help him."

"No way," Terrin declared without hesitation. "If you stay, I stay."

Lyta tried to keep from grinding her teeth. The dentists at Laconia kept threatening to make her wear a mouthpiece at night, as if that were the only time she did it.

"Petty Officer Hayden," she said slowly and patiently to Franny, "get out into the drop-ship right now, that's an order. You too, Terrin...you're working for Military Intelligence, so I can order you around too. Get those data crystals out of here."

Terrin clutched at the heavy box as she said it, as if he were just now remembering he held it. Franny glanced between him and the computer terminal and finally back at Lyta before she sighed in surrender and squeezed Dr. Kovalev's arm before leaving him to run and join Terrin. The turbines of the VTOL transport screamed up to speed a hundred meters away out on the landing pad and Lyta leaned out into the morning sun and squinted at the aircraft just in time to see it lifting off on wavering columns of heat mirage, banking left away from the fighting before it began to rise. She turned back to the lab, still in the doorway.

"Dr. Kovalev," Lyta told the man, "as soon as you're through scrubbing the database, get out to the drop-ship. It'll take our mecha at least a few more minutes to break contact with the enemy and..."

Lyta never really recalled what happened in the next

instant. She'd been standing in the door and suddenly she was on her side, the breath sucked out of her lungs by searing heat. The ground shook, the walls shuddered, and bits of the ceiling collapsed around her, chunks of plaster crashing down in a rain of dust, but all she heard was a shrill whistle. Her thoughts moved in slow motion through a sea of mud and the part of her brain still able to form a thought screamed at her to get up, get moving. Her hands clasped for her carbine; she knew it was still strapped into her tactical vest by its retractable sling, but she couldn't seem to find it.

Through sheer force of will, she forced herself up to her knees, hands flat on the floor for just a few seconds until she regained enough balance to stand. Dust and smoke flooded in through the doorway and into her eyes—somehow, her protective goggles had been knocked off in the blast. She rubbed it away, blinking fiercely until she could see again. Franny and Terrin were down as well, but sitting up and moving. Kovalev had managed to stay on his feet, holding for dear life to the console still, as if he were on the deck of a boat at sea, expecting another wave to crash over the side.

Terrin was trying to tell her something, but she still couldn't hear a thing. She turned away from him, limping toward the door, finally finding the grip of her carbine and pulling the stock into her shoulder. She needed to check on her people.

Outside was a moonscape. The front face of the main building was charred black, matching the bare dirt and pavement, still hissing with the remnants of heat just now radiating away. She saw the bodies of her Ranger squad, sprawled out, smoke pouring off them and she tried to take a step out to check on them but was driven back by the incredible heat.

"Goddammit!" she moaned, the word sounding far away in her battered ears.

The drop-ships. The thought climbed slowly and carefully

through the jagged, broken glass of her thoughts. The drop-ships were burning, twisted, melted, mountains of flame crackling into the sky fifty meters high and a hundred broad, their only escape from this place destroyed in the space of a few seconds.

Something drew her eye, a flash of reflected sunlight off in the distance, a shuttle roaring across the sky.

No, not our only *escape.*

She touched the transmit button on her 'link and prayed that the signal wasn't being jammed, that there was still a chance of getting through.

"Katy!" she yelled, as if she were trying to overcome the blast deafness in her own ears as well as the distance between them. "Get down here now! We need an evac!"

No answer. She slumped against the door frame, then cursed and withdrew as the metal seared her shoulder through her armor and utility fatigues.

Hell with it, then. She checked the magazine of her carbine to make sure it was still seated after the battering it had taken, then pulled the stock into her shoulder and waited.

Good a way to go as any.

6

Commander Kathren Margolis was pissed off.

She was pissed off that her nation and its leader were under attack by traitors, pissed off that someone was trying to kill her, her lover, her friends, her fellow soldiers, and spacers, and Rangers, pissed off beyond belief that the ones doing it were her own people. But most of all, she was pissed at Francis Acosta for puking in her cockpit *again*.

"Goddammit, Francis," she snarled against the gee-forces pressing her back into her acceleration couch. "If you're going to insist on play-acting as my copilot, you have *got* to stop doing that!"

"I'd be happy to," Acosta gritted out past clenched teeth, not even trying to wipe up the mess he'd left on his control panel, "just as soon as you and 'Colonel Slaughter' cook up a new cover for me."

"Shit," she drawled the word out, spinning the shuttle into a barrel roll to the right to avoid the laser targeting her from the bird on her tail. "You keep reminding me you're a major in military intelligence, you could pick whatever cover you want. I think you just like being where the action is."

If Acosta had an answer for her, he clamped it down along with his jaws in a desperate attempt to hold whatever was left in his stomach inside. She had more important things to worry about. The gunships hadn't even tried to take her or Duane on, rightly figuring the assault shuttles would tear through them like they weren't there, but this new force of drop-ships had come with its own escort, four assault shuttles of their own. And they were being complete pains in her ass.

"We got missiles," Acosta warned, finding his voice from somewhere, pointing at the flashing icons on the threat display. Four of them had separated themselves from an enemy bird and were flashing across the screen with depressing speed.

"I see 'em," she said curtly. "Launching countermeasures. Hold on for evasive."

"Oh, Mithra's bloody horns," Acosta moaned.

She stood the attack craft on its tail and burned upward, the turbines shrieking in protest, heat and stress warnings flashing yellow on her screens. She ignored them, ignored the proximity alerts and the tactical display trying to remind her she couldn't outrun missiles. She didn't have to. She just had to get high enough for this to work. And not pass out.

She tightened her core muscles and tried to stop her blood from retreating to her extremities and send it back where it belonged, to her brain. The flight suit helped, but only so much, and a human body could only take eight gees plus for so long before it lost consciousness. A black tunnel was closing in on her vision, the banshee scream of the jets seeming to grow distant and the missiles were still catching up, but she kept what attention she had left on the altimeter.

The shuttle was on the edge of space when she cut the atmospheric jets and hit the plasma drive. Her bird nearly shook itself apart despite the thin atmosphere, would have been destroyed completely by the thermal blooming if she'd tried it at a lower altitude. The flare of plasma from the extra-atmospheric drive propagated through what air there was and slammed into the enemy missile like a wall of star-bright heat.

Propellant ignited and blew the warheads only a few hundred meters behind them and a wave of pressure pushed her over the edge into the darkness of that black tunnel. She blinked at the warbling call of the alarms and realized she'd passed out. If she'd left the fusion drives burning, she would have been heading for orbit, but she'd only risked a two-second burn and she grabbed at the control yoke, desperately trying to pull the shuttle out of the beginnings of a flat spin back into the soup.

Acosta was limp in his restraints, head lolling and a line of drool hanging out of his mouth.

"Acosta!" she snapped. "Wake up, damn it!"

He mumbled incoherently, eyes blinking and face turning green as the rotation hit him, growing faster with each second.

"What the hell?" he mumbled, covering his mouth with a hand, she supposed to arrest the incipient nausea.

"We may be about to die," Katy explained, switching back to the turbines, "and I didn't want you to sleep through it."

She fed power to the jets, bleeding just a fraction of it off to the landing thrusters, gradually pulling the bird out of the spin. She didn't tell Acosta, but her heart felt as if it was about to beat its way out of her chest, and the adrenalin didn't stop pumping just because the shuttle stopped spinning. She felt sweat collecting against her skin, cold and clammy in the vicelike grip of the flight suit and if it didn't affect her grip on the steering yoke, it was more from the absorbent coating than her lack of nerves.

Did I used to be this jittery? She couldn't remember. She remembered the doing, but not the feeling. The emotions were muted by the wave of sensory input and the need to filter it into something useful. Maybe it had always been like this and she forgot every time, the way her mother had told her women forgot how painful giving birth was between one child and the next.

Like now. No more time for thinking or feeling, just reacting. She was coming straight down over two of the enemy assault shuttles, their crews occupied with an attempt to bottle in Lt. Duane. The kid was in trouble—*kid, right. He's a year younger than me*—and he wasn't going to be able to avoid the cross-hatch of laser bursts much longer.

"Target me the one to the north, Francis," she ordered.

He didn't respond, perhaps not trusting himself to open his mouth just yet without another incident, but she saw the reticle on the weapons display floating over the enemy shuttle to the left of the screen. It locked onto the bird with a steady green and a pleasing, bloodthirsty tone.

"Eat this, damned traitor," she murmured, flipping the arming switch for two of her bird's anti-spacecraft missiles and squeezing the launch trigger.

Something jolted the assault shuttle, the sort of feeling she remembered when she'd been driving the rover back home on the backroads and she'd passed over a tree root. The missiles had cut loose from the launch bays on puffs of inert gas, dropping just far enough for the solid-fuel rockets to ignite away from the fuselage. Twin vapor cones were just visible in the targeting screen as the missiles went transonic, spearing downward into the enemy shuttle.

It didn't even try to evade, didn't have the time. One second it was curving slowly around Duane's bird, setting up for a shot, and the next it was an expanding ball of fiery plasma, a star rising in miniature before what remained surrendered to gravity. The remaining two in the formation broke off, tearing away at maximum acceleration, while the last, stuck in patrol above the battlefield, turned and bore down on her.

Young. Clumsy. No combat experience.

And quickly dead. She had the shot long before he did and the burst of laser fire from the shuttle's chin cannon tore off his portside delta wing with a flare of sublimating metal and ionized air. A better pilot could have survived it. Shuttles had power to spare, and with enough power, you could fly a brick. But he didn't have the training and he didn't have the nerves. He tried to hit the belly jets full bore and the strain was too much for the already wounded airframe. The fuselage split down the middle just behind the cockpit. The section with the jets shot upward, suddenly lighter by tons, while the cockpit and crew compartment fluttered into the mountains. She didn't bother to track it, didn't want to see the puff of dust where it hit.

Instead, her eyes were focused on the valley floor, on the hellfire blooming on thermal where Wholesale Slaughter's drop-ships had been. Katy didn't get motion sickness, hadn't thrown up once in her whole life, yet now her stomach dropped and nausea clawed at her.

"Duane," she called, hoping the jamming would be lifted now that two of the birds were gone and the other two scattered. "Hold those other two assholes off. I need to land."

"Land?" Acosta asked, his voice pitched high. Then he looked where she was staring, and the breath went out of him like he'd been punched.

"Jesus," she hissed, not a curse but a prayer. "Let him still be alive..."

"Mithra save us..."

Logan didn't know who had said it. The IFF transponder display was fried, along with his radar, lidar, and everything else that had made the Sentinel a command platform. He appreciated the sentiment, but he wasn't sure God was listening.

Perhaps it was a blessing that the IFF was down, because he didn't want to see how few of his mecha were still fighting. He couldn't make much out through the smoke, the visibility down to maybe fifty meters on a side, barely enough to see the group of three others standing beside him.

His father was there, his Sentinel resplendent with the crest of the Guardian across its chest, amazingly almost unmarked after the seemingly endless battle. Next to him, unwilling to leave the side of his commander, was General Anders. His mech was the same model but the armor over his chest and legs was cracked and flaking off, huge sections charred and smoking, as if he'd thrown himself between Jaimie Brannigan and all the incoming fire headed his way. And perhaps he had.

Logan's own Sentinel wasn't much better off, what wasn't solid red and inoperable flashing yellow in warning it soon would be. It was upright though, and the plasma gun still worked. Enough for a last stand, and if this wasn't a last stand, he'd never see one.

"Here comes the next wave," Anders said, his voice hoarse, dry.

Logan could see them, a dozen assault mecha charging through the billowing clouds of impenetrable smoke like demons straight out of Hell.

This has to be someone's *version of Hell.*

He fired, shuffled sideways, dragging an uncooperative left leg, and fired again once the capacitor banks recharged. One of the traitors went down, a Golem, hunchbacked and ugly and now a burning ruin, its pilot trapped inside. How many enemy mech pilots had he killed today?

Not enough.

Anders went down first, a laser slicing through his mech's

left arm, amputating it at the shoulder. The loss of tons of weight threw the general's Sentinel off balance, sent it stumbling to the right and directly into the line of fire of someone's ETC cannon. The cannon rounds pierced the reactor shielding on the strike mech's back and Logan thought he might have seen an ejection pod burst out of the Sentinel's chest and hurtle into the smoke before the mech's reactor blew in a starburst of plasma plumes.

Logan had been too distracted by the loss of Anders' machine. He didn't see the missile until it was too late, until it was so close all he could do was try to turn. It hit his Sentinel's already-balky left leg and everything was light and intense heat and a vibration violent enough to slam his head against the cushioned collar. He felt everything tilting, and thought for the briefest of moments that he had a concussion until he realized the mech was collapsing, its left leg blown off at the hip.

The fall took an anguished eternity and when it finally ended, he was thrown against his restraint straps with enough force to drive the wind out of him. The impact of the fifty-ton goliath smashing into the dirt reverberated through his gut, rattling his teeth, one dull pain merging with another and leaving him hanging, helpless, too stunned to even cut loose his harness.

Through the cracked and scarred transparent aluminum of his canopy, Logan could see the enemy mecha thundering across the ravaged valley floor, heading for him, ready to smash his cockpit underfoot and put an end to everything he'd ever imagined. His father's Sentinel interposed itself between Logan and impending death, as looming and legendary and larger-than-life as Jaimie Brannigan had always been to him. His weapons fired in quick succession, ETC cannon, then laser, then 20mm Vulcan, timed to keep any one of them from overheating.

Cannon rounds were streaking only meters from his cockpit, ionized flares through the smoke-filled air, passing on either side as if he were favored by God, protected by the hand of the Beneficent Spirits, the *Spenta Mainyu.*

"Son, get out of there," Jaimie told him, his voice staticky and garbled over Logan's damaged communications gear, barely audible over the roar of the Vulcan and the chatter of incoming fire. "You have to make it, you and Terrin. You have to..."

Whatever divine will had been protecting the Guardian of Sparta melted away. Tungsten slugs from Electro Thermal Chemical cannons, propelled to hypersonic velocities by their plasma ignition systems, converged on his father's Sentinel, at least three sizzling vapor trails terminating in the strike mech's cockpit.

Logan's mind was shaken, concussed, perceiving the world through a fog of unreality, and he tried to convince himself he was hallucinating. But the nightmare wouldn't end. Gouts of sun-bright plasma streamed from the ruptured fusion core of his father's mech, consuming what was left of the cockpit and blowing the left arm off from the torso. The severed limb crashed to the ground; Logan felt the vibration through the ground, through the metal and BiPhase Carbide of his cockpit, but he couldn't hear the sound over the roaring in his ears.

The Guardian of Sparta was gone.

And he was next. He could see the mech that was going to kill him, an Agamemnon, focused on him like a laser, its Home Guard camouflage pattern mocking him with the familiarity of an old friend. It would lumber past, crushing him as an afterthought, and that would be the end of the Brannigan line and the successful end of the coup...whoever was leading it.

Is it worse to die not knowing who's killing you?

The Agamemnon made it to within fifty meters of him

before the sky ripped open and Mithra destroyed it with the wrath of his holy fire.

That was the first thought through his concussion-addled brain when the lightning-bolt streak of ionization lanced into the enemy mech. The second, fighting its way up through clouds of haze, was that an assault shuttle had just fired a laser from somewhere above him. He couldn't see it, but he could see its handiwork. A line of divots in the earth tracked their way to the next mech running through the clouds of black smoke, the 20mm Vulcan cannon rounds hammering into the torso of the enemy Peregrine, cracking its armor and penetrating through to the cockpit. The ostrich-legged scout mech stumbled and went down in a heap, legs snapping off and tumbling away.

The exhaust of landing jets began clearing the smoke away, sending streams of it billowing out to the sides in roiling swirls as the assault shuttle descended. The laser fired again, spearing through a Nomad strike mech and passing on to sever the left arm of the assault mech directly behind it, and the charge lost steam. The remaining machines began to dig in and turn, heading back to their landing zone.

Logan squeezed his eyes shut for a second, forced his fingers into fists, trying to slug his brain into motion. He managed to find the quick-release for his harness and yank it, gasping as he spilled out of his seat and his shoulder hit the canopy. Pain ignited like a brushfire in his chest and he thought he might have cracked a rib during the crash, but the discomfort helped him to focus. He pulled the latch for the canopy and kicked it open, gasping at the pain in his chest and then choking from the breathtaking, oven-like heat outside.

His vision swam with the pain in his ribs and the concussion and the lung-searing heat and when he saw a shadow approaching from his right, he clawed blindly at his shoulder holster, trying to pull his pistol before a hand grasped his shoulder.

"It's me, Logan."

He blinked tears from his eyes and finally saw Terrin's soot-stained face above him. He felt an instant's relief, and then a renewed pain for the news he'd have to deliver.

"Dad," he said, barely able to utter the words. "He's dead."

"We know," Terrin told him, his long, lean face twisting with grief Logan could tell he was barely keeping in check. "We saw from back at the facility."

"We," he'd said. Logan abruptly realized Franny was with him, along with Dr. Kovalev.

"Where's Lyta?" he asked, letting Terrin help him to his feet.

"She and the Rangers who survived," another paroxysm of pain on his brother's face, "are trying to round up the pilots who ejected. We've already radioed the others to abandon their mecha and get into the assault shuttle."

"Come on, sir," Franny urged him. "We have to go *now*, before the enemy regroups."

She was carrying a case, and he realized it was the same one she and Terrin had used to store the data crystals from Terminus.

"We'll lose everything," Logan said, looking around them at wrecked machines and dead men. *We've already lost everything.*

"Not as long as the two of you are alive," Dr. Kovalev interjected, nodding toward him and Terrin. "As long as a Brannigan lives, the fight isn't over."

Logan saw Lyta Randell leading a handful of mech pilots toward the opening ramp of the assault shuttle, thought he saw Valentine Kurtz among them. He forced himself to breathe, no matter how much it hurt. He still had people counting on him.

"Let's go," he agreed, nodding to Terrin. "Let's get to the *Shakak* while we still can."

"You need to be in the sick bay," Katy told him.

She was a solid support under his right arm, and he needed it just to walk. Logan never thought he'd regret the artificial gravity Terrin had conjured up for them, but right now he could have done without it.

He shook his head and kept walking toward the bridge.

"The docs are busy enough right now," he told her. "They can take care of me later."

Lyta was already on the bridge, leaning against the railing, her head hanging. Logan had never seen her look so utterly defeated, but he understood. They'd failed. The bridge crew seemed to sense it; none looked up from their stations, none would meet his eyes. Except Kammy. The big man shuffled up to him almost reluctantly, putting a massive hand on his shoulder.

"I'm so sorry about your father, man," he said.

Logan nodded his gratitude, unwilling to try to speak. It was, he thought, a statement on how the spacer looked at things that he'd considered the personal loss before the fact they'd lost the head of their government.

"Did the fleet catch up with you?" Katy asked him, helping Logan over to one of the auxiliary fold-down acceleration couches and depositing him gently in it. "Did you have to fight them?"

"No," Kammy told her, and Logan could see the relief on his face. "We were able to outrun them by making them think we were heading for the jump-point, then doubling back. They'd already built up enough momentum, it took them hours to catch up and you guys were on board by then." He winced. "Well, the ones who came back. Damn, it sucks about the drop-ship crews. And Captain Ford..."

He fell silent and Logan slumped back into the chair, eyes closing, trying to keep from crying in front of the bridge crew. But it needed to be said.

"Ford and the entire Arbalest platoon," he listed, as if he were carving the names on a memorial. "Tracey, Mercouri, Paschal and Corraface." He could see them as they passed in review in his memory and faded out, taking a piece of his soul with them. "Paskowski..." He couldn't keep his voice from breaking. "Prevatt. Coughlin." They'd been with his platoon before he'd even formed Wholesale Slaughter, back when he'd been in the Spartan Mobile Armor Corps. They'd followed him along with Marc Langella and now all of them were gone.

Katy's hand grabbed his, squeezing it tightly.

"The rest made it, but a couple of Hernandez's people are pretty badly injured."

"Plus Kallias, Benitez and Butler from the squad I took down," Lyta contributed, not looking up.

Silence fell across the bridge, perhaps awkward, perhaps respectful.

"We'll, uh...," Kammy stuttered. "We'll be at the jump-point in a few minutes. No one's close enough to stop us."

"Sir." It was Shelly Nance, the ship's communications officer. She looked up, her eyes wide. "Colonel Conner, there's an incoming message from Sparta. It's for you."

"Put it on the main screen," he told her.

The face on the screen was familiar. He couldn't place it at first, but he knew he'd seen it before. Attractive in a harsh, cold sort of way, like a naked blade, her blond hair pulled back tight into a bun, her eyes as cold as the core of an ice giant. She wore a Spartan military uniform, Mobile Armored Corps, and suddenly he remembered her name.

"Logan Conner," the woman said, her voice as smooth and cold as her eyes. "I am Rhianna Hale."

"Shit," Lyta hissed. "Of course it would be her."

"Wait, pause it," Katy said. Nance seemed hesitant, glancing between Katy and Logan, but she touched a control and the glacial eyes froze on the screen. Katy turned to Lyta. "Who's Rhianna Hale?"

"She's Duncan Lambert's niece," Lyta told her, almost spitting the words. "Her mother, Duncan's sister, swore up and down she wasn't involved in the coup, begged the Guardian to be lenient with her family, promised they would be the most loyal citizens of Sparta and support him in the Council if he didn't exile them."

"And they were," Logan admitted. "The Hales have backed Dad in every Council vote for the last twenty years. And Rhianna...she's a decorated officer in the Mobile Armored Corps, no black marks on her record at all, as far as I know."

"There weren't," Lyta declared sourly. "Keeping track of her career was one of the responsibilities General Constantine shifted off on me in an attempt to groom my future career...once I got tired of playing in the dirt, he always says. She's had a spotless career, never shown any hint of being disloyal. But I never liked her."

"Play the message, Nance," Logan ordered. The woman nodded and resumed the playback.

"Colonel Conner," Hale went on, then paused with a hint of sneer on her lips. "So convenient that the Guardian's son is the youngest colonel in the history of the Mobile Armored Corps, isn't it? I'm sure there was no nepotism there. That won't be a problem anymore, of course. I have a proposition for you, Logan, one you'd be wise to consider. Leave here, leave Spartan

space and never return and we won't come looking for you."
Now the sneer was outright with no attempt to hide it. "You can
even maintain your little make-believe mercenary company."

A breath caught in Logan's chest. She knew. She knew
about Wholesale Slaughter, which meant she probably knew
about Terminus. And if she knew, that meant Starkad knew.

"If you do that for me, Logan, if you stay away and don't
interfere, we won't have any more unpleasantness and no one
else has to die. If you're stubborn, though, if you're so full of
your own ego and self-importance that you put your own
aggrandizement over the good of Sparta, like your father and his
grandfather before him, then it's the people you've left here on
Sparta who you care about who will pay the price."

"Who the hell is left?" He hadn't meant to say the words
aloud, didn't like how they sounded when he said them.
Rhianna Hale couldn't hear him—the message had been
recorded and sent out nearly an hour ago—but she had an
answer for him, nonetheless.

The camera angle had been a closeup of her face and shoulders, the wall behind her blank and featureless. Now, it
widened out and he saw she was in the Guardian's private
offices in the palace. He knew the room well, had spent most of
his formative years in and out of it. The Brannigan family
portraits had already been stripped off the walls and replaced
with a poorly-done painting of Duncan Lambert.

Soldiers dressed in Home Guard body armor, their faces
hidden behind the darkened visors of their helmets, pulled a
tall, powerfully-built man into the room. His head was covered
with a dark, cloth hood, his hands bound behind his back with
plastic flex-cuffs, but he wore a Spartan Mobile Armored Corps
uniform and there was something familiar about his gait and his
carriage. The guards held his arms while Hale reached up and
yanked the hood off.

General Donnell Anders had survived the ejection from his mech, though the bruising across the right side of his face showed it hadn't been pleasant. He was gagged beneath the hood, a broad strip of tape across his mouth, but in his eyes was pure hatred. He struggled against the hands holding him once he saw the camera pickup, but one of the guards put the muzzle of a carbine under his chin and jabbed him sharply. Anders grimaced and fell still in their grasp.

"I'm sure you remember General Anders," Hale said, running a gloved finger down the bruised side of the man's face. "He's just one of the officers loyal to your father who we've managed to capture alive. How we deal with these men and women is entirely up to you, Logan. If you're a good little exile and keep your nose clean, they'll eventually be allowed to settle somewhere comfortable, possibly one of the more remote colonies, once we've established they won't be trouble. If not…" She shrugged. "Well, we could simply keep them locked up in an off-world prison the way your father did. But that seems cruel. We'll likely just kill them, quickly and mercifully."

The camera zoomed in again, pulling in close so all Logan could see was her face.

"Logan Conner," she said, eyes narrowing as if she were considering the significance of the name. "Conner. You were so afraid of people knowing you were your father's son you wouldn't even use his name. You've been running from your legacy, running from your responsibility, running from your family's heritage for years now." She snorted a humorless laugh. "Well, now you can just keep running."

The view drew back out as if to show him the painting of Duncan again, to drive the point home.

"Sparta," she declared, "belongs to the Lamberts."

Nicolai Constantine hadn't expected to wake up.

He supposed, if he'd had the time to think about it before the drugs had kicked in, he would have wound up in some sterile, white-walled cell buried deep inside Argos or, worse yet, Stavanger. So, perhaps waking up with his head against a cold, damp stone floor in a cramped, darkened room was an improvement, but not by much.

His mouth tasted like some small mammal had crawled inside and died, and he spat reflexively, wiping at his lips with his jacket sleeve before he realized what the motion signified. He wasn't restrained and he was wearing the same clothes he'd had on when he'd gone to visit that traitorous bastard Wesley Martens. He sat up and began patting himself down, searching for the various weapons and communications devices he kept hidden in his clothes as a matter of course. He scowled. They were gone. He'd likely been thoroughly searched, probably scanned. They hadn't left him so much as a throat lozenge.

Or shoes, he noted, staring down at his stockinged feet. The light in the room was natural and came from the only window, along with a chill, damp breeze and the unmistakable crash of waves on a coastline. He moved over to it, trailing fingers along the slick surface of the bare stone walls. The window was narrow, so narrow the builders hadn't bothered with bars or grating.

It was night and the sky was shrouded in grey clouds, backlit by a moon somewhere behind them, giving just enough of a glow to make out some of the details of the rocky cove below.

Far below. He was in a tower or turret of some kind, ancient grey blocks polished smooth by the centuries, looming at least a hundred meters over the jagged rocks of the coastline. It wasn't just the splash of the tide hitting those rocks, either. There was a whirlpool out in the cove, roaring its defiance to the shore, daring anyone to test its resolve.

They could have made the window two meters wide. No one would try to escape.

Unless the designers hadn't wanted to leave room for suicide. That thought was discomfiting. He turned away from it and away from the window, examining the door instead. It was thick wood, strapped with steel and seemed as ancient as the rest of the construction. No electronic locks to hack, no ID plates to spoof, just a door several centimeters thick and bolted from the outside.

Where the hell am I?

The bolt scraped open and Constantine took a step backward, the damp finality of the far wall slapping against his shoulders quicker than he'd expected. Rusty hinges shrieked in protest as the door swung open and the harsh glare of naked, white light flooded in from the hallway, stretching a long, human-shaped shadow in its wake.

The woman was not tall, nor large, nor imposing, and yet Constantine did not underestimate her for all that. He didn't recognize her, but he recognized her uniform and the insignia on her left breast pocket and her right sleeve. She was Starkad

Intelligence, a full colonel. Behind her, a pair of Supremacy Marines loomed, weapons ready should he become troublesome.

"I have a feeling," he said, "that I'm not on Sparta anymore."

"Good evening, General Constantine," the woman said without malice. "I'm Colonel Laurent." The corner of her mouth quirked up. "You can consider me your counterpart in our government, though of course, without your experience or accomplishments."

"I don't know about that. Getting me here was quite the accomplishment." His brain was working now, clawing its way out of whatever anesthetized stupor he'd been kept in for the flight to wherever he was. "You wouldn't have risked this if it hadn't been part of something bigger. And as big a fool as Martens is, he still wouldn't have worked with Starkad unless he was sure there'd be no recriminations for him and his family. This is a coup."

"It was a coup," she corrected him, hands clasped in front of her. "Now, it is a regime change, and a *fait accompli*. Jaimie Brannigan is dead and Rhianna Hale is the new Guardian of Sparta."

The wall had been a barrier behind him. Now, it became a support because his legs had no strength. She could be lying, playing an elaborate mind game with him, but it fit with the facts he knew. It meant there would be no negotiations for his release, no rescue mission. He would be here for the rest of his life.

However long that ended up being.

"General Constantine," she went on, not seeming to take any pleasure in the words or in the announcement of the coup, "I have been ordered to use chemical interrogation on you, to strip your psyche bare and mine every piece of valuable information you've collected over the last twenty years. Before I am forced to carry out this order, I felt I had to give you the chance to talk voluntarily, because I respect you and the job you've done."

Interesting. Perhaps I could pretend to play along, buy time... But no, she's far too intelligent for that.

"If you respect me, Colonel Laurent," he said, standing straight, moving away from the wall, "then you already know what I'll say."

She nodded, what seemed like genuine regret passing over her face.

"I do."

She motioned to the Marines and they moved past her, coming into the cell to grab him by the arms and pull him toward the open door.

"Welcome to Maelstrom Strand, General," she said, her voice falling behind him as he was marched down the narrow hallway. "I'm afraid it's your last stop."

The ice giant hung in a dull torpor, barely visible in the distant light of the red dwarf at the system's center. Even in the enhanced optics of the cabin's holographic viewport, it was grey and featureless, lifeless.

The perfect backdrop for this meeting.

Lyta Randell hugged her knees to her chest, curled into a ball on a sofa way too comfortable to be furniture on a starship. Kammy had gotten carried away during the refit, not that she could blame him. He was working on a cost-plus contract from a Dominion government, why not splurge?

No more contract now. No more government support, no more government. At least not one they'd recognize if they were ever able to go back.

Logan still looked shell-shocked days later and a dozen light-years away. He was slumped across the conference table of what Kammy had jokingly referred to as the *Shakak's* "flag cabin." The actual sleeping compartment was through another hatchway, and this was more of a VIP reception and planning area, but she thought it made Kammy feel more important.

Katy sat next to Logan, hands massaging gently at his shoulders, her face still stricken. It seemed to Lyta as if Katy hadn't been more than a meter away from the man since they'd returned from Sparta, and she wasn't sure if it was because he needed the support, or she needed the comfort. Not that Lyta blamed her. She could have used the support herself.

"Shouldn't we have some sort of ceremony?" Terrin wondered. He had a bottle of water he'd brought with him from the galley when they'd left dinner to reconvene here, but he seemed to be using it more as a stress-relief device than for drinking, squeezing it and twisting it until she wanted to smack it out of his hands. He seemed uncomfortable sitting in on the planning session, or perhaps he was uncomfortable that Franny hadn't been invited. "I mean, for everyone we lost?"

"You need to talk to them, too, man," Kammy said to Logan. Lyta blinked at the grim sobriety of the words. That wasn't like Kammy at all. "Everyone's kind of walking around in a haze. They gotta know we have some sort of idea what's going on."

"I do," Logan admitted. He nodded to Terrin as well. "And we do need a ceremony. But before we can tell the crew what's going on, we have to figure it out first." He shook his head slowly, his eyes fixed on something light years beyond the bulkhead of the cabin. "I have no fucking idea what to do next. We have four mecha in the cargo bay, no drop-ships, nowhere safe to go to get more within twenty light-years and I don't even know if our credit accounts work anymore."

"We have a company of Rangers," Lyta added, then winced

and corrected herself. "*Most* of a company of Rangers. We might be able to steal what we need."

"Maybe," Logan admitted. "But what are we going to do with it if we get it?"

"What about the other fleets?" Terrin wanted to know. "Lyta said something about how Starkad made Dad deploy them away from Sparta so Hale could pull off the coup. Couldn't we go hook up with them and get them to back us?"

Logan met her eyes with an expression of guilt, and she shared the feeling.

"There's something we haven't told the crew," Lyta said. "Another message Hale sent out broadband back home and probably to every Spartan-held system, too." She shrugged. "It's mostly rah-rah bullshit about how we're just one big, happy Dominion no matter who the Guardian is, and how it's their duty to support whoever the Council chooses as Guardian, blah, blah, blah."

"But at the end of it," Logan interjected, "she pretty much warns all the Navy forces deployed at the lines that they left their families back home and she knows where they live. She invites anyone who can't bring themselves to do their duty to Sparta to resign immediately with no recriminations."

"But they won't do that, will they?" Terrin asked, face screwed up in an expression of disbelief. "They wouldn't just abandon Dad like that!"

"Dad's dead," Logan reminded him quietly, pain still tugging at the corners of his eyes as he said the words. "But no, you're right, not all of them would abandon his memory like that. But enough will. Enough we can't take the chance of trusting them, of putting everything we have left in their hands."

"Maybe once we figure things out," Katy suggested, her voice rough and hoarse, as if she hadn't been sleeping. "Maybe if we can get a good base of operations and a network of some kind, we can get ahold of them, try to pull them in."

"Pull them into *what*, though?" Kammy asked. He was staring at Logan, not in anger but as if he kept expecting him to say something to make sense of it all. "What's the goal here, boss?"

Lyta frowned at the big man.

"What do you mean? We have to take down Hale. She's nothing but a Starkad puppet. If she stays in power, we're handing over our government, our *homes* to our enemy."

"That's part of it," Kammy admitted. "But people ain't gonna risk their lives and their families without a clear goal."

The ship's captain pulled a chair out from the conference table and sat down opposite Logan. It still struck her as odd, having normal planet-side furniture in a starship, but this ship didn't maneuver with reaction engines, which meant no worries about sudden acceleration. The only thing that would shake them up was if something big hit them, and at that point, they'd have more to worry about than loose furniture in the cabins.

"Boss," Kammy went on, "the crew of the *Shakak*, the ones who were here with Captain Osceola, do you know why we all stayed on after he was gone?"

"They're your people," Logan attempted. "They knew you'd have been his choice..."

"And the money's good," Kammy allowed, waving them both away. "That wouldn't be enough. Not when we're risking our life every time we go out. There're no milk runs with Wholesale Slaughter. No, man, we all stay on because we believe in what we're doing, because we believe in *your* mission. We believe in you, because you've put your ass on the line right beside us. If you want to take down this bitch Hale and save your home and all that shit, you'd better be laying yourself out there as the one to lead the charge and be the one who's going to take your dad's place."

Logan rubbed at his eyes, unwilling to meet Kammy's. "I don't know I'm ready to do that right now. It feels like there's a million years between where we are now and even the idea of me taking Dad's place. I think right now, we need to concentrate on finding somewhere to hang our head, getting some support." He looked over to Lyta. "What about Clan Modi? They sure as hell have the most to lose if Starkad doesn't have to worry about Sparta anymore. The Supremacy will roll right through them the first chance they get."

"That's the problem," Lyta said, shrugging. "Starkad *will* roll right through them, and take us with them. There's no point in trying to get help from someone unless they can actually help. If we set up on a Modi world, the odds are we'll be pulling up stakes and running within months."

She unfolded from the couch and stood, touching a control on the table and bringing up a holographic map of the Dominions. Sparta and Starkad were the largest, but next to them, outlined in red was... "The Shang Concord," she declared. "They've been rivals of Starkad for centuries, economically, militarily...they might be very interested to learn how involved Starkad was in the coup and what it might do to the balance of power."

"Why not the Imperium then?" Katy asked her. "Mbeki isn't any fonder of Starkad than Shang, and they're even stronger."

"Mbeki's had an official truce in place with Starkad since the end of the last Border War. They're not going to break it without some sort of unprovoked aggression against them."

"I don't like it," Kammy said, mouth twisting as if he'd bitten into something sour. "Cap'n Osceola and me dealt with those Shang bastards more than once and I'll be damned if they didn't try to swindle us every time. I wouldn't trust them to give me a straight answer if I asked them for the speed of light in a vacuum."

"General Constantine never cared much for them, either," Lyta admitted. "But it's them or nothing." She ran a hand through her hair. It was greasy and knotted; she needed a shower. "At least, there's nothing else I can think of."

Logan nodded slowly.

"We'll contact them," he decided. "The worst they can do is say no."

"Shit," Kammy said, snorting in disdain. "You wish that's the worst they could do."

8

Nicolai Constantine's breath was a deafening rasp in his own ears, drowning out the echoing tap-tap-tap of his boot soles on the marble floor of the great hall at Laconia. The carbine seemed at once impossibly heavy in his hands, weighted down with the judgement of God, and yet pitifully light and inadequate to the task at hand.

He needed grenades, armored vehicles, mortars, missile launchers and a host of other equipment he wasn't going to get. The insurrectionists had made sure of that when they'd seized the North-side Armory and destroyed the others. The smoke from the demo charges still rose into the darkening sky, an obscene tombstone hanging over the men and women killed in the blast. So many had died...and so many more would.

Constantine ducked into a nook in the wall, kicking a stand with a potted plant out into the middle of the concourse to make room for him to shelter. He'd taken cover by instinct, by the internal clock telling him he'd been out in the open for too long, and it proved itself right yet again. A stream of fully automatic fire hammered into the wall only centimeters from his head, shattering ceramic tile into grenade fragments, peppering his left cheek with half a dozen stinging wounds.

"Action front!" he yelled back to the Rangers following him, leaning out and throwing the carbine up to his shoulder.

The shooters were thirty meters down the corridor, streaming out of a T-junction, a full squad of troops in the grey-camouflage armor and full-face helmets of the Home Guard. None of his Rangers had joined the Insurrectionist forces, thanks be to Mithra; it wasn't too difficult to figure out who to shoot. He put a three-round burst into the lead trooper, catching the man in the mirrored visor of his helmet and shattering it and the skull beneath in a spray of red. He collapsed forward, tumbling as he hit, leaving a trail of blood across the marble floor, and the next trooper spun down just behind him, catching a shot to center mass from one of the Rangers following Constantine.

There were two ways to handle that sort of kick in the teeth. His Rangers would have assaulted through it, taken out the opposition and then gone back to see to their wounded, but these weren't Rangers. Home Guard soldiers were well equipped, but there was a reason Sparta went to war with its Mobile Armored Corps and Rangers and left the Home Guard at home. What was left of the squad scrambled backwards towards the cover of the intersecting hallway, one of them, to his credit, grabbing the wounded trooper and dragging him with them.

"Move!" Constantine yelled to his platoon, waving them forward.

He was a captain, he shouldn't have been leading from the front, and he knew it. But this wasn't an ordinary battle and he didn't want to take the chance of an enlisted man hesitating because he thought he saw a friendly officer where he should have seen an Insurrectionist.

And frankly, he was pissed and wanted to shoot some traitors. The Guardian had been assassinated by his own security forces and the only thing standing between Duncan Lambert and the throne of Sparta was Jaimie Brannigan and the men and women loyal to him. And he was betting one of those men was Alexander Drew, the Adjutant General of the military base at Laconia. He'd received the distress call from Drew's private line fifteen minutes ago, saying he was trapped in his office by Insurrectionists and he didn't know who to trust beside Constantine.

Drew had too much sensitive intelligence in his head and his personal files to let the traitors get their hands on him...and the man had been a friend of Constantine's father back when they'd attended the Academy together. He was a military officer and personal feelings shouldn't have mattered, but they did. It was a fortunate turn of fate his feelings and his duty happened to align this time.

Constantine jogged up to the T-junction and put his back against the left-hand wall, edging forward until he could take a quick glance around the corner. If he'd had time to equip himself with full combat gear, he could have just angled his rifle around the corner and scanned the other side with his combat optics, avoiding the possibility of getting his head blown off.

And if "if's and but's" were fruits and nuts...

He was lucky he had the carbine and a tactical vest full of loaded magazines—some of his Rangers hadn't even had that much and had been forced to scrounge what they could off enemy casualties.

No gunshots met his lightning-quick glance, and he hadn't seen any startled enemy troops either. He took a knee and ducked around again, longer this time. The corridor was empty except for a couple of blood trails. They'd retreated.

Up and moving again, coughing. There was a thin haze of smoke in the concourse, from what he didn't know. The fire suppression systems should have put out anything the rebels had started.

I don't remember the smoke.

He nearly stopped in his tracks at the oddness of the thought, but he forced himself to shake it off and keep running. He didn't have time to stand around trying to figure out the mysteries of life. There was a mission to accomplish.

What mission? Was I even at *Laconia that night?*

He snarled at the voice; it wouldn't get out of his head. He couldn't afford distractions.

There. There was the office, the outer doors sealed, their wooden façade chewed away by gunfire and explosives, revealing the thick metal beneath. He found the intercom and punched the button, hoping the gunfire hadn't damaged it.

"It's Captain Constantine," he said. "Are you still there, sir?"

"Nicolai," General Drew's voice answered, incredibly clear for such a battered intercom speaker. "I am unlocking the doors. Come in, but only you. I do not trust anyone else."

Constantine waved at his platoon to stay back. He frowned. It was strange, the smoke had grown thicker. He couldn't make out more than their silhouettes against the ruined, cracked walls of the concourse. He wasn't coughing anymore, though. The smoke was more like a fog, a vapor...

The door locked clicked as it released.

"Come in. Quickly."

He didn't remember the door opening, but suddenly, he was inside. The interior office seemed untouched, just as he remembered it, almost as if all hell wasn't breaking loose outside. The hand-carved bust of the first Emperor, Hellenus. The book-shelves an anachronistic touch General Drew insisted on keeping around. Constantine had always wondered how many of the physical, paper books the man had read but he'd never had the nerve to ask.

The general was standing behind his desk, hands clasped behind his back, staring up at the portrait of his wife and son, both of them killed during a pirate attack while they'd been visiting her parents back on Nike. It had happened twenty-five years ago, when Constantine had been a young boy, but the man had never let them get too far from his thoughts. He'd never remarried, just plunged into his career and climbed every rung of the ladder.

"Damned pirates," General Drew murmured. "All this time and we still haven't taken care of that problem, Nicolai. Why do you suppose that is?"

"That's a bit above my pay grade, sir," Constantine admitted, impatience growling inside his chest. "We need to go, sir."

Drew glanced back at him, annoyance on his dog-jowled, deeply-lined face.

"You're an intelligent man and a military officer, Captain Constantine, give me your best opinion."

He hissed out a sigh.

"Yes, sir. The pirate leadership is decentralized and their base camps are mobile and constantly changing. Committing enough forces to pin them down would leave us open to attack from Starkad."

"And just what do you think this coup is, young sir?" Drew cocked an eyebrow. "Or do you think Colonel Duncan Lambert came up with this all on his own? Lambert is many things, but a strategic mind is not one of them."

"We have to go, sir," Constantine repeated, wondering if he was going to have to physically remove the man from the office. "The Insurrectionists are all over the base and my men are outside."

"The insurrection is all over this city, son. And with good

reason. Our Guardian, tasked with protecting his people, has let pirates, and brigands, and bandits ravage our colonies, steal our treasure and murder our citizens because of his inaction and lack of imagination."

Constantine's blood froze in his veins and his fingers tightened around the pistol grip of his carbine.

"Sir, what are you saying?"

The man's dark eyes were filled with fire, with more passion and anger than he'd ever seen in them. A pistol had appeared in his hand from somewhere, as if produced by magic.

"You have a chance here, son, more of a chance than my own wife and child. You have a chance to be on the winning team."

"No," Constantine insisted, shaking his head. "No, it didn't fucking happen like this! This is not what happened!"

He clenched his teeth, raised the rifle to his shoulder and fired a burst into the chest of the man, the wraith, the phantom who wasn't the General Alexander Drew he knew, the General Drew who'd been killed by the rebels that night. The muzzle flash from his carbine seemed to expand and consume everything in his vision in a soft, white glow and he couldn't see the office, couldn't see the base, couldn't even see himself.

Everything was fading, but through the haze he heard voices, distant and muffled.

"His conditioning is deep. This is going to take a while."

"That's all right." He recognized that one, pictured her in a Starkad uniform, Intelligence. "We have the luxury of patience."

Darkness claimed him and he heard no more.

Logan tried not to breathe too deeply. The air stank of death and decay, as if the rot had worked its way deep into the heart of the planet.

"Why the hell did we have to meet this guy in the middle of a swamp?" he wondered, eyeing the surrounding jungle with suspicion, his hand not straying far from the pistol at his belt.

The assault shuttle had landed on a finger of high ground stretching out into the wetlands, fringed by cypress trees. They grew on the land and in the water and everywhere in-between and it was hard to tell where one ended and the other began in the gathering dusk. He slapped at a mosquito, wondering how effective the sonic bug repellant at his belt actually was.

"Be happy he met us at all," Acosta told him. He didn't seem bothered by the insect life, just by the waiting. He paced back and forth in front of the open ramp, a silhouette backlit by the interior lights. "I don't care what Colonel Randell says, Shang wasn't exactly thrilled about hearing from us. It took every single contact General Constantine had ever passed on to me to get us this face-to-face, and they weren't about to do it somewhere Starkad might have an intelligence asset." He waved around them at kilometer after kilometer of nothing. "Hell, they didn't even want to have a ship sitting in space next to ours for a telescope to get a shot of. This shithole has maybe ten thousand people on the whole planet and I'm pretty sure they're in some sort of exile prison."

"Perfect place for one," Logan murmured.

His eyes went back to the horizon, where he'd been searching for the last two hours, waiting. And there it was, finally.

"Aircraft," he said, nodding toward the south. "Not even a shuttle."

"Harder to trace back to them," Acosta judged. "Like I said."

"You going to keep being all passive-aggressive, Francis?" Katy asked, coming down the ramp behind him.

"I don't know what you're talking about, Commander Margolis." Logan could almost hear the scowl in his voice even without looking at him.

"I'm sorry no one thought to invite you to the strategy session," Katy said, sighing like a patient parent. "But we were all pretty rattled. We value your contacts and your knowledge, honest we do."

"Game face on, Acosta," Logan told him, still watching the approaching lights. He judged by the speed it was a ducted-fan helicopter. *Probably flew it out from the prison colony. That way they could say they were running a maintenance inspection or something. Plausible deniability.*

He was proven right a moment later when the vaguely disc-shaped aircraft began an almost straight-down descent, the belly fans kicking up a fountain of grass and stray water droplets. The landing lights blinked dutifully, flashes of red and yellow blowing out the details of the night sky, and he squinted against the glare and the dust and debris, refusing to raise a hand to shield his eyes out of what he admitted to himself was likely stubborn pride.

Logan tried not to let his hand rest on his gun butt, though the temptation was strong. The Shang Concord hadn't been a direct military threat to Sparta in over a century, but neither had they been a friend. He suspected, but couldn't prove, that they funded some of the pirates he'd taken down in the last year. It was an open secret Starkad funded a few of the bandit gangs, both as a source of intelligence and a distraction for their enemies, but they weren't the only ones, just the most obvious.

If there was anything Shang excelled at, it was keeping secrets.

The canopy of the flitter popped open and a long, slender figure exited the cockpit with machine-like efficiency, not a motion wasted. The lights of the aircraft's control board teased at his features, revealing a hint of a high cheekbone, the perfect curve of an aquiline nose, a few stray, midnight-colored curls slipping out the sides of the dark skullcap men of rank in the Concord wore. His clothes matched the cap, trim and conservative down to the flat, black gloves.

Dark eyes gleamed in the light from the shuttle, regarding them one at a time, judging and assessing. He wasn't visibly armed, and neither was the flitter, but Logan didn't make any assumptions he wouldn't have armed support nearby if he needed it.

"You may call me Mr. Salonga," he said. He speared Logan with a glare. "Are you the heir?"

"I'm Logan Conner, son of Jaimie Brannigan. Thank you for meeting us, Mr. Salonga." Logan paused, waiting for the Shang representative to respond, but the man remained silent, still focused on him. "There's been a coup on Sparta," he went on, the words feeling awkward and strained. "Rhianna Hale, the niece of..."

"My government knows of the happenings on your home-world," Salonga interrupted. "There is little that occurs in any of the Five Dominions that escapes the eye of the Concord. You have asked for this meeting and someone has agreed and sent me to listen to what you have to say. Endeavor to tell me something I do not already know."

Asshole. Logan bit down on his instinctive response, sensing it might have been impolitic. *Okay, he wants brass tacks, I'll give it to him.*

"Starkad's behind this. Hale is their puppet. Once they finish off Clan Modi, Shang is likely next. If you back me, supply me, give me weapons and funding, I'll take Hale down and remove the Starkad influence from Sparta. Even if I lose, it will distract Starkad enough to keep them out of your hair for a while."

Salonga nodded, the straight line of his mouth bending just slightly, as if he appreciated the brevity and efficiency of Logan's statement.

"Do you know why the Concord has seen far fewer wars than any of the other Dominions?" the Shang representative asked.

Logan blinked. It seemed a sharp left turn in the conversation and it took him a moment to bring together an answer. Acosta was quicker.

"Astrographic isolation," the Intelligence agent said. "You had us between you and Starkad, Modi between you and the Mbeki Imperium. We were concentrating on Starkad and Modi isn't strong enough to threaten you."

"Not inaccurate," Salonga admitted. "But incomplete. The reason we do not become embroiled in your wars is that we mind our own affairs. This matter between you and the Starkad Supremacy is not our concern, and will not be unless and until the Supremacy makes the mistake of thinking we are vulnerable simply because we are reluctant to interfere in the dealings of others."

"Won't your superiors want the chance to assess the situation themselves before they make a decision?" Logan's chest was tight with frustration, with the inescapable feeling of things slipping away from him, but he tried to keep it out of his tone. There was always the chance he was misreading things, or maybe the man was testing their resolve...

"My orders were clear before I was ever allowed to meet with you," Salonga told him.

"Then why come at all?" Logan snapped, finally losing patience with the man. "Why drag us out here if you already knew the answer?"

"Just because we are unwilling to become embroiled in your war does not mean we have no counter-offer." Salonga spread gloved hands, smiling thinly. "We would be more than willing to offer sanctuary to you and those with you for as long as you might require it. For a price."

"Three guesses what the price is." Katy had taken a step back up onto the shuttle's belly ramp, as if she were getting ready to run.

"Your discovery of the Imperial research lab at Terminus did not go unnoticed by our intelligence corps," the Shang operative confirmed. "We want whatever you discovered."

"And of course," Acosta said, "with the Imperial technology, you won't have to worry about Starkad trying to expand into your territory." He shook his head, the expression on his face perhaps denoting disgust or perhaps professional admiration.

Shit. Logan wished he'd been able to convince Lyta to do the talking. He was a mech-jock, not a diplomat. It would be so damned easy for him to screw this up...

"I'd be willing to share the data we extracted," he countered, the words tasting sour on the way out, "in exchange for a base of operations and financial and material support. Failing that, I have no interest in running and hiding from this fight and the data will be going to whoever is willing to fight beside me."

Salonga did something Logan hadn't thought him capable of. He laughed. It wasn't a pleasant sound.

"Colonel Conner," he said, still chuckling, "were you under the misapprehension we were going to give you a choice?" He gestured out into the tall grass waving in the warm, fetid wind. "You are, right now, being covered by a platoon of Shang infantry. If you attempt to move back toward your shuttle, you'll be disabled and your pilots will be killed. Once your comrades on your ship hear of your predicament, I'm fairly certain they'll turn over the data to preserve your life."

Logan blew out a heavy sigh. It was always a relief when the other shoe dropped. He tapped a control on his 'link surreptitiously, as if hitching up his belt.

"Now," he said.

The stuttering wasn't loud, more of a hammer-on-a-board sound, but the cadence was clearly gunfire run through an integrally suppressed Ranger weapon loaded with special, subsonic ammo to avoid the snap of a conventional round breaking the sound barrier. It was the sound of short bursts, but a *lot* of short bursts all firing at once. The tall grass moved, thrashed, exploded, and somewhere a single unsuppressed gunshot rang out, solitary and desperate.

Then silence.

"Clear," Lyta reported into Logan's earbud.

"Get the Rangers back to the shuttle," he told her, eyes still locked on Salonga. Those eyes didn't seem nearly as arrogant and in-control anymore. He could have sworn he saw the reflection from a thin sheen of sweat on that perfect brow. "Lyta, get the shuttle ready to go and tell Kammy to plot a direct burn to the jump-point."

Salonga made a break for it. Logan had sensed it coming and had a step on the man, grabbing him by the back of his jacket collar and slamming him to the ground. The Shang operative was taller than him by nearly a head, but Logan had him by ten kilograms, all of it muscle. He knelt into the man's chest, drew his handgun and put the muzzle under his chin.

"Logan...," Acosta blurted, but stopped himself from finishing the admonishment.

Smart. Keep your damn mouth shut, Francis.

Salonga's skullcap had fallen off, letting loose a mass of dark curls, but the man hadn't seemed to have noticed. His entire concentration was on the gun digging into the flesh of his neck and the eyes of the man whose finger was on the trigger.

"Let me tell you what's happening here, Mr. Salonga. Your

platoon of soldiers is dead." Behind him, he could hear the boot-steps of the Rangers as they trotted across the clearing, heading for the ramp. "We're going to get on the shuttle and take off. If anything on or around this planet tries to stop us, the *Shakak* is going to blow them out of orbit." He cocked his head to the side, curious. "Did your intelligence sources happen to mention that it's the only fucking ship in the Dominions with a stardrive and Imperial weapons systems? Because it is. You might want to warn your people to stay out of its way. Nod if you understand me."

Salonga's head moved up and down just slightly, constrained by the gun barrel.

"Good. That's short term. Long term, I *am* going to take down Rhianna Hale and I *am* going to be the Guardian of Sparta when it's all over. So, your Concord bosses have three choices, as I see it. Stay out of this fight, which is what they want to do anyway. When it's over, things will be just like they were. Or, the wrong decision, come in on Starkad's side. In that case, when I get done taking back my home and my fleets and my military, you can consider Sparta and Shang at war." Logan withdrew the muzzle just slightly, just enough for Salonga's head to tilt downward and meet his eyes. "Or, they can be smart. They can back the winner, come in on my side. Then, once things are over, you'll have an *ally* in Sparta, not just a neutral rival." He suppressed a feral grin. *This* was his idea of diplomacy.

He could hear the shuttle's turbines screaming now, enough to drown out any more words. He slowly and carefully stood, letting the pressure off the Shang operative. The man didn't move, still eyeing Logan uncertainly.

"Think about it," Logan shouted over the jets, backing toward the belly ramp.

When his heels touched metal, he turned and jogged

upward into the aerospacecraft, the ramp rising beneath him before he'd even stepped off of it. Lyta was making sure her Ranger platoon was strapped into the passenger seats behind the cockpit, but she looked up at his approach.

"No casualties," she reported. "For us."

The shuttle lifted off the ground and Logan grabbed the back of a seat and fell into an acceleration couch beside hers, strapping in as they roared away from the swamp.

"I'm sorry," Lyta told him, leaning in close. "This was my idea."

He shrugged. "It didn't go as bad as it could have."

"We still don't have a base," she lamented, head falling back against the neck cushion of the seat. "We don't have anywhere to go for support."

Logan grunted softly, eyes hazing over in thought.

"You know," he finally said, "I think we just might."

9

Josephine Salvaggio clamped her jaws together against the yawn trying to fight its way free. She remembered a time when she would have let it loose, not cared what anyone thought of her for it, but those days were gone. She wasn't the "interim military commander" of Revelation anymore, she was just the "minister of defense," which was a damned aggrandized title for the commander of a company of mostly scout mecha and a few lightly-equipped infantry.

But everything about Revelation was overblown, including their "planetary government." "Planetary." *Yeah, if one small, seaport town hooked up by railway to a few farming outposts constitutes a planetary settlement.* Their politicians sure loved to talk, and David Carpenter, the duly-elected Planetary Governor, was perhaps the worst of them. She didn't check her 'link readout, but she judged he'd been droning on for nearly an hour and she had to pretend to be interested if she was going to get the funding her people needed.

Carpenter was a tall man, always seeming as if he were on the edge of malnutrition, his face gaunt and spare beneath the scraggly salt-and-pepper beard. His wife was just as thin though not quite as tall and, thanks be to Mithra, not nearly as talkative. She watched her husband with the sort of fond, almost worshipful look that made Salvaggio want to puke. The rest of the elected Council and cabinet ministers watched from the perimeter of the round conference table with varying degrees of interest and boredom, reminding Salvaggio of a picture of an ancient painting she'd seen once called The Last Supper. She didn't remember whose supper it was or why it was their last one, but everyone in the painting had the same sense of "oh my God, this is so important" in their faces. Except this one weird looking dude who seemed like he wanted to start a fight.

Maybe that's me.

"Governor," she said, raising a finger to interrupt him as he went over the same figures for what had to be the third time, "might I be allowed to make a salient point?"

There were a few dirty looks. Some of the Council members still hadn't forgiven her for taking over the colony after she'd freed it from the brigands who'd set themselves up as the ruling class.

Shitheads should have paid me on time, then. Girl's got to make a living. Damn good thing for them Wholesale Slaughter came along and offered to cover my expenses or they'd be fighting off another bunch of bandits or pirates by now.

"Of course, Captain Salvaggio," Carpenter said with a polite nod. "You had a thought on the reconstruction budget?"

Yeah, I got a thought, you officious coot. My fucking thought is you've been "reconstructing" this place for a year and you still ain't built the important things.

"The last communication I had with Colonel Slaughter was a few months ago," she said, standing, palms flat on the table. It was cheap plastic and creaked beneath her weight. "In it, he stressed the importance of our finishing the mech fabrication plant above all other priorities."

Mithra's bloody horns, I sound like one of them now! Spenta Mainyu save me from fucking bureaucrats!

"We all appreciate everything Colonel Slaughter and Wholesale Slaughter have done for us," Genevieve Gayou said, leaning forward, fingers clasped in front of her as if in prayer. "But he doesn't live here, and our needs are many…"

"He may not live here," Salvaggio cut in, "but he *paid* for that fabrication plant and you'd better have a damn good reason not to have spent the funds he gave us for the project he *thought* he was paying for."

Several uncomfortable glances at each other sidelong and much silence met her statement.

"That's what I fuckin' thought," she murmured. A few eyes widened and she knew she'd said it too loud.

She sighed, about to try to offer a compromise when the door to the council meeting room slammed open and Yuri stumbled in, out of breath, his wild mane of grey-streaked hair even more out of control than usual.

"Momma!" he called to her. She winced at the old nickname. She'd tried to get her people to start calling her "Captain Salvaggio" to sound more professional and less like a crime boss, but it was an uphill battle. "We got…" he gasped for breath. "…incoming shuttles. They'll be landing in ten minutes at this course and speed."

"What?" she blurted, shooting to her feet. "Why didn't we pick up their mother ship before she reached orbit?"

"The orbital sensors didn't pick up any fusion drive flares," Yuri said, hands resting on his thighs as he caught his breath. He must have run all the way there from the Security Station…what had used to be called the city jail. "I don't know how they missed it!"

The hall exploded into a gabble of confused voices, people springing to their feet without any idea of what they were going to do or where they were going to go. Not Salvaggio, though. What had begun as utter panic subsided into something less fearful but equally curious. She knew exactly who could sneak up on them like this, but not why he would be here.

There was a chime on her 'link, the notice of an incoming call. She saw from the address that it was a radio signal being relayed by satellite rather than another 'link address in the city.

"Salvaggio here," she spoke into the external pickup rather than using her earbud, thinking this was probably something everyone needed to hear. The buzz of voices died down as they waited for the reply.

"Josephine," the voice was small and tinny over the external speaker, but they all recognized it nonetheless. "This is..." A hesitation. "...Colonel Slaughter. Sorry to drop in unannounced. Pick me up at the port. We need to talk."

"Sure thing, Colonel," she said, shooting a stink-eye at David Carpenter, wondering what he'd have to say now about how they'd spent their money. "I bet there's a lot to talk about."

"Holy shit." Salvaggio looked like a cow ready for slaughter, right after the butcher had slammed it between the eyes with a maul. She sank back in the rickety, hand-made chair in what had been the constable's office before someone had gotten the idea to start calling it the planetary security center. "So, you're really the son of the Guardian." She winced. "I mean, the late Guardian, God rest his soul."

"I am," Logan said, pacing from the desk to the window. He'd tried to sit down, but he couldn't manage to shake the restless feeling in his gut that he'd wasted too much time. "I was born Logan Brannigan, but I've been calling myself Logan

Conner since I entered the Academy to avoid anyone knowing who I was and treating me different."

"You might want to consider going back to Brannigan," Terrin suggested. He sat on a corner of the office's desk, which the town constable might have objected to if he'd been invited to the meeting. "Not many people who don't know you are going to get worked up about following Logan Conner."

"Wait a second," Salvaggio interrupted, pointing an accusatory finger at Terrin. "That means you're the Guardian's son, too!"

Terrin nodded, grinning. "Younger. Not interested in being a soldier or a Guardian though. I'm a scientist."

"I was holding the son of the Guardian of Sparta prisoner," Salvaggio muttered, eyes glazing over. "Goddammit, I could have asked for *such* a ransom..."

"I often wonder why I broke you out of jail," Lyta commented from where she leaned against the wall by the door. She wasn't in combat armor, but she still carried a carbine slung across her back, as if she expected the enemy to land at any second.

"Okay," Salvaggio said, shaking her shoulders as if she were trying to get rid of regrets over lost opportunities. "Your dad got killed, you've got a traitor on your throne. I understand all that. But why did you come *here*? To hide until the heat dies down?"

"No." Logan felt his shoulders tightening at the insinuation he'd hide out and he forced himself to loosen up. Salvaggio was probably going off what *she* would do in his circumstances. "I came here to find a place to build up our forces and start preparing to take back Sparta."

"Build up *what* forces?" She waved a hand expressively. "You told me you weren't able to contact the rest of your fleet."

Logan shared a look with Lyta and she rolled her eyes. He knew she still thought this was a crazy idea.

"Wholesale Slaughter," he explained. Salvaggio blinked in obvious confusion and he went on. "We can't reach the other Spartan forces and we wouldn't know who to trust if we could. We can't trust the other Dominions not to turn us over to Starkad to try to curry favor with them. But we do have all the mercenary units we brought under the Wholesale Slaughter umbrella. And I want to bring them all here."

"Whoa!" David Carpenter had been sitting in the constable's swivel chair, which was a good deal more comfortable than the other chairs in the office, but now he popped to his feet, face like a prairie dog alerting on a hawk. "Here? Are you nuts? We don't have any real defenses here, no spacecraft besides a couple cargo shuttles!"

"We can help with that," Lyta told the governor. "Once we get enough forces, we're going to go out and...appropriate what we need from the enemy."

"Steal it, you mean." Salvaggio's tone was dry, a small smirk passing across her face.

"In wartime," Logan corrected her, "you aren't stealing, you're appropriating. And we can get what we need to set up defenses for this world."

"You're talking about turning our home into a battlefield again," Carpenter accused. "We haven't even finished rebuilding from the last time we had to fight for our independence."

He seemed shaky on his feet, steadying himself against the desk, and Logan felt suddenly guilty.

"I won't lie to you," he told the older man, "it might come to that. I can only tell you if Starkad gets their way, no one is going to be independent for long. Leaving loose ends isn't Aaron Starkad's way." Logan shrugged. "If you don't want us here, if you want us to leave, we'll go."

Where, he had no idea, and he was praying very hard Carpenter wouldn't take the chance he was giving him.

David Carpenter rubbed his palms across his eyes as if the light from the overhead lamp was hurting them, turned away and stepped around the desk. He pulled the window shade aside and stared out into the street. Logan wondered if he was imagining the town on fire, the streets filled with the dead and dying, the way it had looked after the battle with Starkad.

"No," he said, his voice a sigh of regret, and Logan's gut went cold at the thought the man was about to kick them out. "No, I won't ask you to leave," he clarified. "If it weren't for you and your people, we would have nothing. We'd either be under Starkad's thumb, or dead." He laughed, a harsh sound totally devoid of humor. "And if it does come down to Starkad or your own government's traitors coming here to dig you out, we can always hide in the canyons again and wait them out. No one wants to stay here forever. No one who has anywhere else to go."

Logan controlled the sigh of relief he couldn't quite suppress, releasing it slowly and almost silently. He didn't want to seem desperate.

"Thank you, Governor Carpenter," he began, but the older man cut him off.

"I don't want your thanks," he said, rounding on Logan, "I want you to make me a promise. If you win this, if you wind up ruling Sparta again when all this is over, I want your word you'll come back here and take us somewhere fit to live. Somewhere we won't be squeezed into a small slice of the planet because the rest isn't livable, somewhere we won't have to be constantly on guard for pirates and raiders who want to take what's ours."

Terrin chuckled softly and Logan stared at him as if he'd lost his mind, but his brother shrugged and pushed ahead.

"You know, the thing about nice, safe places, sir," he told

Carpenter, "is there are already people there running things. I believe I heard a lot of people complaining about her..." He jabbed a finger toward Salvaggio. "...being in control, taking away your self-determination. Are you going to be willing to live by someone else's rules, pay their taxes, work where they say you work?"

"He won't have to," Logan declared. "Mr. Carpenter," he said with grim resolution, "if I can win this, if I live through it and I am the Guardian of Sparta at the end, I'll find you a home wherever you want to go. And I'll make sure you govern yourselves when you get there."

Carpenter peered at him through narrowed eyes with an air of suspicion and paranoia earned through long and difficult experience. Finally, though, he offered a hand in bargain and Logan shook it.

"What now?" Salvaggio asked him.

"Now, we send out the word," Logan told her. "The *Shakak* will hit the closest systems and use their communications networks to get on the mercenary job net and contact every mercenary unit we've contracted out as part of Wholesale Slaughter and bring them here."

"What if they don't want to be revolutionaries?" Salvaggio wondered. "We're talking about mercenaries, you know. Real ones, the kind who fight for money, not patriotism. What makes you think they'll fight for you?"

"Will you?" Lyta demanded, stepping over to the woman, almost nose to nose with her. "Will you fight for us?"

"For you? No." She grinned lopsidedly. "for the prospect of a piece of the action if you win...sure. I didn't get where I am by avoiding risks."

"There you go, then." Lyta patted Salvaggio on the shoulder with awkward comradery. "We just have to hope the rest of them are as bad at calculating the odds as you are."

10

Come on, you sorry sons of bitches!" Valentine Kurtz yelled into the general communications net loud enough to cause a burst of feedback in Logan's headphones. "You think you're gonna beat Starkad armor or worse, Spartan mecha with that kind of sloppy piloting? Hundred-meter separation in open ground, fifty meters when you're in tight like here in the canyons! Creighton, if you like D'Agostino so much, you should get with him after the war and make some beautiful babies, but right now you need to back the hell off!"

Logan laughed softly in the privacy of his mech cockpit. Kurtz had missed his calling; he should have been a trainer at the Academy. The two platoon mates from the imaginatively-named Bulwark Universal Private Military Company mumbled apologies and the lead mech, D'Agostino in a patched and pieced-together Reaper, picked up its pace, moving further down the broad canyon the locals called the Run. The afternoon sun beat down straight into them and he didn't envy the ground troops being trained by Lyta and her Rangers.

"Aren't you being a little hard on them, Val?" Logan asked, shuffling his own Scorpion closer to Kurtz's Golem. The two mecha represented half of all they had left, and they'd only managed to get them down from the *Shakak* by borrowing a cargo shuttle from one of the mercenary companies who had answered the call. "Not like they've had to fight anything but half-trained pirates before."

"Yeah, well, I'd be yelling at you, too, boss," Kurtz told him, "if you weren't my boss. You're driving that thing like it's a freaking cargo truck."

Logan winced, partly because Kurtz wasn't wrong. "I'm not used to the feel of this thing. I thought the Sentinel took some adjusting, but this Scorpion's even worse with the digitigrade knee joints. I don't know how the hell Paskowski did it."

He was almost able to say the man's name without the excruciating tightness in his chest now, over three months later.

"I still keep expecting him to saunter into the ready room every morning," Kurtz mused as if he were reading Logan's mind, "just a couple seconds before the morning meeting, and then Ford would roll her eyes and tell him if he wasn't five minutes early, he's late."

"And Paskowski would say 'if he wants me to be here five minutes early, he should schedule the meeting for five minutes earlier.' That always drove her nuts." He sighed. The pain was still there. He wondered how long it would last. "Come on, Val, we got four more companies to run through the tactical lanes, let's get moving."

"Companies," Kurtz scoffed, following along behind the Scorpion's slow shuffle with the stiff gate of the Golem. "They're a bunch of damned scout mecha and a few beat-up old Reapers or Agamemnons at best. I don't know how we're gonna take on line units with this kind of shit, Logan."

"We'll get them better machines," Logan assured him. "We just need the men trained."

"I'll do what I can."

"Colonel Brannigan, sir, this is Lewis at the Security office." The voice intruding on Logan's headphones was young and hesitant, one of the locals they'd been training to help monitor communications and orbital sensors. "We have another ship making orbit. The *Shakak* says it's got clearance and it's landing a couple of heavy-lift shuttles in a few minutes down at the spaceport. They wanted me to let you know it was a Captain Bohardt and that he wanted to meet you there at the port. He says he has something for you."

"Roger that, Security," Logan replied crisply. "For the record, a ship is a she, not an it."

He didn't bother correcting the kid for calling him "Brannigan" instead of "Conner." It had been happening with the mercenaries and the locals so much lately, he'd just started to accept it.

"Sorry, Val." Logan pulled the Scorpion up short, scraping its giant, oval footpads against the sandstone of the canyon floor and awkwardly swiveling the massive strike mech back the other direction. "Guess you'll have to run this bunch through without me. Bohardt's people are here, finally."

"I didn't expect them to show," Kurtz admitted. "It's been what? Almost two months now since you sent the word out?"

"Yeah, but from what Kammy said, it's getting harder to make it through Starkad and Spartan space. I imagine Modi's pretty paranoid now, too. Not everyone has a starship that can bend space."

We could have had a couple more, if they'd waited just a few months. He shook the thought off. *Or Starkad could have them.*

Probably best to leave what-ifs in Mithra's hands.

He thought of Ford and Paskowski and his father and had the unworthy thought that perhaps Mithra was no longer on their side.

"Holy shit," Logan breathed the words, shielding his eyes from the afternoon sun so he could stare up at the mech coming down the cargo shuttle's ramp with heavy, clomping steps.

It was sleek and deadly, plastrons extending up from its shoulders to give extra shielding to the missile launch pod on the left shoulder and the 30mm Vulcan cannon on the right. Its left hand was articulated, while the right ended in a plasma gun. It was a Vindicator, right down to the Spartan Mobile Armored Corps markings on the chest plastrons.

"You like it?" David Bohardt asked him, grinning broadly.

The man had given him a perfunctory handshake and greeting when he'd disembarked the Bastards' makeshift drop-ship, a converted heavy-lift cargo shuttle, but he'd been occupied with staging the unloading of their mecha and people for the last half an hour, leaving Logan waiting and wondering why the man had insisted he meet him at the landing field. And then the Vindicator had come down, last of all the Bohardt's Bastards machines. It stopped at the foot of the ramp as if posing for them.

"It's a beauty," Logan admitted, circling around the assault mech. It looked like thirty-five tons of pure death and part of him ached for a chance to pilot it. "Where the hell did you *get* it, though?"

Bohardt was still smiling but with a bit of an evil glint to his eye.

"We liberated it from some pirates who'd raided a Spartan military cargo transport," he admitted. "They'd taken the haul back to their base and wound up selling off most of it, but their captain kept this one for himself." He snorted. "Not that he knew how to even use it. Couldn't get past the military lock-out codes."

"But you could?" Logan asked, eyeing him sidelong.

"Hey, we weren't always mercs." The man spread his hands. "Some of us were in the Spartan Mobile Armored Corps back in the day. Anyway, we *had* intended to return this to the Spartan military...until we heard what was happening on Sparta. That's when I thought a mech like this would be better off with you."

Logan blinked at the statement, wondering if he'd heard the man right. The canopy had popped open and the pilot who'd walked the Vindicator down the ramp was climbing down the ladder rungs built into the side of the machine.

"I...uhh...," Logan stumbled over his words, glancing back and forth between the Vindicator and Bohardt. "I'm deeply grateful, Captain, and it couldn't come at a better time, but why wouldn't you just keep it for yourself?"

"Honest and truthful, sir," the mercenary said with a shrug, "if it were just Colonel Jonathan Slaughter I was dealing with, I definitely would. But since it's Logan Brannigan, the rightful heir to the Guardianship of Sparta, it only seems right to give it to you."

He'd been stunned before, but now the overwhelmed feeling of gratitude was replaced by a gut-deep fear. They'd done everything they could to keep this operation off the radar, not springing the truth on any of the PMC's they'd contacted until after they arrived. And he hadn't had the chance to tell Bohardt yet. If anyone knew who he was and where he was...

"Bohardt, how the hell did you know that?"

He hadn't meant the words to sound as harsh and accusatory as they did, particularly after the gesture of gifting him the Vindicator, but he had to know. Bohardt didn't seem offended. Instead, he laughed, as if this was the reaction he'd expected.

"Don't worry," he assured Logan, "your meet-up here is still a secret. But one of the reasons we took so long to get here was, we ran into someone who wanted a ride out here and it took a while to vet their credentials."

Logan had been too wrapped up in his conversation with the mercenary officer to notice the woman walking down the ramp behind the Vindicator until she was almost on top of them. She was an unassuming figure in dark, homespun robes and a hood half-covering her face, neither short nor tall, the sort of figure who could blend into a crowd. When she threw back the hood, the face it revealed was young, the dark brown hair pulled back into a simple bun over dark eyes.

"Mira!" Logan's mouth dropped open. Of all the people he might have expected to see, she had been close to the last. "What are you doing back here? The last time I saw you, you made it pretty clear you never wanted to see this place again."

Her mouth twisted in a wry smile so much older than the years of her appearance.

"I have discovered over the last few years, Colonel Brannigan," she said, her voice sounding somehow deeper and rougher than the last time he'd spoken with her, "that fate does not give a damn about what we want. I'm sure you've found the same thing as of late."

"How did you find out about me?" he asked her. "How many people know?"

"It's my job now to find things out. And in the process of my job, I've found some things you might like to know."

"Such as?" he invited, waving a hand in a prompting gesture.

"I have been on spaceships and space stations for the last two years," she said, arching an eyebrow. "What I have to tell you, I will say sitting at a real wood table on a comfortable chair, eating a steak not made from soy and drinking water not recycled from my own piss."

"You know the place better than me," Logan said. "Lead on."

"I don't mean to be rude," Terrin said, arms folded as he sat and watched Mira eat, "but who *are* you?"

"Oh, yeah," Katy said, elbows on the table, hands encircling the beer she'd ordered. "You never did get to meet Mira."

Mira hadn't stopped eating her steak, but she'd looked up at the mention of her name, taken a sip of water and then gone back to chewing.

"Mira worked for Lana Kane," Katy explained, pitching her voice to carry to all the people gathered at the longest table the largest restaurant in Revelation City had to offer. It was hand-polished wood and would have fetched a pretty penny even back on Sparta. She looked down the table at the gathered Ranger and mech officers and the mercenary commanders. "Kane was a facilitator on Trinity back when we passed through there looking for Terrin and Franny," she explained, nodding to the two of them, seated next to each other.

She didn't have to explain what Trinity was. The space station was notorious as a meeting place for bandits, pirates, smugglers and mercenaries, and Momma Salvaggio had, until recently, provided a cheap workforce to the station from the younger adults of Revelation as a way for them to repay the debt they owed to her. Lana Kane had been one of those young adults, but she'd built herself a thriving business of her own as someone who brokered meetings, introductions and exchanges of information. She'd been entrusted with the data crystals from Terminus and then held them hostage as a way to get Logan to liberate Revelation from both Salvaggio and Starkad.

"She died in the battle to retake this place," Katy added

quietly.

Mira did stop eating at that pronouncement, not in surprise but in what might have been a pang of grief for her friend.

"Mira led us here from Trinity when we were trying to find you," Katy finished, speaking to Terrin and Franny this time.

Acosta sat silently to her right, waiting with hands folded, ignoring the drink he'd ordered and glancing back at the waiters as if considering whether or not they should be chased out of here so they wouldn't hear anything top secret. On her left, Logan sipped at his drink and waited patiently. She knew him well enough to know he was worried. He got quiet when he was worried and the first few hundred times she'd tried to get him to open up about it had convinced her to let him stew in his own juices for a while until it passed.

She wasn't sure this one was going to pass.

"Now that we're all caught up," Logan finally said, once Mira's steak was down to the T-bone, "let's have it, Mira. Why did you come here and what did you want to tell us?"

"I've been working on Gateway," Mira said, wiping the corners of her mouth with a napkin. "Trying to set myself up with the same sort of business Ms. Kane had, but with a higher class of clientele."

Katy nodded understanding. Gateway was a larger, grander version of Trinity, a place for making deals and meeting clients, though the market there was grayer than it was black. Under-the-table arrangements were made on Gateway, but they more often involved corporations and politicians than they did pirates and mercenaries. Gateway was where they had gone to hire Donner Osceola and his starship, the original *Shakak* when all this had begun.

"Ms. Kane had contacts, leverage," Mira went on, "and I used those to establish myself. I began to do business with intelligence assets from Clan Modi and the Mbeki Imperium, passing information and payments back and forth between people who would rather not have been seen together. It was from one of my contacts in Mbeki that I discovered who you really are, Colonel Brannigan."

Katy frowned at that. People kept calling him Brannigan, assuming he had the same last name as his father, and it bothered her, though she wasn't sure why. Maybe it bothered her because it didn't seem to bother him. And maybe it was because she knew Logan Conner so well, but knew nothing of Logan Brannigan.

"How did they know?" Logan asked her, his voice calm but his eyes intense. "Were you able to find that out?"

"They learned it from agents in Starkad. Apparently, their new Intelligence chief, a woman named Laurent, knew your real identity and knew Wholesale Slaughter was a cover for a Spartan deep-cover operation."

"Did you say Laurent?" Lyta Randell asked, leaning forward in her chair, as if she might spring right out of it.

"That's the name I read in the files I stole," Mira confirmed.

"Shit." Lyta sat back in her chair, eyes glazed over as if she were in shock, and Katy wanted to ask her what was wrong, but Mira was still talking.

"So far," she said, "I have received no indication any of them know about Revelation. That is, Starkad knows you were here once, but they don't know you've returned or turned it into a base. They also don't seem to be aware of your extended Wholesale Slaughter project, bringing in other mercenaries under your company banner."

"We haven't exactly been keeping that a huge secret," Katy said, frowning.

"They've been preoccupied with other things, I'm sure," Mira pointed out, arching an eyebrow. "As a matter of fact, their preoccupation is the reason I'm here."

"She found us on Gateway," Bohardt explained around a mouthful of his own steak. The man could polish off a meal, Katy judged. "One of our guys was talking up Wholesale Slaughter, trying to drum up some recruiting for you, the way you said, and she collared me in a bar and told me we needed to keep our damn mouths shut."

"As I understand your situation from Captain Bohardt," Mira said, "you have plenty of mech pilots and infantry, but you lack machines."

"It's worse now," Logan admitted, a spasm of pain flickering across his face so briefly she wasn't sure anyone else could have caught it. Maybe Lyta and Terrin. "We had to abandon almost all our mecha on Sparta when..." He swallowed hard. "...when my father was killed. We have the four mecha that were on the *Shakak* being repaired at the time and now the Vindicator David picked up for me, and that's it."

"And most of the machines our subcontractors brought with them," Kurtz pointed out, a bit sourly, as if it were a sore spot for him, "are older and lighter."

"Starkad is heavily involved with the Spartan coup," Mira said, steepling her fingers in front of her. "Not just with supplying and supporting Rhianna Hale's forces, but also with keeping their forces deployed at the borders to avoid letting any rogue Spartan vessels escape. And their Intelligence network is spread as thin as their fleet, sniffing out opposition in the Spartan military and on colony worlds. It's left them stretched thin, drawn troops away from key areas that are now vulnerable."

"Key areas like what?" Acosta asked, speaking for the first time since she'd begun. The Intelligence officer didn't seem inclined to trust her. Katy wondered if he were right to be suspicious, wondered if she wasn't so accepting because she *wanted* Mira to be a friend, because they so desperately needed one.

"Have you ever heard of Farsund?" Mira asked, directing the question to Acosta.

"I think so," he said, nodding slowly as if trying to jog the memory into the front of his brain. "I think I read a report on it a couple years ago. Isn't it an arms depot?"

"Farsund is the planet," she corrected him. "The arms depot is technically called Eitri Base. It's the depot for Starkad's frontier with Clan Modi, so it's heavily stocked for the inevitable attempt to take back the Disputed Systems from Modi. Mecha, ammunition, weapons, spare parts, drop-ships. And it is currently guarded by one Supremacy Navy cruiser."

She smiled broadly and Katy found herself mirroring the expression.

Logan sat back in his chair, arms folded, expression sober and thoughtful, ignoring the chatter and cross-talk among the others. Katy was silent, watching his reaction. She had her own thoughts, but she was waiting to see what he would do, if he was ready to take the next step. She wondered if she wanted him to. It was necessary, it was what was right for his people, for Sparta. But what was it going to do to Logan Conner? Would he even exist anymore?

"Ladies and gentlemen," he said, finally, not raising his voice but cutting through the buzz of conversation just the same. "I brought you all together for a purpose. It was my government's, as you know now, but it was also my own. For a long time, I have made it my own, personal mission to rid the Dominions of pirates and bandits and hijackers." He reached out a hand and took hers, squeezing it tightly. It was, she knew, his own little way of letting her know he would never forget Ramman, that he knew she would never forget it, either. It was one of the reasons she loved him.

"And I'm still committed to that goal. But for now, I have a greater responsibility, to my crew, to the nation and people of

Sparta, and to the Five Dominions as a whole. We have to depose the traitor Rhianna Hale and reclaim the Guardianship, not because I want revenge for my father, although I do admit I burn to avenge his death. Not because I want the throne..." He shook his head, lip curling in distaste. "No. If I'm being frank with you, speaking soldier to soldier, I have no desire to rule. I've accomplished more in the last two years as a mercenary than I ever did as the son of a Guardian. Nor is it because I want a Brannigan on the throne, contrary to the propaganda Hale is spreading."

He stood, pacing back and forth along the line of the table, hands clasped behind him. "No, the reason Hale must be overthrown and Sparta retaken is that Starkad can't be allowed to control Sparta, can't be left unchecked. If they are, the entire Five Dominions is going to be thrown into a war that will destroy everything left of the Empire, destroy everything we've managed to rebuild since then." He paused, running his eyes over the mercenary captains he'd invited to the meeting. Salvaggio, Bohardt, Chen, Russell, Franco and Solana. "Some of you may be wondering if this is what you signed up for, if we're not in over our heads. Others may be thinking of the endgame, of the reward if you take down a Dominion, put a king in place. And there will be rewards for those who survive, trust me. But to do this, to pull it off..." He shook his head, laughing softly, without humor. "It's going to take everything we have.

"And the first thing it might take is our honor. We've spent the last two years fighting, hunting down, killing pirates and bandits and hijackers. But if we're going to get the weapons and ships and supplies we need, pirates and bandits and hijackers are exactly what we're going to have to become." He let out a breath in a sigh of regret. "And may Mithra have mercy on us all."

11

You know, you didn't *have* to come, dude," Kammy said quietly, giving him a sidelong glance from the captain's station.

Terrin Brannigan tried to swallow the frog in his throat and affect a smile, though he couldn't take his eyes off the main screen and the countdown to the jump.

"Is it that obvious?" he wondered. "I shouldn't really be nervous after everything, right? I mean, it's not the first space battle I've been in. Besides, if I'm not your engineering officer, who else you got who actually knows anything about how the drive works?"

He wiped sweaty palms on the shirt of his Wholesale Slaughter utility fatigues. Theoretically, they all should have been wearing Spartan Navy uniforms, but they simply didn't have enough and somehow, the Wholesale Slaughter gear seemed more appropriate to the task at hand. He'd gotten used to the crossed swords and laughing skull, as gaudy and cliched as it had seemed to him at first.

"Don't let Kammy scare you, kid," Tara Gerard told him, sprawled casually at her station. He was fairly certain she enjoyed the artificial gravity more than any of them. It was hard to look intentionally casual in free fall. "We're happy as hell to have you along. You're like our good luck charm."

"It's true," Nance said from the communications console, though Terrin thought her tongue was planted firmly in her cheek. "We've never lost a space battle when you were along."

"Yeah, but you're like, second in line to the throne behind your brother," Kammy objected, forehead creasing as he seemed to be thinking about the mechanics of that. "That makes you like a spare heir, right? And since Jonathan..." He scowled. "Dammit. Since *Logan* is like, always on the front lines trying to get himself killed, shouldn't we keep you someplace safe, just in case?"

"Oh, sweet Mithra, you do *not* want me as a Guardian," Terrin insisted, eyes going wide. "It took Starkad twenty years to figure out how to depose my father. I probably wouldn't last five minutes." He paused and took a breath, still feeling an emptiness inside his chest whenever he thought of his father's death. "I'm a scientist, not a soldier or a politician. I don't *want* to be anything more than a scientist, and as soon as all this is over, I'm going right back to *just* being a scientist."

"Ten seconds to jump," Kammy announced, touching a button to transmit the announcement over the ship's public address system. "Everyone to battle stations and prepare for immediate enemy action."

The jump made Terrin's skin crawl. He knew it affected everyone differently and some it didn't affect at all, like his brother. It gave him a feeling like he'd been stretched out too far and hadn't quite rebounded back all the way, not something he could adequately explain in words. He didn't have the time to think about it, since general quarters sounded with a nerve-jangling klaxon the second they were through.

"Enemy vessel at L5 position between Farsund and its

primary moon," Tara reported immediately before Terrin could even make sense of the data on the main screen.

"Full power to the drives," Kammy said, his voice flat and businesslike, so unlike his normal cadence. He had really stepped into the captain's role. "Helm, set an intercept course for the Starkad cruiser."

"Engaging," Lt. Commander Bergh confirmed from the helm position. He was Spartan Navy, signed on after the battle at Terminus to take Kammy's old position at the ship's virtual wheel, while Tara had moved into the XO spot. Terrin hadn't spent much time with the spare, soft-chinned man, but he seemed affable enough and competent at his job. "Acceleration analog of thirty-five gravities. Forty. Fifty. We're at full output."

The ship seemed to shoot forward, the view on the screen changing swiftly. It was a simulation, he knew. It had to be. The ship's drive warped the fabric of spacetime around it, including photons, so the actual image from the external cameras would be something psychedelically twisted, incomprehensible to the human mind. The computers took the sensor data and combined it with a decoded and recombined reading of the incoming image to put together the simulation they saw on the screen; but the Imperial systems were so advanced, it was very difficult to tell the difference. The planet and its small, captured asteroid of a moon certainly looked real enough.

Farsund itself was green and blue and white. Mostly white, which meant it was currently in ice age and had been since before humans entered space for the first time. He'd studied up on the world during the week-long voyage, which helped distract him from thinking of Franny, who'd stayed behind on Revelation to help refit the mercenary ships' tactical networks and get everyone on the same combat programming. Farsund had been a civilian colony once, before the fall of the Empire, then had been briefly conquered by the Jeuta before Starkad and Modi had banded together for a brief moment in their long history of warfare to drive the genetically engineered species out of the Dominions. After Farsund had been taken back, there'd been none of its original colonists left alive and no one had wanted to resettle the place, so the Supremacy Navy had set up a military base.

"Twenty minutes till intercept," Tara announced, tracing lines on her touch screens with the forefingers of both hands, her motion like a conductor leading an orchestra. "No sign he's picked us up yet."

Starkad undoubtedly had satellite surveillance on the jump point, but most systems would be on the lookout for the tell-tale thermal signature of a fusion drive. It was impossible to hide, and until they'd found the *Shakak II*, there had been no way to sneak through a jump point, which had saved their lives over and over. They couldn't have even made it to Farsund without passing through Starkad-held jump-points, but even if anyone had noticed their passage, the drive field distorted the light around the *Shakak*, which prevented it from giving a clean reflection and made it very difficult to even identify it as a ship.

Hmmm. There must be some way to use the distortion to simulate the signature of a different ship. I wonder if I can get Franny to help me run some numbers on that when we get back...

"Oh, she's seen us now," Tara said, cutting into the equations he'd been spinning through his brain. "Burning this way at six gravities. Updated intercept time is seven minutes, thirty-three seconds."

"Too fast," Kammy muttered, shaking his head. "Dude isn't going to be able to do much once he reaches us."

Terrin knew from experience how miserable six gravities was on a conventional starship using a reaction drive. Just staying conscious was exhausting after a few minutes of the increased perceived weight, much less thinking.

"He's panicked," Tara assessed, sniffing in a dismissive sort of way, as if it were someone else's problem. "He's looking at something batshit crazy and..." The woman squinted at the screen, then adjusted the view, zooming in on a section of the planet as if the oncoming warship wasn't important. "Holy shit," she murmured. "You seeing what I'm seeing coming around the terminator of the planet?"

Terrin tried to get a look at whatever it was, but he couldn't make heads or tails of the sensor data, though it obviously meant something to the two of them. Kammy's grin was so wide it looked as if it would split his broad face in two. He touched a control on his console and leaned over the audio pickup.

"*Ho'onani*," he said. It was his nickname for Lyta Randell. He'd told Terrin it meant "beautiful" in some ancient language he'd learned from his great-grandmother. "We got a repair dock in orbit here and sensors say there are two Starkad destroyers being serviced there."

There was a long, silent pause and Terrin wondered if she'd heard his message. She was with Logan and his makeshift mech company in one of the converted cargo shuttles Bohardt's crew used as a drop-ship, borrowed for this mission, and it was entirely possible the thing's comm systems had gone down again.

"I got you, Kammy," Lyta's voice came over speakers concealed in the fabric of the walls, sounding as if the woman were standing right beside him. "We're going to call an audible. I'm transferring to Duane's assault shuttle with a boarding party. After we drop Logan, you'll take us in range."

"Yes, ma'am," Kammy acknowledged, laughing in appreciation.

"Is everybody forgetting we still got this guy coming toward us at six gees?" Terrin wondered, pointing at the tactical display, where a very large, red icon was still approaching.

"Have faith, dude," Kammy adjured him, frowning. Then his voice slipped back into what Terrin had come to think of as "command mode." "Time till they're in range of the main gun?"

"Three minutes, twelve seconds," Tara provided.

"Capacitors charged?"

"Would I take us into battle if they weren't?" She sounded offended by the notion.

"Target their drives."

"They have deflectors on full power." It wasn't exactly a warning, more of an observation by the Tactical officer. So far, conventional ship's deflectors hadn't done a whole lot against the *Shakak*'s particle accelerator except prolong the process. "They're launching anti-ship missiles. Three of them. Estimated time of intercept one minute."

Terrin's eyes went wide. That was overkill; one of the gigantic missiles was enough to take out a starship, and even a Starkad heavy cruiser only carried four of the behemoths.

"They really are panicking," he realized.

"Yo, scientist," Kammy said, casting a sidelong glance that might have been nervous. "You sure this thing can take a fusion blast that size? Like, if they all hit us at once?"

"Am I sure?" Terrin repeated, a catalog of test results running through his memory. "No, I can't be certain. The Navy never tried anything quite that powerful, probably because they didn't want to damage the ship. Theoretically, it's possible for the drive field to overload if you pump enough energy into it."

"And what the hell happens if it overloads?" Tara asked, spinning in her seat to stare at him, appalled.

"It'd collapse," he explained. "We'd be left sitting with no momentum right where we were when it failed."

"Totally naked to whatever this joker shoots at us," Kammy surmised. He rolled his eyes and turned back to Tara. "Target the missiles and take them out."

"Retargeting on the closest of them," she affirmed, finger tracing spirals on her screen. "Firing in ten seconds."

The beam itself was a barely-visible blue glow in a vacuum, but the computer simulated it as it did everything else it considered important, drawing a line of white fire between them and the approaching fusion flare of the missiles, each of them the size of an assault shuttle, armored with centimeters of BiPhase Carbide capable of shunting off the primary laser on a heavy cruiser for at least one or two shots. Where the white fire connected, a flare of expanding gas formed a small supernova and that was something the computer didn't *have* to simulate.

It all had a distant quality to it, though, and Terrin wondered if it was because of the artificial gravity. He'd experienced it before on the original *Shakak*, but the grueling agony of constant acceleration and maneuvering had given immediacy to the fight, brought home the life-and-death stakes. They were travelling at a few percentages of lightspeed now, but sitting on their butts as if it were all a simulator back on Sparta. It was easy to think it wasn't real.

"That's two of them down," Tara announced.

"That's enough," Kammy decided. Retarget the cruiser and tell me when the capacitors are recharged."

"That last one is gonna blow in ten seconds," Tara said, her tone matter-of-fact.

"Yeah, I know." A bit of Kammy's native accent worked its way back into his neutral "starship captain" voice, just a hint of how nervous he was. "Carry on."

Terrin tried not to move his lips as he counted down the seconds inside his head. When he reached zero, he squeezed his eyes shut and... *Yeah, there it is.* A trembling, a vibration through the ship, not like an impact but more a wave tossing them sideways, like a rowboat on a lake hitting the wake of a ferry. He forced his eyes open and checked the readings from the field generator.

"We had some feedback," he reported. "It dampened the field output maybe twenty, twenty-five percent for a few seconds, but it's back to full strength now."

"Yeah, let's make a note of that," Tara cracked. "Don't let them shoot fusion missiles at us anymore." She sobered at a quelling glare from Kammy. "Thirteen seconds until the capacitors are charged for another shot," she added. "Still two minutes to intercept range."

"We're back up to full acceleration analog," Bergh said, cool and unruffled. "Everything is stable again."

Kammy turned back toward Terrin, frowning massively.

"Dude, can you stop with the damned tapping?"

Terrin looked down, realized he was tapping his toe against the deck unconsciously, the nervous energy working its way out of him. He planted his foot firmly against the deck, then offered an apologetic shrug to Kammy.

"He's firing his primary laser battery at us," Tara said, pointing at the screen.

The Starkad cruiser was close enough for the computer to give it physical features instead of a generic red delta threat icon. It shone bright silver in the reflection of the starlight, a wedge-shaped monster against the white and blue circle of Farsund. A line of scintillating red shot out from its dorsal laser batteries, again a computer-generated convenience, since there was nothing to refract the beam of photons in the depths of space. The crimson light splashed in surreal spirals around the periphery of the *Shakak*, distorted away by the drive field, but again, Terrin noticed a slight dip in field efficiency.

"About a five percent drop in stability," he said. "He's at extreme range though. That laser could bring us down maybe thirty percent up close."

"Also good to know for future reference," Kammy allowed, grudgingly. Terrin thought he looked disappointed that his shiny new ship wasn't quite as invulnerable as he'd hoped.

It's science, not magic.

"Let's not give him the chance for another shot. Tactical, are we within maximum range for the main gun?"

"Not *optimal* range," she equivocated with something of a scowl, "but yeah, we'll put a hitch in the bitch's step if we hit her from here."

"Target her laser emitter and fire."

Mithra alone knew what the particle cannon fired, because the Spartan Navy's best researchers hadn't been able to figure it out. Terrin suspected it was antihydrogen, but Dr. Kovalev insisted it couldn't be, due to the output from the test bed, though he had no real suggestions as to what else it could be. Whatever it used for ammunition, it splashed into the nose of the Starkad cruiser with a devastating flare of vaporized metal, a halo of burning gas surrounding the bow of the starship. The cruiser sailed through the cloud, still in one piece, but the sensors told the real story.

"I'm reading a huge thermal bloom all down their dorsal weapons mount," Tara said, her teeth showing in a smile that wouldn't have been out of place on a stalking wolf. "That laser focusing is so much junk now."

The star-bright fusion fire expanding from the cruiser's drive bell abruptly winked out, leaving behind a glowing after-image in Terrin's vision.

"Did we disable him?" Terrin blurted, knowing it wasn't likely but hoping they'd been lucky.

The words had barely made it out of his mouth when he saw the white jet of flame surging from one of the ring of maneuvering thrusters circling the aft end of the cruiser just fore of the drive bell.

"She's pulling a skew-flip," Kammy judged. "She's making a run back for the planet, hoping to use their orbital defenses against us."

"Gonna take her forever to decelerate after that high-gee burn," Bergh said.

They sounded so calm, Terrin thought. As if this were just another day, just a drill back at the proving grounds, or a computer simulation. A year or two ago, he might have thought they actually weren't nervous, weren't afraid of dying. He knew better now and he envied them their ability to hide their fear.

"Hit them before they restart the main drive, Tara," Kammy told the Tactical officer. There was a tinge of regret in the order, a hint of wistfulness.

"Capacitors will be recharged in ten seconds." Tara's hand hovered over the firing control, watching the power reading travel up the scale from red toward green.

On the main screen, the cruiser was still traveling toward them on its momentum from the boost, its aft end swinging slowly around even under the full thrust of the steering jets.

They're trying to move a hell of a lot of mass. Physics doesn't change just because you're desperate.

"In range," Tara droned, her attention fixed on the readouts. "Capacitors fully charged. Firing now."

The shot was perfectly placed, striking the cruiser at the juncture of the drive bell and the radiation shield, spearing through to the fuel tanks for the maneuvering thrusters. The particle beam burned through the thinner armor there, undeterred by the electromagnetic deflector screens, and the propellant for the steering jets detonated in a rocket blast opposite the thruster already firing. Bereft of its fuel feed, the controlled thrust ended and the entire load of propellant burned off in a giant torch from the starboard aft of the cruiser, a signal flare begging for help when none would come.

"That had to have jacked up the fuel feed for their main drive." Tara leaned back in her seat, smacking a palm against her console in triumph. "They can't maneuver and they can't boost and that thing's gonna drift right out of the system unless they hit the gravity well for the gas giant sometime next year."

"It's worse than that," Kammy said, not sounding near as happy about it as his Tactical officer. "With the velocity they built up, even if they do try to evacuate in their shuttles, they'll never have enough fuel to get back to Farsund."

"Damn," Terrin whispered, the realization hitting him. "As long as the reactor holds out, they'll have heat and oxygen, and they can get water from their recycling plant, but..."

"They're going to run out of food," Kammy finished the thought for him. "That's why in a war, there are trans-Dominion treaties about aiding stranded vessels. And if we were in a war, and we were fighting for the Spartan Navy, which we technically used to be, I'd be forced to stop and help them. But since Starkad didn't bother to declare war, and since we're not working for the official Spartan government anymore, and don't have the time, or energy, or personnel, or supplies to deal with a shitload of enemy prisoners..." The big man hissed out a breath. "Well, the poor bastards are on their own. Bergh, take us into orbit. Tara, get ready to target their orbital weapons platforms."

Kammy hit the intercom control. "Colonel," he transmitted, "the Starkad ship is neutralized. Tell your pilots to get ready. You are cleared for launch in fifteen minutes." He shot a grin at Terrin, though it didn't seem to reach all the way to his eyes. "Now the fun really starts."

12

Stardrives were nice for a ship, but Kathren Margolis enjoyed the gut-level thrill of the boost. It pushed at you like a bully on a schoolyard, trying to find out just how much you could take. She reveled in it as it slammed her back into her acceleration couch, an insistent detractor trying to tell her no, she *couldn't* fly that fast, but she did it anyway, to spite him.

Farsund screamed toward her, closer with every second, the abstract lines of white and blue and green acquiring texture and depth with proximity. Mountain ranges capped with trackless glaciers split the primary continent in two, the ice growing thicker near the poles until it squeezed everything else out, turning what would have been an ocean in a warmer climate into chains of saltwater lakes. It was starkly beautiful, a place she could have seen herself visiting for a cross-country skiing vacation, though she wouldn't have wanted to live there.

Their target was as close to the equator as it could be without setting it afloat in the middle of the narrow ocean ringing the planet's center, one of the small, isolated strips of green amidst all the white. She couldn't see the missile batteries or the coilgun turrets from the upper atmosphere, but she knew they were down there, ringing the Starkad base like spines on a hedgehog. These weren't pirates or second-rate bandits, ripe for the picking. If she didn't take out their air defenses, the drop-ship was as good as dead.

Drop-ship my ass. It's a beat-up old cargo shuttle, the best the mercs could afford, with some armor and a chin cannon slapped onto it.

The Supremacy troops below weren't just going to wait for her to come to them, though...they were coming to her. A squadron of dual-environment fighters was climbing to meet them, already rising above the towering mountains, wicked, silver darts on roaring turbojet engines. If she'd waited in the almost thinner reaches of the upper atmosphere, she would have had a greater advantage. The fighters were powered by small fusion plants, but their turbines were smaller, more fragile and more prone to overheating. In the near-vacuum at the edge of space, there was nowhere to bleed off that heat.

They knew that, too, though, and they'd be very happy just to sit down in the soup and wait for her.

Nothing's ever easy.

"Have you ever taken on fighters before?" Acosta asked her from the right-hand seat. At least he didn't sound like a nervous mother this time. *Maybe I've killed all his fear instincts after so long flying with me.*

"In training," she told him, biting down on the mischievous smile that wanted so badly to break through. "Simulators and shit."

"Oh, great," he muttered, shaking his head.

Finally, she gave in and laughed. "We'll be fine, Francis. Just man the Vulcan, I'll take the laser. Don't waste ammo."

"What about our missiles?" he wondered, already toggling through the control board to transfer the 20mm rotary cannon mounted in the wing to the trigger on his steering yoke. "They can't have much in the way of anti-missile defenses on those fighters."

"We need the missiles to take out the anti-aircraft batteries," she reminded him, making sure the capacitors for the laser were fully charged. "Just trust me."

The fighters broke wide and banked around as she descended, trying to box her in and she shut out Acosta's questions and ran down a technical brief to herself about the capabilities of the enemy birds. Starkad Falk Jagerfly air-superiority fighters, top of the line but mostly used for planetary defense. 20mm chin cannons but they couldn't carry much ammo for them. A laser not much more powerful than a scout mech could carry, which wouldn't do more than bake the paint on an armored assault shuttle. Four anti-aircraft missiles each, and they'd be counting on those to do the work for them. Their warheads weren't large and they didn't have much range, but they could kill her jets if they managed a tail shot and they wouldn't do a damn bit of good for her control surfaces if they hit a wing.

She had the power and the speed, but the fighters were feathers on the wind, maneuverable as all hell, and they'd try to use that to keep her distracted so the ground batteries could deal with her. They also had next to no armor and could be brought down with harsh language if you could manage to hit them.

You're the hotshot pilot, babe. Time to show these Starkad assholes how it's done. Think you can outmaneuver me in those little freaking toys, huh?

"Hold tight, Francis."

There were things you could do with a shuttle you wouldn't even think of doing with a fighter, simply because they weren't nearly as durable. She cut power to the main engines and used the maneuvering thrusters and belly jets to send the shuttle tumbling into what would have been a flat spin if she hadn't immediately powered out of it, lighting up the drives again, pushing her back into her acceleration couch with a punishing, excruciating gee-load.

The air went out of Acosta in a high-pitched wheeze, like someone squeezing a balloon in their hands and she hoped he wasn't about to throw up. She wouldn't blame him if he did, because her lunch was knocking at the door of her throat. But the maneuver had flipped her end for end and put one of the enemy fighters right into the targeting reticle of her laser. Lightning struck, a static charge following the ionized air from the superheated blast of photons, as if Zeus himself was smiting the swing-wing dart out of the sky.

There wasn't much left of it after the laser pulse cored it through the center. Plasma from the small fusion plant and pure, ambient heat from the high-energy photons turned thin BiPhase carbide and metal to vapor and spread it over the sky in a yellow and white brush stroke across the blue canvas.

"They're launching," Acosta warned her, his words muffled as if he were shoving them past the acceleration and the incipient nausea. "We have two missiles inbound." She saw him reach out against the gee load and flip three switches on his control console. "Launching countermeasures."

She heard the gentle bump-bump-bump of the electrostatically-charged chaff dropping from ports in the wings, saw them bursting with miniature sun-flashes of thermite, the perfect mix of ingredients to confuse the missiles on their tail. Katy banked left and climbed, using the shuttle's superior power to her advantage, knowing the Falk Jagerfly fighters would have to follow. They'd committed, and whatever their nationality, they were pilots and she knew pilots.

"All three missiles scratched," Acosta reported.

He really was good at this job now, though she'd never admit it to him. For someone whose training as a copilot had consisted of a two-week familiarization course from Military Intelligence before his assignment, he'd managed to make himself dependable at least as flight support. She still wouldn't have trusted him to fly the bird himself, but then, she didn't trust *anyone* to fly her bird.

"Two of them are pursuing," he went on, his eyes glued to the sensor readouts. "One is circling in patrol above the base."

"I see them."

She'd pulled up into a steeper and steeper ascent until she had the assault shuttle standing on its tail, riding the candle, forcing the fighters to run their jets close to the redline. She knew they'd have to launch missiles again rather than continue to chase her higher into the edge of the atmosphere, and they did. Two more streaks of fire arced away from the Falks at twenty gravities of boost, more than a human could take and stay conscious.

"They just..." Acosta began.

"I know."

She cut power and flipped the shuttle end for end in the space of three seconds, watching the missiles get way too close before she switched off the turbojets and hit the fusion drive for just a fraction of a second. They were high in the atmosphere, high enough and with the air thin enough she was fairly certain the plasma wouldn't cause a shockwave and knock them out of the sky. A 300-kilogram sack of concrete slammed Katy back into her acceleration couch and she tasted blood in her mouth where she'd slipped and bit her own lip, but there was no time to give in to pain or weakness. They were plummeting planet-ward, depowered, a giant dart heading not just towards unforgiving land but right into the firing arc of all those ground defenses.

"Shit," Acosta blurted. She could hear his breathing, heavy and frantic beside her as he watched their descent on the screen. She could feel it in her gut, the free-fall, zero-gravity sensation she'd learned to love.

She powered up the turbines with a touch on a control beside the steering yoke, but instead of pulling up, she added their boost to their own gravity-aided course. The free-fall sensation went away, replaced by the sheer terror of accelerating straight down.

"What the hell, Katy?"

"This is gonna hurt," she warned him.

On the tactical display, the view of the Starkad base was magnified by the external cameras, a series of huge, fortified warehouses and smaller base housing, and at their perimeter were the two missile batteries. Rectangular pods mounted on motorized gimbals, the launch batteries were rising up on their mounts, spinning in place, hunting for her, guided by the radar dishes emplaced between them. She toggled her targeting screen to the shuttle's multi-purpose missiles, guided the targeting reticle over the emplacement to the north of the base and thumbed the launch control.

She barely felt the missile separating out of the internal weapons bay, didn't watch the tactical screen to see if it flew true. She put all her strength, all her concentration into yanking up on the steering yoke, throttling up the turbines as the shuttle slowly, reluctantly pulled out of the power dive. She hadn't been lying to Acosta. It hurt. Every muscle in her body seemed to cramp at once and she let out an involuntary scream of pain, rage, and frustration, but she kept pulling on the stick and the nose came up and up and...

Sweet Jesus!

She didn't even have the breath left to speak by the time the shuttle began to arc upwards, only meters above the roof of the central warehouse, each crack and rut and moisture stain in its tar-black surface visible in the finest detail as it slid by beneath her. A fireball rose above the roofline, red and angry against the afternoon sky, just a flicker of an image out of the corner of her eye before the shuttle pulled up and away. The missile had hit, hopefully on target.

Her forearms quivered with the effort of holding the steering yoke against its stops, keeping the belly of the shuttle only meters above the rising face of the rugged hill behind the paved landing field. She was sure the enemy fighters were still incoming, but she'd have to trust Acosta to watch them.

"The two we left up high are still five kilometers away," he told her as if he'd read her mind. He was squeezing the words past the stress, but he hadn't passed out yet, which was impressive. "The last guy is coming in at our four o'clock, five hundred meters!"

"Priorities, Francis," she growled, wishing he'd started with the last bit.

She jerked the control yoke to the port just as the warning chime let her know the fighter had missile lock on her. He'd taken a chance, launching from about three hundred meters away, and it was the wrong call. The missile streaked by, too close to have time to curve around and follow her, slamming into the hillside instead. Dirt and rock exploded away in a cloud that rolled across the valley, billowing up around the shuttle and twisting in tight curls as the jets roiled through it.

She stayed low, circumnavigating the edge of the valley, trying to stay below the firing arc of the weapons emplacements and keep the fighters from launching their remaining missiles at her. Buildings flashed by the edges of her wings, the surrounding hills blurring into a haze of green and brown.

"Get ready to fire," she told Acosta, toggling to the laser. "You won't have much time."

She curved tight, kicking them around with a brief burst from the belly jets to claw an extra degree of turn, bringing the nose of the shuttle in line with the row of air defense turrets.

"Now!"

Katy triggered the laser and it seemed to split reality in two, cleaving through concrete bunker and metal framework with a scalpel that could slip between atoms. The remaining missile launch pod vanished in a fireball of flash ignition, engulfing everything around them, including the radar dishes and the machine gun turrets guarding them. She pulled away from the expanding inferno, not even noticing Acosta had managed to get a shot off until she heard him whooping loudly.

"I got the coilgun!" he bragged, pounding a fist against the console like a rookie just out of flight school scoring his first kill.

"Good shot," she said, without sarcasm for once. It had been. He'd had maybe two seconds to target and fire, while under about four gees of pressure.

She risked a look at the rear cameras as she pulled up to meet the remaining fighters, saw the entire grassy plain behind the base burning, clouds of inky black smoke pouring off the defense emplacements.

"Drop-ship One," she transmitted, "you are clear for landing."

"What about the fighters?" he reminded her, gesturing above them.

"Oh, I think we can take care of those." She toggled to missiles, now that she didn't need to save them for the air defenses. "If they're stupid enough to stick around now, they deserve what they're about to get."

Seat restraints bit into Logan's shoulders and he bit down on the mouthpiece inside his helmet to keep his teeth from clashing as his chin thumped against his chest. Hundreds of tons of drop-ship and mecha and human cargo jolted back and forth as the craft settled into the played-out hydraulics of the landing gear. The touchdown was much rougher than Logan was used to, but he didn't know whether to blame it on the Bohardt pilot or the half-assed cargo shuttle the woman was forced to fly. He hoped it was the ship, because he didn't have any spare pilots.

"Wholesale Slaughter, follow me!" he yelled, hitting the control to free his Vindicator of its restraint gantry as the boarding ramps lowered.

This would have been a perfect time for an air drop, but half their mecha didn't have jump-jets, they had no single-use drop harnesses and the damned ship wasn't equipped for it anyway.

So, we do it the old-fashioned way.

He stomped down the ramp, feeling it lurch beneath him, the weight of his mech wrenching its hydraulic lift mechanism beneath him. He hit the jump-jets right off the end of the metal, an awesome sense of freedom filling his chest as the Vindicator flew. He hadn't flown in so long, had felt for a year as if his feet were nailed to the ground, weights strapped to his shoulders.

He heard a whoop in his headphones and would have believed he'd uttered it unintentionally if he hadn't seen Kurtz's Golem arcing down beside him, landing within a few meters of his. First Platoon rumbled out behind him, the last of the Wholesale Slaughter mecha, two more Golems, a Valiant and the Scorpion, piloted by the surviving senior officers from his company. Behind them were the reserves, the heaviest mecha in Bohardt's Bastards, who were the best trained and equipped of the mercenary units they'd signed on. David Bohardt led them personally in his Valiant assault mech, and he wasn't worried nearly as much about the man or those who followed him as he was about their machines.

Just have to take care of that today.

"Here they come, boss," Kurtz said.

Logan missed the sensor arrays and command-and-control consoles from the Sentinel, but he didn't need sensors to see the enemy. They were rushing out in front of God and radar, piling through the broad doorway of a massive hangar, two heavy platoons, all of them assault mecha. His mouth watered at the thought of what else was in the hangar, but he kept his thoughts on the task at hand.

"Bohardt," he ordered, breaking into a long, loping run towards the enemy, "my people are going to engage. Circle around and secure that hangar before they get any more pilots geared up!"

"Gotcha covered, sir." Bohardt's tone was relaxed and laconic as usual. Logan wondered how the man had ever wound up a hired gun. If he'd been one of Logan's platoon leaders, he would have had him heading for Command School as soon as he was eligible.

"Wholesale Slaughter, spread wide and take these Starkad assholes down."

He launched a spread of missiles from his shoulder pod, the Vindicator's stride dragging a half-step as the weight shot away. A dozen other streaks of white arced out alongside his, and the Starkad mecha were launching as well, the missiles crossing each other in mid-air like a volley of arrows at the onset of some medieval scrimmage from old Earth.

He didn't raise a shield to fend off the flight of enemy projectiles, though. His strategy was to not be there when they hit. He jammed his heels into the jump-jet pedals and the Vindicator soared upward, topping the downward arc of the incoming missiles. Lasers and ETC cannon rounds ripped past him, but none of the enemy rose to meet him, and he'd fought enough battles to know why. Starkad warriors were many things, but cowardly wasn't one of them. Being a coward in the Supremacy military was a good way to get yourself executed, which meant they weren't holding back because they were afraid.

They were holding back because their leader was hesitant, probably either young or long past their prime, stuck out here in the middle of nowhere, guarding weapons for other men and women to use, to go obtain glory for the Supremacy. Hesitant leaders trained their troops to be hesitant, and they didn't lead from the front.

He zeroed in on an Agamemnon positioned between the two parallel wedges of mecha, right where a by-the-book, unimaginative armor officer would be. The Agamemnon tried to raise its arm-mounted laser, but it was too late, Logan was already firing. A gout of ionized gas heated to plasma by the Vindicator's fusion reactor, held together and accelerated by a magnetic field, caught the Starkad mech in the right shoulder and burned through the armor, the actuators, the power couplings and most of the joint, leaving the right arm hanging by a fragile thread of metal cable, the charred end of the power coupling sparking fitfully. The Agamemnon stumbled, off-balance from the sudden shift of weight, and had no time to adjust before Logan's Vindicator landed nearly on top of it.

Logan's plasma gun would take a few more seconds to recharge, but his 30mm Vulcan was lined up perfectly with the Agamemnon's cockpit and he'd toggled his firing control to the rotary cannon before the mech's feet touched the ground. He saw the man's face through the transparent aluminum slats of his cockpit canopy, through the narrow opening of his helmet, just revealing the nose up to the forehead, pale and glistening with a thin sheen of nervous sweat. His eyes were wide, beneath the rim of his helmet, the muscles of his face tensed as if he were biting down on his mouthpiece and Logan was sure he could sense fear in the man, not of dying but of something so much worse: failure.

Logan squeezed the trigger and the Vulcan roared its indifference to the Starkad pilot's fear. 30mm tungsten slugs blasted through the BiPhase Carbide frame and the transparent aluminum panels and all the young man's dreams of glory and fears of failure disappeared. His mech didn't fall, just stood motionless, a ghost machine waiting for orders from a dead pilot.

Logan used the ghastly memorial as cover, stretching his Vindicator's right-hand plasma gun around the side and firing a blast of starfire at the closest machine in the second wedge formation, a Lykos, long-limbed and rangy with an ETC cannon mounted along its right arm. The enemy mech's cannon thundered almost simultaneously, the round slamming through the back of the dead Agamemnon, coring its fusion reactor in a spray of plasma plumes. Logan jumped backwards, just a tap on the jump-jet controls with the balls of his feet, enough to take the Vindicator ten meters, clear of the blinding spray of ionized gas and the halo of burning metal and give him a straight shot at the Lykos with his Vulcan.

The plasma blast had charred a crater in the right chest plastron of the Lykos, but hadn't nailed the cockpit and hadn't managed to disable the right arm and the cannon it held. The mech was slow to react, the movements of its arm jerky and spastic as it tried to realign its main weapon, and he wasn't sure if that was from damage to the machine or the effect of the heat of the plasma impact on the pilot. He was about to try to finish the job when someone took care of it for him, a glowing spear of tungsten moving so fast, all he could see of it was the heat of its passage ionizing the air behind it. The Lykos was caught in mid-step and unlike the Agamemnon, it went down, crashing into pavement already cracked by seasonal temperature swings and fracturing it to small chunks of cement.

Logan scanned back and forth, searching for a target, but there were none. The enemy mecha were burning, motionless, two ejection seats floating back to earth on parachutes the only indication of survivors.

"Casualty report?" he asked brusquely, not wanting to give in to the premature elation of a skirmish won.

"Minor damage," Kurtz told him. "This was a bunch of scrubs," he added, echoing Logan's earlier judgement. "They never expected a real attack here, the smug, overconfident shitheads."

"They only have so many troops," Logan reminded him, "and they have them spread out way too thin. Bohardt," he called. "What's your situation?"

He could see the man's IFF transponder, knew he was in the hangar, but the smoke and dust clouds from the mech battle blocked his view of the building.

"There were a few dismounts," the mercenary captain replied, "but we cleared them out pretty quick." He paused and Logan thought he could hear the grin in his voice. "It's everything we thought it would be. You might want to come take a look yourself."

"Roger that." He switched frequencies back to Kurtz. "Val, set up a defensive perimeter around the drop-ship, get Captain Grant and his Rangers out here to pull security, and send in the pilots and crews. I'm going to go see what all the fuss is about."

He took the Vindicator through the drifting smoke and past the unadorned concrete-block bunkhouses where the base personnel made their barracks. Heads popped out of the side doors, tiny figures carrying rifles. He swiveled his torso to the left and cut loose with the machine guns mounted in a niche of his chest armor, spraying the side of the barracks with 6mm rounds. Chips of concrete block fragmented and sprayed shrapnel and the heads and the rifles ducked back inside. He hoped they stayed there. Starkad was the enemy, but he didn't want a massacre.

The hangar lay beyond two featureless warehouses, each a good twenty meters high and probably two hundred meters on a side, and the hangar was at least as big as either of them. Behind it stood a beautiful sight, squatting in bulbous, utilitarian ugliness on the broad, unpaved landing field behind the hangar: half a dozen Starkad drop-ships, just waiting for flight crews to come and fire them up. It would take Starkad military activation codes, but luckily, Mira and Acosta had provided them, and they'd brought the pilots along with them from Revelation.

Bohardt's two platoons of mecha were spread around the front of the hangar, its broad doors gaping open now, though he imagined they could be shut tight against Farsund's savage winters. A Reaper and a Golem moved aside to give his Vindicator space to pass and he stepped up behind Bohardt's Valiant. The man had his canopy open and was leaning out onto the edge, staring as if he had to see with his own eyes to believe what was in front of him.

Row upon row of mecha were lined up in the hangar, a full battalion worth of them. Arbalest missile carriers, Scorpion and Nomad strike mecha, Valiant and Agamemnon assault mecha and Peregrine scouts. It wasn't quite the arsenal Logan had seen on Terminus, but these were far more useful since they didn't need antimatter to power them.

"Mithra's bloody horns," Logan murmured. "I don't know if we have the space for all of them on the ship."

He hadn't realized he still had the general frequency open, not until he heard the reply from Katy.

"Well, then, Colonel Slaughter, sir," she said, her tone light and teasing, "I think I have some good news for you. The *Shakak* just sent me a message to relay to you. You know those two destroyers we saw sitting in the repair docks in orbit? Well,

Lyta just told us she checked them out on the other shuttle and one of them is just about fully operational and we can definitely sail it out of here."

He very nearly didn't reply, the gears in his brain already turning. Getting the destroyer back would be a challenge. They couldn't go through the more settled Starkad systems, but taking a Starkad destroyer through Modi space would take some bribes...

"Tell Kammy to get a flight crew over to the destroyer," he said. "The access codes Mira gave us should work on the ship, too. We can send at least two of the drop-ships to dock with it."

Below him, he saw the Ranger squad escorting in two dozen mech-jocks, his own people and the mercenaries, enough to load up a full company of the Starkad mecha at a time.

"Holy shit, boss," Bohardt said, a tinge of wonder in his voice. "This is really gonna work, isn't it?"

He grinned at the obvious disbelief on the man's face, visible clearly as he leaned out of his canopy, helmet off.

"David, we're Wholesale Slaughter," he told the man. "This is what we do."

13

They're looking better," Kurtz said a bit grudgingly. "Maybe having the new machines is making them think more about what the hell they're doing with them."

Logan tapped his fingers on the desk, watching the recording of the tactical exercise with half his attention while the rest shifted platoons and companies and wondered if he could get away with deploying mech-jocks from one mercenary unit into one of the others without everyone screaming their head off.

"Look there, though," Hernandez said, scowling as she pointed at the two-meter wide screen they'd set up in the Security center, which Logan had taken over to use as his operations headquarters. The display was currently divided into multiple sections and Hernandez was indicating the view stretching from the mouth of the Run to the first curve, where three of the four mecha in the picture were within about thirty meters of each other. "Third Platoon of Bulwark Universal is still sloppy as shit with their interval."

"Yeah," Logan agreed. "I've been thinking about splitting

them between Bohardt's platoons and replacing them, if I can get everyone to agree. They need better leadership."

"You're the boss, boss," Kurtz reminded him. "They all agreed to that and they'll do what you tell them."

Logan grinned at Kurtz's naïve faith but said nothing. Lyta wasn't so reserved about it, but then, she never was.

"He's the boss," she told Kurtz, snorting derisively, "but he's also smart enough to know that just because you can get away with ordering your people to do something doesn't mean they'll understand your reasons or believe in them." She leaned back against the wall behind what had once been the desk of the town constable. "You can get away with that shit in a battle, when everyone is worried about living through the next minute and most of them want someone to tell them what to do. But when you give boys and girls time to think, time to complain to each other and stew in their juices, well…"

"We're not a Spartan line unit here, Val," he told Kurtz, trying to be gentle about it. The man was the most loyal officer he had. "Right now, we can't just ship a problem soldier out to some unit in a backwater outpost and forget about them. We need every man and woman who can pilot a mech out there fighting for us."

Kurtz rubbed at his eyes, suddenly looking exhausted.

"I know you're right," he admitted. "It's just not what I'm used to." He gave a sideways glance at Logan. "Okay, since we're being all open and sensitive and shit, and explaining everything to the troops, maybe you can explain something to me. We're training all these guys pretty damn hard these last few weeks, but who are we training them to fight?"

Logan frowned in confusion and Kurtz raised a hand to forestall his objections. "I mean, it's all well and good to raid some convenient Starkad base for weapons, but Rhianna Hale is just tightening her grip on Sparta while we sit here training.

What's our objective here? Are we fighting Starkad or are we fighting Hale?"

"The real enemy is Starkad," Lyta declared before Logan could answer. "This whole coup was their doing, especially that new intelligence chief Laurent, and I'm all for making them pay for it."

"Speaking of intelligence," Hernandez said, hiding a yawn behind her hand, "wasn't that weird chick supposed to be briefing us tonight?"

Logan had to tighten his jaws against his own yawn. The damn things were always contagious. They'd been working sixteen-hour days for so long, he couldn't even remember a time when he'd gotten to sleep before midnight.

"Katy's bringing her down from the *Shakak*," he said. "She had to make a covert run back to Gateway station."

"I'm not comfortable loaning out our most advanced weapon to her," Lyta said with an expression like she'd just bitten into something sour.

"We wouldn't have most of our weapons without intelligence she provided," Logan reminded her. "Sometimes, you just have to trust."

"General Constantine never was big on trust."

The door from the outside wasn't locked, and Katy didn't bother knocking, just pushed through, emerging from the outer darkness looking maddeningly fresh compared to the rest of them.

She got to sleep between jump-gates.

"Welcome back," he told her, offering a genuine smile despite his exhaustion. "How was the trip?"

"Boring, thankfully," she said, kissing him briefly but without embarrassment. There'd been a time when they had both been too sensitive about discipline and the idea of fraternization between officers to even hold hands in public. "The fake registration we copied from Bulwark Universal's freighter worked like a charm."

"How about you, Mira?" Logan asked the woman. She'd stepped in behind Katy, silent and enigmatic as always, closing the door behind her before she said a word. "Was the trip worth it?"

"You tell me," she replied. She sat in the vacant chair beside the desk, folding her hands in front of her like a poker player who'd just been dealt a royal flush. "I was able to call in a favor with a woman of my acquaintance who is an operative for Clan Modi. She has sources within Starkad Intelligence, and she is fairly certain she's discovered where they are holding General Constantine."

"He's alive?" Logan asked, gaping at her in disbelief. "Why the hell would they keep him alive?"

He winced, not realizing how it had sounded until after he'd said it. But Lyta was nodding.

"That's a damned good question," she said. "He's incredibly dangerous and they have to know that. But they also know he's carrying a lot of secrets around in his head that aren't recorded on any database, secrets too dangerous to write down. This Colonel Laurent might consider them valuable enough to keep him alive." She nodded to Mira. "Is he on Stavanger? The dungeons under the palace?"

"No. According to my source, it was considered too dangerous to keep him anywhere he might have contacts, unknown allies."

"Does it even matter by now?" Kurtz wondered. "It's been months now. No one could hold out that long under chemical interrogation and all the other high-tech shit Starkad has. He's probably told them everything."

"Nicolai Constantine has been Sparta's chief of intelligence for twenty years," Lyta said, glaring at him balefully. "You don't think he has conditioned barriers in place to prevent that? No, he'll die before he reveals anything." The wince was just a barely perceptible flicker around her eyes, one Logan was sure no one else would have noticed. "The question is, where is he being held, and can we get him out before it comes to that?"

"I can only answer the first part of that," Mira said. "Do you have a star map of the Starkad Supremacy in there?" She nodded toward the main display screen.

Logan began scrolling through the control screens for the office's systems, upgraded by Franny to include all the data from the *Shakak*.

"Where's Terrin?" he asked Katy as he pulled up the correct map for Mira. "Still on the ship?"

"Sleeping, I guess," Katy said. She chuckled. "Or well, whatever. He went back to that loft he and Franny are renting above the spice shop. He was dead tired, but he hasn't seen her more than a couple days in the last two months, so..."

"Shouldn't Acosta be here for this?" Hernandez wondered, glancing around as if she expected the man to come through the door, sensing someone was having an important conversation and he hadn't been invited.

"Your intelligence agent already knows," Mira said. "I told him along the way."

"He's still on the *Shakak*," Katy supplied. "There were some modifications to the ID codes he wanted made to the captured destroyer."

"Here it is," he said, casting the map to the big screen.

Starkad was a jagged, misshapen thing, huge and jutting into everyone else's territory, a reflection in hyperspatial dynamics of the way they'd dealt with their neighbors over the centuries. The Dominions had all coped with the chaos of the Empire's fall, the Jeuta incursions and the Reconstruction Wars in their own way. Sparta had tried to make up for in strength what they lacked in size, building up their defenses, tried to make themselves so fortified that no one would dare to attack them. Mbeki had emulated the empire, expanding quickly while the taking was good, before things had solidified. They'd made themselves large and decentralized, not leaving a central hub where an enemy could strike and decapitate their government or military. Shang had made it their business to know everyone else's business, to keep track of every nuance of Dominion politics and use it to their advantage in trade and foreign policy, made their economic connections indispensable, made it too costly to disrupt. Modi had clambered desperately for any handhold to let them stay independent, had tried to ally themselves with anyone who would have them to keep from being swallowed up.

Starkad had reacted to the chaos by lashing out, by challenging everyone around them. They'd overreached, been driven back time and again, yet never overthrown. Logan remembered one of his military history professors at the Academy saying that Starkad figured as long as they were pushing outward, no one would have the time or energy to push back. And maybe they were right.

Mira reached out to the control pad with a questioning look and he nodded for her to go ahead. She magnified one of the Starkad systems near the border with Mbeki, nearly as far from Sparta as possible and still remain in the Supremacy. It was a G-class star with no recorded name, just a string of letters and numbers floating in space beside it on the map and four planets orbiting it. She spread her fingers across the control pad and the rocky iceball at the edge of the system disappeared off the corner. The gas giant and its captured-asteroid moons drifted off after it, then the asteroid belt, while on the other side of the picture the star itself faded with its charred and brittle close companion. When her fingers left the pad, the picture was zoomed into the second planet out from the star, twisting, braided clouds rolling over what seemed like a solid ocean blue, twin moons orbiting it in a complex pattern.

"This used to be an Imperial colony," Mira explained. "It's mostly water, with just a few archipelagos, but it was naturally habitable and didn't require a terraforming investment, so they made an attempt to settle. It failed. The twin moons cause erratic weather patterns and periodic flooding that inundates all but one small section of one island, so it wasn't economically viable, and they couldn't find any colonists who wanted to live there. They left a military outpost, but it was abandoned when troops began to be recalled during the collapse."

She sneered.

"Starkad found it and built a prison. Historically, it's been used for political rivals of whichever house has been in power, but currently, it has only one guest. General Nicolai Constantine."

"Well, I'll be damned," Lyta said, almost under her breath. She offered Mira a rueful grin. "I take back everything I ever said about you."

Logan was still leaning across the desk, staring at the star map, barely listening to their exchange.

"That's a *damned* long way across Starkad territory," he said, half to himself.

"The *Shakak* can make it," Katy assured him, resting a hand on his shoulder. "They can't catch her. Half the time they can't even *see* her."

"It's not as if we have any choice here, Logan," Lyta pointed out. "Leaving aside the possibility that this Laurent woman might actually crack General Constantine, the fact is, we need him. Mira has provided some very useful intelligence so far, but Constantine knows where the bodies are buried, knows who buried them. He could make the difference between winning this thing and losing it."

"This won't be like Farsund," he warned, grim certainty weighing him down like a sandbag across his shoulders. "This isn't some isolated supply depot. This is a prison, and if Constantine is there, he's going to have high-ranking Supremacy Intelligence officers interrogating him. Which means at least one cruiser, assault shuttles, Marines, maybe a company of first-line mecha."

"I'm afraid my stock military access codes won't break into their security systems, either," Mira admitted. "This will be strictly a Supremacy Intelligence operation with constantly changing random computer codes."

"We'll need Franny," Logan decided. He ran a hand through his hair. It was getting long again. *Should I cut it or let it grow, keep cultivating the rogue, outlaw image with the mercs?*

"We're doing it," he added, almost an afterthought. *As if there'd really been any doubt.* "Despite the fact they might be expecting us to. You were right, Val," he told Kurtz. "We need an objective, but we need one that's more about winning this war than getting revenge. We have weapons, we have troops. Now we need connections." He let his eyes travel across theirs. "You saw what happened when we tried to get aid from Shang with no friends to smooth the way. They considered us an opportunity, nothing more. With Constantine, we have connections."

"You're the boss, boss," Kurtz repeated his earlier statement, though with less conviction.

"There's no names on any of the planets or the star," Hernandez said, tracing a line around the world with her finger on the screen. "Just numbers. Don't they have names?"

"Not official ones," Mira said. "I'm told among the locals, the star was known as Leucothea and the planet was named

Nereus. But the island where the blacksite prison was built has an official name, both in the Imperial records and in the Starkad military maps." She pointed to the one dot of black in the sea of blue.

"It's called Maelstrom Strand."

How long has it been?

Nicolai Constantine rocked back and forth, arms clasped around his legs, pulling them closer to his chest, trying to conserve warmth. It didn't seem to help. He couldn't stop shivering. He kept hoping he'd succumb to hypothermia and slip away in the night, quietly, painlessly, but they wouldn't let him. They had to be monitoring him, checking his core temperature. Whenever it dropped below a certain threshold, he'd feel a warmth from beneath what looked like stone floor. There were heating coils beneath the floor, medical sensors built into the walls, security monitors concealed somewhere he couldn't see. The cell wasn't what it seemed. Nothing here was. The appearance was medieval dungeon, but that was just a mind game.

Unfortunately, it was a very well-designed, very effective mind game, one he was losing.

He was scared, terrified every waking moment. And *every* moment was waking. He hadn't slept in days.

How long has it been? How long since I slept?

He'd fool himself into thinking he'd nodded off without realizing it, but he knew it wasn't true. They were keeping him awake somehow, keeping him scared and confused, trying to break him down.

Subsonics, maybe. It's what I'd use.

"You deserve this, Nicolai."

He blinked, raising his head, trying to open his eyes against the salt and rheum built up in them. It was *her* again. She seemed so real, as beautiful, bold, and brave as she'd been over twenty years ago, her long, auburn hair flowing down across her shoulders, her eyes green and piercing.

"Maggie," he tried to shout the name, but it came out as a whisper through cracked and bleeding lips. "You can't be here."

"Why?" she asked, a scorn to her tone she'd never had when she'd been alive. "Because it's too dangerous? You already let me die once."

A spear of pain stabbed through his chest, as surely as if Maggie Conner had thrust the blade into him herself.

"I couldn't be there," he insisted, the protests sounding weak in his own ears. "I had orders to secure the armory at Laconia!"

"Orders from my husband?" She cocked an eyebrow at him, skeptical, accusing. "Do you think he knew, Nicolai? Do you think that's why he sent you away instead of keeping you at the palace to protect me?"

"No." Constantine shook his head. It was a violent motion, so harsh and abrupt it rattled his teeth. "No, Jaimie couldn't have known. I never told anyone...and we were never alone again. It was just the one time..."

"You said you loved me, Nicolai. But you let me die. You let them kill me when you could have been there to save me." Her perfect lips twisted in a snarl. "You deserve this. You deserve to be punished. You should die here alone, forgotten, despised."

"I've tried to protect your sons," he pleaded with her. "I've done the best I can."

"You've failed them too." Her words were as cold as the storm-wind off the ocean, as cold as the slick dampness of the floor. "You let everyone you love die."

Constantine wept, praying to whatever gods might be listening to let him die and knowing they would never be so merciful.

"I don't know how much longer he can take this, physically."

The man was short and soft, and Laurent would have called him despicable if she were indulgent enough to allow her personal feelings to interfere with her job. He was technically a doctor, but "interrogation specialist" was probably a better description of his field of expertise.

"It's your job to make sure he lasts as long as is necessary, Dr. Whitmore," Laurent told him. She didn't meet his disapproving glare, simply stared at the monitors, watching Nicolai Constantine slowly crack to pieces in front of her in infrared and thermal. "We're dealing with an exceptional mind and we'll have to bring it right up to the edge to get what we need from it."

"I must say, I still don't understand what he could tell you that you couldn't just get from the files Hale seized on Sparta."

"Nicolai Constantine is legendary for his personal approach to spying," she told him. Her predecessors in this job wouldn't have bothered to explain their actions to underlings and functionaries, but she was of the opinion that people could do their jobs more efficiently if they knew the why as well as the what. "He has connections, contacts...*friends* he calls them, from Modi to Shang. People who'd be executed if any official record of contact with him existed. Exposing them could cripple entire governments. The *threat* of exposure could put them under our control." She traced a line down the monitor with a fingertip, wondering how long she could have endured the privation, the subsonics, the cold. "The end goal of this is to reunite the Empire, Doctor. With as little violence as possible."

She was telling him, but she knew she was trying to convince herself.

It wasn't working.

"Are you worried about the heir?"

Laurent glanced up sharply at the question. It wasn't pertinent to the task or Whitmore's part in it. Just blatant curiosity and she was tempted to tell him it wasn't his place. She didn't. It helped, sometimes, to talk through her own thought processes and he was someone she was fairly sure wouldn't be able to use it against her.

"Logan Brannigan," Whitmore clarified, as if she might have thought he meant the scientist, Terrin.

"He's resourceful," she conceded. "Almost recklessly brave. But he has at most one real warship and no more than a company of mecha. He's an annoyance, nothing more. I know where he is and, more importantly, he doesn't know I know. Once I've dealt with General Constantine, once you've wrung everything useful from him, we'll take care of the young Brannigan." She sighed with honest regret. "It's a shame. There are so few good men out there and we're going to have to kill so many of them."

14

I still don't understand why we had to come on the destroyer," Corporal Glover said, tapping his gloved fist against the hard, plastic arm of the narrow acceleration couch.

Lyta glared at the enlisted man and he stopped the tapping. There were too many of them squeezed into too small a compartment, hanging in seats oriented the wrong way for the sense of down the ship's thrust was giving them, and her nerves were as frayed as any of them.

"Because," Francesca Hayden said, more patiently than Lyta would have, "the *Shakak* propels itself by expanding and contracting spacetime. It doesn't actually accelerate. The freighter is accelerating at one gravity. If we launched from the *Shakak* in this transfer pod, we wouldn't be able to match velocities with the freighter because we'd be motionless in space relative to it. We had to launch from a ship accelerating at the same rate."

"Shit's complicated," Glover lamented. "And it took forever to get out here."

He was right about that, at least. Even pushing it and accelerating between gates at a punishing three gravities, the trip to the intercept had taken nearly two weeks, days of it spent sweating whether their cover registry would be accepted by Starkad traffic control. She'd made the argument during the planning session back on Revelation, suggesting they could use the fusion thruster they'd installed on the *Shakak* for maskirovka, to conceal her true nature from casual observers. Kammy had explained they couldn't carry enough fuel for the drive to actually match velocities for the freighter. And this was her plan, so…

"Launching in ten. A woman's voice came over the transfer pod's speakers, sounding distant and tinny. She nearly wouldn't have recognized it as Commander Shelly Nance's. *That's* Captain *Nance now.* Master of the newly-christened Wholesale Slaughter destroyer *Avenger.* "Five, four, three, two, good luck Rangers. Launching."

Quick-burnout, solid-fuel boosters roared in feral rage and suddenly, what had been "back" was now "down." She couldn't see out of the pod because the pilot's station had been removed to modify it to carry a platoon of Rangers and a technical crew, including Franny. Its flight was completely automated, which made Lyta nervous as hell. She didn't trust computers. Which was funny, since the uncrewed freighter they were about to board was run entirely by computers.

"You're right on course," Nance announced. "You should be docking with the freighter in thirty seconds."

That was dangerously close in astronautical terms, especially for two ships accelerating under fusion drive in deep space, but it had been necessary. The whole mission was insanely dangerous, but absolutely necessary. *Even if Logan and I are the only ones who understand that.*

Terrin certainly hadn't. The blow-out between him and

Franny when he found out she was going to be going along with the platoon of Rangers in the infiltration team had been epic to behold. The highlights of it still reverberated in her head, echoing her own doubts.

"We are risking just about *everything* on this!" He'd yelled, throwing his hands up in the air, angrier with her and Logan than he was with Franny. "How the hell can it be worth it to send our only two ships that are worth a damn and all our senior leadership after just one man?"

She guessed they'd patched things up before they'd departed for their ships, Terrin for the *Shakak* and Franny to the *Avenger*. She hoped they had. This wasn't a time to be holding grudges. *Not against each other, anyway.*

"Hold on," Nance warned. "It's going to be a rough docking."

Metal struck metal like a gong sounding at the temple in Argos, and she jerked against her restraints, feeling as if she'd been ground under a giant boot. Breath gushed out of her explosively, and no sooner had she been tossed forward than she recoiled back into her seat, left without even the air in her lungs to grunt at the pain. It took her a moment to realize that "down" was now toward her feet, due to the way the pod was oriented to the freighter's thrust.

"Mithra's bloody horns!" Glover wheezed. "You can say that again!"

Franny was unstrapping already and Lyta envied her the resilience of youth, or perhaps it was the desperation of knowing how little time they actually had. The young CPO lunged for the pod's airlock, unlatching it with strength Lyta wouldn't have expected from someone so skinny, throwing it aside and heading straight for the security pad on the freighter's inner lock.

Lyta pulled the quick-release on her harness, and stumbled

to her feet, feeling a twinge of pain in her left knee from an old injury she'd aggravated during the docking. She felt as if she should be in as great of a hurry as Franny, but knew there was no good reason for it. The freighter had no crew Lyta needed to subdue, just a security system the techs would have to worm their way into and erase any sensor records of their boarding.

"Lyta, it's me." She heard Logan's voice in the ear bud of her 'link, relayed from the pod's internal communications system. The *Shakak* had been shadowing the *Avenger*, guarding their backs in case this system wasn't as deserted as they thought. "The *Avenger* is heading back to Revelation." That was no surprise. The destroyer would have no excuse for showing up in the Leucothea system and wouldn't have been able to keep up with the *Shakak* at any rate. "We're falling back now. We'll jump into Leucothea seventy-two hours after you and head straight for Nereus. Once we reach orbit, Starkad is going to detect us and go on alert, so you have to get Constantine secured by then."

"Roger that," she replied. "It'll get done."

"Lyta." A different voice. Terrin's. "I know Franny's busy right now, so could you give her a message from me when you get a chance?"

She felt like snapping at him, something officious about how a mission was no time to be getting emotional. Then she remembered how badly she wished she could have said goodbye to Donner Osceola one last time.

"Sure, Terrin."

"Just tell her...I'm sorry, and I love her."

"I'm sure she already knows both of those," Lyta said, bemused at the idea that little Terrin Brannigan, the precocious eight-year-old she'd met almost twenty years ago had, somewhere along the line, become a man. "But I'll tell her anyway."

"Good luck, *ho'onani*," Kammy said, the last voice she'd hear before the *Shakak* went out of range. "See you on the other side."

Watching Nicolai Constantine eat was making Ruth Laurent hungry. Her stomach growled but Dr. Whitmore pretended not to notice, so she didn't bother to apologize. On the monitor, Constantine sat cross-legged in his cell, the plate in his lap, shoveling the food down as if he hadn't eaten in days.

Which he hasn't.

"How long of a break do you want to give him?" Whitmore asked her. "Medically, I would say he needs two nights of rest, minimum, before we start again. Anything less and he'll go catatonic."

"I might give him three," she mused. "Make it nice and long and comfortable. Even give him a blanket, or a cot, make him think we've given up. Then start it over again, even worse. Revolutions happen in times of rising expectations, so my history instructors said, and so do interrogation breakthroughs. If he's convinced himself it's hopeless, that there's only misery and death in his future, he'll simply accept it. Giving him comfort makes him remember things can be better, if he cooperates."

Whitmore eyed her carefully, as if trying to control his expression.

"I knew Colonel Kuryakin," he said, "and Colonel Grieg, the men who came before you. When I heard of how quickly you ascended the ranks to get this job, I had concerns you might not be ready for it. That you might be too soft."

"And now?" she wondered.

"Now, I think those men were amateurs."

"Colonel Laurent, this is Captain Marshall in traffic control." The voice came over the PA speakers in the control room's ceiling. Laurent had left instructions for the staff here at the Strand to refrain from calling her on her 'link unless it was an emergency, mostly because she disliked being tethered to it, unable to get away from the day-to-day minutiae. "You know the scheduled automated freight shipment that made orbit a couple hours ago, ma'am?"

"Yes," she said, suppressing a sigh of frustration. Marshall was one of those officers who needed their hands held every five minutes. If their forces weren't stretched so thin as it was, she would have had him replaced. "I am aware of the freighter. You reported on its arrival *three times* now, Captain Marshall."

"Yes, ma'am," the man went on hastily. "The thing is, though, they dropped a cargo shuttle a couple hours ago, once they hit orbit and it landed out by the north loading dock, like they all do, you know..."

"The *point*, Marshall," she reminded him, grinding the words out.

"Yes, ma'am. Well, we sent out a crew to unload the shuttle about twenty minutes ago and you know how the crew chief usually sends up a lading report once they get inside, to make sure the shipment actually has everything it's supposed to?'

Her eyes frosted over and she felt for her gun in its holster. Marshall couldn't see it since the call was audio-only, but he must have sensed the silence was a bad thing, because he went on quickly.

"Well, that's it, ma'am. The chief hasn't sent the lading report and they're not answering the comms down there. I tried to check in with the security monitors, but the security center says they're just getting static." She heard the shrug in his voice. "Lt. Scott in Security says they've had a lot of problems with moisture getting into the communications circuits and that he hasn't detected any alarms. He says it's probably nothing..."

"No, you were right to bring it to my attention," she admitted reluctantly. He was only right because he was too damned stupid to do the correct thing on his own. "Send a security patrol to check it out. If it's simply a bad circuit, they can call for a repair team."

"Do you really think there is anything wrong?" Whitmore asked her, his tone striking her as curious, as if he'd welcome an interruption from the isolation and boredom of the Strand.

"Out here?" She shook her head. "But Colonel Kuryakin told me, always handle each situation the correct way and you'll never be caught unaware when the unexpected occurs."

"He was a smart man. How did he wind up getting killed?"

She regarded Whitmore sidelong, trying to determine if the question had been disrespectful. She needed him for now, so she decided it hadn't been.

"Colonel Kuryakin forgot the most important rule of all," Laurent said. "No matter how good you think you are, there's always someone better. Or just luckier."

Francesca Hayden tried not to look at the bodies. They were the enemy, of course, but they'd been simple loading dock workers, functionaries who never made a decision in their lives more crucial than which pallet to off-load first. It didn't seem fair they had to die for the sins of men and women who would never set foot on a battlefield, never once get their hands dirty or put their lives at risk. It was the blood of the common soldier soaking into the cement of the loading dock floor, diluted by the puddles of rain blowing in through the open doors out to the landing pad.

Maybe rain, she corrected herself, maybe sea spray. You couldn't get away from either of them in this place.

She shook the sight of the bodies and the smell of saltwater and salty blood out of her thoughts and kept searching through the facility's database. The worm she and the other techs had developed from the freighter's computer records had worked, but just getting into a system didn't tell you how to use it or where to find the information you needed.

"Time, Hayden," Lyta reminded her.

The Ranger colonel was anonymous under the hooded poncho she'd stolen off one of the bodies, her suppressed carbine held down by her side, out of sight as she watched the doors into the main building.

"Just another second, ma'am."

George Easton looked up from the terminal he was tapping into with the worm module, his big eyes getting even bigger.

"Do you need help, Chief?" he asked her, sounding very much like he wanted to be the one to step in and be the hero.

"No, Petty Officer Easton," she snapped. "Get back to rigging the loop on the security cameras before someone realizes what's going on in here."

"Yes, Chief," he said dutifully, eyes returning to his task.

She hated being called "Chief." "Chief" was some old, crochety NCO a couple years from retirement who never had time for a family and drank himself to sleep at night. She wasn't even thirty, way too young for the rank if there hadn't been so few technicians assigned to Wholesale Slaughter and if she hadn't had so much combat experience.

Not that I wanted *combat experience...*

"Here it is, ma'am."

Lyta was suddenly at her shoulder as if she'd materialized there, staring at the schematic she'd pulled up on the screen.

"There are the holding cells," Franny said, pointing at a

block of rooms in the tower of the castle-like prison. "That's the only section drawing much power pretty much every day, so the one with General Constantine has to be in there."

"Anything in there about how many troops they have on site?" Lyta asked, her eyes scanning back and forth across the screen as if she were memorizing it.

"No, but I found references in the lading lists about two drop-ships that landed here and no mention of them leaving." Franny waved off to the west. "There's another landing pad that way and they might still be here. Each one of them could hold two platoons of mecha. Also, there are two full floors of barracks drawing power, but I don't know how many Marines and armored troops that might mean."

"All right," Lyta said, voice pitched louder, addressing the platoon of Rangers arrayed behind cover around the loading dock, their weapons pointed outward. "Third squad, Bravo team, you're staying here with the techs. Chief Hayden, keep trying to break into the security system and give us access to their internal sensors. If you manage it, break radio silence and let me know, otherwise sit tight and stay quiet. Everyone else, with me."

The Rangers moved out of their defensive positions and began stacking on either side of the wide freight doorway, the soldier walking point crouching just to the right of it. Lyta put a hand on Franny's shoulder, grabbing the armored vest she wore under her poncho and giving it a tug as if to remind the younger woman it was there.

"You got your sidearm, right?" she asked.

Franny nodded, her hand automatically going to the butt of the weapon in a holster attached to her vest.

"If it comes to it, don't hesitate. Promise me."

"Yes, ma'am."

The promise came easy. Keeping it might not, but the

colonel had work to do and she wasn't going to make things harder by forcing the woman to worry about her. A hollow formed in her stomach as the point man ducked around the door frame and headed out, the others filing through behind him, with Lyta following behind the first squad. They were gone in seconds and it seemed incredibly quiet and empty in the dock, each shadowy stack of palleted crates hiding an enemy waiting to jump out and attack.

"I'll keep an eye on the hallway," Sgt. Todd, the team leader offered.

Franny had gotten to know her on the voyage in on the freighter. She was a solid, unflappable junior NCO, and Lyta must have thought she was dependable or else she wouldn't have left her to guard Franny and the other two techs, but there were still only the four Rangers left with them.

We'll be okay. There's no reason for anyone to come down here as long as George got the security footage looped in time...

"Patrol coming!" Sgt. Todd snapped, pulling back inside the door. "Quick, push those bodies under cover! Franny, you and the techs pretend to be working the cargo...try to get them to leave."

"Shit!" George blurted, eyes darting around as if searching for a route of escape. Franny saw him looking at the door and the open ramp of the cargo shuttle.

"There's nowhere out there to hide," she warned him, judging the man was about to panic. She was terrified herself, but facing the harsh emptiness of the island scared her more than staying under cover and facing Starkad Marines. "Keep your head and go pretend to be working the pallet jack."

The motorized jack was still halfway down the shuttle's boarding ramp, exactly where it had been when Lyta's troops had ambushed the work crew sent to unload the bird. George ran over to it but balked when he saw one of the Rangers pulling a body away from it, leaving a trail of blood. The Starkad dock worker had been tall and long-limbed, with a horsey face and dark eyes. His eyes were frozen open in shock, the face pale, his lips parted in a rictus of pain and fear. George stared at the dead man, hands going to his mouth as if he thought he might throw up.

"Hurry!" she urged him. "Pull the pallet down over the blood."

George skirted as far away from the dead body as he could, circling around the pallet jack and grabbing the control bar at the other end. Franny left him to the task, hoping he'd figure it out in time. She shooed Grimmett, the other technician, away from the control board and out to one of the pallets already offloaded, then went to work on the display screen, pulling down the evidence of their hack and replacing it with a lading list.

The Rangers had barely pulled the last of the bodies behind stacks of crated supplies and joined them in the shadows when the Marines walked through the broad entrance to the dock. Franny pulled the hood of her stolen poncho over her face and tried not to look them in the face. There were only six of them, armored but not bothering with helmets, walking casually as if they expected to find everything normal, their time wasted.

Good. Keep thinking that.

The leader was a lanky, young man, younger even than her, his blond hair buzzed almost down to the scalp and a sergeant's stripes on his shoulder. He had cruel eyes, she thought, grey and lifeless. His rifle was tucked under his arm, hanging from a sling but readily accessible and looking somehow deadlier than the guns of the Rangers, even though it was close to the same design.

"Who's in charge down here?" the young sergeant demanded, his tone impatient, annoyed.

Shit. Shitshitshitshit…

"Umm, I am, Sergeant," she said, cringing as her voice cracked at the end. "What can I do for you?"

"You can tell me why the hell you haven't filed your damned lading report," he snapped. His eyes narrowed as he looked her over. "Who are you, what's your rank?"

She froze, her mouth half open, racking her brain, trying to remember if she'd seen the name or rank on any of the bodies. George, of all people, saved her.

"Oh, Petty Officer Antonelli," he said, leaving his power jack sitting at the foot of the ramp and rushing over. "Did you check on that short I told you about in the comm panel?"

She stared at him wide-eyed for a beat before figuring out exactly what he was saying.

"Oh, no, damn!" she clucked. "I'm so sorry to waste your time, Sergeant…" She looked down at the name tape on his chest. "…Carter. George told me there was a short in the comms panel and I got so involved trying to resolve the shortfall in the lading report for the shuttle I forgot to check it."

Sgt. Carter glared at her, the scowl on his harsh face looking incredibly skeptical.

"You're Petty Officer Antonelli?" he asked. He brought his wrist-mounted 'link up and checked the readout. "You're Petty Officer *Stephen* Antonelli?"

"Yeah," she nodded, smiling weakly. "My…umm…my parents wanted a boy, you see…"

She saw his hand on the grip of his rifle, saw his finger drifting toward the trigger. Her arms were inside the poncho, her hands hugged to her chest in an instinctive protective stance against the cold and the fear, and the grip of her pistol was right there, at her fingers. She didn't remember making a decision, didn't remember pulling the gun from its holster or raising it to shoulder level. All she could remember, all she *would* remember to her dying day was the look on Sgt. Carter's face when the muzzle of the handgun came level with his eyes. She'd thought they seemed cold and lifeless, but now they were animated, incredibly mortal and desperate to cling to life.

She pulled the trigger. It was as if a snake had struck her and she jerked back at the recoil and the flash. It was a horrible shot and if she hadn't been holding the gun centimeters from the man's face, she would have missed altogether. She didn't. Everything that made Carter the man he was splashed backwards into the faces of the female Marine directly behind him and she choked and spat and wiped at her eyes. There was a moment that seemed to draw on forever, an emotional shockwave rolling back from the muzzle of her pistol that buried the reaction of the Marines in mud. It didn't reach Sgt. Todd and the Rangers.

She didn't even realize they were shooting at first, the muffled reports from their suppressed carbines beneath the register of hearing blasted by the sound of her own gunshot. She saw the Marines directly in front of her jerk back, their faces distorted in what might have been anger or fear, but what was most likely pain. She didn't see the bullets striking them until one took a hit to the neck and red sprayed across the others.

She heard the burst of return fire, though, the sharp, jackhammer chatter, cutting through everything else, saw the muzzle flash swinging her way and knew she was going to die. Something hit her in the shoulder, knocked her down, crushed her beneath its weight. Her head smacked against the floor and stars filled her vision, their song a ringing in her ears.

Was I shot? Was that what getting shot feels like?

She'd dropped the gun somewhere along the way and there was something wet on her hands, something warm and sticky. Was it her own blood? Was she bleeding out on the floor? There was someone lying on top of her. She'd been dazed and it had taken her a second to realize it but now she felt the weight pressing against her chest, blocking out the light. She felt around the edges of the person, felt the same wetness coating their poncho.

Poncho. It was one of the techs.

It was George Easton. She rolled him off of her and a unveiled a tableau of blood and death. The Starkad Marines were down, dead twice over, riddled with multiple bursts from the Rangers. One of them, a young enlisted soldier, was switching out his empty magazine as she watched, his face pale but his jaw set in determination. She didn't want to look down, didn't want to see George dead from a bullet meant for her.

He gasped and so did she. The man was alive. His eyes were squeezed shut, his puffy face screwed up taut with pain and blood was soaking his poncho through a ragged hole through the right side of his chest.

"Help!" she shouted, scrambling out from beneath him, gesturing wildly at the Rangers. "Help, he's been shot!"

"Watch the door!" Todd ordered, slinging her carbine and rushing over to George Easton's side.

George had his eyes open now, wide with pain, his breath ragged and wet and blood flecking around his lips. Franny didn't remember taking his hand, but she was squeezing it now.

"Damn it, Easton," she moaned. "Why'd you have to go and do that?"

"Shit," Todd murmured, pulling at the poncho, trying to look through the hole.

The Ranger NCO yanked a wicked-looking knife out of a sheath on her chest harness and began cutting the rain jacket away, then the fatigue shirt beneath it. The skin of George's chest was pale and almost hairless...and ripped by the ragged hole from a bullet. Blood didn't spurt, but it welled steadily, more than he had to spare.

"Think he's got a collapsed lung," Todd said softly, as if to herself, as she pulled a sealed pouch from her thigh pocket.

She ripped the plastic open and unfolded a smart bandage, something Franny had seen demonstrated in training but never used in real combat. Todd's surprisingly long and slender fingers spread the malleable plastic over the wound, pressing down the adhesive edges. Beneath the opaque, drab-green surface of the bandage, a clotting agent was pouring into the wound, followed by a sealant to temporarily close it. It would take time to work, but she knew it should stabilize him until they could get him back to the *Shakak*.

If they got him back. If *any* of them got back.

"Anyone coming?" Todd called to the rest of her fire team, set up by the door.

"Negative," came the response from the same pale enlisted man Franny had seen reloading earlier. "It's clear."

Todd went silent and Franny thought she was listening. The wind was howling outside, the waves crashing onto the rocks with roars of fury. Maybe enough to cover the shooting.

"Chief Hayden," Todd instructed her, her voice calm and firm, "please pick up your sidearm and holster it."

Franny blinked as if waking from a dream, then began to search on the floor around her. The 10mm pistol lay beside the foot of the loading dock computer terminal, its muzzle stained with burned, sticky blood. Her hand shook as she picked it up and cleaned the goop off the end of the slide with the cut-away remains of George Easton's poncho before shoving it back into her holster. It took three tries to slide it home, but at least she remembered to keep her finger away from the trigger.

"Okay," Todd said, just the slightest bit of uncertainty in her voice and her darkly intelligent eyes, as if she was trying to convince herself along with the rest of them. "I can't think of anyplace else we could go that would be better to dig in than right here. Endicott." One of the Rangers at the door looked up at her name being spoken, though she kept her carbine pointed out into the hallway. "Get on the pallet jack and start stacking them up in front of the door. We can't block it off entirely because Colonel Randell will be bringing General Constantine back through there, but make a tunnel the bad guys will have to come through to get to us."

"Yes, Sergeant," Endicott said, slinging her carbine and running back toward the cargo jack.

"McCallister," Todd went on, this time to the pale man. "Police up the weapons and ammunition from the Starkad Marines and divvy them up. Make sure Chief Hayden and Petty Officer Cooper each get a rifle and ammunition."

Franny felt her stomach twisting and bile rising in her throat at the thought of shooting someone again, but a glance at Mary Cooper, huddled behind a stack of shipping crates, shivering and pale, firmed up her resolve.

"Cooper," she said, forcing steadiness into her voice. "Help Endicott with the pallets."

The Navy tech stared at her doubtfully for a moment but finally nodded and pushed herself up from the floor.

"I'm going to help set up the defenses," Todd said, running a hand across George's forehead, wiping away the cold sweat. The man's eyes were closed and he was breathing easy. "He's anesthetized by the bandage. He should be out for a few hours. Why don't you find something warm to cover him with while we take care of the rest?"

Franny didn't respond, but rose and began hunting around the small break area behind the control console, searching for a jacket.

"Oh, and Chief," Todd added, making Franny turn back to her. "You did the right thing. If you hadn't shot him when you did, more people would have gotten hurt. Or killed. Including you."

"Thanks, Sergeant."

She tried to let the Ranger's words comfort her, but the vision of the Marine's death, of the results of what she'd done, wouldn't cease replaying itself over and over behind her eyes. And with it, the conviction she hadn't saved them from their fate, only delayed it.

Something nagged at the back of Ruth Laurent's consciousness, refusing to allow her to enjoy her dinner. Not that it was anything to write home about. Rations on the ass-end of nowhere tended to be consistently bland, soy protein paste and spirulina powder twisted and stretched out and seasoned until you could almost be fooled into thinking you were eating chicken, or pork, or beef, and pasta, or rice, or bread. But not quite.

Still, she was used to it. Running Colonel Kuryakin's errands, gathering intelligence from every corner of the Supremacy and out in the Periphery, she'd eaten plenty of what seasoned spacers called "ship food." She could let her hunger and her imagination and a lot of salt bridge the gap between soy and algae and whatever it was pretending to be.

Not today.

She set down her fork and let her eyes wander around the break room. It looked like every other break room in every other shithole outpost she'd ever visited, which was disappointing. The exterior of Maelstrom Strand promised something myste- rious and anachronistic, something more like the cells, but all of that was a psychological ploy, the whim of some forgotten Supremacy Intelligence chief who had more style than sense. The staff areas, the living quarters, all the functional, pragmatic sections of the prison were your basic, military blah.

"Damn." She suddenly remembered what was nagging at her. She pulled her 'link off her wrist and patched into the base's command net. "Security," she snapped.

"Yes, ma'am," Marshall answered immediately.

"Did you ever get the report back from the loading dock?"

"The...oh, umm...no, ma'am, I hadn't heard back from Sgt. Carter yet. I just thought if anything was wrong, he would have called by now."

"Goddammit, Marshall, don't they teach you idiots *anything* in the Academy nowadays?" The words had erupted out of her before she realized she'd just quoted Colonel Kuryakin word-for-word. Except he'd been talking to her.

"Well, it's just, we've been kind of busy, ma'am," Marshall tried to explain. "We kept detecting this sensor anomaly in the direction of the jump point and it doesn't seem to make any sense on any of the instruments."

Laurent felt the hair on the back of her neck stand up, and she slowly pushed herself away from the table.

"What *sort* of anomaly, Marshall?"

"Ma'am, it can't be a ship. There's no fusion signature and it looks as if it's accelerating at like twenty or thirty gravities, and no one could live through that. It's got to be a problem with the satellites and I just haven't been able to... Oh, *shit!*"

"Marshall, don't make me come down there and beat you to death," she growled.

"Colonel Laurent, the anomaly is a ship! I mean, it turned into a ship and it's launching shuttles! I think those are dropships! Oh, Mithra's bloody horns!"

Laurent forced herself to remain calm. The man was about

to hyperventilate, and her yelling at him would only accelerate the process.

"Marshall," she said, slowly and clearly, "my cruiser is still in orbit and so is your picket ship. Contact the captains and tell them they are ordered to engage the enemy vessel and launch assault shuttles to deal with their landers. After you do that, I want you to call down to Captain Scheer down in the hangar and tell him to fall out with his mech company and be ready to repel an assault. Do you understand all that, Captain Marshall? Repeat it back to me."

"Yes, ma'am, call Captain Waters in the picket and your captain on your cruiser and tell them to engage, then call Captain Scheer and tell him to fall out his mecha. Got it, ma'am."

"And there *is* just the one ship, right?" she asked, biting down on each word.

"Oh, yes, ma'am, definitely! There was only the one anomaly!"

"Good. Then get to it."

She stood, unmoving for a moment after cutting the connection. It was an attack, perhaps by Spartan loyalists but more likely by the heir, Logan Conner. The sensor anomaly Marshall had described matched what they'd found when they studied the tiny transport Logan's brother Terrin had piloted from Terminus to Trinity. She'd been afraid the Spartans might have found other ships, and time had proven her right.

Logan had made a mistake coming here, though. She knew the losses he'd suffered during his escape from Sparta. Hale had reported he'd had to abandon his whole force of mecha during the evacuation. Their Imperial-tech starship might have gotten them here, but it wasn't going to let them sneak past her security or break General Constantine out of...

The sound was like distant thunder and she had to listen

again for a moment to make sure she'd actually heard it. She tried to pinpoint it and finally decided it had come from above, through the next floor up, but what was it?

There it was again, and suddenly she *knew* what she was hearing. Gunfire. *Inside* the building. When the alarm klaxons began to ring only a moment later, she was already moving, drawing her sidearm and heading for the stairs.

"Security!" she yelled into her 'link. "Get me all the Marines you have available to confinement level four now! We have enemy forces inside the base!"

The loading dock...it had been them. They'd come in on the cargo shuttle, stowed away on the freighter. And there was only one person Logan Conner would trust to do that. Lyta Randell was here.

How many more of these? How many more drops? How many more battles before my luck runs out and the percentages catch up with me?

It was an odd set of questions for a mech-jock, not the sort Logan usually asked himself in the middle of an operation with his stomach rushing up into his throat from a drop. But he'd begun to ask them more and more since the death of his father. Every soldier thought about dying at some point, usually after the first time they heard a shot fired in anger, and he'd made his peace with it like everyone in his profession had to. Yet somewhere in the depths of his unconscious, he'd always thought that at some point, perhaps after ten years or even twenty, he'd leave the life of a combat soldier behind. Perhaps he would become an instructor or even work for his father as a military liaison.

All the thoughts of the future had died along with Jaimie Brannigan on the fields of a small valley in the Bloodmark

Mountains. He'd keep fighting because he was a Brannigan, and Brannigans didn't give up the fight, but the odds of coming through all this alive seemed smaller every time he strapped into his mech.

One fight at a time. Just take one fight at a time.

"We'll be in position for drop in one minute, boss," Muller reported. Randy Muller had been Bohardt's best drop-ship pilot and now he was Wholesale Slaughter's best. "Taking minimal ground fire. The assault shuttles suppressed it good. I can see three...no, four fires burning where the air defense turrets were."

Katy had his back. She always did.

"After we're clear, I want you and Claremont to take off and swing wide," Logan told him. Greg Claremont was the other drop-ship pilot, a man who he'd pulled over from the Cossacks. "I don't want you guys taking damage in the ground battle and leaving us stranded here. I'll call for you when we're ready to un-ass the area."

"Got it," Muller acknowledged. "The report from orbit is, that picket ship is launching assault shuttles to interdict, but they won't get here before you and your people drop."

Nothing they hadn't expected. This was all running close to the edge. Terrin had been right about that, even if he'd been angrier about his girlfriend going on the mission than he had about the risk to the rest of them. They were risking it all to this one toss of the dice. No, not *they*. *He* was risking it all. It was his call, it was on his shoulders. Everything was on his shoulders.

"Ten seconds to drop," Muller droned. "Nine, eight, seven..."

Logan wanted to offer a prayer to Mithra, to the *Spenta Mainyu*, the Beneficent Spirits, for aid and safety and victory. He tried to think of one in the seconds before the floor dropped away and he fell into the dark, but the only thing ringing through his head was the graffiti he'd seen in the mech bay of every drop-ship he'd ever flown in: *Here we go again.*

He could see the enemy already from two hundred meters up, a company's worth of them, pouring out of a decidedly modern looking hangar behind the anachronistic lines of the stone tower, the power behind the illusion.

"Launch on them now!" he snapped. "Don't let them get into formation!"

Jump-jets were roaring in his ears, shaking the structure of the Vindicator, but he managed a lock on the first Starkad mech heading out of the hangar, a Valiant. Starkad liked the machines, but he thought they were too tall, too slender, too big a target for an assault mech. He struck a blow for the Spartan choice, the Vindicator, with a volley of four missiles launched mid-flight. He wondered how many would manage it, if he could count on the mercenaries to get a lock in the midst of a drop, but the smoke trails from behind him answered the fear. Missiles rained down and the response was what he'd hoped.

A proactive commander might have ordered a launch on the dropping Wholesale Slaughter mecha. A forethoughtful commander might have told his pilots to fire at the drop-ships as they passed slowly over, before they could pull up and head out for their patrol, taking out their hope of egress. This commander was neither. He just charged through the missile barrage and took the damage to try to get his troops into position for an attack. It wasn't as bad as standing there, much better than retreating back into the hangar, but it told Logan what he needed to know about the Starkad Captain. He wanted to get into just the right formation, into just the right position to do what the book told him he ought to do. Just the type of commander who was begging for someone to get inside his OODA loop.

Logan made a decision fifty meters off the ground.

"Bohardt, Salvaggio, head for the flanks and box them in! Kurtz, Hernandez, follow me and take your platoons right down their Goddamned throats!"

Another risk, another roll of the dice letting the whole pot ride. One after another, following his gut and praying to Mithra he didn't lose it all again. He just didn't know any other way to lead.

Three of the Starkad machines were down, either destroyed or badly damaged by the missiles, all of them near the rear of their formation, the last mecha out of the hangar. It gave them a sort of leaning-forward formation, heading straight into the center of the flat table-land on which the base was built, with a gap in their left rear. It was there Logan aimed his jump, stretching out the flight until the heat warnings were flashing and the cockpit was a convection oven and his jets were about three seconds from shutting down or blowing apart.

The Vindicator's foot pads struck rock and the jets cut off, their absence a cool breeze through his cockpit. He'd spun around at the last second, facing the rear of the enemy formation even as they skidded to a halt, turning with obvious desperation, firing wildly. Lasers and ETC cannon rounds from the Starkad weapons ripped apart the gathering darkness, creating an impressive light show but not hitting a damned thing.

When Logan fired his plasma gun, the round found its target, hammering through the rear shielding of an enemy Golem, sending up a miniature supernova as his reactor flushed violently and consumed half its torso with it. He didn't even have to think about transitioning to the next weapon and the next target. His fingers worked the toggles automatically, nudging the control stick to rotate his upper torso just a few degrees until the targeting reticle lit up green and he squeezed the trigger. The 30mm Vulcan made a sound like a god clearing his throat, the tungsten slugs chipping away at the shoulder plastron of another Valiant, leaving the inner workings of the joint exposed and vulnerable.

He was about to fire his plasma gun into the naked shoulder joint when someone else fired a laser into it from just behind him and blew the arm off in a shower of sparks and a cloud of sublimating metal. The Valiant stumbled away, the pilot trying to regain his balance, and Logan fired off the plasma round into the jagged, charred wound where the arm had been. The plasmoid pierced through the cockpit and the Starkad mech's knees locked up in mid-stumble, sending it crashing sideways, nearly colliding with the Agamemnon fighting beside it.

"Pour it on!" Logan yelled, urgency roiling in his gut.

Maybe it was fear and panic sublimating itself into something more palatable to a soldier's mind, but somehow, he knew they had to finish this quickly, that delay would mean disaster. He knew it as surely as he knew his name, something was about to go wrong.

16

Oh, shit," Tara murmured. Kammy had seen that look on her face before, usually after a hard night out on shore leave when she'd had too many tequila shots and was about to decorate the street.

"What is it?" he asked, the question automatic. He was already searching the tactical screen, looking for... "Oh, shit." There it was.

"That's two 'oh, shits,'" Terrin said from behind him. "That can't be good."

The kid was trying to sound light, bantering like one of the bridge crew, but Kammy could tell he was scared. *He has every reason to be.*

"The Starkad captains aren't stupid," Kammy told him. "They're not just accelerating at us balls-out the way the others have." He pointed at the main screen, where the sensors displayed the positions of the enemy vessels in relation to the *Shakak*, the planet and the jump-points. "The cruiser is staying up at the L5 position, while the picket ship is maintaining a geosynchronous orbit. And they both just launched anti-ship missiles at us."

"We can outrun those, right?"

It was a dumb question. The kid *knew*, better than anyone, that they could outrun the missiles. But Kammy didn't get impatient because Captain Osceola hadn't become impatient with him when he'd been a dumb kid.

"We could," he explained instead, "but they know we can't. We can't be running all around the system dodging missiles because we have to be available to pick up our shuttles."

"Oh." Terrin's voice was small and so was his posture, as if he were trying to shrink down into his chair.

"Orders, Captain?" Bergh asked from the helm.

Good question. Damn, I miss Captain Osceola.

"We're going after the picket," he decided. "We're going to fight him in close, make sure the cruiser can't stand off and take potshots at his leisure. Take us to him, full acceleration. Tara, target those missiles." He nodded toward the red dart shapes accelerating far too quickly towards them on the screen. "Wait until the last second to take them out, though. I don't want to advertise our range."

He glanced back at Terrin, a thought creasing his forehead.

"Hey, Engineer, I got a question. We did all our testing out in Spartan proving grounds in the system's asteroid belt. So, tell me 'cause I got no idea, how close to the planet can we use the stardrive?"

"When I took the courier out of Terminus," Terrin said, fingers working as if he were moving thoughts around in his mind, "I'm pretty sure it activated the stardrive somewhere around the LaGrangian points between the planet and its moon." He shrugged. "But I *was* unconscious from the acceleration of the ship's atmospheric thrusters, so I can't say for sure." Terrin winced, as if he'd just realized how that sounded. "Give me a couple minutes of computer time and I'll figure it out."

"You got a minute and thirty seconds until we hit high orbit,

Terry," he said, unable to keep from calling the kid by his old nickname or to keep the exasperation from his voice. "Work fast."

The dark, swirling mass of a continent-size storm was already taking up most of the main viewscreen's optical camera feed and the planet seemed too damned close as it was, but it didn't seem to be affecting their drive yet. In fact, he was fairly sure he could see the first of the anti-ship missiles cutting across the blue swathe of endless sea, visible now on the optical tele-scopes, which meant...

"Firing," Tara announced.

The missile died spectacularly, if predictably, the explosion enhanced by its proximity to the outer reaches of the atmosphere. Auroras spread downward through the magnetos-phere, the polychromatic display of a massive fusion blast, bright and beautiful as a poisonous flower warning the world of its deadliness.

"We got another coming in off our firing arc," Tara said. "Taking helm control."

"Helm control to Tactical," Bergh confirmed, a formality. Since she doubled as Executive Officer, Tara had override at her station.

The view on the screen tilted off in the direction of the nearest of the planet's twin moons, towards the enemy cruiser.

"Ten seconds to recharge," Tara said. "Missile impact in two minutes."

Another formality. He could read the display as well as she could. But you said it out loud so everyone on the bridge could have a picture of what was happening in case there were casual-ties in the command crew and one of them had to take over. Kammy wished he could say it was an academic precaution, but he'd been there when it had happened.

He knew Tara would be concentrating on the missile and

the main gun, so he kept an eye on the enemy ships. The picket ship was content to stay where she was, knowing they'd have to come to him, counting on his heavy armor and help from the cruiser to destroy the *Shakak* before she could get too close. The cruiser though, she was moving.

"The enemy cruiser is accelerating at six gravities," Tara warned before he could announce it himself. "She's running in hard on us, Kammy. She's not going to let us get away with it."

She was right. Whoever was commanding that ship was outthinking him, guessing his capabilities and not letting it take them off their game. The cruiser was burning hard to intercept them before they could do to the picket ship what they'd done to the missile. He wouldn't launch again, not when they were this close to the other Starkad vessel, but...

"How long till she's in laser range?" he wondered.

"About..."

There was that damn rumbling again, the effect the drive field threw off when it was destabilized by external energy, a vibration not through the superstructure of the ship, he knew, but through the fabric of spacetime.

"Now," Tara finished, wincing.

The screen had gone red with the computer's representation of the laser strike and a warning was sounding, a day late and a few credits short.

"We lost ten percent power to the field on that shot," Terrin told him. His eyes were flicking back and forth from the engineering readouts to the hand-held tablet he'd been using to input the calculations on the field. "Back to full power now. By the way, I think we can use the drive field up to the edge of the atmosphere. If we try to use it any lower than that, the gravitational warping effect of the planet is going to pull us right into it. Like, towards the center of the planet."

"You *think*," Kammy repeated. "Well, that's just something I'd like to *know* at this juncture, Terry."

"Firing," Tara Gerard put in. He'd almost forgotten about the missile...

The laser hit just as she tried to fire the main gun and *something* happened. He didn't know what it was, but he could tell it wasn't good. There was the normal disruption of spacetime, though Mithra alone knew when he'd started referring to that as normal. But there was a flash as well, like a wall of static electricity crackling through the space around them, as impossible as he knew that was. The displays flickered in and out and it seemed as if his consciousness did as well.

When the tactical readout came back to life, the missile was still there, still coming. Tara looked at him wide-eyed, shocked, which so wasn't a good sign.

"Commander Gerard," he said sharply, trying to snap her out of it. "Can you tell me what the hell just happened?"

"Mithra's balls!" she blurted. "How the hell would I know?"

"It's the drive field," Terrin said, hands gripped to the arms of his seat as if he expected to float away. "The particle accelerator uses the field to focus the beam, at least that's what we think happens. The laser hit just as she fired and there was extensive particle scattering, which weakened the drive field even further." He scrolled through the display, making a face like he'd been kicked in the gut. "We're down fifty percent and it's building back up slowly."

"Yeah, our speed's way down, Captain," Bergh noted. "Maybe five gravities acceleration analog, down to about three kilometers a second."

"If that missile hits us," Tara noted, as if he hadn't already thought of it, "we're dead."

"Is the damn gun working still?" he asked, eyes going back

and forth between the two of them. "*Can* it still work while the field is all wonky?"

"Not full power," Terrin gave him the answer he hadn't wanted but had definitely expected.

"Well, try it anyway," he told Tara. "We're close enough, we just have to damage the thing's guidance and get out of its way!"

Close...yeah, we're closer than I ever wanted to be to a ship-killer missile.

It was clearly visible in the optical view, an evil, black wedge shape against the day side of the planet, the flare of its fusion drive backlighting it. It was two hundred megatons of death and they were nearly naked.

"Firing again," Tara said, a hopeless note in her usually defiant voice.

They were hit again, harder this time, shaking the ship like the biggest dog in the universe had sank its teeth into them, but they got the shot away first. The pale blue tendril of the particle beam was barely visible, fainter than usual, but there was a definite reaction when it struck the ship killer. Metal flared away, heated to a gas, a jet of white plasma gushing out from the side of the missile.

Hope burned in Kammy's chest. They'd hit the fuel supply, igniting the metallic hydrogen pellets. The push wasn't much, but it was enough to send the missile off course, and they were too close for it to correct in time. It had been accelerating at twenty gravities for minutes now, and to turn around and curve back to them would take just as much thrust and even more time.

Saved by physics yet again. *Thank you, Mithra. Or Katy's Jesus. Or his great-grandmother's gods, Maui and Pele and Ku. Don't want to leave anyone out.*

"The drive field is weakening," Terrin warned.

Kammy thought he heard Donner Osceola's voice in his ear,

whispering with his cynical growl, "Don't be thanking anyone just yet."

"How far are we from the picket ship?" he asked.

"Shit Kammy," Tara drawled, "another thirty seconds, we'll be smelling what he had for dinner!"

"Target him with everything we got. Lasers, coilguns, missiles, I don't care how unlikely it is to take him down, keep firing and fire the damn main gun, too, even if it's weakened."

"Doing it," she acknowledged. "But what about the cruiser and that laser?"

"We get in close enough, he won't be able to use the laser."

That's the plan, anyway.

The computer simulated the outgoing laser and the hail of tungsten slugs pouring from the coilguns but didn't need to provide special effects for the missiles flashing away on solid-fuel rockets that only outpaced them because the drive had been weakened. It wasn't much, mostly designed for anti-missile use, though it wouldn't have scratched the paint on the ship killer. It certainly wasn't going to destroy a picket ship, but it kept them occupied, made them waste their main laser on the missiles and coilgun rounds, forced them to power up their deflectors.

They were too close now for the cruiser to use the laser, so damned close to the atmosphere he felt as if he could a roll a window down and take a whiff.

"Drive field status?" He hadn't meant to bark the question, but everything felt wrong. He'd gotten too used to the new technology making him feel invulnerable and here he was getting his ass kicked and it was starting to piss him off.

"Back up to seventy percent," Terrin said, sounding enthusiastic about it. Kammy supposed that meant something good, but he just knew enough science to captain a ship.

"Bergh, I want you to take us so close to that asshole's starboard flank we rub bumpers."

Bergh was a professional, and not just a professional spacer like Kammy or Tara. He was Spartan Navy and he did what his captain told him no matter how bugnuts he thought it was.

"Everybody strap in," Terrin advised. His eyes were wide and Kammy thought he knew what they were trying to do.

Kammy tightened his harness, just in case. They were so close to the picket ship, he could read the stencil across the side. SS *Skjold* it said, and he assumed that meant something nautical in whatever language they'd gotten it from. Then the drive field touched the *Skjold* and something tried very hard to throw him through the opposite bulkhead.

That was what it felt like, when he was slammed against his harness and the compartment swam around him as if the entire universe was spinning, and he was fairly certain he'd killed them all. And then it ended as abruptly as it had begun, it ceased and they were still and the ship was apparently facing in the opposite direction and unmoving, or at least only moving as fast as gravitation was pulling it.

"Where the hell did he go?" Tara asked, staring at the sensor display.

"Check the atmosphere," Kammy suggested, hoping he was right.

"Holy shit," she said.

"Is that a good 'holy shit' this time?" Terrin wondered.

Tara pinched her fingers against the touch screen and the optical telescope zoomed down into Nereus' atmosphere, showing a comet streaking groundward, trailing glowing white fire. Kammy barked a laugh.

"I knew it! I knew that would work!"

"You did?" Terrin asked, face pale, eyes full of doubt. "Because I kind of thought the field would implode and we'd wind up atomized."

"Well shit, Terry," Kammy said, blowing out a heavy sigh, "I'm glad you didn't tell me that. Is the field still up?"

"It's propagating." There was wonder in his eyes, as if he'd believed they'd broken the ship. "It should be at full strength in a couple minutes."

"Good. Where's the cruiser?"

"I got her," Tara said, pulling up part of the screen to show him the tail end of a fusion drive, burning hard away from them. "He's decelerating hard, burning off the gee load he built up. I think he's going to pull back out and assess the situation, maybe ask for further instructions." She smirked. "All that military bullshit for running away because he thinks we'll kick his ass."

"Let him run," Kammy decided. "Our job's not to chase him down, it's to clear out the area. Phillips," he said to their new communications officer, "let them know downstairs our part of the fight's over. It's all up to them now."

17

Get that damned door open!" Lyta Randell yelled over her shoulder, then winced as a 6mm round ricocheted off the wall beside her head, sending out a spray of stone chips.

She put her cheek back against the stock of her carbine and hunted for a target. The Starkad Marines down the hallway were trying to stick their heads around the corner at random intervals, putting a burst downrange and then ducking back. They were trying to pin Lyta and her Rangers down, no doubt hoping to hold them in place until reinforcements arrived, which was exactly what she was hoping to avoid.

The toe of a combat boot stuck out from around the corner, just a small mistake, someone shifting their weight in preparation to lean out and fire a burst. The target was only a few centimeters long and fifteen meters away, only exposed long enough for her to fire a single round. The end of the boot jerked backward, leaving a trail of blood and a high-pitched scream warbled back over the kettle-drum echo of gunfire. The unfortunate Starkad Marine pitched forward, landing on his left shoulder. He apparently hadn't had time to find his helmet, not that it would have saved him at this range, and his eyes were wide and white and terrified.

Lyta tried to remember a time when she'd hesitated to pull the trigger, a time before this had all become so easy. She was sure there had once been a version of Lyta Randell who'd been innocent, who'd been horrified at the idea of killing someone, but she couldn't recall that woman, couldn't remember ever being so young. She shot the enemy trooper in the head, ignoring him afterwards, her eyes only open to threats.

"I got it!" Glover crowed.

She risked a look back and saw the Ranger NCO yanking at the heavy, centimeters-thick metal of the cell door, his electronic cracking module still affixed to the ID plate on the wall, blinking a cheerful green to confirm that it had accomplished its task. The door opened reluctantly and one of the other Rangers jumped in to help Glover push it aside. Lyta was past them in a single, long stride, pausing only for a moment to let her eyes adjust. The chamber was dark, gloomier than the dimly-lit hallway, the only light from a narrow window letting in the cloud-wreathed glow of the double moons. A chill dampness filled the air and the stone floor was precariously slick beneath her boots and her jaw clenched at the thought that General Constantine had spent *months* living in this hellhole.

He was huddled in the corner. It took her a moment to spot him, crouching in the shadows, hands hooked into claws as if getting ready to pounce. His hair was down to his shoulders, his beard long and grey and tangled, and his eyes gleamed with feral rage in the faint moonlight. She heard a low growl coming from his throat and thought for a long, sickening moment he might try to attack her.

"General Constantine," she said loudly and firmly, taking a step toward him, trying to bring her face into what little light there was. "It's me, Lyta. We're here to break you out."

He slowly rose to his full height, eyes seeming to finally focus on her.

"It's another trick," he declared. His voice was rough, raspy, unmodulated, as if he weren't used to speaking. "It's just you Starkad bastards trying to break me again."

She'd considered the prospect he might not believe it was them, thought long and hard during the voyage about how she might convince him. It was why she hadn't worn a helmet despite the risk, knowing he'd need to see her face.

"Maybe it is," she conceded, shrugging as if the thought wasn't concerning. "But you won't find out unless you play it through."

She had her hand on the dart launcher she'd brought along with them, just in case, but the words seemed to penetrate, and he nodded slowly.

"All right. At least it'll pass the time."

"Stay behind me, sir," she instructed him. "Glover, you ride the General's six and eat a bullet for him if it comes to that, clear?"

Glover's face was pale beneath the rim of his helmet, but he nodded.

There was still intermittent fire coming from down the hallways and she'd frankly had enough of it. She pulled an antipersonnel grenade from her vest, twisting the arming dial to three seconds and pulling out the safety pin.

"Grenade!" she yelled before bouncing it off the far wall and around the corner.

She draped herself over General Constantine, putting her body armor between him and the blast, tucking her head down just before the concussion hit. Pressure contracted her sinuses and pressed at her chest, but no fragments made it around the corner. Suppressed carbines barked as her platoon rushed the enemy positions, but they faded quickly.

"Clear!" Lt. Grant called back to her.

She grabbed General Constantine by the arm, a stab of shock going through her at how thin and frail the arm felt in her hand, and pulled him with her, heading for the emergency stairwell. The elevators were a no-go, not least because they'd planted charges on the rails in the shaft ten minutes ago. The real professionals, people like Colonel Laurent, would go for the stairs anyway, but she wanted to make sure they only had to watch for threats from one direction.

They'd passed by interrogation centers, medical labs and monitoring rooms and the part of her that had worked intelligence for so many years wanted to burst in and grab whatever data they could recover, but that wasn't the mission. What data Starkad had managed to get was burned. The objective was the man.

"Go! Go! Go!" she urged the squad on point, motioning for the stairwell door, unmarked and set back in a dark corner of the cell block.

The squad split off into two teams through the door, half moving up to cover their approach and the rest heading down, with Lyta, General Constantine and Sgt. Glover behind them while the squad she'd taken into the cell block followed. Another fire team was covering the approaches at the ground floor, and the last was still—she hoped—at the loading dock.

"Sgt. Todd," she said into her throat mic, "do you read?"

"You're five by five, ma'am."

Lyta hissed out a sigh of relief the woman was still alive and kicking, not least because it meant Franny was still safe.

"Keep your eyes open. We're heading down."

"Yes, ma'am," Todd acknowledged. "My eyes haven't closed yet."

Francesca Hayden knew there was no reason to keep trying to break into the security monitoring system, that Lyta and the others would be back at the loading dock any minute, but it gave her something to do. And anything was better than sitting around watching George Easton breathe and waiting for someone to come try to kill them.

George was asleep, or unconscious. She wasn't a doctor or a medic, so she didn't know which. She kept checking to make sure he was still breathing, that he wasn't bleeding again, but there was nothing else she could do for him. This, though, she could do. The Starkad Intelligence encryption system was tough, the toughest she'd seen. It made cracking the codes to access the systems of the destroyer seem like a cakewalk and she was sure she'd run out of time before she got in...and then, suddenly, she was. She had an even dozen cracking programs stored in her 'link and it had, of course, been the twelfth and last that did the trick.

She scrolled past the things she might have found useful half an hour ago, like Marine troop files and mecha arming and storage data and went directly to the base's security camera monitoring system. There were hundreds of cameras in the base, but most were inactive, emplaced in unoccupied cells or empty wings and she wasted nearly thirty seconds cycling through them before she found the first live one. It was a conference room, or a break room or something with lots of chairs and tables and, in this case, people hiding underneath them. Noncombatants, she assumed, probably medical technicians or maintenance workers.

I'm a technician and I just killed a guy and I'm sitting here with a rifle over my shoulder.

It was almost another minute before she found what she was looking for. Lyta Randell and her Rangers were coming down the back stairwell, a line of black-clad figures moving cautiously but quickly. At their center was Nicolai Constantine, though she only knew it through process of elimination. She'd seen the man only months ago and wouldn't have recognized him now. His face was pale as death, his hair and beard in a wild, grizzled tangle and he'd lost at least ten or fifteen kilograms from a tall, lanky frame that couldn't spare it. He seemed a walking skeleton and she wondered how much was left of the man they'd all known.

She followed the Rangers down the steps, making sure there were no Supremacy Marines along their route. She saw nothing and was beginning to wonder if the Marines were huddled under tables alongside the other personnel.

No, Lyta always says, whatever other failings Starkad Marines might have, they aren't cowards.

So, where the hell *were* they? She'd seen a few dead bodies, but that couldn't be all of them. Were they outside?

She risked scrolling away from the view of the back stairwell, past a few unoccupied rooms, past a small garage with two cargo trucks and a ducted-fan helicopter and finally to another staircase. It had to be near the front of the building, the side facing inward toward the landing zone where two Starkad dropships still sat, empty and unpowered. As she followed the cameras down from the top floor, she saw them. At least a platoon of Supremacy Marines in full armor were strung out over two floors with a uniformed woman at their lead, already pushing open the door to the ground floor...

"Sgt. Todd!" Franny yelled, twisting around to where the Ranger NCO was leaning against the interior of the door, waiting for Lyta to arrive. "There are Starkad Marines coming down on a different staircase! They're behind Lyta and the others!"

Todd didn't waste time responding to her, just waved acknowledgement.

"Colonel Randell, this is Sgt. Todd," the woman said, her voice muffled and barely audible over the wind rushing by the open cargo doors. "Colonel Randell, do you read?"

She touched something on her left arm and Franny thought she must be switching frequencies.

"Lt. Grant, this is Sgt. Todd, do you read me?" Lt. Grant, please respond." She cursed, this time loud and clear even over the background noise. She looked back at Franny. "I think we're being jammed. They're trying to cut her off before she can get down here with him. I have to go warn her." She gestured to one of the other Rangers. "Corporal McCallister, with me. The rest of you, guard the techs."

Todd and her corporal sprinted out of the door to the loading dock without hesitation or precaution, leaving the two Rangers glancing at each other doubtfully, as if they would rather have gone with their team leader. Franny wrapped a hand around the pistol grip of her stolen rifle and stood at the edge of the door, staring down an empty hallway and fighting an insane urge to run after them.

Sweat trickled cold down between Lyta Randell's shoulder blades and she shuddered at an itch she couldn't scratch. It was too empty, too clear. This base was too big for there to be so few troops. Something was wrong.

Not much I can do about it. The damned stairs only go two directions.

They were finally at the ground floor, though she had to wait a landing up with General Constantine while the squad walking point checked the exit. The stairwell was gloomy and claustrophobic, built from the same stone as the outside wall and lit only by an occasional chemical striplight, the steps moldy and slick under her boots. She'd tried pulling down her night vision goggles, but they robbed her of too much depth perception and she'd nearly slipped twice before deciding to just deal with the dark and keep her balance.

Constantine hadn't said a word since he'd left his cell, for which she'd been grateful given how ragged out and close to the edge he'd seemed. But now, waiting on the dim and lonely landing, he turned to her and asked her a question, his voice quiet and full of broken glass.

"Is Jaimie really dead?" A long pause gave her time to consider whether she wanted to tell him the truth, but he went on. "They told me he was. That woman Laurent told me he was, that Rhianna Hale had taken the throne. Is it true?"

"It is," she said, deciding she owed it to him to be honest. "But Logan and Terrin are alive, and free. They're here, along with Wholesale Slaughter, to get you out."

"Oh, sweet Jesus," Constantine moaned, almost under his breath.

"Since when are you a follower of the Old Religion?" she asked him, too surprised to contain the question.

He eyed her balefully.

"Mithra is a warrior god," he told her, bitterness strong in his voice. "A god of the victors. Christ is Lord of the weak and helpless. I have been too long weak and helpless here."

"We're clear, ma'am," Lt. Grant called back over her ear bud. "Moving out."

She shuffled carefully down the steps to the ground floor, pulling Constantine along by the shoulder, afraid to let him go lest he collapse. It was brighter on the ground floor, the illumination coming from ornate light fixtures five meter above them in what seemed like a cross between a lobby and a conference room, with an open tile floor and a low wooden platform stage against one wall. At the center of the first floor were the elevator banks, two for personnel, one for cargo, and around the other side of them, she knew, was the loading dock.

The lead squad had already moved around the curve of the lift station, Lt. Grant with them, and his platoon sergeant, Danielle Amato, was at the rear of the squad trailing her and General Constantine. Grant had insisted she stay at the center of the formation and, for once, she hadn't overruled him. Keeping Constantine safe was the purpose of the mission and she couldn't bring herself to leave him to anyone else's trust.

The position put her about halfway across the open area when a door on the far wall burst open, just around the curve of the passenger elevators, and Starkad Marines came pouring through.

Another set of stairs, she had time to think. She wanted to blame Franny or herself, or *someone*, but the truth was, they'd gone into this mission nearly blind and this was the sort of chance you took.

Time seemed to slow down, the classic tachypsychia of a gunfight, bundled together with auditory exclusion and tunnel vision. At the end of that tunnel was Colonel Ruth Laurent, leading her Marines, a rifle at her shoulder. Lyta could have fired first, but she had another duty. She yanked Constantine behind her with one hand, raising her carbine with the other, opening up on the Supremacy Marines, but just a half second too late.

She didn't hear the shot that got her. She remembered being told no one ever did.

Ruth Laurent had never fired a rifle in combat before, never shot one anywhere but a tactical range during the training sessions Colonel Kuryakin had required for his field agents. She'd kept them up since taking over as head of Intelligence simply because it had seemed the responsible thing to do...and also because it seemed to garner more loyalty from the Marines she often brought along for support. She wasn't one of them as Colonel Grieg had been, nor did she have the fearsome reputation Kuryakin had gained in his youth as a mech-jock, so performing well on the combat simulators and the tactical ranges was a way to earn their respect.

The rifle seemed to kick more than it had at the range, seemed to weigh down her arms more. The targeting reticle in the optics danced around as she tried to hold it steady, but she pulled the trigger anyway, knowing she didn't have the luxury of time, knowing if she didn't fire first that Lyta Randell was going to.

Incredibly, miraculously, Laurent did. She'd aimed for Constantine despite her history with Lyta Randell, simply because the man was the greater danger to the Starkad cause, but the Ranger colonel put herself between the general and danger. And paid the price. Laurent couldn't tell where she'd hit the woman, but she thought she saw a spray of blood just before the Ranger officer spun to the ground.

Feral satisfaction spread through her core like a shot of whiskey, warming and tingling and making her long for more. She shifted her aim. Just one more burst and she'd take out Constantine, too, and three of the biggest threats in the Spartan government would be gone: Jaimie Brannigan, Nicolai Constantine and Lyta Randell.

Something yanked her from behind, pulling her back towards the stairwell door, pulling her out of the way of gunfire she hadn't heard. Rangers were running back from around the corner, firing full auto on the move and Marines were jerking and falling all around her, rounds smacking into the wall behind her until she was back around the curve and inside the stairwell door. She turned and glared at the Marine who'd grabbed her, a senior sergeant with dark, expressive eyes visible through the faceplate of his helmet.

"I had them!" she snapped, still absorbed with the bloodlust of the moment, not even thinking about her own troops. "I could have killed him!"

"No, ma'am," the sergeant told her with a note of reproof in his deep and resonant voice, "they could have killed you. And it's my job to keep you alive."

Laurent deflated like a balloon stuck with a pin and she finally lost the tunnel vision and noticed the wounded Marines being pulled into the shelter of the stairwell by their fellows.

"Where's Lt. Gault?" she asked the sergeant.

"Out there, ma'am," he replied, motioning with the barrel of his rifle. "Dead. Just like we'll be if we chase after them now."

"Goddammit," she hissed, slamming a palm into the wall, smooth and modern here away from the medieval façade of the exterior wall. "Goddammit! We lost." The realization stung, a whip across her back. "We lost him."

"Ma'am," the sergeant said, "with all due respect, we haven't lost as long as we're alive."

She looked at him sharply.

"What's your name, Sergeant?"

"Fuchs, ma'am. Jacob Fuchs, Gunnery Sergeant," he added, and she sensed a slight reproof there. She'd been calling him simply "Sergeant."

"Well, Gunny Fuchs," she told him, "you're on my personal guard from now on. Ranking NCO and you report directly to me. You can pick your team when we get back." She sighed and leaned against the wall, still infuriated but unwilling to spend any more energy on a lost cause.

"Assuming Lord Starkad doesn't have me summarily executed, of course."

"In that case, ma'am," Fuchs said with an unflappability she envied, "I sincerely hope he doesn't."

18

Logan smoothed his only clean pair of utility fatigues down, checking their gig line in the mirror. When he looked up at his own face, he thought he saw lines etched into it he never remembered noticing before.

"I wish I had a dress uniform," he said, shoulders sagging. "Hell, I wish any of us had dress uniforms."

Katy's hand trailed across his shoulder and he saw her in the mirror as she leaned her cheek against his arm. There were still faint streaks on her cheeks where she'd been crying. He hadn't cried. He wasn't sure if he could, not since his father had died.

"This isn't a dress uniform sort of assignment," Katy said softly. "Lyta knew that."

"We used to call her Aunt Lyta, Terrin and me," Logan mused, slipping an arm around Katy, absorbing her warmth, her strength. "She stepped in after Mom died and made sure we didn't get ignored when Dad was swamped with the work of being Guardian, of trying to repair the damage of the coup. She's always been there for us."

"She was proud of you," Katy assured him. "She was proud

of the man you'd become. The *leader* you've become. She told me so."

"It doesn't feel right, just...tossing her away out here in the nothing. She deserves a state funeral, the recognition for what she did for Sparta."

"It's what she wanted. Recognition was never important to her, you know that." Katy slipped her hand into his and squeezed tightly, then urged him toward the hatch. "Come on, it's time to go say goodbye."

The passageways of the *Shakak* were silent. The crew he and Katy passed were a procession, dressed in their best and each of them wearing matching expressions of shock and disbelief. Most were ahead of them, already on their way to the hangar bay, the only compartment in the ship large enough for them all to gather together. Logan had waited until close to the announced time for the service, both for decorum and because he hadn't wanted to stand around and attempt to seem stoic when all he really felt like doing was crawling in a hole and pulling it in after him.

He and Katy took the lift down to the bay, claiming a car for themselves. She didn't let loose of his hand until the doors slid aside and they stepped out onto the hangar bay. There was an abrupt silence, the muted buzz of conversation only detectable in its sudden absence, and three hundred heads turned their way. Some of the faces were stricken, some were respectfully grim, others seemed unaffected. Most of those were the mercenaries. They'd only known Lyta Randell by reputation.

He stepped through the crowd, returning nods and handshakes, until he reached Terrin, Franny and Kammy. They huddled together for support, shoulder-to-shoulder. Franny sniffled fitfully, wiping the back of her hand across her nose, while Kammy seemed so much smaller, shrunken in on himself. His broad-featured face had collapsed like some giant stone monument, broken and fallen amidst the ruins of the past.

Logan offered Terrin a hand, but his brother swept him into a hug and held him tight with an arm around his neck. He felt the sob shaking the younger man's shoulders. Katy was there, too, embracing them both and he wished he could have kept his head buried between theirs, shielded from the reality he had to deal with. But hundreds of people were waiting, not just to pay their respects but to receive some sort of reassurance.

And who the hell's going to reassure me?

He broke away from Terrin and Katy and turned back toward the crowd, looking past and over them at first, not quite ready to meet their eyes. The hangar bay itself drew his gaze, so marvelously different than anything else he'd ever seen on a Dominion starship. The assault shuttles and the dropships in a conventional ship were nestled into niches surrounding the pressurized section of the bay, open to the vacuum and accessible only through airlocks. The armor there, at a warship's ventral hull, was some of the thickest, and centimeters of it wrapped the shuttles and landers up, keeping them safe during combat.

The *Shakak* had no such worries, since the stardrive itself shielded them from attack. She also had no need for evacuated niches and airlocks because the same technology that had allowed Terrin to give her artificial gravity could be used to create an impermeable atmospheric seal across the mouth of the hangar bay. They didn't leave the bay doors open when not launching shuttles, but that was more for psychological comfort than physical safety.

It was awe-inspiring to stand beside the massive drop-ships, towering nearly fifty meters above him in the largest open space he'd ever seen inside a starship, and think that the whole bulk of the *Shakak* had once been underground on Terminus, had blasted up and off the planet's surface and up through the atmosphere. It had taken very nearly all the antimatter the ship had retained after centuries in hiding on the Imperial outpost, but something this huge had flown in the sky. He wished he could have seen it, since it would likely never happen again.

The shuttles and the drop-ships and loading equipment all looked down observantly at the silvery metal capsule set below them, just in front of the gathered crew, near the bay doors.

Major Lee, Lyta's Executive Officer caught his eye, looking a question at him, and Logan nodded. It was time.

"Rangers!" Lee bellowed. "Attention!"

The company had already been gathered together on one side of the gaggle of the ship's crew and as one, they snapped to attention.

"Lt. Grant!" Lee snapped.

"Here, sir!" Grant responded.

"Sgt. Preston!"

"Here, sir!"

The roll call went on through the whole company, each man and woman sounding off at their name and rank, until Lee finally hesitated before calling one, last name.

"Colonel Randell!"

No response.

"Colonel Lyta Randell!"

Logan wasn't certain, but he thought he heard a break in the man's voice as he called her one, last time.

"Colonel Lyta Ellen Randell!"

There was silence.

Lee did a perfect about-face and saluted Logan.

"Rangers lead the way, sir!"

"Indeed they do," Logan agreed solemnly, returning the salute.

Now it was Kurtz's turn, looking out over the mech-jocks,

both those who'd come with them from Sparta at the beginning of all this and the ones who'd come aboard from the mercenary units they'd signed on.

"Wholesale Slaughter Armored Corps!" There was just the hint of a drawl in his tone, the accent of his colony-world youth coming through when he yelled. "Attention!"

His about-face was not nearly as textbook as Lee's, but the salute was just as heartfelt.

"Armored Corps present, sir."

Tara Gerard piped the ship's crew to attention, a ceremony none of them had ever participated in before, Logan knew. They'd had to practice it in small groups during the flight into the system. Once they were all in some semblance of order, Tara saluted Kammy who, in turn, saluted Logan.

"The crew of the *Shakak* is present, sir," Kammy told him. The words held the weight of worlds.

"At ease," Logan told them.

He took a breath and was about to begin when he noticed movement at the back and nearly did a double-take when he saw General Constantine shuffling up from the lift banks, supported by a medical orderly. The medic didn't seem happy about the man being out of bed, but wasn't arguing with him either. The General had found utility fatigues somewhere that fit him and his hair and beard were neatly trimmed. He still had a gangly, skeletal frailty to him, and would until he'd gotten another week or two of steady rations into him, but he seemed almost human.

Logan wondered for just a moment if military procedure demanded he turn the formation over to the general, but he dismissed the idea immediately, and not just because the man was still in a fragile state. This was his crew, his mission.

Logan sucked in a breath, forced his breathing and heartrate slower, and looked the gathered men and women in the eye.

"We are here today to honor a soldier," he said. Franny had offered to set up an amplifier, but he'd learned long ago how to pitch his voice to carry. "For all she accomplished in her life, Lyta Randell was always proudest to have been a soldier, a Ranger in service to Sparta and her Guardian. She devoted her life to it, sacrificed everything for it."

His throat seemed to close up on the words, the pain squeezing at his chest. He closed his eyes and steadied himself.

"And in the end, she sacrificed herself to accomplish her mission because she believed with all her heart that the mission comes first. It defined her. She once shared with me a quote from an empire of old Earth known as Japan, from a class of warriors called the samurai. 'Death,' they said, 'is as light as a feather, but duty is heavier than a mountain.' I was just starting the Academy at the time, and it seemed obvious to me. Duty, honor, sacrifice, that was what all of us believed in. Death was far away and glorious, something that might happen to someone else, not to me or my friends. Or my family."

Logan shook his head.

"I should have known better. Lyta knew. She knew and yet she kept going, kept fighting. And the best way we can honor her memory is to do the same. I won't lie and tell you Lyta is the last of us who'll fall in this fight. But I will swear to you that I will not give up on the cause Lyta fought for and died for. I'm going to take back Sparta. I am Logan Brannigan and this I swear to you, and to her."

He regarded the silvery lozenge-shaped capsule, the final home for her physical remains.

"If it were up to me, I would take her home with me when I go, inter her in the holy ground of the Resting Place of the Guardians. But her wish, recorded on the day she'd joined the Spartan military, was to make her home here, among the stars. Today, we honor her wish. But when the time comes, when we're back home, when Sparta is no longer under the thumb of the Starkad usurper, there will be a monument to her right beside the one I build to the memory of my father, the Guardian."

He came to attention.

"Wholesale Slaughter, attention!" Every man and woman straightened, even Constantine and his medical orderly. "Present, arms!"

Logan saluted and the others followed, except Kammy. He walked slowly, deliberately to the docking bay control station and touched a panel. The bay doors began sliding apart, curtaining in on each other as they melted into the sides of the bay, and beyond them was harsh, white glare of Saraswati, the system's primary star. It washed out the other stars, jealously claiming the blackness for its own. The light flooded in, but the atmosphere remained trapped, kept in with an energy field he couldn't begin to understand. He wasn't even sure Terrin understood it. They just knew it worked.

In the front rank, lined up with the bridge crew, Terrin spoke softly, and it took Logan a moment to realize he was saying a prayer for the dead.

"Death has freed them from the material bondage," he murmured. "They have shed their frail earthly clay and departed this life to live hereafter in the realm of the spirit. Their earthly work is done and they have laid down the burden that pressed heavily on them."

Katy was praying as well, her lips moving silently, her left hand sketching a cross even as she held her salute.

Lyta's burial capsule slid forward, propelled by the electromagnetic launch strip built into the flight deck, gradually building speed as it traversed the three hundred meters between the formation and the open bay doors. There was an almost imperceptible shimmer as it passed through the field and kept going, its momentum carrying it slowly outward, bound eventually for the star.

"Order arms!"

As one, the salutes came down and the bay doors began to slide shut.

"Wholesale Slaughter, fall out to your duty stations."

The formation began to melt away, slowly at first, reluctantly. The ones who'd known her didn't want to leave, didn't want to believe it was over. The ones who hadn't didn't want to abandon their comrades in their hour of suffering, or perhaps, Logan thought uncharitably, just didn't want people to think they were assholes. But there was work to be done and, at last, even Kammy was gone, leaving him standing in the docking bay beside Katy, Terrin and General Constantine. And his orderly, who still refused to leave his side.

The general pushed the medic away and stepped up to Logan, hands on his hips. The man still looked about a hundred years old, though the haze had dropped away from his eyes after the medics had cleansed his system of the psychoactive drugs Starkad had forced into him.

"You're in no shape for this, sir," Logan told him. "Give it another few days, get some more strength back."

"The hell with that," Constantine said, dismissing the notion with a negligent wave of his hand. "You think I'm going to do any good staring at the fucking walls back on Revelation, boy?" He snorted a laugh. "That Starkad bitch wanted to squeeze the secrets out of me because she thinks what I know is dangerous, and she's damn well right it is."

Constantine seemed to waver for a moment and Logan thought the man was wandering back into the mental caverns he'd dug to escape the interrogations, but instead, he was crying. It seemed disrespectful to acknowledge weakness in Nicolai

Constantine, but Logan hesitantly reached out a hand and clutched the man's frail shoulder.

"It's the drugs," Constantine insisted, wiping at his eyes but not pulling away from Logan's touch. "The docs tell me I'll be prone to mood swings until they're completely out of my system."

Logan tilted his head, unable to keep the skepticism out of his eyes.

"Oh, all right, damn it, and I owe her something. I owe Lyta my life and, the way I see it, the only way I have of paying her back is keeping you idiot kids alive. And I can't do that sitting around feeling sorry for myself." He grinned and while it lacked, the utter, infallible confidence of the Nicolai Constantine Logan had known since childhood, it was close enough.

"All right," he decided. "Katy, prep your shuttle and get Acosta. The two of you are going to drop General Constantine on Guajarat." At her nod, he touched her arm, shooting her a warning look. "Get out quick. We're too hot to handle right now and I don't want someone IDing you."

"I am a doddering old fool," Constantine declared as if he were jumping into the middle of a completely different conversation. "This all started with you," he said to Terrin.

The younger man started as if he were waking from a dream and Logan thought he'd probably still been lost in memories of Lyta.

"What?" he grunted, then remembered who was speaking to. "I mean, sir?"

"This all started when you found Terminus," Constantine clarified. "It was the spark that lit the fuse."

"You think this was all my fault?" Terrin asked, face going white as if the General had put into words something he'd already been considering.

"No, of course not." The general waved the idea away. "*Someone* was going to find it, it was inevitable. But it was just as inevitable that it would upset the balance of power. We," he waved his finger in a tight circle indicating himself and Logan, "all thought it would be Sparta that kicked it over, but we underestimated Starkad. We all underestimated this Ruth Laurent, wherever the hell she came from. She caught us with our pants down. I've been reacting since Terminus, letting Starkad make the first move. That ends today. Today, I'm the one kicking over the anthill."

He sneered, and in the cunning, chill hatred of the expression Logan finally saw a hint of the man he knew.

"She's going to wish she'd killed me."

19

I feel like this is the second or third time I've said this to you since we've known each other, Colonel Laurent," Aaron Starkad said, a thin smile covering what Laurent could guess was cold rage, "but please tell me why I shouldn't have you taken out and shot."

"I deserve it, sir," she admitted, not flinching from the judgment.

She *should* have been flinching. She should have been sweating and shuddering, because he was very capable of doing just that. Colonel Kuryakin had told her the tales of Lord Aaron's wrath. But she'd had the entire trip back to prepare herself. A couple of stiff drinks before walking into his personal offices had helped.

"I failed to anticipate the heir would have the intelligence assets to locate Maelstrom Strand or the military resources to launch a successful attack on it." She shrugged. "It wasn't likely, and our military units are spread thin supporting Rhianna Hale, but there's no excuse for not being prepared. I can make it up to you sir, if you give me the chance."

Lord Starkad circled around her, treading carelessly on the

real tiger skin rug on his office floor and falling heavily into a leather-upholstered sofa. It was showily casual, but she could sense the lithe agility and strength of the man in the movements. The muscles of his arms and chest played beneath his tight, silk shirt and she understood very well how he'd earned a reputation as a lady's man. Rhianna Hale had to practically pry herself off him to leave and execute the coup.

"Tell me," he urged, gesturing invitingly but not offering her a seat.

"He's lost Lyta Randell," she explained. She tried to keep her eyes off his, instead letting them wander around the opulent trappings of royalty. "She's been his military advisor and infantry commander from the beginning, and a close personal friend of his and of Jaimie Brannigan before him." A pair of swords, their blades narrow and curved, their hilts unguarded, were crossed above the sofa, shining in the soft light of the crackling fireplace. "He's going to be off-balance without her, hurting and itching for a fight to get revenge. If we attack him, he won't run, he'll stand and fight."

"Attack him *where?*" Starkad demanded, leaning forward, elbows resting on his knees, as if he were about to leap up and throttle her at the wrong answer. "Do you know where he is?"

A painting of a young woman in an off-the-shoulder white dress, filmy and spectral, carrying a laundry basket on her shoulder beside a river, the frame gilt wood.

If I tell him he could still have me shot then send his generals in without me.

"Revelation," she told him.

His eyebrow went up and he grinned.

He always appreciates irony.

"Oh-ho!" he said. "Returning to the scene of the crime, is he?"

"He's gathered together several mercenary companies there,

bringing them all under the umbrella of his Wholesale Slaughter cover. He's been using them to clean out pirates and bandits all across the Periphery and the Disputed Systems."

His gaze sharpened, eyes narrowing in realization.

Just because he's an egotistical bastard doesn't mean he's not smart.

"You knew this already. You've known it for a while now, haven't you?"

"I have," she admitted.

"Yet you said nothing till now, did nothing." He seemed more intrigued than enraged. "Why?"

"Because he was using them to hunt down pirates and bandits, sir," she said without a hint of apology. "Which is not only the right thing to do, but also frees up any of our own forces which might be called on to deal with them."

"The right thing to do...," Starkad repeated, wonder in his voice, mouth nearly dropping open. "Mithra's bloody horns, my dear, it has indeed been a day since I've heard those words from someone occupying your position. My, my, how quaint."

He rubbed his palms together lightly, eyes clouding over in thought for a moment. She thought she knew the man by now, but she still didn't know if this was for show, if he'd already made up his mind and was simply toying with her.

"You did fuck up," he said, finally, with the gravity of a judge ruling on a case, "but you also gave me Sparta. And a wise man once said, if your subordinates are too terrified to fail, they'll never try."

"Who said that, sir?"

"I did. Just now."

He smiled broadly and hopped up from the couch so suddenly she had to restrain herself from jumping backwards. He went to a polished, wooden bar and retrieved a crystal decanter and two glasses. He poured something amber-colored and alcoholic from the container and handed one of the glasses to her. He offered a toast and the crystal clinked gracefully as the glasses touched.

"To second chances," he said, then downed the entire contents of the glass in a single swallow.

She knew better than to sip it. She tilted it back and drank it as a shot, closing her mouth tightly to keep the burning, bitter taste inside, to keep from coughing it back up.

"My father," Starkad told her, "was a vindictive man, Colonel Laurent. You may have heard stories about me, but you'll have to trust me when I tell you my father was so much worse." He shrugged. "I may have picked up one or two of my worst traits from him. And yes, I *do* know they're my worst, but a man has to have his hobbies. But I do endeavor to learn from the mistakes of others, and one of Lord Bran's biggest was the way he kept his generals and admirals terrified of him. Incompetence is never acceptable," he warned her, raising a finger, "but failure happens when we take risks, and some risks are worth taking."

She tried to let herself breathe again, hoping she wasn't being premature.

"And if you're wondering why I don't correct my reputation," he said, pouring himself another drink, "it's because being an ogre is sometimes convenient." He offered her more of whatever it was and she shook her head. "I'll task Admiral Longoria with assembling the task force. General Hoenig will be in charge of the ground forces and will have final command, but I will instruct him he should follow your recommendations."

"Thank you, my lord," she said, not having to pretend to sound grateful. "I know he has to die, but I have to admit, it's a shame. This man, Logan Brannigan or Logan Conner or whatever he chooses to call himself, is a born leader. I wish to Mithra he were one of ours."

"If I thought he would accept," Starkad said, with more fore-thoughtfulness than she'd believed he was capable of, "I would offer him a position as my vassal. But a man like that would never serve under another. Too much pride runs through those Brannigan veins." He chuckled and the illusion of personality was washed away in the ruthlessness of it. "Not to mention, we've killed the last four generations of them." He eyed her coldly. "Make sure it's five."

"I don't know about you guys," Josephine Salvaggio said, raising her hands palms out, "but I'm totally good with running."

Logan eyed her sidelong, remembering Lyta was the one who'd always kept the woman in line and wondering if he was going to have to do it himself now.

"Now, Josephine," David Bohardt said quietly, almost gently, "that ship has gone and sailed. We keep running, pretty soon there ain't going to be anyplace left to run."

Josephine? Logan thought. He looked across the conference table at Katy and she nodded in confirmation. *Holy shit. When did* that *happen?*

"We're making a stand," Logan declared. "If we leave, they'll sweep in here and probably leave a garrison, and this place'll be the property of the Starkad Supremacy in all but name. If they don't just decide to ship all the colonists to their work camps for cooperating with us."

"If they blow up the cities to get to us," Salvaggio pointed out, "it's all gonna be the same to the people we leave here homeless and destitute. After we're all dead," she added, glaring at Bohardt.

The other mercenary captains didn't seem inclined to

comment, the ones who disagreed with Logan's decision content to let Salvaggio speak for them.

"That's a point," Logan acknowledged. "Which is why I propose this."

He nodded to Franny and she pulled up a schematic on the operations center's main display. It showed Revelation City along with the other settlements, but the area to the north, toward the canyon they called the Run, was highlighted in yellow.

"They're going to have to come to our strength if they want to break us. We want to preserve as much of the city as we can, so my plan is to use the time we have to dig entrenchments in the hills to the north and set up our heaviest armored forces there. That should draw their mecha outside of town and minimize the damage. We'll have what heavy weapons emplacements we can spare dug in at the far end, just outside the Run, which is where we'll keep our mobile reserve."

"Starkad will still put ground troops in Revelation City," Major Lee said. His voice was quiet and reserved, his posture stiff and uneasy. Logan knew the man still wasn't entirely comfortable taking over from Lyta, but he needed him to speak his mind.

"They will," he agreed. "Which is why the Rangers and most of the infantry from our other units..." The mercenaries, he meant, though he didn't like to differentiate them from his own people because he wanted them to feel part of Wholesale Slaughter. "...and whatever volunteers we get from the Revelation militia will be set up at key junctures to slow them down. You'll be in command of the infantry units in the city, Major Lee. What I want from your force is mobility. I want them in whatever fighting vehicles we have available, technicals, trucks, all-terrain vehicles, whatever we have. They're to pin Starkad down for as long as they can, then move on to the next crossroad and do it again. I also want charges planted to block off key intersections to keep the Starkad Marines from flanking our infantry and pinning them down."

Lee nodded, a thin smile of appreciation spreading across his narrow, hard-edged face.

"Not bad," he admitted. "Starkad will constantly be taking and retaking the same ground and never accomplishing anything." He shrugged. "Eventually, they'll get tired of chasing their tails and just wipe out the whole city, though."

"If they have the available firepower to do that," Logan reminded him, "then they'll have already defeated our armored and air assets and we'll have already lost." He waved at the representation of the town on the display. "The infantry fight is to keep them occupied." He gestured to the pilots, clustered in a tight group, Spartan Navy and mercenary flyers, all Wholesale Slaughter now. "The fight in the air is to keep them occupied. The real fights are going to be the Armored assets on the ground, and our warships in space."

"I'm worried about that, bro," Kammy admitted.

He was in his utility fatigues, but the top was pulled down to his waist, exposing a sweat-soaked tank top. Kammy was too large for the heat down here planetside, even with the best the locals could do with indoor climate control, but Logan had wanted the big man here in person for the planning session. The *Shakak*'s captain had been keeping to himself since Lyta's funeral, hiding in his cabin whenever he wasn't on duty, and Logan needed to make sure he was engaged with the defense strategy.

"The *Shakak* is a better ship than anything the Supremacy has," Kammy went on, "but you've been there, you've seen what happens when we have to face multiple capital ships and we can't maneuver."

"It's the power source," Terrin interjected, finally finding something within his area of expertise. "I think if we had anti-matter power for the drive field, nothing in the whole Dominion could touch us. But all we have is a fusion plant, and the field isn't strong enough to hold up when a lot of energy is poured into it from the outside. It's inherently unstable to begin with, for practical reasons if nothing else, since a stable expansion field would mean nothing could ever come close to the ship so no one could enter or leave it. But that means it wants to collapse and it needs constant, stable energy input to keep it from collapsing."

"Bottom-line it for us, Terry," Kammy urged.

"We can outrun anyone," Terrin declared. "Nothing out there with a conventional fusion drive can keep up with us, not even a ship-killer missile. But when we're trying to stay in one place and defend a position, we're vulnerable. They can just sit back and pour missiles and lasers at us until the field collapses."

"We have the destroyer," Katy pointed out. "We have the cargo ships the other mercenary units came here with."

"Those cargo ships won't last a damned minute," Salvaggio opined. "You'd be better off sending them off to hide, because anyone who crews them and tries to take on Starkad cruisers is committing suicide."

"The destroyer can help," Kammy admitted. "But it can't take on a cruiser by itself. Our best bet would be to have Nance sit back in a LaGrangian point and take potshots at them, keep them distracted. But it all depends how many ships they bring after us."

Logan chewed on his lip for a moment, moving chess pieces around in his mind and coming up with a gambit he was sure no one would like.

"We're all agreed the cargo ships are part of the Wholesale Slaughter TO&E, right?" he asked, meeting the eyes of Bohardt, Salvaggio, and the other mercenary commanders.

TO&E, Table of Organization and Equipment, was all the gear and weapons native to a unit. They'd understand the reference, all of them being former military.

The others shared uncomfortable glances, all of them finally settling on Bohardt as their spokesman.

"We signed on with you, Boss," he assured Logan. "But if we lose those ships, we ain't getting anyone out of here, win or lose."

"We'll hold two of them back," Logan decided. "The *Venture* and the *Wayfarer* will head out by the ice giant, powered down." Those were the most lightly armed and armored of their cargo ships, the least likely to survive a space battle. "They'll each carry a couple of our drop-ships. We won't be able to use them for the fight anyway. That way, if we need it, we'll have a way out." He looked around the conference table. "Any objections?"

He was sure he saw some doubt in a few eyes, especially those of the owners of the other cargo ships, but no one else raised a concern.

"What good are the cargo haulers anyway?" Kammy wondered, earning a dirty look from one of their captains, a gaunt woman with a greying mohawk. "Sorry, sis," he said, touching a hand to his chest in apology, "but they're not warships. They could do all right against pirates, but we're talking Starkad cruisers here."

"Terrin," Logan said, "we've got a few dozen spare fusion reactors for the mecha between all our ships and their repair bays. How hard would it be to turn them into mines?"

"Shit," Kammy blurted, frowning as he considered the idea.

"Not too difficult," Terrin said. "Not from a technical standpoint," he added. "I'd have to get with the ships' engineering crew and some of the repair techs to see how fast we could rig it up."

"There's a reason no one uses mines though, boss," Kammy reminded him. "If they're 'dumb' mines, just sitting there until the ship gets close enough, the deflectors will knock them away, and if they're computer controlled with maneuvering rockets, the ships' ECM systems will screw up their guidance."

"If they have the time," Logan agreed. "But what if one of the cargo ships builds up six or seven gravities of steam and then launches the mines ahead of it like a shotgun? We could mount them to short-range rocket engines, maybe strip them off the reloads for our mecha launch pods."

"That's fucking suicide!" the gaunt woman snapped, her eyes going wide.

"It'd be a damned close thing," Logan admitted. "The ship would have a skeleton crew and they'd have to eject right after they launch the mines."

"That's ballsy," Salvaggio admitted. "Who's gonna volunteer for it, though?"

"Are you kidding?" a small, frail-looking man with a shaven head covered in tattoos piped up, his voice surprisingly deep for his frame. Theon was his name, Logan remembered. Grant Theon, captain of Bohardt's ship, the *Ambrose Light*. "Getting a chance to destroy a damned cruiser with a cargo hauler? I'll do it! Live or die, they'll tell that story for centuries."

"Well, listen to you," the mohawk woman said with a sharp laugh. He couldn't remember her name, but he knew she worked for the Cossacks under Captain Bakunin. "You think I'd let you take all the fucking glory, Theon? You and that damned rust bucket?"

"If we both live, Marie," Theon told her, "I'll buy you a drink on Gateway at the *Tia Juanita*."

"You think you're gonna get lucky with me that easy, you old goat?"

There was a general chuckle around the conference table

and just a tiny fraction of the weight on Logan's shoulders seemed to fall away.

"Boss," Bohardt said slowly, almost reluctantly, "you know I'm in this with you. But I have to ask, because we're all thinkin' it. This is Starkad we're talkin' about. They might be spread thin right now, but spread thin for us and for them is two different things. If they come after us here with everything they got, we ain't gonna' be able to pull this off."

Logan tried not to wince at the question. Not that he hadn't been expecting it.

"I understand that, David. And if any of you want to pull out, I completely understand."

He saw Valentine Kurtz bristle at the pronouncement, but it had to be said. So much of this depended on the mercenaries sticking with him. If they changed their mind, he had no legal authority behind him, nothing but a threat of force he didn't want to use and that might backfire on him if he did.

"And maybe you're right," he acceded, shrugging casually. "Maybe I'd be smarter to run, to preserve all the forces I have, hit and run, make myself a thorn in Rhianna Hale's side and give Starkad a wide berth. You know what would happen then, David? Josephine? The rest of you?" He met their eyes, one at a time, making sure they understood what he was asking. "How do you think we'd live, then? How would we get supplies? Food? Fuel? Spare parts?"

"We could raid for them...," Salvaggio began, then she stopped mid-sentence,.

"Exactly." He nodded. "We'd start raiding, telling ourselves we were justified because it's a war. And the war wouldn't end, because with Starkad backing Hale, we'd never beat her through attrition. They'd just keep making up her losses, and we'd keep raiding, and what do you think we'd become after a few years of that? If we were still alive?"

"Pirates." Katy fairly spat the word.

It seemed to echo across the room, impacting them physically. The air went out of Bohardt as the thought sank home.

"Starkad will come here, ladies and gentlemen. And maybe we win, or maybe we all die. But I'd rather risk it all in open battle here, fighting the real enemy." He stood from his chair, leaning on the conference table with open palms. "I am Logan Brannigan, and I mean to be the Guardian of Sparta, as my father was, and his grandfather before him. I'm going to liberate my people, not prey on them. Mithra forbid, we may wind up having to kill my own countrymen in battle, but I won't scavenge the carcass of my nation."

He straightened, stretching his hand into the center of the circular table.

"Win or die. Who's with me?"

Katy was first, followed only a moment later by Terrin, then the rest of his Spartans and Kammy, their hands resting on top of his. Slowly but in a rising tide, the others joined, until they all stood together.

"All right then," he said. "Let's get to work."

20

They'll know we're coming," Eric Hoenig declared as if it were the prophecy of an oracle.

The general was, Laurent thought, trying to look purposefully stoic and momentous, staring out at the stars through the transparent aluminum of the *Orkla's* observation bubble, his arms across his chest, chin tucked into his chest. All he needed was a long, red beard to match the red stubble on his head and he could have passed for a Viking captain of another age heading from Denmark to England.

"Of course, they will," she agreed. "There's no way to hide a task force this size."

She could see two of the other five cruisers burning at one gravity on candles of fusion flame thousands of kilometers away in a globular formation. They were slightly brighter stars among a vast and wonderful firmament, but not hard to spot if one knew how to look.

Each carrying two companies of mecha and two more of Marines.

"It's very pretty up here, sir," she said carefully, not wanting to offend the man. He had a reputation for being prickly. "But

I'm sure you didn't just invite me up to the Observation Deck to look at the stars. Is something wrong?"

Because we're going to be jumping again in ten hours and I could really use some sleep.

"I need to know you're sure," he confided, his beady, brown eyes moving beneath heavy brows, peering out at her like bugs sheltered under a rock ledge. "About the enemy disposition," he amended. *Just in case I'm some kind of idiot.* "This is an awfully big risk. These ships are needed elsewhere."

Ah. He's got nerves and wanted them soothed somewhere private. This was certainly the place for a private conversation. No one but the universe to overhear them.

"Lord Starkad believes they're needed here," she reminded him. "But yes, I'm certain of the enemy strength. They have no more than eight companies of mecha and only two of them are composed of line-quality machines." *Stolen from us.* She didn't add that aloud, though. "The rest are outdated, obsolete or pieced together from spare parts. They have one company of Spartan Rangers along with possibly as many as five to eight companies of lesser infantry, some in lightly armored vehicles. Two true military assault shuttles and a few armed landers that won't last long in air combat. They only have two honest-to-God warships, a destroyer and the Imperial-tech cruiser they stole from the old outpost at Terminus."

The part of her that had worked intelligence for the last ten years bristled at sharing out state secrets so freely, but Lord Starkad had assured her Hoenig had been read into all the details of the Terminus operation.

"The Imperial ship concerns me," Hoenig said, frowning as if this were some sort of shameful admission.

If it didn't, you'd be a complete moron.

"It's beyond anything we can build now, but it's not magic. From the reports I audited, it can be damaged if enough fire is focused on it. Its greatest advantage is speed, but that's only an advantage if they run."

"And what if they do? This mission will be meaningless if they don't stand and fight."

"Logan Brannigan is not the running type. He *wants* to fight us. We're going to give him what he wants."

Hoenig nodded, and she thought he was satisfied.

Perhaps a bit too *satisfied.*

"Make no mistake, sir," she warned him, "these people are not going to roll over and die. We *are* going to take losses, perhaps heavy ones. But as long as we don't do anything stupid, victory is inevitable."

What she'd said was necessary. Hoenig needed the reassurance, big, red-bearded baby that he was. Yet they made her intensely uncomfortable, reminding her of a phrase Colonel Kuryakin had shared with her once. Something about famous last words.

The plains outside Revelation City were almost pleasant at night, the unrelenting heat of the day giving way to a high desert chill, the brutal punishment of the primary replaced by the magnificent light show of a cloudless night and a million stars. Logan lie motionless beside her on the blanket, eyes fixed on those stars as if he thought the answers to their problems were hidden among them.

"I'd use nukes if I could," he confessed softly.

Katy blinked and rolled over, one arm falling across his chest, wondering if she'd heard him right.

"Nukes?" she repeated. She wanted to whisper though she didn't know why. There was no one out there with them, no one for kilometers around. The groundcar they'd taken pinged quietly in the cooling night as metal heated up on the drive out contracted again.

"On Starkad," he clarified. "On their ground forces. If we didn't have to worry about the civilians here, I'd use nukes. It's the only way I can see to make up for the difference in forces." He shrugged and she could feel the play of his muscles in his chest. "Unless the interdiction in space goes better than how I'm thinking it will."

She shuddered and she was certain it wasn't just the night air.

"Do you think Starkad would use them? I mean, out here, away from any witnesses, they might be able to get away with it."

"No." His response was firm, confident. "Aaron Starkad is going to want proof I'm dead. Otherwise, the possibility I'm alive out there somewhere would give hope to loyalists."

He spoke of his own death so easily, so calmly, and she was sure he wasn't just putting on a front. For the others, perhaps, but not for her. She knew him too well. He'd accepted it, accepted not just the possibility but almost the certainty of it.

Impulsively, she leaned up and kissed him, her lips lingering on his, fingers entangled in his blond hair. When they parted, her breath came shorter, not merely from desire but from something warmer, deeper.

"I need you to do me a favor," she said.

"Anything," he said. She could tell by the earnest certitude of his voice, his gaze that he meant it.

"Starkad will be here in a couple days, and sometime before that I need you to marry me."

He sat up quickly, mouth falling open.

"Really?" he blurted, and she laughed softly.

"Yes, really. No matter what happens, I want us to be husband and wife when we face it."

"But there's no time for a wedding," he said, panic she hadn't seen at the thought of his own death coming into his eyes as he realized it. "We'd have to start the ceremonies tomorrow with the silver coins, and then the lamps have to be lit the next day..."

"Not a Zoroastrian ceremony," she corrected him. "I want us to be married with a Christian ceremony."

"You do?" he asked, looking almost as equally dumbfounded as when she'd suggested getting married in the first place.

"Later, when we're back on Sparta and you're the Guardian, we can have a Zoroastrian wedding. I know it's politically necessary. But right now I'd like one in the name of the God I believe in."

"What made you decide to return to the Old Religion?" he asked. She didn't think there was any disappointment in his tone, only honest curiosity.

No better time to be curious about religion than when you're sure you're going to die.

"I don't find comfort in Mithra anymore," she confessed. "He looks too closely at what I've done, the mistakes I make. Jesus recognizes I'm human and fallible. He knows I can't find perfection on my own"

"You *are* perfect," he said, arms going around her. "And yes, I'll marry you with a Christian ceremony, or any other kind you want, you know that. I've wanted to marry you since I first met you."

He pulled her into a fierce kiss, holding onto her as if he was afraid something was about to tear her away. The warmth of his chest burned against hers, a second sun in the cold of the night.

As prisons went, it wasn't bad.

Donnell Anders set his fork down onto the empty plate with a clatter of metal on ceramic and sat back in his chair. Plain wood, just like the table, unfinished and rough, but comfortable. The house wasn't his own, was small and undecorated, devoid of anything more dangerous than a butter knife, but it wasn't a cell and food and drink and even entertainment of a sort were all available.

No connection to the open net, of course, nor any other communications with the outside world. He wasn't even entirely certain where on Sparta he was being kept and the guards stationed outside weren't forthcoming. There were mountains outside, but not the Bloodmarks, which ruled out Argos. Maybe Engyon, or somewhere near it in the far south. He'd never been there, but he recalled there being a mountain chain just outside the city.

Does it matter? Are you going to escape into the wilderness, climb the mountains and steal a shuttle, hijack a starship and join some resistance?

Not if he wanted his wife and daughters to live through this. That much had been made clear to him.

He nearly jumped out of the chair when the front door opened, but settled back down when a pair of armed soldiers strode through, rifles levelled. Behind them, one hand resting on the butt of her holstered pistol, was Rhianna Hale. She seemed more severe than the last time he'd seen her, back before the coup, her dark hair pulled back tight in a bun, lines of stress aging her face by a few years. She still wore her Spartan Armored Corps uniform, though it no longer bore a major's rank on the collar. Replacing it was the symbol of the Guardian, and he felt a flash of impotent rage at the sight.

"Good evening, General Anders," she said, her tone casual. "I trust you're not finding your confinement too arduous?"

"Surprisingly, no," he acknowledged. He felt a stubborn

urge to refuse to speak to her. It was what a younger Donnell Anders would have done, but age and experience had taught him that those sorts of games accomplished nothing. Getting your enemies talking was a victory in and of itself. "Though I admit to being confused as to why."

Hale laughed, a cold and harsh sound, like the polar winds across the glaciers. She pulled a chair out from the table opposite his and sat down. The guards remained two meters away, rifles trained on him.

"And what purpose would that serve, Donnell? To prove how tough and unyielding I am? I think I've proven that point."

She leaned back, propping a boot up on the edge of the table.

I eat there, he thought churlishly, but didn't say.

"Donnell, tell me something, when you were the head of the Guardian's armies, did you consider yourself a servant of Sparta, or of Jaimie Brannigan?"

"I considered them one and the same," he said, not willing to be pulled into the word trap. "Jaimie Brannigan always served the needs of the people of Sparta."

"And now?" she prompted, turning over a hand. "Nothing will bring Jaimie Brannigan back to life. I am the Guardian now, however you may feel about my methods of achieving the position. Are you still loyal to the people of Sparta, or were those empty words?"

"You are not best serving the people of Sparta." He was probably making a mistake, he knew, but she wasn't stupid. She'd know if he was simply pretending to go along with her. "You've subverted the good of Sparta to the purposes of the Starkad Supremacy."

"I'm using Starkad as they're using me," she argued, waving his objection away. "I'm allowing them to bleed themselves dry hunting down loyalists and holdouts, while I preserve my forces...Sparta's forces. When I've consolidated my power, they'll turn their attention to Clan Modi, seeking to use their newly-secured alliance with Sparta to expand."

"Mithra's horns," Anders hissed the words, leaning forward. The motion drew a threatening motion from the guards, but he ignored it. "You mean to betray them."

"They're the enemy," she reminded him, not even bothering to deny it. "How can you betray the enemy? I mean to do what your former leader, Jaimie Brannigan lacked the balls or," she shrugged, "to be generous, the political capital to do. I mean to rebuild the Empire with Sparta at its head. Lord Brannigan thought it was always something for the future, for some nebulous period when we had more troops, more technology, more weapons." She sniffed her disdain. "A true Guardian needs none of those. They simply need the will. The will to make the sacrifices that need to be made, to take the chance."

"You'll break us," Anders warned her, fear prickling across the hair on the back of his neck. "You'll destroy us going against Starkad."

"Perhaps I will," Hale admitted. She brought her feet down from the table and rested her hands palm-flat on it instead, her face drawing closer to his. "But at least I'll make the attempt. The question is, will you let me make it without you?"

"The hell?" The words escaped of their own volition before he'd even considered them. "You can't be serious!"

"You're a patriot, General," she said. "And so am I, though you may not believe it. I did what I did because Eoghan Brannigan subverted our system of government, our way of life in an attempt to aggrandize his own family. I don't blame his grandson. Jaimie did what he thought was right, but it couldn't be allowed to continue. The Guardianship is *not* hereditary, it's *not* a Goddamned birthright for the Brannigans to hand from generation to generation."

"So, you won't be grooming your own replacement then?" Anders assumed. "You'll be happy with the Council's choice, whoever they may be?"

"Now that the deadweight has been cleansed from their ranks, I will," she shot back. "I didn't do this to establish a Hale legacy, whether you believe it or not! I took the life of a good man, and I'll kill many more if I have to, in order to save this nation from those who would have turned it into a kingdom like the Supremacy!"

He wanted to rail at her, wanted to rage for the heroes who'd died fighting her people, but he remembered something General Constantine had told him during what the older man termed "leadership counselling." No one, he'd said, is the villain in their own story. Rhianna Hale *was* a patriot. She *did* believe she had the best interest of Sparta at heart. She might be dreadfully, disastrously wrong, but simply dismissing her as a demon wouldn't change anything.

"Let's stipulate for a moment that I accept what you're saying is true," he allowed. "Why do you think I would join you? And more importantly, why would you trust me if I did?"

"Sparta *is* going to war with Starkad," she said. "I am the Guardian and I will make it so. You know as well as I do you're a more experienced general than any other I have, and you know having you will mean a better chance of victory in a war that will be fought whether you join me or not." She shrugged. "Knowing you as I do, I doubt you can bring yourself to turn me down."

Damn the bitch. The thought wasn't without admiration. Because she was exactly right.

21

Dearly beloved, we are gathered here in the sight of God," Revelation City's only priest of the Old Religion intoned solemnly, "and in the face of this company to join together this man and this woman in holy matrimony..."

The man was plump in the face, his cheeks red from the late-afternoon sun and the heat and sweat stained the armpits of his ornate white robes. He reminded Logan of the family chef back in the palace, except Chef Phillip had a big, blond handlebar moustache and Father Daniel sported a full beard. At least the priest had dressed up for the occasion. Logan and Katy both wore their duty clothes, a flight suit for her and fatigues for him. The witnesses were no better attired, all of them just coming off duty and ready to head back on just as soon as the ceremony was complete.

Katy though...Katy didn't need a formal dress. She didn't need anything. She smiled beside him, looking as happy as she had since he'd known her, and he was certain he wasn't biased in the thought that she was the most beautiful woman in the entire universe.

"...which is commended to be honorable among all of God's

children, and therefore is not to be entered into lightly by any, but reverently, discreetly, advisedly and solemnly. Into this holy estate these two persons present now come to be joined. If any person can show just cause why they may not be joined together, let them speak now or forever hold their peace."

"Here they come!" Tara snapped. Kammy could see it himself on the sensor display, but he let her talk. It helped her think things through. "Three, four, *five by Mithra*, six.... *Six* Starkad cruisers through the jump-point, Captain."

"All Wholesale Slaughter vessels," Kammy ordered, trying to channel Donner Osceola as he always did in times such as these, "move to attack positions." He turned to Bergh. "Take us into weapons range, Helm, maximum acceleration."

"Aye, sir," Bergh said crisply. "Maximum acceleration."

"Drive field at one hundred percent," Terrin announced. It wasn't any more necessary than Tara's observation, but he'd been trying to get the kid into the habit of letting him know the status of the field on a regular basis, so he let it go. "All systems nominal."

He'd thought about trying to make Terrin stay on one of the ships they'd sent out to the ice giant to hide, but he couldn't bring himself to suggest it. Terrin had been with them from the beginning, near enough, and he was one of the crew now.

Besides, Logan probably already tried to talk him into going, and if the Boss decided not to force the issue, neither will I.

"They're gonna target us with their lasers the second we're anywhere close to in range," Tara judged. "Which should be just another three or four minutes at this speed."

The enemy ships were probably in optical range by now, but the simulation on the main screen was so high-quality he nearly couldn't tell it from the real thing. Six of them, gigantic, rough-hewn mountains burning straight for them at three gravities, while they rushed into the breach at the equivalent of thirty gees. Their wedge shapes were arrows of glittering silver, lit up by the miniature suns at their tails, fusion flames confined by magnetic fields.

"They think we're just gonna sit in front of them and go into defensive mode," Kammy mused. "Let's try to use what we got how they won't expect. Helm, take us up forty degrees on the Y axis relative to the ecliptic."

"Forty degrees Y axis, aye," Bergh confirmed.

He couldn't feel a thing, couldn't feel the change in direction or the brief interruption of the drive field as Bergh switched it off to kill their forward momentum, then bumped it to full power heading at a steep, upward angle compared to the course of the Starkad cruisers. Their lasers could be fired off their X axis, but not more than a few degrees. If they wanted to keep the *Shakak* at bay, at least one of them was going to have to...

"Ships at the north and northwest position in the cluster are turning," Tara announced.

Kammy nodded. He'd expected it. The fusion drives had cut off and the flare of maneuvering rockets lit up the ventral bow of both cruisers on the hemisphere of the globular cluster at the north side of the ecliptic. "North" was a relative term in space, but you had to describe directions somehow, and this was intuitive while some arbitrary numeric system wouldn't be.

"The rest are proceeding toward Revelation," Tara added.

Kammy turned to the communications officer. "Signal the *Avenger* and the *Ambrose Light* to target the southern ship in the formation." Back to Bergh at the Helm. "Set an intercept course for the two ships they tasked for us, but don't make it easy for them."

"Aye, sir. Heading in."

"Marriage is the union of husband and wife in heart, body and mind," the Father went on, the corners of his mouth turning up the only indication he was having a good time. "It is intended for their mutual joy and for the help and comfort given one another in prosperity and adversity."

We've certainly had our share of both, Katy thought, tightening her grip on Logan's hand.

What if they didn't live through this? What if this was the end of their journey?

"Through marriage, Logan and Kathren make a commitment to face their disappointments, embrace their dreams, realize their hopes and accept each other's failures. Logan and Kathren will aspire to these ideals throughout their lives together."

Logan was beaming at her, despite the unfamiliar ceremony, just happy to be with her, the way he always was. He might have been the son of a king, but his wants were as simple as any other man, someone to be with him, to love, to grow old with and raise a family with.

Will we have any of that? Does it matter as long as we both found what we were looking for?

Terrin was standing beside Logan, the best man. He might not have always been there, definitely not when she'd first met the two of them, but now he was Logan's friend as well as his brother. To Katy's side was Franny, as cleaned up and presentable as any of them had been able to manage at short notice. It might have been Lyta Randell there had this all happened a few weeks earlier, but Franny was a good choice for maid of honor. She'd become important to Katy simply because she was important to Terrin, and Terrin was as much her brother now as he was Logan's. She thought she saw Terrin and

Franny sneaking glances at each other during the ceremony. She wondered if they were thinking about doing the same thing someday.

Probably not a Christian *ceremony, but still...*

"Who stands present with Kathren as she enters her life with Logan?"

"I do," Kammy said from behind her, taking the place of her father. The big man's voice broke slightly at the words and fond warmness spread through her at his obvious emotion.

She wished her mother and father could be here for this moment. She hoped they were still safe, that all this strife hadn't touched them in their little pocket of heaven in the heart of the war.

"Do you, Logan, take Kathren to be your wife, to live together after God's ordinance in the holy state of matrimony? Will you love her, comfort her, honor and keep her, in sickness and in health, for richer, for poorer, for better, for worse, in sadness and in joy, to cherish and continually bestow upon her your heart's deepest devotion, and forsaking all others, keep yourself only unto her as long as you both shall live?"

"I will."

"Drive field down to sixty percent," Terrin said, fingers digging into the armrests of his chair, trying not to clench his teeth. It felt unnatural for a spaceship to shake like that, and it was worse that it didn't seem to bother any of the others.

They're probably just better at hiding it.

"Capacitors recharged," Tara Gerard droned, always so frosty in combat, so unlike her normal, fiery self. "Targeting cruiser one and firing."

Cruiser one and two, that's what they'd been calling them.

As if one weren't enough, as if they weren't dealing with *six* of the damned things. Just narrowing it down to the two, trying to slice it into manageable chunks.

The particle beam cannon fired again—*was this the third time? The fourth?*—and the Starkad cruiser's portside stern erupted in a fountain of liberated energy, hundreds of tons of metal turning violently into gas, then into plasma. Smaller jets followed, burning atmosphere from breaches in the hull. The drive cut off and the cruiser began to drift, the gas surging away from the hit acting as its own, unplanned maneuvering thruster.

"Cruiser one is down," Tara announced, then added quietly, "the bastard. Two is maneuvering, capacitor recharging."

"Drive field back to eighty percent," he put in, having to force himself to look away from the spectacle of the dying cruiser to check the reading. "Should be one hundred percent in..."

The second cruiser's laser fired, the range closer now, and Terrin jerked against his restraints as the drive field contracted again, rattling the hull and them with it.

"Drive field fifty percent." *Damn it.*

"Kammy, we got cruisers three *and* four turning back to us," Tara warned. "Ten seconds till capacitors are recharged."

"Status on the *Avenger*?" Kammy asked her, still as placid as a mountain lake.

"*Avenger* is engaging with cruisers five and six near the LaGrangian points. *Amber Light* is approaching six at four gravities acceleration."

Terrin could feel a surge as the drive field regenerated, but not fast enough, not with three cruisers...

"Do you, Kathren, take Logan to be your husband, to live together after God's ordnance in the holy state of matrimony?"

Logan felt light-headed. It was ridiculous. He'd faced death so many times he'd lost count, led dozens of men and women into battle where the very fate of worlds was on the line, and he was nervous as a kitten at the prospect of marrying the woman he loved? *Ridiculous.*

"Will you love him, comfort him, honor and keep him, in sickness and in health, for richer, for poorer, for better, for worse, in sadness and in joy, to continually bestow upon him your heart's deepest devotion and, forsaking all others, keep yourself only unto him as long as you both shall live?"

The priest was looking at Katy and so did he. They'd been through so much, seen death, devastation, and betrayal, yet somehow she was more beautiful now than the day he'd met her.

"I will," she promised.

"What token of your love do you offer?"

This had been the tricky part, given the time constraints. No one outside the very small Christian community in one of Revelation's more remote outposts had any idea what a wedding ring was, so they'd had to have them custom fabricated and they were still hot from the polishing wheel only an hour ago.

He slipped the gold band onto her finger, hoping his hands weren't so sweaty he'd drop it.

"With this ring, I thee wed," he repeated the words as he'd been instructed.

When she put the simple, unmarked band onto his left ring finger, it felt strange, almost unnatural. He'd never worn any sort of jewelry, but it was more than that. There was a weight to it, a permanence.

His pulse was beating so loudly in his ears, he almost missed it when Katy said the same phrase back to him.

"With this ring, I thee wed."

"In as much as Logan and Kathren have consented together in marriage before this company of friends and family and have pledged their faith, by the power vested in me by the Holy Church of Our Lord and Savior Jesus Christ, I now pronounce you husband and wife."

The priest grasped their entwined hands in his and smiled as he squeezed them tightly together.

"What God has joined together, let no human put asunder."

A cheer went up from the witnesses gathered, and Tara Gerard whooped wildly, having preceded the wedding celebration by at least an hour or two. She didn't have the bottle of wine in her hand *now*, but he'd certainly seen it there less than ten minutes before the ceremony.

Logan swept Katy into his arms, laughing with sheer joy, all the nerves and doubts suddenly gone, and kissed her in the warmth of an alien sun.

"Hey! Hey!"

He didn't register the shout at first over the cheers and laughs of his friends, but it persisted like the buzz of a mosquito past his ear. He broke his embrace with Katy and saw the young man running across the plain from town toward the clearing where they'd had the outdoor ceremony. Logan recognized him immediately as one of the teenagers they'd left on watch in the security center, keeping an open ear for the communications line.

"Shit," Katy murmured beside him.

"Sir!" the boy gasped, out of breath as he reached them, eyes flickering in confusion to the priest. "Sir, we just got a relayed message from one of the ships we sent out for sentry duty!"

Logan nodded understanding. They'd had several of the older cargo ships, useless for a fight but usable as scouts to keep an eye on adjacent systems.

"It was the *Kraken*," the kid reported dutifully. "In the Verdant system. She said the Starkad fleet just jumped into the far antipolar jump-points." The messenger sucked in one last deep, shuddering breath before he settled into a normal voice. "They're coming, sir. They'll be here within a day."

Logan met Kammy's eyes and the big man nodded.

"All spacers to their ships," Logan said, his voice losing its earlier joy, returning to the flat, businesslike tones of war. His thumb rubbed the unfamiliar metal of his wedding ring. "All mech pilots to the hangars."

He gave Katy one last kiss before they began striding across the field, heading off to battle. Behind him, he heard the priest murmuring a soft and fervent prayer.

"Hail Mary, full of grace. The Lord is with thee. Blessed art thou amongst women, and blessed is the fruit of thy womb, Jesus. Holy Mary, Mother of God, pray for us sinners, now and at the hour of our death..."

Terrin was watching the *Avenger*. He didn't know if anyone else had the attention to spare for it, but he felt as if someone should watch. Shelly Nance had been the Communications officer on the *Shakak* since day one, had turned down an XO posting on another Navy ship despite her promotion to commander, just to stay with Wholesale Slaughter. She'd been given her own ship, the captured Starkad destroyer, just in time for this battle, been sent head to head against a cruiser, a ship with twice her armor and firepower. She was less than ten thousand kilometers from the lead Starkad cruiser, their missiles crossing the distance between them, passing by each other en route, running through clouds of electrostatically charged chaff, targeted by waves of tungsten slugs from the point defense coilguns.

"Firing," Tara said, and he looked away for just a moment, seeing the beam from the *Shakak's* main gun splash across the nose of cruiser two. "Shit, we got missiles inbound from three and four. Four, no, six of them. They're not messing around. Cruiser two is damaged, venting atmosphere, but she's still operational. She's turning, pulling back."

Three battles happening hundreds of thousands of kilometers apart, the light of the events lagging over a second behind reality, and even the one he was involved in personally seemed far away to him. In high orbit around Revelation, *Ambrose Light* was still boosting straight at cruiser six, firing off every weapon she had to interdict the incoming missiles, sublimated metal gassing off her nose in a halo of light as the Starkad laser bit into her. She wasn't turning, wasn't trying to present her drive bell, just charging straight in.

"It's suicide." He hadn't meant to say the words out loud, but he saw Kammy's eyes flash his way. There was annoyance in them, anger, but it melted away when the big man saw where he was looking. There was pain in the captain's eyes, but he kept his demeanor calm and firm.

"Bergh," Kammy ordered, "lose those missiles."

Another shudder, a distant hit from a laser.

"Damn it," Bergh muttered, uncharacteristically. "Every time they hit us, we lose ground."

A jolt, closer this time, from the nearer of the two Starkad ships. Terrin clenched his jaw, checking the readouts.

"Fifty percent field propagation," he said, feeling a tightness in his gut as the field closed in around them. "If we get hit again like that, it's going to collapse."

"Get us moving, Bergh," Kammy said. It was obvious he was trying to be calm, trying to be in what Terrin had come to think of as his "captain mode," but he leaned forward in his chair, his fists clenched, tension pulling at the sides of his broad face.

"The more strain we put on the drive field, the longer it takes to repropagate," Terrin told him, trying not to sound as desperate as he felt. "We're going as fast as the field will let us go."

"Which isn't fast enough to keep ahead of those damned missiles," Tara informed them.

The red arrowhead icons were gaining on them, slowly but surely, as inexorable and unstoppable as death.

"Cruisers three and four are taking a twenty-five-degree angle on us," Tara warned. "At this rate, they'll be in position to hit us again in thirty seconds. And those missiles will be on us faster than that."

"Helm control to tactical," Kammy ordered sharply. "Tara, spin us and target the missiles. Try to keep them between us and the cruisers."

Terrin wanted to scream at him not to turn, not to stop accelerating away from the lasers, but there was no right answer and the missiles would kill them faster. If they could keep the missiles in the firing arc of the Starkad cruisers, the enemy wouldn't be able to fire the lasers at them without destroying their own ship-killers. This was why he was a scientist and not a military officer.

He forced himself to look away from the ship-killers, back at the *Ambrose Light* and the *Avenger*. The *Ambrose Light* was coming apart, her nose sheering off in a flash of igniting oxygen, but she was close now, so very close...

The mines launched from her hangar bay, rigged on short-range rocket engines, tiny red fireflies swarming out into the path of the Starkad cruiser, unavoidable, far too close for countermeasures, only a hundred kilometers away. Fusion explosions in space were white globes. He'd seen them before, sometimes from far too close, but this was like nothing else he'd experienced. Dozens of white spheres sprang up so close together they were a solid wall, eating away at the hull of the Supremacy warship, stripping its armor away, each opening up holes for the next. The maneuvering rockets at the nose of the cruiser blew in yellow and red flares of solid fuel, sending bits of wreckage spinning away, leaving the ship impossible to steer.

And the *Ambrose Light* was still boosting.

She had to have been travelling at hundreds of meters per second when she struck the damaged nose of the Supremacy ship. Their forms merged, the rounded oblong of the cruiser, pragmatic and ungainly, and the iron wedge of an axe-head as big as a mountain, briefly forming something new and monstrous. Until the reactors blew and a new star shone in the system, lighting up the night side of Revelation.

Grant Theon, that had been the man's name, the captain of the *Ambrose Light*.

There was no gasp, no exclamation on the bridge, not even from Terrin. By then, he'd known. He knew what was going to happen to all of them.

"Firing main gun."

One of the ship-killers winked out of existence and the seconds began to tick away again, the others still creeping closer. They were wolves surrounding a hiker deep in the woods, a man of an old Earth who had only an ancient muzzle loader for a weapon. Except these wolves were machines who wouldn't be scared off, wouldn't shirk from taking the losses, trying to get him before he reloaded.

On the tactical screen, Captain Nance's ship, the *Avenger* disappeared behind a supernova flash of fusing hydrogen and all her telemetry disappeared from the IFF display.

"Dammit, Shelly," Tara hissed, her voice breaking. She shook her shoulders as if she was trying to bring herself back to the job at hand. "We've lost the *Avenger*. Cruiser five is intact but showing signs of structural damage on thermal. She's not launching drop-ships yet."

"Drive field strength is rising again," Terrin said. "Sixty-three percent now. If we can keep those lasers off of us for a couple more minutes, we should be back to full strength."

"The missiles will kill us before that," Kammy told him. "Bergh, cut the drive to bleed off our momentum, then take us south thirty degrees on the Y axis and lose those damn things. Bring us back up to reengage."

Smart. The missiles were full involved, accelerating at twenty-five gravities for the last few minutes. With the drive field weakened, the *Shakak* couldn't outrun them straight ahead, but the missiles were restrained by Newtonian physics and the ship wasn't. It would take them an hour to decelerate and then accelerate again and, by then, the battle would be over.

The downside, of course, being...

"Cruisers three and four are re-orienting," Tara warned. He could see the Starkad ships maneuvering. Their captains were playing it smart, not burning after the *Shakak*, knowing she couldn't move too far from Revelation, that she'd have to come back to try to keep them from landing troops. "Firing more ship-killers. Four missiles launched."

Damn it, how many of those things did they have?

"Helm control to Tactical. Target cruiser four and fire."

Terrin knew. He knew deep inside his gut it wasn't going to work this time. There were too many of them and they had the *Shakak* right where they wanted her. When the lasers hit this time, the field instability threw him against his harness so hard he nearly separated a shoulder, snapping his head forward and then back hard into the seat. Pain exploded behind his temples.

Someone cursed aloud and the lights dimmed on the bridge.

The stress snapped a power junction. Mithra knows what else it broke.

"Damage report!" The voice was Kammy's but Terrin's vision was swimming and he couldn't quite focus on the man.

Well, I might have a concussion, he thought but kept to himself.

Damage control was crewed by an NCO, Petty Officer Stout, one of Franny's crew. Franny was in the auxiliary control room, the backup for him, and he wished she were here. He wanted to be able to say goodbye.

"We have power failures to all auxiliary systems," Stout said. "The conduits we set up when we redesigned the interior have mostly failed."

Terrin forced his eyes to focus on the display in front of him, knowing Kammy would be counting on him.

"Drive field at thirty percent and falling." It hurt to say the words, and not just because it meant they were going to die. His head and neck were one giant mass of pain and the only reason he wasn't holding his head in his hands was because of the agony in his right shoulder.

"Bergh, get us out of here." Kammy's voice was strained, beyond the limits of his ability to hide the fear or stress or whatever it was he was feeling. "Get us off the course of those missiles."

And then a star went supernova.

At least that was how it seemed when the main screen whited out, when the bridge flickered and went black. Something punched Terrin in the gut and twisted him around, shaking his brain just a little more inside his skull. Feeling washed out of his body, leaving him tingling and numb, as if every nerve had shorted out and had to reboot.

He was floating. He didn't realize it at first, thought the falling sensation in his gut was from the concussion or the pain or maybe nausea from his injuries, but then he saw debris floating across the bridge, past the flickering static of the displays they'd installed, bits of dust and small, red globules he knew from experience were blood. The main holographic screen slowly revived itself, a testament to the technological prowess of an empire long dead.

Just like us.

Kammy was lolling, his head limp and bobbing with his breath, blood leaking in a slow but steady stream from a cut across his forehead, his eyes shut. Bergh was shaking himself, hands gripping the sides of his console as if he thought he were about to float away despite his restraints. Tara didn't seem outwardly injured, but her eyes were out of focus and she moaned softly, hands pressing at the sides of her head.

"What happened?" he croaked. No one else was asking and he was honestly curious. The lasers hadn't done this. The only thing that could have brought down the field that quickly and violently was...

And then he knew. The Starkad bastards had set the ship-killers off all at once, right at the limits of the drive field. The focused energy had overloaded it without killing them. His displays were dead. They'd been part of the refit and hadn't survived the stress.

"Why are we still alive?" he wondered after no one tried to answer his first question. "Why haven't they finished us off?"

This time, his words seemed to penetrate the fog over Tara Gerard's mind, and she looked straight at him, a deep sadness in her eyes.

"They know we're helpless," she said. "And they know this ship is full of priceless Imperial tech. They don't want to destroy us...they're going to board us."

22

We have drop-ships inbound." Katy heard the words over the cockpit speakers but couldn't identify the voice. Someone from the mercenary tech crew in the operations room watching the orbital sensors. "All..." They trailed off and had to start again. "All Wholesale Slaughter ships are out of the fight. The *Avenger* and *Ambrose Light* are destroyed. *Shakak* is drifting outside lunar orbit."

Her stomach twisted, more nausea than she'd felt in years of zero gravity and crushing acceleration. Shelly Nance was dead, and Terrin and Franny and the others on the *Shakak* might be. Even if they weren't, they were helpless and vulnerable.

"Fuck," Acosta said fervently, and she thought for a moment the man had feelings until he kept talking and ruined it. "We've completely lost our space cover."

"Two Starkad cruisers are completely destroyed." *Well, here comes the good news of the old good news-bad news joke.* The voice from the base in Revelation City sounded firmer, more resolved. "One is damaged and unpowered, drifting in high orbit. We have thermal blooming from her hangar bays, and she hasn't launched. The other three cruisers have launched drop-ships and assault shuttles. ETA is five minutes."

She said nothing for a moment, the cockpit silent but for the roaring of the atmospheric jets taking them higher into the atmosphere, out of daylight blue and into star-filled black, towards their fate. The wedding ring seemed to weigh down her left hand, unfamiliar but not unwelcome, reminding her of what she was fighting for.

"All Assault elements, this is Assault One."

Usually, in combat with the people she knew, the people she'd trained with, none of them bothered with call signs. They were playing mercenary and mercs didn't tend to use them, just called each other by name. But these pilots were fairly new to her and she hadn't wanted to take the chance of calling the wrong name in the heat of battle. Besides, it didn't do any harm to remind the guns-for-hire they were officially part of a real military force now.

"We have nine drop-ships inbound and six assault shuttles. Assault One and Two will engage the enemy assault shuttles." That was her and Lt. Duane, the only two real assault shuttles in their arsenal. The rest of her squadron were civilian landers upgraded with weapons and jury-rigged armor. "All other Assault elements will target the drop-ships. Do *not* let them get through. Every ship you take out saves lives on the ground, your friends' lives." She bared her teeth, putting a bit of venom into her tone. "You know what Starkad Navy crews think of mercenary gunship pilots? They say you're the dregs, worthless, with no real air-to-air combat experience, only good for strafing ground targets. What do you say, Wholesale Slaughter, are you going to prove them wrong today?"

"You bet your ass we are!"

"Damned right!"

She grinned. The targeting screen was lighting up with red icons burning down from orbit.

"Don't tell me, tell them. All Assault elements, break and engage." She switched to a private frequency with Duane and her voice lost some of its bravado. "John," she said, calling him by his first name, which she almost never did, "the goal is to keep their gunships busy. Don't get decisively engaged if you can help it. Hit and run, you got me?"

"Yes, ma'am." Lt Duane sounded ready, his voice even and unemotional, trying to imitate the combat pilot ideal. "See you on the other side."

She noticed Acosta's silence, which seemed strange to her, and she let her eyes flicker away from the target displays to look sidelong at him. His face was invisible inside his helmet, the light from the displays reflecting off his visor.

"Hey Francis," she said. It took a moment, but he turned his head and she could just make out his dark eyes through the tinted polymer. "I never asked you, but are you a religious type?"

"Not particularly," he said. There was no wavering or fear in his tone, but perhaps a fatalistic acceptance. "I always figured if there was a God, it's nothing like we think or could even imagine. I doubt any creator would give a shit about us in particular, as individuals. And the whole idea of an afterlife never made any sense to me. Why should there be anything after this one?" He shook his head, his whole helmet moving slightly with the motion. "When you die, you die. That's it."

"Okay," she replied, blowing out a sigh and letting her attention drift back to the controls. "Good talk."

"Katy," he said, and this time there was something softer in his voice. "We'll get through this. I may not believe in Mithra or Jesus, but I believe in Logan Brannigan."

"Damn right we will, Francis."

The enemy assault shuttles were visible now, running a wedge formation twenty kilometers ahead of their drop-ships. Just about in range.

"Air to air missiles armed," Acosta announced, running ahead of her intent. "Optimal launch range in five, four, three, two, one..."

She'd toggled the missiles to her control yoke, and when he reached one, she pulled the trigger. The fuselage shuddered as the weapons separated and ignited, one after another streaking free of the launch bay trailing angry red sparks of light from the solid-fuel rocket engines. The white streaks of smoke wove a web between them and the Starkad assault shuttles across the black sky, missiles from her and Duane crossing only meters from incoming enemy weapons.

Roll, climb, spin, dive, it all seemed to merge together into a ballet, the steps of a dance repeated so often they were instinctive. Flashes of motion, proximity alerts, and grunted warnings from Acosta all painted a three-dimensional picture of the world that she sensed more than saw. Gee-forces pinned her against the seat, tossed her back and forth, bruised her legs, her back and her shoulders in an abusive relationship with Isaac Newton that she couldn't bring herself to walk away from. She didn't think, she *couldn't* think, not with so much data pouring in at her, so much pressure crushing her. She could only act on instinct.

Her instincts guided her closer, tighter, latching onto the enemy shuttles to keep their own missiles away and hers on target. Somewhere above, below, beside her the other birds of Wholesale Slaughter's Assault squadron tried to make their way clear of the enemy attack, tried to pierce through to the drop-ships. If the numbers had been even close to even, her duty as squadron leader would have been to hold back and direct the attack, but that was a luxury she didn't have. Her shuttle was more valuable as a weapon than as a command and control platform.

Missile warheads erupted in sprays of white, red and yellow, intercepted by the tungsten slugs of Vulcan cannons or self-destructing as they approached too close to the shuttles that had launched them, adding another level of distraction. With each layer of data, she narrowed her focus, allowing the information to wash over her in a wave, letting a bit here or there stick. Duane was in trouble, in the process of being trapped in a pincer by two Starkad assault shuttles and probably seconds from death. One of the mercenary birds had already been shot down, its burning remains tumbling back toward Revelation. Two of her missiles struck a Starkad assault shuttle in the port-side wing and sheered it off, sending the aerospacecraft into an uncontrollable spin, maybe not dead but out of the fight.

She snap-rolled away from what her gut told her would be a laser shot from a Starkad shuttle and she turned it into an attack run on one of the two birds going after Duane. They were occupied, distracted, and one of them was nice and fat and juicy inside her targeting reticle. She fired her laser, the burst of coherent light tearing into the enemy shuttle, coring it like an apple. Plasma plumes blasted away from what was left of the craft, a supernova suspended in the upper atmosphere, an aurora spreading across the sky around it.

Another mercenary down, one of Salvaggio's makeshift assault shuttles coming apart in a shower of debris, the wings tumbling away in opposite directions, the screams of the pilot ringing in her ears as the cockpit plunged downward. She wanted to yell at him to eject, but if he could have done it, he would have already.

But one got through. She recognized the IFF signal of Assault Six, Bohardt's best pilot, a woman named Crowley. The elation of seeing the blue icon penetrating the blocking formation and jet through to the drop-ships pulled Katy out of the instinctive trance into which she'd fallen for just a moment, long enough to watch Crowley fire off all four of the missiles they'd rigged to hardpoints on her wings. The missiles streaked away just as a laser blast from one of the Starkad shuttles burned through the mercenary craft mid-fuselage.

Katy gritted her teeth and had to fight not to squeeze her eyes shut. She'd liked Crowley. She hadn't like all the merc pilots, but she'd liked Crowley. She followed the missiles in, trying to urge them home with her fervent hopes, but two were picked off almost immediately by the drop-ship's point defense turrets, falling away in glowing clouds of chaff. She winced at their failure, losing the other two for just an instant and believing they'd all been taken out.

The drop-ship was a massive ocean-liner on a sea of fire, ponderous and ungainly. When the last two missiles hit, it was less an aerospacecraft falling out of the sky and more as if one of Argos' skyscrapers had caught fire and toppled slowly to the street below. Katy wanted to cheer, but she'd spent too much time watching the enemy dying and not enough making sure she was still living.

The laser burned only two meters from her starboard wing, whiting out the optical cameras and the searing heat flooded the cockpit in an instant, nearly making her pass out. She slugged her brain back into motion and pushed the controls down into a steep dive, the gee forces nearly finishing what the heat had begun. Levelling off out of range, she checked the sensors. Four enemy assault shuttles left, seven drop-ships and, opposing them, her, Duane and three...*No, dammit, two*...of the mercenary landers.

"Duane, you and..." *Shit. What's his name?* "...Bolivar gun straight at the drop-ships. I'll take care of distracting the assault shuttles."

"Aye, ma'am," Duane responded, his tone doubtful.

"Are you fucking nuts?" Acosta asked. "There are *four* of them."

"I can count, Francis."

Two of them were converging on her six, boosting in behind her, unwilling to launch missiles so close to the flight plan of their drop-ships, and lining up for a straight laser shot instead. Katy pulled up sharply, kicking in a boost to the belly jets to push her nose up. She felt as if she was being crushed beneath a giant boot, and the fuselage *creaked* from the strain and structural integrity warnings flashed, but she ignored them, knowing an overhaul in the repair hangar was the least of her worries.

The two Starkad birds streaked by her on either side, wicked, flat black darts, and she nosed down again, the strain of the gee-load coming off her chest. She hissed breath back into her lungs and nudged the control yoke to the starboard, bringing the targeting reticle over the tail of the craft to her right and firing just before it began to peel away. A spear of ionized air connected with the enemy shuttle's port wing, a cloud-to-cloud lightning bolt that was only an after-effect of the burst of coherent light. Sublimated metal glowed in a halo and the port wing disintegrated, taking with it most of the port fuselage. The cockpit came apart, blasted by explosive bolts, and the crew's ejection pod rocketed away.

Katy whispered a silent prayer for their safe landing, unable to bring herself to hate even an enemy pilot facing the uncertain fate of a combat ejection.

Then she killed their friends. The pilot of the Starkad shuttle on her left had understood her maneuver just a heartbeat later than his wingman and made the wrong choice in response. He should have peeled off left, out of her targeting arc, but he hit the throttle instead. He must have been convinced he could outrun her since she'd bled away so much speed. And he might have, but he couldn't outrun the last two missiles her shuttle carried in its weapons bay.

Katy put the glowing cloud of wreckage behind her and banked to port on instinct, knowing she'd been flying straight for at least ten seconds, which was five seconds too long.

"They got another one!" Acosta wheezed against the unyielding press of the boost, the acceleration she couldn't get away from, both salvation and torturer. She checked the sensors and saw he was right. Another of the drop-ships was tumbling out of the sky...and then, less than a second later, so was Duane.

One of the assault shuttles had risked a missile and it had blown the tail right off Duane's bird, plasma streaking out and consuming what was left. Duane's copilot was Grant Coffee, a hulking giant of a man next to Duane's meter-seven, dark-skinned to Duane's ruddy complexion and an inveterate practical joker to Duane's straight man. They were both gone in a second.

The last of the mercenary landers tried to pull up, tried to get away from the enemy shuttle on her tail, but it was too late. Katy couldn't even tell if it was a laser that brought her down or a burst from a wing cannon. One moment she was there and the next she was gone, and Katy was alone in the sky with two assault shuttles...and three missiles boosting her way at twenty gravities.

"Fuck you," she said, her knuckles white on the control yoke.

She aimed straight at the closest of them, shoving the throttle to the limits, not listening to the alarmed cries of the overheat warnings, not trying to evade the laser burst passing close enough to burn away the control surfaces on her starboard wing. The capacitor banks for the laser were still charging so she opened up with the wing gun, the 20mm Vulcan shaking the bird with its dull vibration.

Pockmarks rolled across the nose of the enemy shuttle, explosive rounds igniting against the shield of the Starkad nose armor, searching for a weak spot and finding one. The bird nosed down, her engines still burning but out of control, a dart aimed at the hard deck below. Katy felt a moment's exultation, believed for just the space of a second that she might take out the last bird and then bring down the drop-ships and save everyone.

The missile that took off her portside wing disabused her of the notion. She reacted instinctively, keeping the throttle maxed out, not trying to turn, knowing you could fly a brick if you had enough power, and a fusion reactor was a hell of lot of power. Alarms were buzzing all around her, warnings to eject, warnings of structural failure, warnings of overheating, so loud they even overpowered Francis Acosta's terrified yells.

But if she left that enemy assault shuttle flying, he could provide air support, maybe enough to turn the battle. She hit maneuvering thrusters, meant for use in a vacuum, in micro-gravity, spinning her shuttle around 180 degrees. The starboard wing sheered away from the structural stress and what was left of her bird screamed in protest.

"Sorry, girl," she murmured.

The enemy shuttle was three kilometers away, right on her tail. She centered the targeting reticle and fired the last shot from her laser before fuselage integrity failed, the engines ripped away from the rear of her plane and she and Acosta fell out of the sky.

23

Our birds are down, sir."

The announcement was delivered from the tech in Operations with the sobriety and reluctance of a priest at a funeral service for a nonbeliever. Logan sank into the easy chair of his Vindicator, his mind filling with fog. *Our birds are down.* A much cleaner way of saying "your wife is dead."

He didn't reply immediately. He couldn't find his voice, couldn't force his brain to form the words. In the end, what brought him out of the fugue was the thought she might merely be saving him a spot in the afterlife.

"How many got through?" he asked, keeping his voice clear and strong, not letting on to the young mercenary technician how much he wanted to curl into a ball and cry.

"Six drop-ships. They're making for an LZ just your side of the city, towards the Run."

Six heavy companies of mecha, at least two more of Marines, maybe three. Half again their numbers, approximately. Not impossible odds, but long ones.

"The anti-aircraft batteries are trying to get a shot at them, but the course they're taking is going to skirt the emplacements."

The boy sounded apologetic, as if he personally had positioned the coilguns and missiles. He needn't have. They were working exactly as he'd intended, to funnel the dropships away from the city, keep the fight out in the wilderness, to spare the civilians.

He said a prayer to Mithra for Katy's safety, hesitated, then whispered one to Jesus as well, just in case. The sun was getting lower over the plains outside Revelation, but he calculated there would still be time to do battle in the light.

"Logan," Kurtz said over his helmet's headset, "she'll make it. She's punched out before." There was pain in the other man's voice, and Logan knew Valentine Kurtz didn't believe it any more than he did, but he appreciated the lie.

"I know she will, Val," he lied in return, trying his best to convince himself. The truth was, she might have simply preceded him to the afterlife by a few hours. Or minutes.

"Wholesale Slaughter," Logan said, broadcasting over the general frequency, addressing all of his troops. They were spread out behind him, under the cover of the Run, the canyon walls guarding them from anything but a direct overhead view. Kurtz was the closest of them, his Golem hunched and intimidating at Logan's right hand. "We've lost space cover; we've lost air cover. We are all that's left between Starkad and the people of this colony, between preserving hope of returning Sparta to rule by her people and generations of rule by Starkad. We are all that's left between stopping the Supremacy now or letting them plunge all of the Five Dominions into a war worse than any we've seen since the fall of the Empire."

He wished he could look each of them in the eye, not least because he needed to see the belief in their faces, needed to borrow some of it.

"Will you follow me now, Wholesale Slaughter? Will you run into the teeth of the enemy at my side?"

"You bet your ass we will!" He grinned at the harsh rasp of Aliyah Hernandez's response. "We're fucking Wholesale Slaughter. It's what we do!"

A chorus of cheers and affirmations and determined curses echoed over the open channel and he let it build and crash and run its course before he spoke again.

"Alpha and Bravo Companies, follow me!"

"Yeah, yeah," Momma Salvaggio said over their private channel. "We're with you, fearless leader."

Logan stomped on the jump-jet pedals and soared up and out of the canyon with forty other mecha on his heels, none of them heavier than his own Vindicator. Most were mercenaries in mercenary mecha, just what Starkad expected to face, older assault and scout mecha, Agamemnons, Reapers, Hoppers, a few patched-together Golems. Hernandez and Kurtz led their platoons of assault mecha, newer machines mostly stolen from the Starkad outpost, bringing up the rear.

Salvaggio had asked him, when she'd heard the plan, if they were there to keep the merc forces from running. Maybe they were. This was the chanciest part of the battle plan, but he was leading it from the front.

Across the plains between the Run and the city, drop-ships as large as office buildings were turning huge swathes of tall grass into blackened and smoking wasteland, constructing their own landing field with flaming columns of superheated air. The rumble of the landing jets rolled across the plains like the thunder of a distant storm, and boarding ramps were lowering before the drop-ships had even touched down, assault mecha jetting out to meet them, trying to make space for the strike mecha and the Marine armored vehicles to follow.

Logan's Vindicator was edging the red line when he slowly cut the jets and hit the uneven ground running at top speed. He felt as if he were running out to face the enemy alone, a suicidal rush to atone for the lives he'd lost, for Marc Langella, Donner Osceola, Paskowski, Ford, Prevatt, Coughlin, Lyta...for Katy and Terrin, he was sure. For Dad.

It was an illusion, both the responsibility for all the deaths and the thought he was alone. Other machines were keeping pace, running in a wedge with him at the point, not quite visible out the corner of his vision, indistinct blue triangles on the IFF display. They ran forever and the drop-ships never seemed to get any larger, as if they were mountains in the distance, always just at the horizon no matter how far or fast you drove.

And then, like those mountains, they suddenly loomed large, and the shapes pouring off them that had seemed human sized against a conventional shuttle were suddenly ten or fifteen or twenty meters tall, titans of armor forged from the blood of previous generations. Missiles began to fly a kilometer away and he didn't have to order his troops to return the indirect fire. They'd drilled for this moment over and over until the movements had become automatic and the commands rote recitals of mnemonic routines.

And he said nothing. Company commanders and platoon leaders gave orders and directed troops and there was nothing for him to say that wouldn't distract. He was there to lead, to lead by example this time. He launched two flights of missiles from his Vindicator's shoulder pod before the first of the enemy weapons began to rain down and he jumped again.

Around him, a score of other mecha took to the sky, trying to outdistance the enemy missiles, flying out of the arc of their trajectory, ECM systems humming, filling the air with ionizing radiation. Not thirty meters away, like a drama played out on the screen, a Reaper caught a Starkad missile mid-jump and erupted with flame, tumbling down out of control. Two more machines, light scouts from the Cossacks, flashed red and then black on the IFF, lost to the missiles and then they were down and in the midst of the enemy and everything was confusion and carnage.

Logan fired his plasma gun nearly point blank at the cockpit of a Valiant and inside, a Starkad pilot was charred black, dying instantly. A laser passed centimeters from the Vindicator's left arm and paint peeled away, revealing the bare armor beneath, blacking out the polarized coating over the transparent aluminum of the canopy, and before it adjusted back three tungsten slugs had cracked into the mech's hip.

Logan was moving, spinning, shuffling, taking flight briefly and firing his weapons by instinct. His thumb toggled from plasma cannon to 30mm Vulcan to lasers, to missiles and back to the plasma gun in the space of thirty seconds, firing at targets he never saw clearly other than to check the IFF display to make sure he wasn't killing a friendly.

This was the combat of the simulator, the sort he had never experienced in real life before. Most mech pilots never did, barring a major war. People were dying all around him, many of them mercenaries in scout mecha being sniped by larger machines as they tried to use their speed and stay ahead of firing arcs. His soul burned as if a whip scored across it with each black line in the IFF transponder display, yet he couldn't break too soon. None of this would work if he ran before baiting the hook.

The double-flash of plasma was the sign, the signal the bait had done its job. It was from the first of a line of enemy Scorpions lumbering ponderously away from their drop-ship, twin plasma cannons firing. Two more of Logan's people went down in as many seconds and he knew it was time.

"Withdraw!" he yelled into the general net. "Break contact and withdraw!"

They'd practiced this, too, though it had been harder to simulate. It was easy to run through the routes that would be taken, which platoon would lay down cover and which would move but thinking clearly, moving crisply and turning sharply, were all so much harder when fifty and sixty-ton mecha were stomping across the ground, cracking the clay beneath them, doing their utmost to kill you with every step.

He couldn't be first. Point on the way in, drag on the way back. He wouldn't accept anything else, even when Bohardt and Kurtz and Katy had all argued until they were out of breath. Salvaggio hadn't cared. "Better you than me" had been her exact words. She was still alive, her Reaper one of the first to take to the sky and jet back away from the drop-ships.

A Peregrine stumbled and collapsed in mid-step only ten meters away, dirt and smoke billowing away from its crash, and he checked automatically to see if it was one of his.

No, Starkad. Good.

He wouldn't have brought scout mecha to this landing were he the Starkad commander. Speed wasn't going to help them in this sort of battle, only firepower. Whoever was in charge had gone by the official doctrine, which was fine with him. He'd always been of the opinion that doctrine was nothing but a play-book for the other team to study, though the attitude had often driven Donnell Anders crazy.

This was surely no one's doctrine and it might end with all of them dead, a risk most commanders weren't willing to take.

Most commanders aren't as desperate as I am.

He jetted another three hundred meters away from the drop-ships, dropping abruptly when a missile passed only meters above him, stumbling backwards in a machine never meant to walk in reverse. A Starkad mech was heading straight at him, boosting on brief bursts of jump-jets, hopping between them like a man trying to run on a low-gravity moon. It was a Valiant, and he could tell by the markings it was a platoon leader. Probably a young one, still full of daring and bravado, not yet realizing the loss and pain that came with the life.

The Valiant's laser carved away hundreds of kilograms of armor from Logan's left chest plastron and heat spiked inside his cockpit, driving the breath out of him. He jumped again, just forty meters up and down, quick as he could, not wanting to make himself an easy target, and fired off his last two missiles. One missed cleanly but the other warhead detonated near the Valiant's left leg, peeling off a ton of BiPhase carbide and shredding actuator cables, sending the Starkad mech stumbling to the side.

Training and habit wanted to finish the enemy machine, put a plasmoid through its chest, but the plan was the plan, and part of it was *not* for him to get trapped inside the enemy ranks and force one of his foolhardy friends to ignore everything else and come rescue him. He jetted away, the heat warnings starting to sound as he pushed the system to its limits. The metal mountains of the drop-ships and the charred and burning grass surrounding them had filled his vision for minutes, but now sky-blue and forest-green replaced them.

When he landed, he saw friendlies running beside him and realized they were close to the entrance of the canyon. He checked the enemy on his sensors, not daring to look back for fear of catching a round in the process of slowing down, of letting all this careful planning go to hell for one misstep. The Starkad mecha were pushing across the plain, heedless, certain of their victory and filled with a bloodthirsty urge to finish off their foe.

The mouth of the Run was there, just a few hundred meters away, but incoming lasers and missiles were cutting down machines on either side of him, three more of the mercenary scout mecha falling in the space of three steps. The Starkad armor was close, less than a kilometer and closing. Valentine Kurtz turned with his Golem's back to the wall of the canyon entrance and staggered as a Starkad warhead tore the left arm off of his mech in a fireball and a shower of sparks.

Logan's mouth was half-open in a belated warning, a cry of empathic pain, but on his sensor screens he saw the enemy crossing an imaginary phase line projected across the plain, a point of no return.

"Wholesale Slaughter Reserves!" he yelled into his helmet pickup, as if the added volume could make it happen faster. "Engage now!"

They surged out of the canyon almost ahead of his order, hundreds of tons of heavy metal slamming two-meter footpads into the sandstone with the rhythmic percussion of a Lambeg drum. The Scorpions led them in a solid center core, their ostrich-bent legs throwing up huge clouds of dust and sand, with towering Nomads at their flanks. Behind the cover of the lead rows of strike mecha were Arbalests, a full platoon of them, launch ports open.

Missiles streaked out across the early evening sky, pale white tracks against a blue so deep it was almost purple, one flight after another as the Arbalests emptied their magazines. He had no ammo wagons to reload them, no time or cover to protect the crews even if he'd found the vehicles at the Starkad outpost and bothered to load them onto the stolen drop-ships. He wondered if there was ever time in a real battle, or if some writer of official doctrine had just assumed there would be.

"Alpha and Bravo," he transmitted, "fall in to the flanks and force them into the killing ground."

What was left of the two companies moved to comply, even Kurtz, stumbling along in his one-armed Golem, struggling to keep the unbalanced machine upright. The center of their lines exploded with the lightning-strikes of laser bursts, crackling plasma blasts and ETC cannon rounds, hammering into the Starkad forces still charging into the teeth of the ambush, while the missiles arced downward near the rear, catching the ones who tried to turn back.

Enemy assault mecha soared into the sky, trying to escape the inferno and he leapt to meet them, trailed by the survivors of Alpha and Bravo. They were battered and bruised, their armor scorched and pockmarked, but they threw themselves into the fight with abandon, heedless of their own survival, and he'd never been prouder of any force under his command.

But it wasn't going to be enough. Even as he blasted a Starkad Golem out of the sky with the Vindicator's plasma gun, he could sense the data pouring in from the periphery. A dozen Starkad mecha were burning wrecks at the center of the field, more of them strung out along the center of the valley, but not enough. Not enough of them had committed to the charge, not enough had been taken out by the missile strike. And the enemy Arbalests were finally shuffling into line at the edge of the landing zone, ready to send their own strike downrange into his massed strike mecha.

Should I order them to break contact? Try to retreat back into the Run and save what I can? Will it matter in the long run?

No. The missiles from the Arbalests would savage them during a retreat, and he'd lose most of the strike mecha anyway. He made his decision, and felt the weight coming off his shoulders.

Death is lighter than a feather. Duty is heavier than a mountain.

"Arbalests fall back. The rest of you, close with the enemy, stay too close to let them launch missiles!

He landed amidst the foe, only meters from a Starkad scout

mech and lashed out at it with his articulated fist, smashing its left arm to scrap metal, throwing it onto its back and then savagely stomping downward. Metal crunched beneath metal.

"Wholesale Slaughter, forward!"

24

Whatever the hell you're going to do, you'd better do it right now!"

Tara wouldn't have made a good captain, Francesca Hayden decided. The woman's voice carried through the whole ship's PA speakers, cutting through the commotion and confusion of the *Shakak's* engine room like a Viking horn in a foggy harbor, which she supposed was a good thing for a ship's commander. But the desperation and fear were plain in the words, and that didn't seem like something you'd want the crew to know in a situation like this. It certainly wasn't making her feel any more at ease, though it didn't seem to affect Terrin at all.

"Are you sure this is going to work?" she asked, not looking up from the portable computer terminal she'd brought with her from the auxiliary bridge.

"Hold that damn light steady, Kenny!" Chief Shaw snapped at the enlisted spacer anchored to the deck behind them with magnetic ship boots.

"Sorry, Chief," Kenny said, trying to wipe sweat off his forehead with one hand and hold the portable work lamp with the other. "It's hot in here with the ventilators down."

"Well, it's gonna get a lot hotter if the fucking Starkad Marines burn through the fucking hull and start shooting us, boy!"

They'd actually be pretty *cold*, she thought, but didn't bother saying. She was having enough trouble concentrating on the improvised power routing program she was writing while Chief Shaw and Terrin worked at the bypass.

"No, I'm not sure it's going to work," Terrin said, finally answering her question, his voice muffled, buried half inside the access panel to the main power conduit. "But it's the only chance we have to get the drive working again before those boarding craft reach us." Chief Shaw was unspooling superconductive cable from a coil the size of a truck tire, handing it through up to Terrin, who was...doing *something* with it. She was a computer tech and this hands-on stuff wasn't her area of expertise. "The drive still works...a few laser hits aren't going to take out something made of exotic matter with a neutronium shield. It's just the connections we made to the fusion reactor back when we put this thing together at Terminus that gave out. They couldn't stand the feedback."

"Neither could the fucking power systems," added Chief Shaw. "But the reactor didn't flush. It's still running, just not putting all that energy out anywhere."

Shaw seemed almost happy to have something to keep him busy, no matter how dire the circumstances. The engineering section of the *Shakak* had given the traditional engineer little to do over the last few months besides checking and rechecking power connections and bugging Franny to put more learning annexes on the ship's continuing education systems about exotic matter drive systems.

Yeah, I'll just write those up in my spare time.

As if she understood it any more than he did. Even Terrin admitted to not understanding exactly how the system worked, though he certainly knew more than anyone else on the ship.

"All available security troops to hangar bay immediately!" Tara ordered. "Anyone not in an area vital to repairing this ship, report to the armory and grab a weapon, then get to the hangar bay now!"

Anyone conscious, she amended for the XO. Two of the engineering crew were still floating freely in a corner, one of them moaning softly and holding his head, the other unconscious, waiting for the medics to have someone, *anyone* free to come take them to the sick bay. Kammy was barely conscious himself, concussed and foggy and in no position to command the ship, which was why Tara was giving the orders and the big man was strapped into a hospital bed.

What security do we have left? The Rangers are all down on Revelation. Do we have anyone else?

It didn't really matter. Starkad Marines would blow right through anyone they sent out to meet them short of the Rangers. It was all over if they didn't get the drive field back up and... *Damn it, I'm thinking too much, get back to work!*

If she didn't get the software patch written, just hooking the power back up to the drive wouldn't do anything but burn the whole system out again.

"Okay, I got the main trunk connected," Terrin said, wriggling out of the hole. "Chief, can you re-route it to the other systems?"

"Just let me at it, kid," Shaw said, rolling up his sleeves and pushing past him, legs working as he squirmed into the tight access space behind the bulkhead.

Terrin pushed away and floated behind her shoulder. She didn't dare look up to meet his eyes, but she could smell the sweat and the stale odor of dust coming from his clothes and hair. His warmth radiated through his jumpsuit, stifling in the still, dead air of the engine room, adding to the heat of the portable light. Sweat dripped off her nose and onto the screen of the portable terminal and she wiped it away impatiently.

"Just a couple minutes," she promised him. "Just a couple more minutes."

"I love you, Franny," he said softly into her ear, so quietly she didn't know if anyone else could hear. "No matter what happens, I want you to know I love you."

"I love you too," she whispered, but didn't look up. Couldn't look up. So close now, just a few dozen more lines of code...

The lights snapped back on, and with them the ventilation, humming to life and washing across the runnels of sweat on her face with a blast of cold air. The engineering computer systems began rebooting, and she cursed, knowing she had even less time now. She had to get the patch running before they cycled through the drive power systems.

"Got it!" Chief Shaw exulted, pushing back out of the maintenance crawlway and folding the panel down behind him. "Thank Mithra we got the damn life support back up."

"What about weapons?" Terrin asked him. "I know the main gun won't work without the drive field, but what about auxiliary weapons? Point defense?"

"Not yet," Shaw admitted. "Not till the computer systems reboot."

"Damn it. Bridge," Terrin called, his tone shifting. She assumed he was at the communications panel but couldn't pause to check. "Bridge, this is Engineering, do you read?"

"Yeah, I'm here," Tara answered after a moment, her tone harried and near panic. "Tell me the drive is almost up, because now we have sensors back and there are four boarding pods full of Marines heading this way. We have about two minutes before they're at the hangar bay."

"Not. Fucking. Helping." Franny surprised herself with the

profanity and she thought she saw Terrin glance at her sharply out of the corner of her eye.

"It's coming, Bridge," he promised. "Just a couple minutes."

"There." The word hissed out of Franny like the last sigh her mom had given when she'd pushed her sister out in the delivery room, and for much the same reason. She hit the execute key and the patch flowed down through the hardline she'd hooked into the computer console and into the boot-up process of the system. "That's it."

She looked up at the auxiliary display set on the Engineering compartment's bulkhead just over the main control panel, saw the view from the external cameras. The boarding pods were bare, silver cylinders with disposable solid-fuel boosters flaring at the rear, four separate rockets blending into one glowing exhaust at the rear. There was no perspective in the dark abyss, but she'd seen them back on Sparta in training classes. Each could hold over thirty troops. One hundred and twenty Marines against a few dozen spacers, most of whom hadn't fired a gun except on the qualification range.

Terrin and I may have the most experience in combat of anyone on the ship. The thought was absurd, and absurdly terrifying. She needed to get a gun.

"System is rebooting," Chief Shaw chanted like a mantra, as if the words would force it happen faster. "System is rebooting..."

The boarding pods were so close now, so huge and slow and ever more intimidating than the ship-killer missiles had been.

"It's up!" someone shouted, one of the Engineering crew, not Shaw. "The system's up!"

Terrin was throwing himself across the room to the control board before Franny had the chance to move, cursing the response time on the touch-screens, balky as always just after a reboot. He traced lines from the power supply to the Alanson-

McCleary stardrive in a familiar start-up pattern, the traces lighting up beneath his touch. Franny realized she was holding her breath and tried to force herself to relax.

On the screen, one of the boarding pods fired a missile. It was small and slow-moving, creeping along only slightly ahead of the boat that had launched it. She'd seen those in her familiarization class on Sparta as well. They weren't much, just a dozen kilograms or so of explosives, but enough to blow a hole through the hangar bay doors, and they didn't fire them until they were only a kilometer away.

She braced herself as if she'd be able to feel the blast here, deep in Engineering, squinting her eyes in anticipation...and then they were gone. Where the boarding pods had been, there was nothing but a thinly-spread glowing field of gas and debris and she collapsed to the deck with the sudden and unexpected return of the internal gravity field.

Groans and cries of pain echoed through the compartment and probably throughout the ship, and Terrin was wiping blood from his nose as he pulled himself back to his feet, lunging desperately for the communications panel.

"Tara, the drive is up!" he yelled hoarsely. "Get us out of here!"

Franny yanked the leads out of the portable terminal and left it in place, following Terrin out of the compartment, knowing he was heading for the bridge. Technically, she should have headed back to the auxiliary control room, but she'd stared down death in the claustrophobic confines of the Engineering section and she felt a pressing need to see, to be present for the culmination of the battle. And, if the end came, to face it on her feet beside Terrin, not trapped alone, in the dark.

Crewmembers were picking themselves off the deck all up and down the passageway and at the base of the ladders between decks, and she gave silent thanks to Mithra the *Shakak* was built along horizontal lines rather than vertical ones like a conventional starship. What would have happened to crew trying to make it up or down the central hub in microgravity when one gee cut back in didn't bear consideration.

The bridge seemed deserted, half the crew in the sick bay and Kammy's command position empty. Tara hadn't bothered to move from her station, whether because she hadn't had time or maybe because she hadn't felt comfortable sitting in his chair. She gave no orders, issued no warnings because she was flying the ship herself, having taken the Helm control from Bergh. Franny fell into the unoccupied Damage Control seat and fastened the harness just in case they lost gravity again, while Terrin took his normal position at Engineering.

Franny was no expert on reading tactical displays, but she thought the *Shakak* was heading back toward Revelation and she bit down on what would have been her second profanity of the day. They hadn't been able to take on the Starkad ships at full strength, so how the hell did Tara think they would be able to beat them now, battered, beaten and slapped back together?

"Our power bypass is kind of jury-rigged, Commander," Terrin said, as if he were reading Franny's mind. "If we take another good hit, it'll blow out even easier than the first one did."

"I figured," Tara said, not taking her attention off the controls. "But they're more spread out now, we can hit and run and take advantage of our range. We just have to take out one, that's all. We take out one, I think they'll call their forces back and turn tail. Even Starkad can't afford to lose six cruisers in one fight."

It was a comforting thought, though Franny couldn't have sworn how realistic Tara was being. The fact was, running wasn't an option and they all knew it.

"Oh, fuck me," Tara murmured.

Franny had been staring at the image of the enemy cruisers on the screen and she peered even harder at Tara's softly hissed profanity, convinced they must have launched even more ship-killers, though where they could have stored that many of the huge missiles was a mystery. But she saw nothing other than the mountain-like Starkad ships hovering in high orbit, waiting for them.

"What is it?" she asked, looking from a confused Terrin to Tara. The older woman didn't answer, her face slack with despair.

"The other way," Bergh explained, his voice dolorously resigned. He leaned over to Tara's console and touched a control and half the main screen switched back to a view outward, toward the jump-points.

Ships were popping into existence there, star cruisers, appearing one after another as if they'd never stop.

"Mithra's blood," Franny said in quiet blasphemy. "How many of them are there?"

"Too many, girl," Tara told her, the hope draining from her voice. "Too damned many."

General Hoenig, Colonel Ruth Laurent noted, preferred to lead from the rear.

It wasn't a huge surprise. Men and women who led from the front usually didn't live to win their star. Still, there was some-thing of the nagging cynic she'd become in her observation that Eric Hoenig kept as far back toward the supply train as he could and still maintain control of the battle. She shared a mobile command center with the man, which was tight quarters given the general's girth.

Not that she would have called him fat. Lord Starkad

prided himself on his physical fitness and would never have abided a fat general. But Hoenig had a torso the approximate breadth of an oil drum and a florid, round face, pockmarked from a youth spent on one of the rougher, frontier colony worlds where the best in modern medicine hadn't included acne treatment. His hair was wavy and thick and streaked with grey, and she could smell the oily pomade he used to style it over the stale cologne unsuccessfully trying to mask his body odor.

She tried not to let his personal grooming habits color her estimate of the man's ability. Starkad wasn't exactly a meritocracy, but it would be difficult for a man to claw his way to the top of the military heap here without showing courage and daring in battle. Not this battle though.

She stood in the open upper hatch of the command vehicle and watched a Marine armored vehicle explode. It was nearly five hundred meters away, yet every detail seemed to jump out at her, every shade of red and yellow and white in the fireball, every single fragment of debris rocketing away from the vehicle, the impossible trajectory of the twelve-ton vehicle as it spun backwards in the air and crashed onto its roof. The concussion wave washed over them, shaking the frame of their command car, and the sound punched into her chest a moment later, battering her ears even through the light helmet she wore.

When the car braked to a sudden halt, she came up against the front of the open roof hatch, grunting as the rim dug into the pit of her stomach.

"All columns reverse!" Hoenig snapped into the microphone of his own half-helmet. "Back off fifty meters now!"

Engines revved and their own vehicle began backing up with a scrabble of treads on gravel, back out towards the path to the landing zone, out of the edge of the city. The fifteen armored cars ahead of them spread out of their column and back into a double wedge, facing into the back streets, into temples and churches and housing. And a hundred potential hiding places for mines and IEDs.

"Send a scout around the west side," Hoenig ordered. "Find us a clear route!"

"It's a waste of time." The general glanced at her sharply, but she didn't flinch away. He was nothing compared to Grieg. "The Rangers do not do things by half-measures," she assured him. "They'll have every avenue of approach mined."

"Perhaps," he admitted. "But we must try anyway." He shrugged. "And a scout vehicle only carries three Marines."

She pointedly *didn't* sneer at him, as much as she wanted to.

"We should dismount," she advised. "It will be slower, but we have time and they don't."

"Well, we'll find out in..."

Another blast cut off his words as what she assumed was their scout vehicle ripped apart in a gush of flames almost a kilometer away, a mushroom cloud of black smoke rising into the air, a tombstone for three Marines.

"Well, damn." Hoenig sighed in resignation. "All Marines, park vehicles in a lager formation, guns out, and advance into the city on foot."

The armored vehicles dug up half-meter deep ruts in the half-paved gravel road as they circled into a defensive formation, their ramps lowering like opening maws. Marines stomped out, heavy-footed trots turning into jogs as they formed into double-wedge formations, two light companies, one on each side of the street.

"Captain Vincent, take Bravo company straight south. Captain Skrein, Delta will head west and circle in from the cross streets. Find me the enemy forces and pin them down. Captain Mace, bring your sappers up from the rear and clear a route for our vehicles to come in and support them."

"Move out, Marines!"

"Do you wish to move up and join them, sir?" Laurent asked him with feigned innocence. "To have a better sense of the battle?"

To her surprise, Hoenig laughed at the barb.

"This is a sideshow, Colonel. The real battle will be fought out there." He waved at the plains north of them, toward the canyon. "Even I, a former Marine, know this much. But we will clear this town of the enemy, and perhaps level it in the end, if necessary."

She had no comment for that, finding it depressingly pragmatic and inarguable. So she simply stood with him and watched, both what she could see with her eyes and what made it back from the IFF transponders and telescopic displays laid out before them on the inside of the open hatch. She'd read there'd been experiments with body cams transmitting live images back to commanders, but they were too vulnerable to ECM jamming and spoofs and far too likely to lead enemy troops to a unit's command structure.

So, instead, she listened to the distant chatter of automatic weapons fire, to chains of explosions answered by smaller, individual blasts and guessed from the IFF signals going dark which were IEDs and mines and which were Marine grenades going outward.

"I don't even see them," she commented after the battle had raged for nearly ten minutes, the reports echoing down the streets from the south and the west, cross-chatter coming over company and platoon nets listing casualties and enemy strongpoints. "I haven't seen one of them yet."

"Most of the time you don't," Hoenig said. "But they can't hold. They have no support, nowhere to run but the ocean, nowhere to stand but here. Once we isolate them, we can blast them out, or burn them out." He smiled broadly. "I particularly like that. They run out one at a time, afire, and we can decide whether to show mercy or let them burn."

"I see you love your work, General," she told him. "I wonder how long it's been since you had a shot fired your way."

"If it never happens again, I won't mourn, my dear."

"What's the report from the Armored Corps?" she wondered, trying to take her mind off the inevitable carnage ahead of them.

Hoenig traced a line across the screen, pushing the IFF readouts from the Marines to the side and bringing up the transmissions from the mecha forces.

"They've taken heavy casualties," Hoenig said, not seeming too disturbed by what he read on the display. "But we have the numbers. The outcome is not in doubt. I trust Colonel Kennedy."

Laurent eyed the board suspiciously. *Heavy casualties is right.* Kennedy was getting his ass handed to him by a numerically and qualitatively inferior force. But Hoenig was also correct that they had sufficient reserves to win the battle, as long as there were no more surprises.

"General Hoenig!" one of the NCOs manning the communications hub in the shadowed compartment below called up to the big man, his eyes wide and white in the darkness. "There's a transmission incoming from Admiral Longoria on board the *Orkla*! He says twelve, that is one-two military battle cruisers have emerged from the closest jump-point and are making for orbit around Revelation!"

"The hell you say!" Hoenig exploded. "Twelve fucking cruisers? Who the hell would have twelve cruisers to send out here to this dirtball planet?"

The general glared at Laurent as if she knew and was just holding the answer back from him. Rather than argue with him about it, she shoved the tactical display off the command screens and pulled up the orbital feed. The sensor relay from the *Orkla* told the story, a dozen monolithic pillars of metal arrayed in matching globular formations, the starfire of fusion drives pushing them headlong into the gravity well of the colony.

"They're huge," she murmured, reading the computer designators beside each of the threat icons. "Those aren't mercenary ships, converted cargo runners. Any one of those is as large as the *Orkla*."

The sensor display was overridden by a broad-beam transmission, switching over as if she'd ordered it herself. It was a demonstration not simply of power but of subtlety. Someone was bragging they had the signal spoofing technology to hack Starkad systems from orbit. The face plastered across every single one of the displays was unfamiliar to her, dark and narrow and dangerous, a dagger shaped from volcanic glass.

Eyes so deeply brown they were nearly black bored into her as if the man were speaking specifically to Ruth Laurent rather than to every transmitter on the planet and in orbit around it.

"I am," the man said, his voice deep and sonorous as a professional opera singer, "Admiral Buhari of the Mbeki Imperium. All Starkad forces in this system are directed to withdraw immediately. Revelation is now under the protection of the Imperium, and any further aggression toward its inhabitants or any allied forces in this system will be met with overwhelming action." The corner of his lip curled up just slightly. "And given the imbalance of forces, a confrontation between us would surely lead to your destruction. I wish to avoid this if possible. I do not want to be the man who fires the first shot in the war between us, but if that is the only choice, I have been given clearance to do so. Break contact with Wholesale Slaughter and leave this place while you still have any ships left to take you."

"Bugger," Hoenig said softly, as if he found the information merely annoying.

Laurent couldn't speak, couldn't find the breath. Mbeki here could only mean one thing.

As if some malevolent deity had read her thoughts, the admiral's image was replaced by another, one ever more unpleasant. His eyes were less wild than they had been, his face more filled out and healthy, the hair and beard trimmed neatly, but there was no mistaking the man.

General Nicolai Constantine smiled, and there was nothing but sheer malevolence in the expression.

"I'm assuming you can hear this, Colonel Laurent," he said. "I wonder if you understand your mistake. You're a very intelligent officer, and I respect your ability, so I'd suspect you do." The predator's smile disappeared, all emotion draining away and leaving the countenance of a stone killer.

"The only time I'm not dangerous," Nicolai Constantine informed her, "is when I'm dead."

25

Yea, though I walk through the valley of the shadow of death I will fear no evil.

They were the words from something Katy had called a Psalm. She'd recited it as a prayer for comfort, but for Logan Brannigan, there was no comfort to be had in this valley of death.

Burned, cracked soil crunched beneath the soles of his boots and soot coated the sleeves of his utility fatigues, blackened his hands and face. The heat from smoldering mecha was nearly unbearable, shoving him back and forth between one twisted and blackened metal corpse and another. They were the skeletons of titans, burning with the fire of the wrath of a god, and he was just a mortal trapped among them.

Men weren't meant for this. They'd arrogated themselves, wrapped their fragile, mortal bodies in metal and weapons and the fire from the heart of a star and thought they were as gods themselves, but this was the battlefield of legends, when giants walked among men.

Logan wasn't sure how long he'd been wandering between life and death, searching each blackened and fiery hulk for signs of survivors and finding none. The sun was below the horizon, but between the dregs of the dusk and the glow of the fires, there was enough light to see by, though not quite enough to make out fine details. He wasn't sure where he'd left his Vindicator or where the front lines were. The assault mech was battered and broken, its systems glitching and unusable and he'd left it standing alone amidst a sear of enemy dead. No one had answered his radio calls, nothing had shown up on his IFF display except blinking error messages.

The last thing he'd heard before all of his systems had overheated and gone dead was the arrival of Mbeki, the ultimatum their Admiral and General Constantine had given to Starkad. He'd killed the Starkad mech-jock he'd been fighting, taking advantage of the man's distraction and felt no remorse, but after that last blast of plasma fire, the Starkad mecha had begun to withdraw. It hadn't been immediate, and it hadn't been fast. There had been damaged machines and damaged pilots for their recovery crews to come out and haul away.

Wholesale Slaughter's own crews had taken longer, coming from farther away, deep in the canyon. He'd seen them as he walked, only dimly aware of what they were, what the muted headlights burning on the road from the canyon represented. He'd thought they'd seemed hesitant, probably sure Starkad would try to double-cross them somehow. If he'd had any sort of communications, if he hadn't been two kilometers away across the valley of the shadow, he would have told them to hurry, that lives were at stake.

But then the Mbeki shuttles had begun to land, descending on columns of fire on the opposite end of the valley from the Starkad drop-ships. There was no mistaking them for the ships of any other Dominion military and he knew them by reputation though he'd never seen one in real life. Everyone else chose a lifting body design for maximum aerodynamic capacity, but

Mbeki had gone for sheer power, a squat, bullet shape that maximized cargo space over all else.

Their strike mecha had stepped out first, stomping around the boarding ramps like bulky dockworkers, guarding the way for their own recovery vehicles, for trucks full of medics. He had to make it back to them, take charge of the aftermath. It drove him forward through the heat and the dark and the pain, through the emotional inertia trying to drag him down, through images of Katy somewhere out there in the desolate plains beyond the habitable zones, broken and dying or burnt to ash, a human sacrifice to gods even older than hers.

Was that the sacrifice he was expected to make by Mithra? The death of everyone he loved in exchange for victory, for the salvation of his world? It was the sacrifice his father had been forced to make. He'd lost the woman he loved, lost his father and his grandfather and, in the end, his own life. Perhaps it was the fate he'd chosen, or the one that had chosen him, passed down to him with the death of Jaimie Brannigan. The lot of the Guardian, to walk alone and, in the end, lay himself down for his people.

The truck's headlights pierced through the guttering flames of what had once been a Scorpion strike mech and Logan squinted and looked away as the vehicle swerved through the wreckage, coming straight to him. It stopped two meters away in a spray of dust and ash, the lights cutting swathes through the particulate haze of the fires and debris.

"You are Logan Brannigan."

The voice was familiar, though he was surprised to hear it dirtside. It wasn't often an admiral left his flagship to set foot on a battlefield. The man was tall and slender, a pine tree swaying in the wind, his grey fatigues practical and unadorned.

"I am Emmanuel Buhari, Vice Admiral of the Imperator's

Navy," he said, saluting in the Mbeki way, fist to chest. "I greet you in his name."

Logan drew himself straight and returned the salute, fingers to eyebrow in the Spartan tradition.

"Admiral, I thank you for your actions here today. If it weren't for you, we might still have won the battle, but many more would have died, and the people of Revelation would have been left with nothing but ruins. No matter what happens in the future, you will always have a friend and ally in Logan Brannigan, whether I am Guardian of Sparta or simply the commander of Wholesale Slaughter."

"Oh, I think we can do better than that for you, Lord Guardian."

Nicolai Constantine emerged from the haze of the vehicle headlights, cutting a more dashing figure than when Logan had left him on Guajarat. He wore a fresh set of unmarked grey utilities, plain and pragmatic yet somehow seeming pressed sharp enough to shave with the creases. Pain and fear and the stress of months of confinement had worn new lines into his face, but the gleam was back behind those dark eyes.

"I should have known you wouldn't come back empty-handed, Nicolai," Logan said, offering the man a hand.

"Nicolai is it, now?" Constantine asked, cocking an eyebrow.

"It is if it's Lord Guardian now," Logan replied somberly. The general nodded and gripped his hand tightly.

"I don't know if you heard," he said, not letting go of the hand, clapping Logan's shoulder with his other, "but the *Shakak* survived. There are quite a few injured, but no KIA. Terrin is safe."

Logan sagged against the general's grip just a bit, a measure of relief flooding through him.

"Thank you," he said. "I'm glad to hear it. Down here...we

didn't fare quite so well, I'm afraid. I've been out of contact since my electronics got fried by a heat spike, so I don't know the numbers, but..."

"We just came from the aid station." Constantine's face went grim. "You lost twenty-seven mecha, twenty of those the older machines the mercenaries brought with them, and fifteen pilots. Your commanders are still alive, though Captain Bohardt took a pretty nasty shrapnel hit through his cockpit."

Gears turned in his head, numbers crunching impersonally. The pilots hit the hardest, harder than the machines, but if most of the stolen Starkad mecha were still reparable...but something else was more important. He didn't want to ask the question, didn't want to know the answer.

"What about our assault shuttles?" The words weren't spoken so much as expelled, an agonized sob beaten into submission and released as a tightly controlled question.

Constantine's grip on Logan's arm tightened, as if he suspected he might have to prevent him from collapsing.

"They all went down in the battle, from what I was told. We haven't heard any transponders from ejection pods. We're still looking."

Logan nodded, pushing the older man's hands away, standing on his own.

"The Imperium of Mbeki has pledged its aid to your cause, Lord Guardian," Buhari told him, as if the man had sensed this was the right time to bring up the subject. "This includes mecha and spacecraft, and aid in recruiting personnel if you need it, though despite what I told the Starkad forces here, we are *not* committed to open warfare with Starkad."

The man paced around to Logan's other side, the headlights throwing his jagged, hard-edged face into sharp relief.

"The Imperator is concerned what Starkad will do should they consolidate their alliance with the usurper on Sparta and then finish off Clan Modi." That thin line of a mouth quirked just slightly. "Actually, I do not think it would be disrespectful nor inaccurate to say the Imperator is scared shitless about what a combined Starkad, Sparta and Modi could do militarily. The only question is whether they would try to absorb Shang first or us." He shrugged. "Or, if Lord Aaron is as smart as he thinks he is, they could try to work out a deal with Shang to split out territories. Still, we can't afford an all-out war with Starkad. The distances are too great, and we would have no allies..." He titled his head toward Logan. "Unless Sparta were in the hands of someone who owed us a large favor."

"The Imperator is a wise man," Logan conceded. *Bit of a dick, if I remember right from the state dinner when I was a teenager.*

"I assume you don't want a foreign power making war on your own people," Buhari went on, "but we can give you aid and shelter, and keep Starkad off your back."

"Believe me, Emmanuel," Constantine told the admiral, "it's more than enough. I was thinking we might set up a base here and maybe another closer to Sparta, and we could start with a refit of a couple of our ships and some new shuttles..."

The two men were still talking and Logan knew he should have been paying attention, knew this was vital to their future, but his mind refused to focus. Everything seemed to be faded, washed out, the energy bleeding away from him as the fires guttered and flickered and died and darkness closed in. The discussion of the future, of moving on, was running headfirst into the unbreakable piece of the present he hadn't dealt with, hadn't let himself think about: life without Katy.

Is it worth the living? Am I strong enough to face it?

It would be easy to lose himself in work for the moment, but he'd have to face the reality of it soon enough.

It would have been so much easier if I'd died in the battle.

Even burning up inside a mech cockpit wouldn't have hurt this bad.

He could no longer see Buhari or Constantine, couldn't make out the lines of their faces. Everything was distorted by tears he couldn't remember crying. His breath was coming short and he reached out with a hand blindly, trying to find support against the side of the Mbeki vehicle. Its cold metal was a comfort, a support in the utter blackness. He hoped the darkness hid his tears. They were private, not for strangers, not even for Constantine.

"Logan?" Constantine had called his name more than once; he could tell by the tone. "Are you all right? Do you need a medic?"

He was about to ask if he could have some water, ready to blame the moment of weakness on dehydration, but the words died unspoken. Headlights were coming their way, dipping up and down with the ruts in the dirt road, driving fast, weaving between the carcasses of dead mecha. Not from the Mbeki ships or the aid station they'd set up, but from Revelation City.

He wondered dully if it was yet another crisis, another death, another piece of the life he'd known slipping away.

It was a small, flatbed cargo truck, the sort the locals used to deliver feed for the animals or trade goods from the settlements outside town. All other details were lost to the darkness and the glare of its headlights until it pulled up beside them. Mbeki soldiers, Buhari's bodyguards, had piled out of the armored car and were covering the unknown vehicle with compact, wicked-looking rifles. When the driver's side door opened, it wasn't an enemy soldier who stepped out, or even a Spartan Ranger. It was David Carpenter, tall and grey, looking harried and dirty and somehow...hopeful?

His teenage daughter, Chloe, had hopped out of the other side, ignoring the threatening glares of the Mbeki guards, running around to her father's side and yanking at the rear door there. Carpenter seemed breathless, as if he'd run the whole way rather than driving, and he couldn't quite seem to form a coherent sentence.

"Logan," he stuttered. "I mean, Colonel, umm...Brannigan, I..."

"General Constantine, Admiral Buhari," Logan spoke up, realizing he needed to introduce the man to put the officers' minds at ease, "this is David Carpenter, elected governor of the Revelation colony."

"We were...," Carpenter tried to explain. "That is, Chloe and her friends were patrolling outside the city, trying to make sure none of the Starkad Marines were trying to circle around the town that way, and..."

"Someone give me a hand!" Chloe snapped, head popping back out of the back seat, her bobbed brown hair plastered down with sweat and hardened dust. "She's heavy!"

"They saw her ejection pod," David Carpenter said. The words were drifting past Logan. He was focused like a sighting laser on the combat boot stretched out on the back seat of the truck and he moved forward, needing to see, needing to know. "We couldn't get hold of anyone on the radio."

Chloe saw Logan coming and backed out of the way.

"Be careful of her leg!" she cautioned, but he was already halfway inside the truck.

Katy was lying across the back seat, her left leg wrapped in blood-stained bandages from the thigh down to the knee, wedged into a crude, wooden splint. Her flight suit was charred and blackened, and, in places, he could see where the heat had burned through to the skin beneath. Her hair was seared away on the left side of her head and a burn stretched across her face from temple to jaw, and she was the most beautiful sight Logan had ever laid eyes on.

He couldn't speak, couldn't think, couldn't manage to do anything but scramble across the seat and hold her in his arms, feel her breath, her warmth, just drink in the fact she was still alive.

"Till death do us part," Katy said into his ear, her voice rough and hoarse. "Didn't think you were getting rid of me that easy, did you?"

"What happened to your transponder?" he asked, shaking his head. It was an inane question, but all he could think to say. "We thought…"

"The ejection pod took too much damage," she explained. "It was disabled, along with just about everything else. I was hanging out the open side of the pod when it hit, and I was lucky the parachute shrouds didn't get burned away with everything else." She hissed, and he thought it was her leg or the burns, but the hurt in her face didn't come from a physical injury. "Acosta…Francis didn't make it. He just fell out of his seat when the straps burned away."

"Shit." For all his abrasiveness, Acosta had been a good man.

No, Patrick Bray. Patrick Bray was his real name, Francis Acosta was just his cover. I'll make sure people remember that name, even if we never did.

"Can you get out?" he asked her. "I can bring the medics here if you need…"

"My leg's broken," she said, wincing as if speaking the words made the pain worse. "And I could really use some good drugs. But I'll meet them on my feet."

Between Logan and Chloe, they managed to slide Katy gently and slowly out of the truck, and she slipped her arm around his shoulder and put her weight against him as he helped her step away from the cargo truck. There had been a medic on the Mbeki armored car and the woman was already rushing toward them, kit in her hand and a concerned look in her large, dark eyes.

"Admiral Buhari," Logan said as the medic helped Katy to a seat on the ground, leaning her up against the side of the truck, "this is Commander Kathren Margolis-Brannigan, our assault squadron leader...and my wife."

"When the hell did *that* happen?" Constantine blurted.

"It is an honor to meet you, Commander," Buhari said, nodding to her politely, as if this were a state dinner and she wasn't burned and broken at his feet. "May Mithra grant you both a long life and a large family."

"May Mithra grant us victory," Logan corrected him, his thoughts beginning to firm up.

"This was as close to a victory as we're going to get against Starkad," Constantine warned him. "If we're lucky, we won't have to fight them again."

"I wouldn't count on that," Katy murmured, still listening in despite the occasional pained grunt from the prodding of the medic.

"Today might have been the last shot in the fight against Starkad," Logan conceded, "but it's the first day of the battle to bring down Rhianna Hale. She's been letting Starkad do her dirty work, but starting now, she's going to have to face me herself."

"She's had months now to consolidate her hold," Buhari warned him. "Are you certain you can take her on with what you have?"

Katy answered for him, laughing with the groggy bliss of the painkillers finally kicking in.

"We're Wholesale Slaughter, Admiral," she told the Mbeki commander. "It's what we do."

I suppose I can't blame you for this one," Aaron Starkad admitted.

Ruth Laurent found it amusing to watch the man walk in magnetic boots, as if his natural grace were somehow being mocked by the lack of gravity. The tap-scrape of their passage nearly drowned out his words. He'd seemed oddly reserved since her return from Revelation with the news of Mbeki's intervention. She'd been shocked when he had radioed that he would meet her at the military space station rather than requiring her to shuttle down to the capital or to one of his many family estates. Despite his assurances of his reputation as a moody butcher being nothing but a persona he encouraged, she couldn't dispel the paranoid fear he might just have her spaced without a suit.

Instead, he had brought her down from the main docking bay to a military research lab in a restricted level of the station, far down the hub of the massive, spinning can shape, armored by the skin of a massive asteroid against enemy weapons.

"I knew we were taking a chance Shang or Mbeki might get spooked by the coup," he went on, fingers tracing a course along the handrail overlooking pressurized drydocks, each of them huge, large enough to house a full-sized cruiser.

The drydocks stretched over three kilometers of the length of the broad docking hub, taking up nearly as much space as the occupied sections of the station. She'd never had the opportunity to visit, but she found it suitably impressive and intimidating and she wondered if that was the intent.

"Shang won't get involved," she said. "They have too much to lose. It's your decision, my lord, but I would suggest offering them a deal. They'd be likely to take anything that would expand their territory with minimal military effort, and it would keep them from getting involved covertly."

"I already have," he said, smirking in obvious self-satisfaction. "But yes, it was the smart thing to do."

"If I may say, my lord," she ventured cautiously, "you don't seem overly upset by this."

"I should be," he admitted. "We lost three cruisers, most of three companies of mecha, all our assault shuttles...but things change, Ruth. Things progress. Those were the tools of the old way, and I am determined the Starkad Supremacy will never be caught fighting a war with yesterday's weapons."

They'd made it past the hollow bones of a cruiser, stripped down to its spine and drive mountings, and once they were clear of it, another ship came into view. It was lozenge-shaped, somehow sleeker than a normal cruiser, though nearly as large. Its weapons pods were angular and threatening, but there seemed to be something missing from the design, though it took her a moment to understand what it was.

"There's no fusion drive bell," she said softly. Then the words caught in her throat as she realized what that meant. Her eyes widened and she looked over at Aaron Starkad, who was grinning broadly. "Is that...?"

"That is the product of the courier you and Colonel Grieg

brought us over a year ago," the man confirmed. "That and some recent information gleaned from servers Rhianna Hale discovered at the Nike Technological Institute."

He made a sweeping gesture toward the ship, a showman introducing the next act.

"Colonel Laurent, I would like to present to you the Starkad Supremacy Naval Vessel *Kraken*. The first Supremacy military ship to be built with the Imperial stardrive."

His hand closed into a fist and the smile on his face hardened into a dark determination.

"But not the last."

WHAT'S NEXT IN THE SERIES?

WHOLESALE SLAUGHTER
TERMINUS CUT
REVELATION RUN
YOU JUST READ: MAELSTROM STRAND

SPECIAL THANKS TO:

ADAWIA E. ASAD
JENNY AVERY
BARDE PRESS
CALUM BEAULIEU
BEN
BECKY BEWERSDORF
BHAM
TANNER BLOTTER
ALFRED JOSEPH BOHNE IV
CHAD BOWDEN
ERREL BRAUDE
DAMIEN BROUSSARD
CATHERINE BULLINER
JUSTIN BURGESS
MATT BURNS
BERNIE CINKOSKE
MARTIN COOK
ALISTAIR DILWORTH
JAN DRAKE
BRET DULEY
RAY DUNN
ROB EDWARDS
RICHARD EYRES
MARK FERNANDEZ
CHARLES T FINCHER
SYLVIA FOIL
GAZELLE OF CAERBANNOG
DAVID GEARY
MICHEAL GREEN
BRIAN GRIFFIN

EDDIE HALLAHAN
JOSH HAYES
PAT HAYES
BILL HENDERSON
JEFF HOFFMAN
GODFREY HUEN
JOAN QUERALTÓ IBÁÑEZ
JONATHAN JOHNSON
MARCEL DE JONG
KABRINA
PETRI KANERVA
ROBERT KARALASH
VIKTOR KASPERSSON
TESLAN KIERINHAWK
ALEXANDER KIMBALL
JIM KOSMICKI
FRANKLIN KUZENSKI
MEENAZ LODHI
DAVID MACFARLANE
JAMIE MCFARLANE
HENRY MARIN
CRAIG MARTELLE
THOMAS MARTIN
ALAN D. MCDONALD
JAMES MCGLINCHEY
MICHAEL MCMURRAY
CHRISTIAN MEYER
SEBASTIAN MÜLLER
MARK NEWMAN
JULIAN NORTH

KYLE OATHOUT
LILY OMIDI
TROY OSGOOD
GEOFF PARKER
NICHOLAS (BUZ) PENNEY
JASON PENNOCK
THOMAS PETSCHAUER
JENNIFER PRIESTER
RHEL
JODY ROBERTS
JOHN BEAR ROSS
DONNA SANDERS
FABIAN SARAVIA
TERRY SCHOTT
SCOTT
ALLEN SIMMONS
KEVIN MICHAEL STEPHENS
MICHAEL J. SULLIVAN
PAUL SUMMERHAYES
JOHN TREADWELL
CHRISTOPHER J. VALIN
PHILIP VAN ITALLIE
JAAP VAN POELGEEST
FRANCK VAQUIER
VORTEX
DAVID WALTERS JR
MIKE A. WEBER
PAMELA WICKERT
JON WOODALL
BRUCE YOUNG

www.ingramcontent.com/pod-product-compliance
Lightning Source LLC
Chambersburg PA
CBHW051637180726

48284CB00006B/1770